Getting Past Z

GETTING PAST Z

A Memoir of Things to Come

G. F. Gravenson

Infinite Possibilities
New York • http://www.IPBooks.net

Getting Past Z: A Memoir of Things to Come

Published by IPBooks Inc, Queens, NY Online at IPBooks.net

Copyright © 2025 by Guy F. Gravenson

All rights reserved. No part of this book may be used or reproduced in any manner whatsoever, including internet usage, without written permission of the author.

ISBN: 978-1-956864-94-6

For Dina and P.S.

Part I

CHAPTER 1

Caroline, my aide, was just leaving for the day when Peter's Uber pulled up. Perfect timing I thought. It would be just the two of us for a couple of days. Now, at last, I'd be able to hear his side of the story. That is, if he was willing to share it with me.

He had grown a beard, well trimmed, but a bit too full. It made him look older than his 28 years, which no doubt was its intent. He was dressed in a finely-tailored tweed sports jacket, a nicely pressed pair of tapered slacks and well-shined loafers. Peter, it seemed, had come around full circle from a somewhat sloppy laidback post-adolescent to a fashionable, well-comported adult. Maybe California was having a positive effect, after all.

"I'm so glad you called," I said, embracing him under the archway and leading him inside. "I was wondering about how you were doing these days. Come, put your stuff down and we'll take it to your room later. You want something to drink?"

"I'm fine, Granddad. Your aide? I forgot her name."

"Yes, Caroline. She cared for your Mom at one point early on. And then I rehired her for your Grandma and she's been with me ever since. I don't think I could still be independent without her. She's been terrific."

"I think I met her briefly when I was here last."

"Yeah, she and her partner Chris were at Grandma's memorial, of course."

"And where's Spot?"

"I'm sorry to say I had to put him down about a year ago. He was an old dog, you know. We got him when he was about three, so he was about eighteen or so, almost totally deaf. When your Grandma died he sort of became depressed and wouldn't eat much and whimpered and sort of wasted away. I took him to the vet and we agreed to end his suffering."

"Sorry to hear that. You should get another dog. He was a great guard dog. I can't believe you're here all alone at night. Y'know, they have DogBots now that use facial and vocal recognition and will bark if they hear or see something not in their database. Your phone will suddenly bark," he laughed.

"Oh, I feel quite safe. All the doors now have motion lights above and I have thumbprint readers instead of keys."

"But no cameras?"

"Nah. This isn't a prison," I said, and then to change the subject: "So how was your flight?"

"About what you'd expect. They're reconfiguring LAX again. Putting in facial recognition surveillance cameras and new biometric screenings. There's hardly any service staff left at the counters. It's all AI now. You just tap in your thumbprint, get your QR boarding pass and go."

"Well, customer service is a thing of the past," I said.

"Unless your last name is Bot," he cracked. I laughed along; Peter hadn't lost his sardonic sense of humor.

"So let's sit for a moment. I made a dinner reservation for six-thirty so we're not rushed," I motioned that we move to the living room.

"So good to see you, Granddad," he said, placing his arm around my shoulders and giving me a gentle hug. "The place hasn't changed a bit."

"Well, I removed the family photos on that table over there. Brought up too many memories. What can I say? I'm so glad you called and decided to stay with me instead of Dad. We haven't had a good face-to-face in ages, it seems."

He looked about somewhat uncomfortably. "I guess it was my way of shutting down the sadness," he said, extending his lanky frame on the couch fronting the fireplace. "I just couldn't deal with it."

I opted for one of the high-back armchairs flanking the couch. "God knows, it's been rough on all of us, but that's all behind us now," I said. "Now's the time to heal, to reconnect, not disconnect. So it's great to see you, Peter, after what? A year and a half? Two? You're looking very sharp. You've put on a little weight. I like the beard."

"Thanks, Granddad. You're looking fit yourself. Still working out at the Senior Center?"

"Not so much anymore. A lot of my friends there have recently passed."

"Sorry to hear that. Unfortunately, that's a by-product of old age."

"You think 89 is old? With a little stem therapy I could live to see your grandchildren."

He laughed. "But I know you must still be playing tennis."

"Oh, yeah… keeps me somewhat in shape. Healthy as a hearse—as the old joke goes. But only doubles now. Too old for singles."

"What about pickleball?

I laughed along. "That's not a sport. It's TikTok ping-pong. It's a dumb game. And people near the courts keep complaining about the noise."

"From yelling?"

"Nah, nothing like that. From the ball hitting the paddle. It's like a rifle shot. Bang, bang!"

"So why don't they make a ball out of sponge rubber or industrial styrofoam or even cork? String the racquets like in squash."

"That's the engineer in you," I chuckled. "My money didn't go to waste."

"Speaking of which," he said, "I just received word from MIT that the rest of my debt has been formally paid off. I assume that was your doing?"

"Well, there was a window of opportunity last month to pay off student loans at a ridiculously high discount, so I grabbed it while I could. I took care of Estelle's loan as well. She should be finding out about it soon."

"I can't thank you enough, Granddad. Truly."

"Well, thank the government too," I said. "It was their program after all."

"You know what I think about the government," he said somewhat bitterly. "They graduate you awash in debt, then hang you out to dry."

"Well, we'll have some time together this time to talk about that. I'm not going to try to change your mind about things. It's your life, your choices, your decisions. But the country has been very good to me, very good to Ruthie, to your Mom and Dad, Estelle, the whole family. In spite of what's been happening lately. That's a blip on the radar screen. All in all, we were very privileged to live in the U.S. when we did."

"You put that in the past tense," he noted dryly.

So I did, I thought, when it wasn't my intention. "From my perspective," I said, trying to rectify, "the country goes through good times and bad. But we make it through somehow. We pull together and make it work. That's what we have to do this time, too. You just can't drop out. That doesn't solve the problem."

"I didn't drop out," he said defensively. "I'm working on plans I can tell you about later. I'm still productive. I'm just not suited to be part of a giant utility that only has money on its mind."

"They paid you very well, you once told me. You didn't mind getting your paycheck."

He winced at that putdown. "Did Stella tell you that I quit?"

"Yes, she did. I've known about it for some time now. But then you called to say you were coming East for a few days to do some business. So I thought maybe you hadn't quit after all."

"No, I gave notice. I signed the papers with HR. I had some vacation and severance time coming so technically I suppose I'm still on the payroll."

"Can you..."

"Granddad, I'm outta there. I haven't the slightest inclination to return. I'm not saying that I wasn't treated well. The respect was mostly there. But our philosophies didn't match up. I wanted to work on projects that would eventually put them and other utility companies out of business, you understand. That didn't sit very well with them."

"Well, there are ways to get around the system," I said, not fully understanding what Peter was talking about.

He grinned. "That's what my boss said, when I told him I was leaving."

"Your boss said that?"

Peter was laughing now. "Yeah. The hypocrite!" His comment was supposed to be ironically amusing, yet for some reason it bothered me. "Time to go to dinner," I said, checking my watch. "Our reservation is for six-thirty. We'll talk more over dinner."

I made the reservation at a restaurant in Upper Montclair, certainly not my favorite, but Montclair proper would be crowded on a Saturday night. Add to that my advanced age and a bunch of young people drinking, and I decided on the quietude and safety of a much smaller venue. "Hope you like Italian cooking," I said to Peter on the way there.

"Dinner's on me," he responded. It was a nice grandiose gesture, but we both knew it wouldn't hold.

We got a deux by the back windows where we could see the sunset and enjoy some privacy.

I ordered a bottle of their house red, a flavorful Merlot, and relaxed in their cushioned chairs, certainly a point in the restaurant's favor I had forgotten about. "How's your wine?" I asked.

"Excellent," he said, looking about. "I like this place. Do you come here often?"

"Ruthie didn't care for it as much as another Italian restaurant we went to in Montclair. But this is much closer to the house. Nice comfortable chairs."

"Your driving is still very good, I noticed. There's nothing like a decade-old Honda Accord."

"I hope so. After 85 they begin to question re-issuing licenses here in Jersey. But the statistics show that we octogenarians are the safest drivers on the road. So it's on a case-by-case basis—and they take your overall driving record into consideration. I have an almost clean record. A couple of speeding tickets, that's all. Never been in an accident."

"That's amazing, Granddad," he said.

Appetizers and dips were put before us. I nibbled on some cauliflower and broccoli florets. Playing dumb, I ventured: "So Estelle tells me you're the head of something or other. Against social media, the internet and the like."

"I'm against any invasive medium, anything that falsifies reality, screws up your head, takes over your life."

"That's a tall order," I laughed. "What are you saying?"

"Everything we input is through filters now, Granddad. We used to use our senses and our reasoning to scope out what was real and what was not. Now we use screens and virtual reality and generative AI as convenient go-betweens. We've allowed electronic devices to interpret reality for us. External waves of distracting energy interfering with our own internal natural processes. An intrusion on a massive scale."

"That's not new," I said. "They said the same thing about TV when I was a kid."

"Yeah, but back then TV was a home movie theater. You could escape reality for a couple of hours to relax with the family after coming home from work. TV dinners, remember? Milton Berle. Ed Sullivan. The Honeymooners. The Colgate Comedy Hour. Television was free harmless family entertainment."

"And now?"

"The internet and all these devices streaming social media in your face 24/7 have become our new reality. There's no getting away from them. You can't avoid them. They've infiltrated our consciousness, our every waking moment. Nothing relaxing or entertaining about them. They pander for your attention, your check in, your call back, your excuse for not immediately acknowledging some asshole insurance salesman. There's a new Princeton study that shows they actually cause ADHD, anxiety and depression."

"So, Peter, let me understand: You want to ban devices that carry the internet? Like my smartphone?" I asked pointedly, pulling my new 3D twin-screen from out of my shirt pocket.

"No, Granddad, that's not it. I just want to put some disclaimers in, like a warning label—that what you are experiencing, what you're peering into, is a commercially filtered view of reality. A corporate sponsored, multi-layered reflection of reality that may not correspond to what objective reality truly is."

"A virtual reality."

"Exactly. An augmented, demented reality that's quickly replacing actual reality by using artificial intelligence—with algorithms that mimic rational thought and behavior."

"Like what? Give me an example. TikTok? 4Chan? Instagram?..."

"All of those and dozens more. Like any platform that provides distorted reality information—from any device—your desktop, laptop, tablet, goggles, smartshades, smartwatch, smartphone, whatever. Back in 2023 there was a rap video *Too Much, Enough!* that protested the infestation of social media-driven news into our lives. So we knew back then, more than five years ago, the addiction the Internet was causing. So today it's called the Splinternet because it has literally fractured the country."

"Well, I find my smartphone very handy sometimes," I said defensively. "But I wouldn't say I'm addicted. That's a pretty strong word."

"You weren't born into an age where these devices blaring their social media sites are almost impossible to give up," he said. "For a lot of people in my cohort it's an addiction, like smoking was to yours. I don't own a smartphone or a phartsmone as we like to call it. I carry a cell phone, an old fashioned flip-phone, but I get robotext messages on it just the same, with the same phony sites that get around the blocks to hack into your private space and time, the same clickbait come-ons and shills. It's all the same behind-the-scenes corporations vying for your eyeballs, your ad dollar, your 'like', your upvote. And a lot of that is disinformation and made up stuff to control your thinking, your decision-making, your behavior. That's what's depressing the country now."

"Disinformation."

"It's like when you marveled at the Times Square smoke ring," he went on, script-like, with his analogy: "Smoking was actually good for you, relaxed you, made you sexier than Humphrey Bogart. And then science found the cancer link and the cigarette manufacturers had to clean up their act. That's what I want—for social media sites on the Internet to clean up their act. An honest acceptance of the divisive harm they and their corporate sponsors are causing, like the disclaimer on the side of a cigarette pack."

"So you're saying the Internet has created, over time, this depression over what? Addiction? Disinformation? A false reality?"

"All of that. And look: It's been said that every social movement starts out as an ideal, becomes a cause, and ends up as a business. The Splinternet is a sad example of that progression."

"And that ideal was... what?"

"Its creators envisioned a world-wide communications forum based on facts, not opinions or personal biases or hateful tirades on race, gender, nationality or anything else. Based on proven evidence, not false assumptions, wild speculation or made up reporting. Based on verifiable reviews, testimonials and evaluations from ordinary people, not celebrities or Influencers who get paid off, or from phony businesses or scam artists who want to sell you a counterfeit something or other, or steal your social security number or banking ID, or persuade you to think in some way from some unheard-of 'expert' with questionable credentials and ulterior motives. Plus, there are a number of Influencers—real and AI generated—knowingly putting out dangerous products. Just look at the harm being done to underage kids with those nicotine-filled lip pouches called Zyns."

Peter was all over the lot, I thought, and was regurgitating well-practiced scripts, yet wasn't focused enough to deliver a convincing argument. But he had used the word *Influencer*, and this was my chance to open up the can of worms that had been sitting on my mind's shelf for these many months.

"So you came up with Outfluencer?" I asked; "Which was to counter this entrapment?"

"Frankly, I was task masking at work and I needed some diversion. Everything on social media was upsetting to me. It was so phony, so staged, and so misinformed I could only puke at what I saw and what the gullible public was buying. For instance, one fashion company artificially raised the price of their sneakers 30%, then gave a 30% discount to the first 100 buyers who used a QR code given to them by the company's handpicked Influencer. That sort of thing."

"These promotions have been standard operational procedure long before the internet and social media, Peter. I should know. Just look at direct mail and mail order companies..."

"Sure. But social media was the gold rush. You just had to open a virtual mine and they came running into a virtual minefield. Nothing real, or tangible, or that you can try on to fit. No reliable money-back satisfaction guarantees and free return privileges like most brick-and-mortar stores have. Moreover, brick-and-mortar stores will be there tomorrow and the day after tomorrow. These on-line cons can shut down their sites in minutes and disappear into the cloud, leaving you holding the bag. They know they have young unsophisticated consumers who buy into the latest social media meme without even knowing what meme means. Social media has stolen our innocence, our trust."

"Let the buyer beware," I put in.

"Sure, Granddad, that's always been true. But now these fraudster scams have reached epidemic proportions, especially since the Covid stay-at-home days. You're never sure what you're getting through these sites. Just a lot of unsellable counterfeit crap, basically. In fact, one site on Instagram had the *chutzpah* to actually defend the items they were selling as 'legitimate knockoffs.' You can't make this stuff up!"

"So as The Outfluencer, your mission was to expose all this?"

"I wanted to 'out' those behind the lies, the hype, the phony reviews and paid celebrity endorsements, the huge Influencer commissions. So I started the Outfluencer blog anonymously with a verifiable user rating guide and unedited comment section—kind of like *Consumer Reports* of your day."

"I think they're still in business."

"They are. But you still have to pay to read it. My blog is completely free to all, without a paywall, without even a sign in or password, so viewers know they can speak their mind without being doxxed or harassed. If you want to donate something, it's all voluntary, no pressure."

"I know. Estelle told me about your blog, so I had a chance to look at it. I was impressed, actually. You did this all without any publicity?"

"Well, I did a couple of on-line interviews with my face blurred, and that created some buzz. But it really took off all by itself, because it was something the public really hungered for. So it wasn't like I said, 'and today I'll start this consumer movement.'"

"What about all these other outfluencer sites out there now? I'm reading about Uncle Scam… Scambusters… Scamscan. You've started a cottage industry, you know!"

He shared in my laughter. "Yeah. Well, like everything else these days, you'll find some way to make a buck off someone else's idea. So, these self-appointed 'product-service investigators' are charging a subscription or per-use fee often crediting 'Outfluencer' in their promotions, and, sure, I was very flattered by that at first. But closely reading their reports made clear they were not only trying to copycat me but undercut what my free blog was about. They're opportunists and plagiarists essentially."

"Couldn't you protect yourself somehow?"

"Not without revealing myself. And I wanted to stay anonymous."

"I see."

"But I still had—still have—a hardcore of really discerning viewers who are sticking by my Outfluencer site because they're looking for authenticity, not more pay-for-play fakery. But unfortunately my name was eventually attached to the blog. Believe me, Granddad, I didn't want or need that publicity."

"I can see that. It can get you into trouble. Especially if some business is affected by your outing them."

"So true. I've had some threats made to me personally. So I'm laying low these days."

That was indeed troubling news, especially in light of the recent Mexican cartel incursion into San Ysidro and the explosion of migrant violence there. "Maybe you should think of leaving Southern California and coming back East," I said. "You can always stay at my place. I have a couple of guest bedrooms I'm not using."

"Thanks, Granddad. I'll think about it. But I don't want to involve you in any way."

"You won't, Peter. Nobody in their right mind would come after me. I'm too old to be Influenced or Outfluenced or anything else. And to that point, I've read somewhere your consumer movement is mostly a generational thing. Young people your age. Why is that? It would seem like a good idea to give some voice to consumers of all age groups."

"I don't know, Granddad. My generation picked it up because they're the most vulnerable, the most to be affected by all this disinformation, the hoaxes, the hype. And I'm squarely on the side of more than half the Z's who feel it's up to us to change things because the three or four generations that came before us haven't done shit about it. Sorry if I offend."

Suddenly something he said clicked in my head.

"Is that what this is all about? Why you and your sister had this falling out?"

"I wouldn't call it a falling out necessarily. We both have the same objectives in the long run. We share the same values about the economy, climate change, the environment, abortion, race relations and many other issues. She's a Z too, but has taken an opposite approach: Appeasement. She thinks you can work through social media and make it more accessible, more authentic and truthful. I think that's naive. It's too far gone to salvage. It's no longer social media; there's nothing social about it. If anything, it's *anti*-social media—beamed to a bunch of hunchbacked loners bent over their phones, accepting without question things they've been told will make them healthy, wealthy and wise. Smartphones are making dummies of us all."

"You really think so?"

"Look. I'm a First Amendment freak. I took the Supreme Court's side back in 2023 that social media sites, like newspapers, have a basic right to free speech. But 'free' speech comes at a cost. And that cost is Truth—with a capital T."

"Truth in their reporting, their advertising?"

"Both. Absolutely. Social media sites depend on their advertisers and sponsors for support. And these companies need eyeballs to buy their stuff. And eyeballs are attracted to controversy. And controversy can be artificially produced by deceit and lies. So it can be one big revolving shill. Not every site, but some dot coms should be renamed dot *cons*. That's what social media is facing today and needs to confront because the trend is growing and taking over."

"But you need to be careful, Peter. There are some powerful players here."

"Well, we're not going away. In fact, if anything, we're taking a more radical in-your-face confrontational approach with these rip-off artists. We're fact checking them when they lie, when they can't back up what they're saying. We're calling them out when they're phishing for what's in your wallet or your credit card's CVC. When they're selling you knockoffs and counterfeit shit. Or like when the poor taxpayer, who has no say in the matter, has to shell out millions for the court costs indicting a so-called President. That pay-for-play scam outraged me. And yes, even though I voted for Trump I was part of TIP—that nationwide protest against paying for any part of the Trump prosecution or defense costs at taxpayer expense. I'm proud of it."

"Like holding parades and blocking traffic? Without a permit? Like laying down on Broadway during last years' Macy's Thanksgiving Day Parade?"

"Not my idea. But it gets results. It gets on the six o'clock news. If it bleeds, it leads, right?"

"A lot of young people are getting arrested or doxxed. It goes on their record. Remember Columbia University's Tenttown? Nobody's considering the long-term consequences here."

He paused, thinking carefully how to handle what I figured was to come.

"You protested the Vietnam War. You evaded serving in the army. You were a conscientious objector. Isn't that what they called you back then?"

"You were exempt if you were a teacher. I temporarily went into teaching…"

"To avoid being drafted."

"Certainly. But this is hardly the same thing."

"Hypocrisy has many forms, Granddad," he said, half smirking.

"Yes, it does," I concurred, "Many forms."

I took it all in, but I was upset. He must have found out about my Vietnam War days from his father. That period was something I wasn't particularly proud of, and I wasn't going to lie about it but he had me on the defensive and was muddying up the water with his protest comparison.

"Just for the record, the country was also badly divided then, maybe even worse than it is today. We were fighting a foreign war without the foggiest idea why we were there. Something about the northern part of a country which was communist invading the southern part of the country which was ruled by an autocrat and a poorly trained army. But it really was no business of ours. And once there we had no idea how to get out…so it went on and on. But what you're describing isn't one population invading another like in Gaza or occupying some territory like in Ukraine. It's a domestic internal struggle, not over turf but over basic American values like freedom of the press and protesting peacefully and having a representative Government you can vote in or out. And we know there are still ways to solve the problems without violence."

"Yes," he said, "by capitulating. Giving up and getting lobotomies. I'm not going to be a hypocrite, Granddad. I'm going to go down fighting for these basic values as you put it."

I motioned for the waiter to bring us printed menus instead of ordering through the QR code on the placemats. I knew if I ordered by smartphone, Peter would go on about it.

It was time to play one of my top cards, something that was bothering me for over a year now.

"You're quoted as saying somewhere that there are the Z's and there are the Not Z's. And you stand with the Not Z's. Do you realize what you're saying? How that sounds?"

"Sure I do. I want nothing to do with that part of my generation who play up to the money-grubbing corporations, the zillionaire elites and political slimeballs who control us. At best those Z's are ass-licking wannabes; at worst they're cowardly traitors."

"And it's better to be a Nazi?"

"Yeah... you're going to use that, I knew you'd bring it up, Granddad. I didn't come up with Not Z—that I realize sounds exactly like Nazi. Some anonymous idiot on Gap came up with that beauty to hijack the movement and shut me up. And yes, I stand with the Not Z's, *not* the Nazis."

"How did that misperception happen? How did you get involved in that?"

"Like I said, I was doing live interviews from time to time as The Outfluencer with my face blurred out so I could remain anonymous. One of the interviews was on the popular InterInn platform. And the interviewer asked me, why am I so negative about my own generation, when I have achieved some notoriety being part of it. 'Are you a Z or not?' And I answered, 'I may have been born into that cohort but I have very little in common with them, I don't identify with them and I don't care to be linked to them. I share some of their goals but not their means of attaining them. So, in answer to your question: No, I am *not a Z.*' And I'm guessing someone with a grudge against me—probably because I outfluenced them, who knows?—picked that up and with AI help, digitally turned a couple of syllables around so it came out, 'No, I am *a Not Z.*'"

"Sounds a bit like the Greg Marston-IBM case."

"Except I was on my own, without a corporate safety net."

"So then what happened?"

"So then this line was spread around on social media, not just to destroy me personally, and my blog, but to malign the anti-Z movement. And after a while I got tired of debunking a vicious misquote, so I'm not doing interviews anymore. And I haven't blogged much after that because I figure they now know who's behind The Outfluencer and these bastards can track you anywhere these days. But I'm not going to live in paranoiac fear of somebody coming after me for something I know I didn't actually say. And, I'm taking precautions."

"I'd drop any kind of Z reference altogether," I said. "Give them the satisfaction of winning that round."

"Granddad... "

"If you must, find something else like what you said before: Anti-Z. Or Contra-Z. Why use Not Z when it gets people, especially us Jews, very very upset?" I asked, almost down to a whisper.

He nodded, reluctantly, in agreement.

"It's not getting the attention you want. It's having the opposite effect," I added. "It's inflaming the situation, and dividing your impressionable peers, your vulnerable generation as you put it. It's just fodder for the ultras—right and left. Remember Columbus, Ohio, right after Trump's win? Or Musk's thoughtless salute at Trump's inaugural rally? Or the Powell demonstrations? The anti-Chinese tariff protests still going on? This isn't going to end well. It never does."

Peter took this all in, and had a long sip of wine before he continued.

"This hateful insult, I'm convinced, was put out by the deep state to embarrass not only me but to humiliate and defame our anti-establishment movement. It was brilliant, I have to admit. And it's having an effect, it's true. But the divide is there, for sure. You're either a Z or not a Z. No room for fence sitters. And whatever you want to call us—or the part of my generation that's in opposition and rebellion—we're not hiding, we're not stealing away to Canada; we're standing our ground. We're getting stronger by the day. And we'll be in their face, not on a screen. And we'll be holding up a reality mirror to whatever they do, whatever they say. The masquerade party is over, Granddad. Time for them to take off their social media masks and get real."

We ordered our dinners. I ordered one of the more expensive items on the menu, lobster, while Peter ordered one of the least costly: a stuffed fish filet, believing he would be picking up the check. It was interesting to see how his mind was working these days, knowing that he went through a bullied childhood for skipping a grade and even more stressful adolescence when he got his girlfriend pregnant; had excelled at Massachusetts Institute of Technology and had, I thought, buried much of his formative years in therapy and moving away to California. Still, there was a part of him that evidently held some anger, some resentment of his past. While his older sister by a couple of years, who was even more vulnerable through those growing up stages, presented herself as more in control, better equipped to face reality squarely, without drama or emotional distress.

There was something Estelle told me I needed to flush out. And over dinner, when it came minutes later, was the time I chose to do it.

"Your sister told me you flew in a few months ago just to talk to Gene. True?"

"I needed to talk to an experienced lawyer about my leaving work before I gave notice. I had met Gene some time ago, remember, at Grandma's memorial, and I liked him from the start. I figured he wouldn't charge me a lot for some advice since he was serious about Stella. Y'know, family rates."

I laughed. "Did you factor in the airfare?"

He joined me in laughter. "I was in New York for a convention, all expenses paid by the company … and Gene was the icing on the cake!"

"Ah, those conventions, very convenient."

"He gave me some good advice about what the company could or could not do about my future employment plans. You know, like non-disclosure or competitive prohibition agreements—what I could expect in severance, unused vacation time, extending health insurance and things like that. It had been my first job out of MIT and I didn't know shit. This fish is delicious!"

"He's a good man," I said. "I like him a lot, too. A sensitive guy. He'll make a terrific husband for Estelle."

"You think they're that serious?"

"Well, of course. She's formally engaged, or will be in a few weeks."

His eyes widened. "Wow, that's news! How do you know that?"

"Didn't you... get your invitation?"

"What invitation?"

I suddenly realized I had been thrust into boiling water like the lobster I was consuming. I hadn't the words to go on.

"I guess I'm not invited," he said at last, not concealing the sadness and disgust in his voice.

"There may be some miscommunication here," I proffered. "I can find out one way or the other."

"No, Granddad, don't get involved. It's her party and she can invite whoever she wants. She probably has her reasons."

"She probably thought you wouldn't come in from California. But you would come in for her engagement party, wouldn't you?"

"I don't know. I might have made other plans. When did you say it was?"

"August 26th, a Saturday afternoon."

"Dad is coming?"

"Yes, he's been invited. And I think he accepted. I know he accepted. Estelle told me he had."

"Where is it being held?"

"At my place. I offered the back yard to them... "

"Oh, wow! How many people?"

"Between 70 and 80."

"Holy shit!" he gasped. "Did you know about the party when you invited me to stay with you this week?

"Yes.... but I assumed you had gotten an invitation as well. I... I can't believe Estelle would not invite you."

"We haven't kept in touch that much lately," he responded. "I'm okay with it."

But I knew he wasn't. We ate the rest of our dinners mainly in silence, thinking over this sibling rivalry that developed... when? When Peter skipped a grade in elementary school? Or in High School where Estelle was now only a year before him although she was two-plus years older?

And then Estelle went to Vassar, a preppy small co-ed college near Poughkeepsie, New York, and Peter was accepted to a couple of Ivy League schools, but chose MIT, because of his scientific bent. Estelle went on to get her Masters in Social Work, her passion. Peter went on to do basic research for a new non-polluting cement while working for an advanced degree in hydroclimatology and then accepted a summer's internship with California's San Diego Power & Light Utility which turned into a full time job that fall. Both these kids were high achievers—and both, it seemed to me, had made some well thought out decisions about where they wanted to go in life.

On my way to the bathroom while dessert was being prepared, I slipped our waiter my credit card and told him it was to pay the bill with a 20% tip. Peter was not happy to learn that when I was presented with the receipt to sign. He had his card out for a bill that never arrived. It was emblematic of the events that were to follow.

I thought Peter would stay for another day, but early the next morning over coffee he informed me he was staying the second night with friends in the City. I drove him to the NJ Transit Station in Montclair and we said our goodbyes. There was a lot left unsaid, and a lot of questions I still had, but he told me there were some job opportunities that would bring him East again for more interviews.

"I have a little departing gift for you," he said, reaching into his carryon as we waited on the platform for the train. "Read it at your peril," he laughed, pulling out a thick manila envelope with a flourish.

"What is it?" I asked.

"My rooftop project brought back to life, kicking and screaming. New photos, new schematic plans, a full year's cost analysis, everything. And a special surprise. The first iteration lacked a clean water certificate. I have two independent lab reports that have California credibility at least," he laughed. "And a third in the works."

I was impressed. "Thank you," I said. "A game changer for sure. Gene needs to see this."

"I'm dropping off a copy when I hit the city this morning," he said.

"Please remember what I said last night about all this nonsense with the Zs. You're bigger than that. It'll get you in trouble. And if you decide to come East, you can always stay with me."

"I'll remember, Granddad. I had a wonderful time with you last night. Don't worry."

"Put down August 26th on your calendar. Stay over at my place again. Loved having you."

"I won't go to Stella's pre-nup party without a personal invitation, Granddad; I'm very clear about that," he said defiantly. "I won't crash it."

"Let me look into it," I said. "Could be just an oversight."

"I doubt that," was his retort. "I'm thoroughly okay with it... "

"I'll call or email you when I know something."

"Okay, Granddad. Stay well. Thanks again for everything."

And then the train was there, amazingly on time, we hugged, and Peter disappeared into its interior, unable, I surmised, to find a window seat to respond to my nervously waving goodbye.

CHAPTER 2

It was quite true that Estelle, or Stella as Peter and their contemporaries called her, was throwing the party for her engagement to Gene, but it was also true that Gene was footing nearly the entire bill. His family was quite well off, into construction and law and real estate. An old-line Jewish family, here several generations before the exodus from Europe in the early 20th century. Estelle had done very well for herself, given the fact that she met Gene, not while she was attending Vassar, but a year later at Kiddo's—a tony Upper East Side bar. He was more than a decade older than she, somewhat of a playboy, but definitely looking for a suitable mate. She was about to get her M.A. in public health, and not particularly interested in getting into a long-term relationship but Gene was smitten by her, and persisted in trying to make Estelle see he was serious about her.

That was five years ago or more, and in that period, slowly but surely they had become an inseparable couple. So the engagement party was simply a show-off formality, for the families to meet, and their friends to mingle and get to know one another before the wedding, its date not set or at least not yet announced. But I expected it would be at the engagement party or soon thereafter. If Gene had any reservations about the semi-dysfunctional family he was entering, he kept it to himself. At least he was very kind to me and Ruthie while she struggled to survive at the end. He and Estelle were at the house many times in that dark period. And Ruthie, especially, wanted to see them married. But it was Estelle, not Gene, who kept putting off any engagement talk. Her mother's losing fight against Covid had taken a toll on Estelle's desire to quickly advance her professional career. And then her grandmother's announcement of terminal cancer hardly three years after Clara's passing, further pushed back the couple's plans.

Perhaps it's time to bring Paul, my son, and Clara, his late wife, into the picture. They were both teachers. Paul taught mathematics at a noted Manhattan, New York public High School. Clara taught social studies at a prestigious Brooklyn private school. They were a devoted couple, married to each other since their early-twenties and lived first in a Brooklyn apartment and later bought a house in Edgewater, New Jersey, commuting to their teaching assignments until Clara took a teaching position at a North Bergen high school to be closer to their kids.

They raised Peter and Estelle in relative middle-class comfort, through good economic times and bad. It was always a delight when they came over to spend a day at our place. The kids were well behaved, respectful of each other and obviously very bright, having two teachers as parents. As grandparents, Ruthie and I doted on them—as did Clara's mother, Dinah, who developed Alzheimer's, and now lived in Coral Gables, Florida, at an assisted living compound.

Somewhere, somehow, Clara developed one of the earliest cases of Covid-19 right after she returned from a Florida trip visiting her ailing mother. This was way before vaccines, before even a classification of a highly contractible virus. She had a bacterial infection—the Wuhan Flu, doctors told her—and gave her antibiotics and other medicine that did her little good. It was half-way through the fall semester of 2019-2020, but she had to take a leave of absence from her school, never to return. Her condition worsened and she was confined to their home. Paul hired Caroline Hamilton, a licensed caretaker for her during the day because he was still teaching and Estelle and Peter were out of town at school and couldn't assist.

Then in early 2020 they put a name to the disease but it came too late for Clara. She was in hospital now, unable to care for herself. We came to visit her once, and were shocked. She was wasting away, not wanting to eat, hardly able to converse. And worse, she didn't recognize us at first. She thought Ruthie and I were *her* parents! Whatever this virus was, it was beginning to affect her cognitive functioning. I said to Paul, he should get the kids down there because I didn't think she had much time left. But he was cautiously optimistic there would soon be a cure; that science would come to his wife's rescue; that he would be able to eventually bring his wife back home to Edgewater; that he would rehire Caroline for Clara's rehabilitation and get on with their lives together, forever after.

Which somehow obliquely affected Ruthie's and my plans for the future. We had this big colonial–type house in Upper Montclair, long emptied of our one remaining child, Paul, that was becoming a burden in its upkeep. We were considering selling the house and retiring to Florida where we had friends nearby, and where Dinah still resided so we'd still be seeing Clara and Paul and perhaps even Estelle and Peter when they'd come visit. That was on our radar screen but then Covid and Fate intervened and the screen went blank.

By Easter 2020, it was obvious that Clara was failing, and no amount of intervention would be in time to save her. Plus, she was now in hospital isolation, and Paul and the kids had to go through extreme procedures just to see her. It obviously had a chilling effect on all three. If you remember the times, paranoia raged. No one traveled on public transportation, strict mandates to wear a mask everywhere. A run on Lysol and toilet paper. And in families where some member had caught the virus, they were now masked pariahs, quarantined to their homes, in fear of their lives or of passing the virus on to more vulnerable family members.

And then, miraculously, a vaccine was created. But at that very moment in time, literally in the week of the vaccine's announcement and Estelle's virtual commencement with an advanced degree in social sciences, Clara passed.

Paul was devastated. He couldn't go through with a formal funeral and just had her body cremated without a ceremony of any kind. That was not good judgment on his part, because there was no closure for Estelle and Peter. They mourned for their mother and now for their father, who left his teaching position before the end of the Spring semester and disappeared. He gave the keys to the house to me to give to his kids. He couldn't stay there with Clara's ghost, he said. He would be back when he got his head together. He took his car, left Clara's in the garage for the kids to use or to sell, but no one knew where he was off to. And when he did finally return in mid-summer he was a newly confirmed alcoholic. His appellation, not mine.

I thought he might get better being around the family and getting back to teaching. But he announced that he was retiring. He qualified for a full pension, and now at 58, a small amount of Social Security would also kick in a few years hence. That would be more than enough to live comfortably back in Edgewater, but he quickly put the house on the market. It sold immediately because mortgage rates were extremely low at that time, and he got a great price for the old run-down house. He invested in a two-bedroom co-op on Riverside Drive in Manhattan close to where his school was, so he had some teacher friends to go out drinking with at night. A smart move socially, I thought, but I was troubled by his drinking...

And then disaster struck again, this time closer to home.

Ruthie was having stomach cramps, not all the time, but when they came they were severe. Nothing showed up on a colonoscopy or X-rays. Medications were helping somewhat, but tired her out and she was forced to give up her painting and yoga classes, and jogging in the park, by then her only regular physical activity. I got a folding wheelchair for her when even walking in the park was affecting her balance and making her nauseous. She was afraid to drive her car to the mall and to our local supermarket merely a mile away, so I drove her everywhere now.

"When you push your car beyond eighty," she said ruefully the morning we drove to the gastroenterologist who gave her the devastating news, "it's beyond the speed limit anywhere in the world. You either crash, or you get pulled over. I'm being written a ticket as we speak."

The ticket was for stage IV pancreatic cancer, which had spread to her liver. Ruthie had a few months to live, chemo and radiation treatments only prolonged her decline, and less than three years after Clara's passing, my wife of 56 years, my lovely Ruthie... died peacefully in her heavily medicated sleep at home, now her hospice, a week shy of her 81st birthday. Everybody knew it was coming, so it wasn't a surprise; Paul was noticeably sober, and Peter, who flew a red-eye into Newark from LA, could hardly keep awake during the memorial service held at the Montclair Reformed Temple officiated by its long-term Rabbi, Max Schulman. Estelle was there as well, accompanied now by her boyfriend Gene, who I met for the first time.

And later that day, I, with about two dozen friends and neighbors, mourned her passing with a lightly catered buffet, together with a classical string quartet held in our quiescent half-acre backyard beneath 'Ruthie's Oak'—an ancient oak tree at the edge of the woods she was fond of sketching. Ruthie would have been proud, her gentle spirit looking down from our bedroom window, it was such a lovely affair. And it had an amazing effect on both Estelle and Gene. That evening driving back to Manhattan they laughingly determined that if they ever got engaged, they'd hold a party at my place. As Estelle recounted to me later, "Then, halfway over the Bayonne Bridge, he asked me to move in with him, and I accepted. I knew from that moment Gene was the one."

So I had to know, and soon, whether my loving Granddaughter had formally invited her wayward brother to her pre-nup party, held on the same hallowed ground as the remembrance for my wife nearly six years before. A smartphone call or a Skypescape meeting wouldn't do. Peter's words were coming back to me about screens: I needed a face-to-face.

But this was, indeed, tricky. I wasn't sure if Estelle knew her brother had been in town, or that he stayed for a night at my place. Did she find out I inadvertently spilled the beans that he wasn't invited? And why hadn't his father, who talked with him often, revealed Estelle's intention to him? Was it because Paul too was in on this little dirty secret that Peter wouldn't be invited?

In this case, it seemed, I was the uninformed Johnny-come-lately, and perhaps there was a good reason for it: Since the event would be at my place, I would no doubt have some say in the proceedings. And perhaps Estelle would have figured out that I would be taking Peter's side. For, as it had always been for me and Ruthie, the family's cohesion came first, diminished lately by two profound deaths, even more so. All the more reason to connect, to reestablish loving relationships, to preserve the Myer name, and all the good things that name, over generations, had accomplished.

So I had to walk a fine line here. I needed to be truthful, but tactful. I needed to hear her out about objections to Peter's presence there, and whether a sit-down meeting between them before the event would iron out their differences. There was still time, but it was fleeting. And I had prepared by going over several possible scenarios in my head before dinner at The Backyard, the new iteration of the AOL restaurant that had closed a few years back on Greenwich Avenue in the Village.

It was a fine cool summer evening, and I was certain the outdoor half of the restaurant would be packed. But I had reserved a deux days earlier, so by five-thirty we were both seated in a nearly empty venue, with the best corner table in the garden, Estelle's long dark auburn hair dancing to the barely audible Muzak in the breeze.

"I hope I didn't take too much of your time at work, dear," I said sitting down, for I knew she would have had to leave work early to get to the Village by five-thirty.

"Nah, Grandpa, I knew this place gets crowded for dinner. You did the right thing. And I know you love this place."

"It serves a Vouvray," I said. "The wine bars have it of course but this is the only restaurant I know of that even knows what I'm talking about," I laughed. "And you can't beat eating outdoors on a fabulous evening."

"So, do we order a bottle? Or glasses."

"I have to get back to Montclair," said I, motioning for the waiter. "Glasses this time since there are only the two of us. The next time, if Gene joins us, it will be a bottle."

She laughed. "You know he'll pick up the tab."

I joined her in laughter. "And maybe my Uber back to Montclair."

It was a good start. She was in a good mood. And when the wine was poured, we toasted each other. "To my very lovely, very loving Granddaughter," I said. "And her upcoming engagement."

"And to my Grandpa," she toasted, "who set the whole thing up."

"You mean, your Grandma Ruthie," I said. "I was just an intermediary. She wanted to see you happily involved with someone, you know."

"Yes, I know that. I'm so sorry she left us when she did. And Mom even more so. I miss them both terribly."

We both had a long sip of the delicious white wine. "But I have some wonderful news to tell you Grandpa... "

"Oh?"

"Gene's grandparents are coming to the engagement party. They're coming up from Florida! Isn't that wild? You'll finally meet them."

"You mean I won't be the oldest one there?"

"Bingo!" she laughed. "You'll have someone from the Silent Generation to talk to!"

That was a great line from Estelle, and I told her so.

"They're both in their 90's now, but in wonderful shape I hear," she added. "Gene is going down himself to get them from their home at The Villages and is using the private jet the company leases to bring them up to Newark. And they'll be staying in a luxury suite at the Marriott in Montclair."

"Wow!" I exclaimed, honestly impressed. "So this is on Gene's father's side, right?"

"Yeah. His mother's parents passed away years ago."

"But Gene's parents will both be there, I think you told me."

"Yep. And Gene's older brother, too. They outnumber us Grandpa!"

We laughed together. But there was a serious undertone. Someone from our side, a close relative, an extremely close relative, had not been invited. But why? And that needed to come out over dinner, but the wine needed to take its full effect first.

We ordered dinner, a crab salad for me, a shrimp salad for her—and another round of Vouvray when the plates were delivered. The wine seemed to be working. Estelle was talkative, relaxed and in an extremely good mood. The work that day had been in training—supervising suicide prevention calls—but she was excited that a new AI program had been devised that was getting good results. The operators would still be 'live' in all cases, but the program picked up various verbal signals from the caller and then could determine if the call should be relayed to higher up specialists who would listen in (while making sure the operator kept the caller on the line) and take the bot's recommendation which, if any, local authorities would be immediately dispatched to the call's GPS origin. In other words, the algorithm, not the caller, determined the severity of the call and its specific response. Attempted suiciders, Estelle explained, are too irrational to decide for themselves what they want done at that critical moment. So this completely virtual program would "call the shots, figuratively, not literally speaking," she quipped.

"It doesn't help if everyone is now carrying a 'ghost gun'," I added.

"No," she sadly agreed. "This is a plague, a terrible development. And no one is doing anything about it! The Feds have to step in, but they're leaving it to the States—and it's all the same 2nd Amendment politically correct b.s. You'd think since Madison they'd get it together—but no. Nationally, shootings have quadrupled in the last couple of years and so have suicides. It's overwhelming hospitals and police departments. Overwhelming social services. I need a vacation," she laughed ruefully, downing what remained of her wine.

"I read somewhere that these 3-D ghost guns can even be printed out and assembled by teens. Or they're coming up from Mexico already assembled. I think they're called zirguns, or something like that. They can go through metal detectors because they're ceramic or plastic or some kind of undetectable compound."

"Zirconia."

"Right. There has to be strict laws about this, nationally," I said. No kid under 21 should be allowed to own a firearm, especially if it's unlicensed, doesn't have a serial number that can trace back to the owner and can pass undetected through metal detectors. This is like Russian Roulette but with all the chambers filled."

"Grandpa, modern office buildings have new walkthrough metal detectors, like in airports. My building is so outdated we have an overhead detector from the 1990's in our lobby. But either way, they can't catch these ghost guns. And our security guards are not allowed to frisk or pat down so they're still using wands which are useless, just useless. Some of our clients are very nervous over this, and some of our staff as well. It's becoming scary just going to work."

"Can't you work out of your apartment?"

"I do. Often now. But most of what I do can only be handled face-to-face. We're like dentists. A Skypescape call doesn't fill the cavity."

The salads arrived with our second chilled glasses of Vouvray. I raised my glass, for a second toast.

"To keeping safe," I said solemnly.

"You too," she said, clinking our glasses. "Especially at your age. I'm amazed you're getting around like you are. You're an inspiration, Grandpa."

"Oh, I have help now. You've met Caroline. She takes care of the house. I really don't do much these days. I jog a little and say hello to my neighbors if I see them walking their dogs. I put out food for the deer. I'm playing a little tennis for exercise and pedalling Ruthie's bike to the park to play chess. I'm on the Internet a couple of hours a day to read *The Times* and *The New Yorker*. I look over some investments I have. Sometimes someone calls me on my new smartphone, well, actually last-year's model. It still needs a charger. You want to see?"

"Sure."

I took out my 3D twin-screen fold-out from my jacket's inside pocket and let her flip it open. "Why did you get this?" she asked. "Don't show it around. It's exactly what thieves are looking for these days. And you know the 'gab and grab' routine migrants use. They'll ask for directions and just grab it out of your hands. Let me buy you a pair of earbuds, grandpa."

"Let's take a selfie," I said, leaning towards her, and she towards me. I positioned the camera with an outstretched arm and took a couple of shots. They came out wonderfully.

"A good self-focusing camera," I said. "I really got it for the camera. And sometimes I'll look at social media when I'm bored."

She laughed. "You go to the InterInn site to see Peter's Outfluencer blog?"

"Sometimes. He hasn't been blogging much lately."

"I wonder why," she said sarcastically.

"What do you think of his blog?" I asked.

She shrugged, "It's a clever conceit, I guess that's the word, Grandpa. It's counter-culture, and definitely anti-establishment and some people are into that. Some people need that in their lives, but I don't. I know there are things that need fixing, like the guns we talked about, but the Outflencers aren't going to make much of a difference, one way or the other. We have to look forward and use technology more wisely now, not dwell on the faulty internet culture we had no say in developing."

"He says you're a Z, through and through."

"Well, I'd rather be a Z than the alternative. Can you imagine Peter saying he's a Not Z. I heard the tape and couldn't believe it!"

"He claims his voice was A.I.-altered. What he said, he told me, was, 'I am not a Z.'"

"I know. That's what he says. But the damage has been done. It was the stupidest thing I've ever heard. From a brother who was bar mitzvahed, no less. Well, he's paying for it big-time now."

"What is this thing with your generation," I asked. "Are you as divided as he says to me?"

She carefully cut up a couple of shrimp, and began eating, mulling over how to respond to my question. Finally she said: "I think a lot of this is media driven. I think our generation was very together in the beginning—at least I felt that way all through high school and college. We were very idealistic, and still are. But we weren't making waves, and social media depends on making waves. So this is all about grabbing attention, putting out sensationalist gossip and false reporting, selling questionable stuff you can't return and making tons of money in the process."

"So you're saying the anti-Z people are the ones who are profiting off this division?"

"Well, *we're* not, certainly! We have bills to pay like everyone else, and inflation isn't coming down even with the newly reduced tariffs so everything is still going up, up, up—but I'm not here just to make money. And I don't know of any of my cohorts who are. We're basically idealists, hard workers who are trying to stabilize the country, not tear it apart, not referring to the Internet as the Splinternet. This doesn't help anyone. I'm proud to be a Z, and I think my Z friends—if you want to call them that—are on the right side of history."

"If you truly believe Peter is in it for the money, you and your bro have some real basic differences, dear. He's more socially benevolent than you may realize."

"Well, I know. We agree on quite a few things too, Grandpa. We think Trump's border war is outrageous. Peter's idea of CCC camps to give these immigrants needed skills and teach them English and eventually Green Cards if they stay out of trouble is a workable plan that should at least be tried. We both want a national abortion law that permits abortions at least through 15 weeks of pregnancy. We both want the government to regulate *all* drug prices, generics as well as the patented brands. We want all semi-automatic rifles, and Glock switches banned. We're both concerned about climate change and want the environment to be cleaned up and new limits placed on fossil fuel production. Lots of things we agree on, Grandpa. Peter is really a Z in sheep's clothing.... correction: cheap clothing." She giggled at her own wordplay, now sipping her wine which was having its effect.

"So you don't mind his Outfluencer views."

"Well, there's a limit, Grandpa. He thinks we're all patsies. All easily influenced by what we see and hear on social media. He wants more radicalization when we don't achieve our primary objectives. And not through political discourse either. He wants demonstrations and protests in the streets. He wants immediate change, and that's not what the Z's are all about."

"Evolution, not revolution."

"Precisely. We believe we can work through the political system and put in younger people who are more flexible and open-minded to advance our views. Extremism has never worked in our country and never will. There are just too many centrists who want to move us safely and thoughtfully forward. We're just starting out, we have a long road ahead of us, and we're determined to make a positive contribution to society. Period."

"Well said," I acknowledged.

Estelle was talkative, I thought, and open to discussion. It was time for me to bring up the reason for our get-together, but in truth I was still nervous about it. "Even so, your Dad tells me you're not speaking to your brother these days."

"It's happened before. No big deal."

"Well, it's a big deal if Peter isn't invited to your engagement party, dear."

She looked away, now knowing that his non-invitation had somehow been revealed to me, and thought for a moment on what to say, although I figured she had spent some time already with her response. "I don't think it will matter one way or the other," she said, a little too flippantly to be taken seriously. "My friends are not his friends. I can't imagine anyone even asking about him."

"Oh? Really? I remember you shared many friends in common in High School," I said. "What about your best friend he got pregnant? Is she invited?"

Estelle was genuinely stunned by my shockingly nasty inquiry. "Julie was invited," she responded angrily, her intense eyes meeting mine. "And it's also none of your business who we invited."

"You and your brother used to be so close. He looked up to you. You...."

"Grandpa, that was years, a decade ago. Since college we haven't seen much of each other."

"You want to tell me what the problem is?"

"Dad can fill you in, like he probably has already," she said bitterly.

"Your father is not a very steady jockey these days. I'd rather hear it from the horse's mouth," I cracked, trying to lighten the mood.

She huffed at my rejoinder, then suddenly went serious. "Why do you want to get involved in this? There's nothing to it."

"Well, your brother is in the news these days. You must know that. And so I think this has something to do with that."

"I don't want him messing up my life. Gene doesn't want him messing up our lives. We're better off not inviting him. We just don't want any problems. Things are stressful enough as they are, especially after Madison. Maybe after the party we'll have him over. I'm sorry if his nose is out of whack."

I tried another tack.

"If you invite Peter and he doesn't come, then it's on him. At least you made it possible for him to refuse. But not inviting him will create a rift that will take a long time healing."

She turned away again, now looking downcast before gathering her thoughts. "Grandpa," she said, almost in a whisper, "I love my brother, you know that. We *do* talk on the phone occasionally to keep in touch. I haven't shut him out of my life. But since he moved he's changed. Radically changed."

"How?"

"Look," she said, now facing me again, "Peter was going to be an engineer, a scientist. He was brilliant at MIT. Got the highest grades. Wanted to go into hydroclimatology. He had a dozen offers from big corporations, great money, We talked about it a lot. He had such a great future before him. And his ideas were fantastic. I'm in social services, nothing to do with hydro engineering, but I know some of the agency's poorer clients can't get enough fresh water each day to fully hydrate and bathe themselves and their kids. And Peter had some really cool ideas on how to get more potable water into their hands without having to pay more for it."

"So what happened?"

"You'd have to ask him. I know he turned down jobs that were offered to him here in the East. Then he took an internship with that public utility in California. I think he wanted to do too much, too soon, and the people above him simply wouldn't put up with him. He was young and inexperienced but thought he knew better than his bosses, and he sometimes can be abusive. And then he anonymously started the Outfluencer site. But, ironically, *he* was outed. So he got fired. Or quit. I don't really know the story. But either way, Peter...." her voice trailed off again, "... needs counseling, I could put him in touch with a good therapist out there. But I know he won't listen to me."

"Well, he's been through a lot these last few years, dear."

"We all have, Grandpa."

"He didn't know, he told me, how sick your Mom was. She didn't want to upset him before graduation. So he only found out at the end, when she was practically in hospice, and that was a mistake."

"Look. I'm not going to second guess why Mom didn't want anyone to know about her condition. Even Dad didn't know just how serious it was. Nobody did at the time. This was Covid before it even had a name. And Mom was a very private person, unlike Grandma."

"Your Dad probably knew, but he never said anything to me, or to your Grandma that I know of."

Estelle pondered that for a while: "There was nothing to be said, either way. It was all guesswork, all conjecture. And the Chinese covered it up for a year, remember, so nobody knew anything until the lid blew off."

And essentially she was right, of course. I recalled the early days of Covid and the paranoia and disinformation that flowed from the White House on down. It wasn't that we would all run out to our neighborhood market and buy Clorox to inject into our arms. But that's what Trump was suggesting, though his defenders have always claimed it was a sarcastic play at Fauci. So, we thought maybe Trump knew something we didn't and we wanted to trust him, because there was no one else. And that was the end of his credibility. Forever. And that's when, to my mind anyway, the first crack in the country's eggshell was observed… and widening ever since.

"And now, nearly a decade later? Isn't it time to heal?" I asked, after an interval of our plates being cleared and the overly-suntanned waiter expounding on our dessert choices.

"It's always time to heal, Grandpa. But I sense some people are still in a combative mood."

"Like your brother?"

"I don't know what to make of him anymore, Grandpa," she said. "All this neo-nazi stuff is too much to bear. I know what he's said about it: That the interview was digitally altered to silence him and the Outfluencers."

"Do you believe him?"

"Actually, yes. As a Jew, especially, he would never say such a thing. So I believe him. But he came out too little, too late. This interview finished him off and I think he knows that now and I think he must be depressed about it. I can help him find some therapy that might help. But inviting him to our pre-nup party won't help. It might actually go the other way. And I... Gene and I don't want to take the chance."

"Is this coming from you, or from Gene?"

"Both. We discussed it, and we came to the same conclusion."

Our flans with an overly sweet topping arrived then. But not even the taste of this delicious concoction could wipe away the bad taste left in our mouths about what we were discussing. Estelle was almost in tears now and I shared—no—felt somehow responsible for her sadness.

"I'd like to talk to Gene, if you don't mind, dear. I'd really like your okay with that."

She shrugged. "I don't think Gene will change his mind. And putting yourself in the middle..."

"I just want to see if he's a little flexible on this, that's all."

"Do what you want to do, Grandpa," she said resignedly. "I'll go with whatever you two come up with. I just want the party to be wonderful, that's all. And safe. I just want to break away from all this sadness lately."

"I understand," I said. "It *will* be a wonderful party!"

And then the flan was tummified, as Ruthie liked to say, and the waiter brought out his pocket printer and I swiped and signed, and could see from the corner of my eye, the young couple at the garden's entryway who would be taking our cherished seats, now waving their approval of our departure. We had hardly spent an hour there, but I was no further along into my journey of understanding. I only knew a little more about what was dividing Peter and Estelle's generation, for as Peter had said, now confirmed by his sister, there was a deep divide here. And from my vantage point on high, my out-of-sight, out-of-mind Silent Generation was to remain that way, and just watch from afar, transfixed, mouths agape at our children's children taking conflicted sides in the overheated boxed canyon below.

CHAPTER 3

The one person who would know the most about Estelle and Peter's split would be their mother, of course—since she assigned herself as their official confessor since childhood. She could 'Clarafy' the situation as she liked to put it—but she was now silenced in death. Paul, their newly-annointed alcoholic Dad, tried to fill the vacuum. But my son was incommunicado these days from about five in the afternoon on. His smartphone used to be answered by a lovely young female operator, or rather an AI headshot hotbot who looked you straight in the eye and breathlessly said, 'Paul Myer is indisposed right now. Please leave your name, number, and any message you may have for him, and he'll get back to you. Thank you.'

That was before Paul's smartphone receptionist took a bathroom break—or whatever bots do to get some relief—and now, only insufferable music played in the background to a blank screen and a printed crawl message that instructed one to leave their name and number. No instruction about leaving a message.

But if I called well after noon but before five, I'd just say 'Dad' and Paul would instantly be on the line. Since Ruthie's passing, I had seen a somewhat more concerned son inquire about his father's welfare.

Losing both his wife and mother in such a short period perhaps made him see the fragility of life more clearly; that it was important to spend more time with those you love the most. At least, I thought that was the case before I realized his drinking was getting in the way. Now I wasn't even in the running with those others he loved most: The distillers of a world class Scottish bourbon (Imagine! A bourbon from Scotland no less! but I refuse to become the Influencer promoting the brand)—and his former teacher-friends in the West Side neighborhood he settled into after Clara's passing. And on any particular evening, it seemed he could go either way across the finish line.

But he took my call this Wednesday at around two in the afternoon, and sounded, as he always did in those few precious hours of total rationality, upbeat and sober as a judge.

"Want to meet for dinner?" I suggested.

"Can't tonight, Dad," he said, "But tomorrow night I'm free. I can come out there, so you don't have to train in. If you let me sleep over."

"That's a deal," I said. "See you at six, six-thirty."

"Great!" he exclaimed. "Lots to talk about."

Paul was in computer contact with Peter via Skypescape almost every weekday, but the time differential made it difficult for the two of them to spend more than a few minutes with each other. His father slept till noon, nine in the morning in California, and Peter, now out of work, was also sleeping late into the morning hours. Paul was getting ready to go out at about five in the afternoon, two PM on the West Coast. So the two of them usually connected at four in the afternoon in New York, one o'clock in LA. And as I said, it was almost on a daily basis, weekends excluded.

Estelle thought Peter needed psychological counseling: Paul brought himself in as counselor. He instinctively knew *his* son needed help to work through some crushing defeats—and *my* son, to his everlasting credit—stepped up to the plate. And while Estelle was quite aware of her Dad's now-chronic alcoholism, I'm not at all sure Peter knew, being so far away. Estelle had said to me once, "As long as Dad is not abusive and can socialize in that state, it seems almost therapeutic to me, especially when you consider the alternatives. How long it can go on like this is another question altogether."

If Estelle could tolerate her Dad's drinking, I certainly could as well. Ruthie was somewhat appalled but also came to accept 'Paul's new-found wife' as she crudely put it, soon after Clara's passing. Into her middle years, Ruthie enjoyed moderate drinking herself, but once the stomach pains started, never took another drop, alcohol affecting her medications. And for my part, I disliked most grain alcohol liquors all my life, sticking with a few choice wines and an occasional after-dinner cordial. But in these times, especially these torturous times, it was either alcohol or fentanyl to get through the pain—and going down that wide open highway usually narrowed into a one-way dead-end street for many.

I hadn't seen Paul in over a month now, although we talked frequently on Skypescape or with a smartphone chat. With so many modes of communication, it was almost impossible to find a good excuse for not initiating a conversation or answering the inquiry of a family member or friend who just wanted to check in. But (and here I completely agreed with Peter) it was the uninvited, unwelcomed bot calls that were forcing me to turn off my phone for much of the day. They knew my age, my address and zip code, my credit rating, my two speeding tickets, even details about the recent loss of my wife, and Rachel, our daughter who died when she was ten. So clearly I was in need of added liability insurance on my car, a professional stock advisor, a senior dating site, a local real estate agent, drug discounts and many other limited time come-ons, coupons, "advertorial" scams and QR codes too numerous to mention. Sure, I registered with a 'do not call' governmental program—but it was ineffectual. AI's algorithms had managed to dig the dirt out on me, invading my space, patiently trudging through reams of aged, yellowed, outdated material scattered about in the Infosphere. Privacy, as Peter once noted—alluding to Mailer's masterpiece—was no longer a luxury for the Naked, but now provided comfort only for the Dead.

Paul pulled up in his new EV Kia a quarter after six, and we headed out to Montclair and to La Dolce Vita, my favorite Italian restaurant in the area. The owner, Eduardo, made sure one of his best customers got a choice table, knew the white Italian wine to serve, asked about my health, and made small talk with Paul whom he hadn't seen in months.

After Eduardo moved on, Paul remarked, "It's like a college homecoming here without the alumni."

I laughed. "You gotta be overly gracious these days, what with the restaurant industry on its knees. Did I ever tell you Eduardo sent flowers to Ruthie's memorial?"

Getting Past Z

"No, but I can imagine."

"Before the pandemic this place was overflowing. Had to reserve days in advance. Now look. It's just us and that other couple."

"It's still early, Dad. And it's a Thursday, remember."

"Yeah, but I've been here on the weekend and much later, too. A quarter of the crowd he used to get. They've raised prices so much to cover their expenses, no one can afford eating out these days."

"Or even eating in," Paul added. "Do you know what ramen noodles are now?"

"Is that what you're eating? Ramen noodles?"

He laughed. "Does that alarm you? What does Caroline prepare for you, if I may ask."

"Anything I want. She's a great cook. Chicken, fish, shrimp, lamb chops, veal, but no red meat. Whatever she sees that looks appetizing."

"Well, if it's on your dime, why not?"

"That's unfair, my dear son," I said as snidely as I could. "You know that she's the reason for my still being independent like I am. Do you expect me to go grocery shopping or wait in line somewhere? At my age?"

"Dad, I know what Caroline Hamilton makes a week, for four-five hours a day, tops! And that includes shopping, dry cleaning, putting gas in her car, picking up prescriptions and whatever else she says she does before arriving at your place. She's making twice as much as I did teaching in my last year!"

"So? She's professionally licensed with an agency. You pay extra for that."

He downed the remains of his first glass of wine, and poured a second from the decanter in the ice bucket beside the table. "It's far too much money to be paying for her hospice services. You don't need hospice. In a way, she's overqualified. I did some research on what caretakers make today, long after Covid."

"I don't want to know. She was wonderful with Clara, you even said so at the time. You paid a premium if the aide was caring for a Covid patient. It was risky work. Quarantine, remember? Masks, gloves, the whole bit. And constant testing. You couldn't find good, reliable help. Ruthie asked me to rehire her to help out when she took ill, knowing what your Mom went through, and what Caroline could provide. She's also an R.N., remember. So I kept her on."

"So are you doing this for Mom or for Grandma?"

"I'm doing this for *me*," I said a bit more angrily than I intended. "I know what I'm doing, these days. You just told me I don't need hospice. Do you think I'm beginning to lose it?"

I could see the direction this discussion was taking. The wine was opening up Paul to things he had to know was causing me distress. So, diplomatically, he backed down, but only a bit.

"I'm sorry, Dad; I just don't like to see you being taken advantage of."

"Let me be the judge of that," I said. "There are many other things, much more important things, we need to discuss. My help is not one of them."

I wanted to nail a few things down now, before my son was too impaired. But I think he realized he was driving us back home that night and so he held off consuming his second glass of wine. Instead, he ordered us dinner from the menu on his phone. I had shrimp diablo; he had veal parmesan.

"Did you ask Estelle about Peter when she sent you the invitation to her engagement party?"

"Yes, Dad, I did."

"And what did she say?"

"She told me, Gene and she had decided not to. She's very troubled about her brother lately and adding him to the guest list was just not a good idea."

"And you agreed?"

"I told her it was her party and whatever she decided was okay with me. I promised I wouldn't say anything to Peter, one way or the other. I didn't want to be put in the middle of this invitation crap."

"You realize, of course, that the two of them shared many friends together, all the way back to grade school. And no doubt some of these friends have been invited to the party. And one of her close girlfriends she's invited dated Peter in high school and it was serious at the time."

"You remember that?"

"Certainly. It was one of the things Clara needed to Clarafy. She and Ruthie were on the phone constantly about it. So of course I knew. It was hardly a secret that Peter got that girl pregnant. And they took a trip to Puerto Rico during Easter recess and she got an abortion there if I remember correctly. You must recall that."

"I put that out of my mind years ago, Dad. We all do stupid things in high school. I taught high school math for over 30 years, remember: I've seen much worse."

"So let me understand: This lady is invited and would naturally see her old flame here at the party which could be really problematic?"

"I have no idea. I haven't seen the guest list."

"Estelle told me she's been invited. And Peter has not. I'm wondering if this is the real reason, and not some neo-nazi-concocted excuse."

"Whatever, Dad. She can invite whomever she wants to her pre-nup. Let it be."

Following my son Paul's (not McCartney's) advice, I let it be. But there was one other matter I needed to bring up with my son over dinner.

"How did this rift between Peter and Estelle happen? They were so close at one time."

"Well, for one thing, Peter moved to California. They were on opposite sides of the continent."

"Why did he take that job? I never got a good reason why."

"Well, I think they made him an offer he couldn't refuse. Very good money, and he was supposed to be working on projects that most interested him. A lot of that was bullshit, it seems. They had a training program he went through in his first summer there and expected it to end that Fall and given some mid-level creative responsibility, but it never developed. They misled him on that. Essentially, he was task masking. He never got the chance to put his ideas across."

"The rooftop idea?"

"Yeah, that was one. So he did the prototype himself out-of-pocket. I've seen photos of it and the actual layout plans. And he had a 35-page detailed report he did after he installed it which showed the cost savings over a 3-month time span. The utility wanted no part of it."

"So this had nothing to do with his Outfluencer blog."

"I doubt it. They used that as an excuse to let him go. I think they were looking for something, some slip-up on his part, and this was it. That, and the Nazi reference. Somehow they got his name and once he was outed, he was let go."

"So he didn't quit. He was fired."

"Yeah. I don't think he'd ever admit to that, but more than likely."

"It could have been the utility who altered the Not Z tape."

"I don't think we'll ever know, Dad. But I believe Peter. He has nothing to do with Nazis or antisemites or white supremasists or migrant haters or even those idiots who laid down on the street last Thanksgiving. He's very disillusioned about everything these days."

"I didn't get that impression when he was here," I countered. "He seemed very animated, somewhat defiant even."

"Well, he puts up a good front. Estelle believes he shows signs of bipolar disorder. You know what that is, Dad?"

"Yeah. It's a nice clean-up for what we used to call in my day, manic-depressive."

"So I agree with Estelle that Peter needs to be evaluated by a professional. And the sooner, the better. He's very lost out there by himself. His unemployment insurance will run out before the end of the year and he's drawing down on savings. And even worse, even though he removed the Outfluencer site, he fears there are people out there who want to even the score; who want to harm him."

"He told you that?"

"Yeah. And I know something that will disturb you no end…"

Our entrees came just then. I wasn't at all sure I wanted to hear more, and I told Paul that. "I don't think I want to know," I said, while the plates were being set. "If he feels he's not safe in California I told him he could always stay at my place. It would be safe for him there."

"To your health," Paul toasted. It would be the last glass of wine he would have that evening and I was thankful, at least, for that.

***

Paul got us back soberly and safely to Upper Montclair and it was hardly after 9PM, but we both said our goodnights and went to bed, much left unsaid. I figured Paul was going to tell me about threats to Peter's life, and I knew such news would disturb me no end, exactly as Paul put it. Peter had brought this all upon himself. But he was young and quite naive. In these times, you couldn't just "out" some company, some product or service, and expect no retribution, no payback. There were daily stories now about "California's Cartels"—new domestic terrorist groups up from Mexico, who had nothing better to do than get paid for Peter's body hanging from a walkway above a busy highway.

All this in the "direction of disaster for democracy" as an opinion writer for *The New York Times* recently put it. And if it affected the Z generation the most, as the writer claimed, then Peter, like it or not, was a primary target. Although The Outfluencer had been effectively shut down, it had spawned dozens of wannabes, just as the Influencer movement had a decade earlier.

But worse, the Z generation was split right down the middle—between those White, wealthy and educated, and those of the lower class minorities without the means to higher education and better paying jobs. This was the classic American have-vs-have not entanglement described for decades as confined womb-conjoined twins, now once separated, emerging violently to life.

What I couldn't understand though, was that Peter, highly educated with a comfortable future before him, would take the Anti-Z side. I got that this was not only an economic and racial issue, but a political one; all three dialectical scripts playing out at once. And that Peter sided with the less fortunate, not necessarily because of economic and social injustice cast upon them, but the political indifference to their plight. So long as the Trump government was in power, elected by and for the corporate "vampires" as he put it, there would be no structural social change, but increasingly violent reaction to apathy and an economic recession long past its closing due date. The *United* States of America was coming apart at its seams.

So I had as a grandson, an accredited revolutionary, no longer nameless and faceless, but actively taking part in a startup movement that I predicted would have a short and violent ending. It immediately brought to mind Max Azzarello, the 34-year-old from Florida who immolated himself in front of the New York courthouse where Trump was being tried for the Stormy Daniels hush money payment. Azzarello claimed the U.S. was going through a totalitarian con job and our "post-truth America" would soon be sponsoring a world-wide apocalyptic fascist coup.

Peter seemed quite a distance away from being a conspiratorial nut job, yet it still was concerning to me just how extreme his views were becoming. I didn't quite know how to handle things—whether I needed to sit him down and lecture him about a peaceful interchange of democratic ideas and ideals, or the direction of disaster as *The Times* put it. This Z generation—Z standing for Zapped, again in *The Times* columnist's words—would turn in upon itself, and self-destruct, unless cooler heads prevailed.

But whether the Silent Generation, now itself in its death-throes, would be listened to was very problematic. Few took the advice of their X-odus parents, much less their grandparents. And so, the threats to Peter, and my offer of a hideaway for his safety, would, I figured, go unheeded in any event. Going further with Paul on the subject was both impractical and self-defeating.

"How did you sleep," I asked Paul over coffee and toasted bagels with a schmear of cream cheese and a slice of lox on them.

"Always great to sleepover here again in my room," he answered. "It's still such a country feeling, you can hear the crickets and tree frogs as if they're in bed with you."

I laughed. "It's time you dated again."

"Believe me, Dad, I'm looking around."

"Any good prospects?"

"Yeah, but with a lot of baggage."

"The kids should be out of the house by now. Unless you're looking for a really young lady."

"No, Dad, I'm not. But almost all are divorcees and are still sandwiched between their kids and their parents... with an ex-husband or two lurking around. It's complicated."

"I bet! So you're not bringing a guest to Estelle's party? Y'know, the invitation said you can bring a guest, don't you?"

"No. I'm going stag. And you?"

"Well, I want to have Caroline there that day, just in case I need her for something, y'never know. So I invited her and her partner Chris but he works on Saturdays so only she accepted. She's my date."

"I bet you're the only interracial couple on the floor," was his crude rejoinder. I didn't respond to his insensitive remark but rather thought it best to change the subject.

"Speaking of which, did you know they're putting in a small dance floor in the backyard?"

"What?"

"There's this gal, Doris something-or-other, who's the party coordinator Gene hired to supervise everything—the caterer, the seating arrangement, the music—and she decided to put in a dance floor so if people want to dance they don't have to dance on the grass or the porch. She was out here a few weeks ago and took pictures of everything."

"Well, that kinda makes sense. Weren't they going to use the caterer you had for Mom?"

"John's never handled that many people. He was unsure he could. So Gene knew a caterer who he uses for all the social events his law firm holds. So I said sure."

"And the string quartet?"

"Yeah, they'll be playing for about an hour or so at the beginning. And then a DJ is coming in for the rest of the afternoon. So much for quiescence. But you haven't heard the latest...."

"Oh, Jesus, I can imagine!"

"Guess who's officiating the engagement?"

"Doris something-or-other."

"No. Rabbi Max."

"Aw, you gotta be kidding. Did you tell him this wasn't a bar mitzvah?" he snickered.

"Rabbi Max called me after Gene talked to him and asked if it was all right with me if he officiated the engagement and of course I said yes."

"How do you officiate an engagement in Reform Judaism? I've never heard of that."

"Apparently you can. You can do anything you want so long as the Rabbi gets a piece of the action. For Mom's gravesite and memorial services I donated five grand to the Temple. I bet you didn't know that."

"I assumed you donated something, but you never told me how much."

"And the string quartet was Rabbi Max's idea, because they played at Temple gatherings for many years, and so I paid another five hundred, and tipped them a hundred more."

"They were great. Beautifully touching music. That was a good deal!"

"And for the engagement party, Rabbi Max wants a chuppa, but Gene is taking care of that and the music, the food, the liquor, the chairs, the photographer, the flowers, the suggested Temple donation. Everything. I'm not paying for anything."

"A chuppa? God, what else?"

"An attendant out front to direct cars where to park."

"Oh, shit! I hadn't thought of that. Where will they all park?"

"I agreed to let them park in the driveway oval in front of the house. Gene said he would pay for any permanent damage to the grass. I guess the oval can handle about fifteen or so cars. The rest can park on the street as long as they don't block driveways. And a few guests are coming in from the city by train—Gene is hiring a van for pickups. Remember, there was a response form with the invitation, directions to the house and a question about how you were planning to arrive along with the train schedule."

"Oh, right. I responded I'm coming by car, of course. And I can take some people back with me."

"That's good. Everything seems to be covered. Everything but Peter."

"I can't help you there, Dad. I wish I could, but it's not my party."

"I know that. It's really Gene's party when you think about it. And I think I need to have a talk with him.

CHAPTER 4

Time was running out. The party was less than three weeks away, two and a half to be precise. Now, at the beginning of August families were taking their vacations, getting their kids ready for school, finalizing their Labor Day Weekend plans and then plans for the Fall. Peter's invitation, if there was to be one, couldn't wait for the last minute; it was unfair to him, because I knew he had other expectations to fulfill were he not ultimately invited to his sister's party.

How did I know?

Because I received a Skypescape call a couple of days after dinner with Paul from a lovely young lady. And like you, my dear Reader, at first didn't know exactly who I was talking to. But she quickly put it all in perspective for me.

"I'm Julie Roemer," she said. "And I got your number from Stella. We're friends. We've been close friends since High School. My Mom and her Mom were close friends, too. Now do you know who I am? I'm the girlfriend Peter knocked up."

I didn't quite know what to say. Her rude description of her pregnancy was for effect, I realized, but even so, it took my breath away. "Well... hello," I said, haltingly. "It's nice to hear from you. How have you been?"

"I'm fine, Jerry... if I can call you that."

"Sure."

"I've been in touch with Stella and I believe she told you I was invited to her engagement party. True?"

"True."

"And Peter has not. True?"

"True."

"Thank you. That's all I needed to know. I had to confirm that for myself. Bye now."

"Wait!" I shouted. "Can we talk a little more? Please?"

"I don't think there's any more to be said," she replied. "I won't be coming to Stella's party if Peter isn't there. It's as simple as that. And I told her that."

Wow, I thought, I was completely upside-down in my thinking. Apparently, they were still on friendly terms, perhaps even romantically connected. So I had to back up a bit. "It's still not definitely decided," I said. "I would like Peter there as well. Do you know Estelle's boyfriend Gene?"

"Yes. I've been with Stella on Gene's boat."

"Oh, I didn't know he had a boat."

"Yes, it's a beautiful yacht. Harbored in Westport. But what about Gene?"

"Well, I was going to try to get in touch with him, and tell him I was upset with their decision over Peter. They're having their party at my house, you realize, and so I think I have some say here."

"Good luck with that," she said bitterly.

"Look. While I have you on the phone, can you tell me, please, why Estelle and Gene aren't inviting Peter. What's their real reason? I can't get a straight answer here."

"Do you know Gene's history?"

"I don't know very much about Gene really."

"Did you know his Dad died in the 9/11 attack on the World Trade Center?"

"I thought his Dad was coming to the party."

"That's his step-dad. His mother remarried. His real father was killed that day."

I was dumbfounded. "Oh, I didn't know. I'm so sorry to hear that."

"So Gene is a bit sensitive to people with radical issues these days. And Peter is connected to some radical anti-social groups, I'm sorry to say. He's trying to break away and do his own thing, and I think I'm helping him do that. But things are very dicey out there now, especially since Madison and Trump's migrant mess, I don't have to tell you."

"So this is about security? And for security reasons Gene isn't taking any chances?"

"Gene has a security team connected to his law firm he sometimes uses. They clear the way for him. I know it sounds a bit paranoiac, but you have to see this from his and Stella's perspective. They want a peaceful party away from everything; that's why they chose your place. They were going to have the party on his yacht, but there were too many guests for that. So your backyard was perfect."

"I talked to Peter at some length, Julie. He's not going to create any problems."

"Did you know Peter's been threatened?"

"For The Outfluencer blog."

"For that, and for the Not Z comment. These people shut him down. And they're still threatening him."

"He told me that, yes."

"And did he tell you what precautions he's taken?"

"No."

"Well, I know. He tells me everything going on in his life. Peter and I are still very close as you can imagine. He took the California job to be with me, after all."

"I didn't know that."

"Well, it's true. I never told anyone, even Stella. I was at CalTech, getting my PhD in biochemistry. Peter helped me enormously with writing the thesis."

"So you're calling from California?"

"No, I'm living close to New Haven now. I have a position with a big chemical company here and I want Peter to come East and be with me. We talked about that after he stayed with you a couple of weeks ago."

"So you saw him then?"

"That Sunday. We took the room at The Royale we had booked a week earlier. Then on Monday he had me drop off some updated plans of his with Gene, or rather the firm's front desk receptionist, because Peter didn't want to go through security. He also had an interview the following day which went very well, he told me."

"Why wouldn't Peter want to go through security?"

"Jerry, do you know the new law in California called 'concealed carry'?"

"Not a lot. Some states are allowing people to now carry a concealed weapon if they register it and take some preventative measures. I don't know much about it."

"Every state is different. New York State is still working on a concealed carry bill. So even if you have all your registration papers in order from another state, New York security still won't let you through. You have to temporarily give up the firearm to the security people. They give it back when you leave the building."

"Ahhh," it suddenly dawned on me, "Peter said he had taken precautions. He meant he was now carrying a gun, is that it?"

"Yes. And Gene knows about it, because when I found out I had to let Stella know and obviously she told Gene. And both came to the same conclusion about inviting Peter to their party."

"Ahhh," I said again, now having most of the pieces of the puzzle put together for me. "Now I get it. So if Peter leaves his weapon behind, he can come to the party?"

"That was originally the plan," Julie said, a hint of anger in her voice. "He's known about their objection from the start. We talked about it when I got my invitation and he didn't."

"You mean he already knew about the party and the fact he hadn't received an invitation when we got together a couple of weeks ago?"

"Yes."

"Well, he could have fooled me. In fact, he *did* fool me. I thought I had inadvertently let the cat out of the bag, but he already knew for weeks it seems."

"Yes."

"So this is really simple," I said. "Peter has to promise not to bring the gun to the party and he'll be invited and you'll be coming and that's it! End of story!"

"Like I said, that was originally the plan, Jerry. But his gun is his security blanket now, now that he's been personally threatened. He's exhibiting the same paranoid tendencies of millions of Americans who have already bought into concealed carry when outside of their homes… without having the means of defending themselves… the feeling of being totally defenseless."

"It's still very controversial," I said. "I think the jury is still out on this."

"I think it all depends on the perceived threat level," Julie replied. "And the threat perception is rising everywhere it seems. Some people are terrified of heights, and some people are terrified of depths. And more and more people are terrified of being alone in crowds these days… in light of the Nova rave and Madison, the border war and all that's followed. Agoraphobia. That tipped the scale for concealed carry in many States."

"When he was here, I didn't know he had a gun with him," I put in. "I don't want guns in my house either. So I'm with you 100% on this."

"One of the reasons I moved from California back to Connecticut," she continued, "was Connecticut's legislature defeating the latest concealed carry bill. You can't walk out of your house with a firearm, period. I'm very clear about this with Peter. We love each other, we're soulmates. But If we move in together somewhere in Connecticut, or elsewhere, he leaves his firearm in California with the rest of his anti-Z pals."

"So you're on the same page as Estelle here. But I think you told her you won't come to the party if he's not invited. So I see you're conflicted about this, too."

"If we can work this out, I'll actually be coming to the party with Stella and three other longtime girlfriends, still single I may add. Gene is hiring a limo for us. And I think he's invited some really nice single men from his office. So it's going to be a really great party and I really want to be there, Jerry."

"Ah, ha, some ulterior motives, I see. So in a way this is all in Peter's hands, figuratively speaking," I joked.

Julie laughed along. "Look. Stella and I only want the best for Peter. He's a brother to her, a loving partner to me, a brilliantly creative mind, a wonderful sense of humor. You couldn't ask for a more devoted friend and companion, especially what we've been through together. We... I don't want to let him go! I want to make a life with him, but he's caught up in the times. He wants to make a difference in a world that is getting more and more indifferent to difference."

"I'm not sure I understand," I said.

"Well, we'll talk more about this at the party," she said. "Get Peter to somehow give up his gun, and then I'll see you there, Jerry."

"I'll do everything I can, Julie. Thanks for your call, for laying out things like you did. It's made a great difference."

"Keep me informed about what's going on," she said. "There's not much time left."

Julie was right, there wasn't much time left before the party. I was left with two possibilities: One, call Peter that very day and present him with this ultimatum: He either promises to leave his gun in California, in which case he'd be invited to the engagement party while staying with me—or remain in California with his gun and his paranoia, and lose not only Estelle's, Gene's and Julie's abiding faith in him, but now, my own.

Or Two, call Gene and see if there was not some kind of compromise possible: That perhaps Peter could promise to turn the firearm over to Gene or me or even Doris, the event coordinator, before the party began and then get it back after all the guests had left. Like I told Julie, I didn't want any guns in my house at all, ever, so this second possibility was very problematic for me. But I was willing to bend.

In any event, Gene had to know I sided with him and Estelle in this matter. And I wanted them to know about the call I had just received from Julie. We were all on the same page here. Peter had to decide which was more important to him: close friends and family, or his misguided considerations for his personal safety and wellbeing. An impossible choice, clearly, but one he alone would have to make.

And then, at that very moment, as if by some act of a mystical overseer in this dilemma, my smartphone rang. It was Gene smiling at me over his Skypescape connection.

"Hi, Jerry! I tried to get you about fifteen minutes ago, but your line was busy. Are you free to talk," he asked.

"I was about to call you," I said, astounded by this timing coincidence.

"I think we need to talk about the engagement party some more. There are some details I want to go over with you."

"Yes," I agreed. "The sooner the better."

"How about tomorrow, noon. We can have lunch in our private dining room here."

"Oh... oh fine," I said. "Where is your office?"

"It's in the World Trade Center building. But don't worry about that. I'll have a car pick you up at your place and drive you here. Can you be ready say, around, 11am?"

"Certainly. I just have to tell my aide Caroline that I'll be gone for the day. No problem."

"Oh, that's great. We'll drive you back as well. Now, let me ask you: What would you like for lunch? There's a great deli downstairs."

"Whatever you're having, I'll have the same," I said.

"I like to order their roast beef on rye with a side of spicy mayo. And a Dr. Pepper."

"Make that two."

"Done. My car will be at your place as close to 11 as possible. See you tomorrow."

I realized I had ordered a roast beef sandwich, barely cooked red meat, but it didn't matter: this had to be Fate intervening, and so I was more than willing to accommodate it. For it was so much better that Gene called me and not the other way 'round. I didn't want to become a pest or interfere in their celebratory plans. And now I could bring up Peter without sounding like I was taking sides.

What I needed from Gene was a way an invitation could be sent to him. If Peter declined, then that would be fine; it would be all on him and no one's ego would suffer (and secretly, Dear Reader, I was hoping for that outcome—for it would have ended my narrative peacefully right then and there.)

But you must remember the background story here, as I'm sure you do, since it happened a little more than two years ago, in June of 2026: the so-called Madison Massacre… or MM for short—(as differentiated from the other earlier Madison mass murder just before

Christmas 2024 at the Abundant Life Christian School.) We don't have to go over the grisly details of MM since they're still fresh in most every American's mind. But no doubt even more fresh in the minds of those couples planning engagement or wedding events since that tragic incident.

And yes, this simply wasn't a tragedy for Madison, Wisconsin, where the mass shooting took place. It reverberated throughout the country, like the Kennedy Assassination, 9/11, Lewiston and Uvalde, Parkland and Sandy Hook. And because it happened just days before Trump's massive Declaration of Independence 250th Anniversary July 4th Celebration, it was, and no doubt will always be, regarded as the single most traumatic domestic event of the 2020's—Washington, D.C.'s Insurrection, the LA fires and the Covid contagion notwithstanding. And this is just not my judgment, but almost every newspaper's editorial board from *The New York Times* on down. It could have easily been our country's second Ft. Sumter had not the National Guard been called up in virtually every State to protect vulnerable sites— from religious institutions to malls to children's school playgrounds. And even today, on its anniversary (which just happens to be Trump's birthday as well) and other social occasions where there are masses of people congregating, we are acutely aware of MM's ramifications: We are a nation getting more and more paranoid with the increase of gun violence and the newest security precautions now being taken to mitigate this intensifying plague.

But let me also say here, that by the mid-2020's the country was already defensively arming itself in almost every way conceivable— pepper spray, mace, stun guns, tasers, zappers—and legislative bills for 'concealed carry' were gaining political strength in almost every

State. What was new, of course, was the Chinese-inspired Zirgun—a chemical concoction that was actually a kind of ceramic—stronger than steel that could pass unnoticed through metal detectors—and molded into any kind of weapon using 3-D printing technology for its illegal creation. It did not help that the Chinese gave the Mexican cartels all they needed to manufacture and stealthily export these guns into the United States. It was, as one journalist wittily put it, "[the] first good reason humans have to begin planetary exploration."

But getting back to the Madison Massacre: The perpertraitor, Michael Hammond, had a zirgun pistol on him for his suicide but used a standard all-metal semi-automatic AR-15 kit sold to him at a gun show earlier that year for the slaughter of 32 innocents and the wounding of 46 others, some for life. No one in Madison's All-Saints Catholic Church was spared, including three children, a service dog, and an usher who carried a concealed pistol: you either played dead or were dead. Nor was it, as many people claimed, a miscegenatic hate crime—built around the fact that the bride was White, the groom Black. Hammond was indiscriminate in his hatred: Robotically, he fired at anything that moved.

Nor was he declared insane by the committee investigating the tragedy, even temporarily impaired due to the insignificant amount of fentanyl in his body. He had never been in analysis, much less ever even being seen by a psychologist. In fact, he was, by every account of those who knew him, a 'straight arrow', never having been arrested for any crime or misdemeanor, not even a driving offense. Rather, he was a periodically unemployed Harvard-educated techie, somehow being able to hack into his girlfriend's email, cyberstalking her at will. An operating room nurse, she was now seeing a well-respected orthopedic surgeon at the hospital they both worked at. And now, Hammond knew of their every move, their every plan for their future together.

It came down to pure jealousy and a failed relationship that hadn't even been consummated with an intimate act of any kind, according to the bride's journal. Hammond was enraged that the bride had chosen another instead of himself to marry, when, naturally, he was clearly the better choice, despite what the bride eventually figured out after nearly a year of courtship, wanting only to remain 'good friends' with him.

Of course, we will never know Hammond's true motive for certain, since after destroying the large porcelain and mahogany crucifix hanging above the sanctuary, thereby emptying the last of his magazines, he threw away his AR-15 made fully automatic with a giggle switch, pulled out his zirgun and through his keffiyeh and the elastic band holding his GoPro camera, put a bullet into his right temple. Since he had already killed the officiating priest, there was no one to give him his last rites. And when the police did finally arrive and could attend to the many wounded (including the organist who played dead) they believed, falsely, that it was a Black assassin, someone from the groom's entourage. So they literally stepped over Hammond at first, looking for some Black killer they had reason to believe was still somewhere at large. Luckily the (White) organist was still lucid enough to set them straight before she passed out.

[I know you have your theories and your thoughts on this obscene tragedy still fresh in your memory—and it is certainly not my intent to alter in any way your personal feelings in this matter. I only want to put in context what was discussed in my meeting with Gene Samuels, that I am about to describe, and some of the reasoning behind the security considerations that were facing all of us at the time. I still wish to remain neutral in my authorship, but please understand, recent past events are still fermenting in my mind and may, unwittingly, bias my narrative.]

The limo Gene ordered for me was promptly on time. Caroline had dutifully arrived at 10:30 and, noticing it was going to be a very hot day, had with her a couple of frozen apple juice containers for my trip into the city. She needn't have gone through the trouble since there was a full refrigerated bar containing all sorts of accompanying soft drinks backing the partition between the driver and myself—with the air conditioning turned to the perfect setting. Once we left Upper Montclair, I took out my pen and pad and began working on the agenda I wanted to have with Gene. There were several things to be discussed, and I wanted to put them into some organized fashion so I wouldn't overlook any. They were:

Introduction. Sorry about the loss of his father 9/11. WTC?

My guest list of close friends/neighbors—3 couples, Caroline, Paul (8) accepting.

Bathroom off art studio from the back porch entrance. Sign with arrow in garage.

Rain? Tent or covering for the caterers? The ceremony? Chuppa?

Parking. Be sure not to block driveways along the street. Attendant?

Julie's call to me & Estelle. Coming together in limo? Getting back to city?

Call to Peter with agreement of G/E/J for his invitation. Yes/no, or what conditionals?

If conditional, Security & how I'm proposing to Peter to relieve him of his firearm. MM.

Me as holder, gun in bedroom safe. Give to Doris?

Invitation sent by Estelle to Peter by express mail today if he agrees to all. Coming in?

Pay for something. Flowers for chuppa? Rabbi Max

Caroline to take Monday off. Maybe Paul to stay over with Peter.

So there was lots to talk about. I would write down what was decided. Could all of this be handled in an hour? Twelve items, 5 minutes each? I had my doubts.

And I wasn't at all sure about the position I was finding myself in. It seemed like now I was the go-between between Peter, and Estelle, Gene, and now Julie—something I didn't want to ever happen. But Peter seemed open enough when he stayed over a couple of weeks before. Could I restore that open feeling? There had to be some give-and-take here for that to happen.

The limo took the Holland Tunnel in, and the West Side Highway down to Battery Park. There we made a left and in a few blocks found ourselves at the entrance to the World Trade Center's underground parking garage. But even before we could enter, the limo had to be driven onto a platform, and a tunneled cat-scan produced of its structural integrity and internal contents, myself included. The gate was lifted, we passed in quick order, then drove down the ramp to the designated spaces below. Once parked, the driver, whose name I can't remember now, opened the door for me, and told me to wait for a moment before an elevator until someone from the law firm would be coming to accompany me upstairs.

That happened almost immediately, for I'm assuming that once we hit Manhattan, the driver called ahead to report that we were just blocks away. A young man, nattily attired in a gray pinstriped suit appeared from the elevator, right hand extended for shaking. "Hi, I'm Robert, and I'll take you to see Gene now."

I said goodbye to the driver, complimented him on his driving prowess, and stepped inside the elevator with Robert, expecting to be whisked up to Gene's law firm. But instead the elevator only deposited us to an area off the building's main lobby. It would be here that both Robert and I would be scanned again with the latest in security devices—and I needed to ask Robert what this was all about as we waited in a short line because I saw no walk-through detector before us.

"This isn't just for metal," he explained. "This is an AI program that analyzes shapes we may be carrying on us or in backpacks and purses. It's informally called a ShapeSifter—after shapeshifter I suppose. At any rate it's completely non-invasive, so don't worry."

"You mean it'll spot my zirgun?" I asked, my innocent query designed to scare the living shit out of him.

It worked. "You... .you're carrying a zirgun?" Robert gasped, barely able to contain his fear and amazement.

"Nah," I assured him. "Only kidding."

"Oh, thank God!" he exclaimed, now quite relieved. "That could be a real problem. We'd be detained for an hour while they checked us out. And you'd have to surrender your gun. But that's what the algorithm is supposed to catch. Its data bank holds over a thousand shapes and sizes in any material that could be used as a weapon. Even can look into solid-state batteries for explosives. That's a real advance over wands and the old metal detectors we had to walk through after emptying our pockets."

And then it was time for Robert and I to be scanned with a portable device no bigger nor thicker than a computer tablet. I stepped onto a foot pattern etched into the concrete floor while the security agent simply walked around me raising and lowering its screen, head to toe. No threatening shape was found and the ordeal took but seconds. Same for Robert. And now, turning a corner, we were fronting the elevator bank that would take us to the Erskine & Samuels law offices on the 81st floor.

CHAPTER 5

Their executive board room, which served as Gene's private dining room as well, was somewhat more than expected. A corner office with two large windows facing both North and East, so a fantastic view of uptown Manhattan and the Hudson River and New Jersey streamed into the uncurtained apertures. Robert indicated where I was to sit before he departed: a plush leather chair to the right of the larger chair at the head of the lengthy table, but I wanted to first look at the amazing views before me. And of course 9/11 came into mind as I knew it would. But that Gene had lost his father in that catastrophe was something new and disturbing to me. Why would he choose to put his offices in the rebuilt building at that exact location? Curiosity got the better of me, although I realized it would be a sensitive subject to bring up. Better, I thought, to see if Gene would first breach the subject.

And then, in a couple of minutes, he was there behind me, a manila folder in his left hand. "Quite a view," he said, extending his other hand, "even better when there's no haze in the air. Glad you could make it, Jerry. How was your trip?"

I hadn't ever seen him in a finely tailored suit and tie, for at Ruthie's memorial he was wearing a sports jacket—as I had insisted that the event be informal—and at other times he was wearing a sweater or a leather jacket. I was looking at a reasonably tall, handsomely slim 40-ish gentleman, with a head of curly faintly auburn hair and hazel eyes, who looked ten years younger. Estelle was obviously attracted to him physically, and why not? A good catch, I thought to myself.

"Fine," I said. "I even passed through security." I joked.

He laughed, placing his arm across my shoulders and leading me to my chair right-angled to his. "We have new security devices downstairs which are so much better than what we used to have. They hadn't changed much since the old World Trade Center came down," he said, now slipping into his chair to my left, and pouring a glass of water for himself from the pitcher on the tray separating us. "So this is definitely an improvement. Would you like some water?"

"I'm fine," I said. "They're called ShapeSifters?"

"There is another technical name for them, but informally that's what the public is calling them. We've ordered one ourselves for our outside events. In fact, that's one of the things I need to discuss with you. But later. I'd really like to get to know you better, since Stella speaks of you so highly."

"Well, that goes both ways," I said. "She speaks very highly of you. You two seem to be of the same mind on many things."

"I know. Sometimes I think we're brother and sister, we're that close. But I want to bring up something at the very beginning of our conversation today. And I have to do this because we're not having an attorney-client discussion which would be, of course, privileged.

And that is: Do you have any objection to our conversation being recorded?"

"Recorded?"

"Yes, I have a recording device on me. It's for my review only. I don't want to miss something later on that we agreed upon—or disagreed upon."

"Sure, so long as I get a copy," I said.

"Absolutely," he said. "AI takes care of that. You'll get a PDF transcript sent by email to you even before you get home today so we'll both have a record."

"Your new stenographer?"

"Well," Gene said, a bit too insensitive for my taste, "actually much better than the young lady stenographers we used to use. These AI programs are really amazing. Their algorithms hardly ever make mistakes, and if they don't get a word right in a conversation, they'll flag it. And I can't tell you the amount of cost savings we've made."

"AI is replacing humans everywhere," I said, "so I'm not surprised."

"But human supervision is still necessary," he went on. "In fact, artificial intelligence is creating more human supervisory jobs than ever. It's a misperception to believe we'll all be robots before long. We said that over 100 years ago with Ford's assembly lines—and of course it never happened. We created millions of new jobs, and still are."

"Well, automobiles were a brand new industry. What new industry is creating those kinds of jobs today?"

"Healthcare, for one," he said. "It's one of the most challenging new industries out there. We're all concerned about our physical, mental and emotional states, the environment, the appeal of psychotropic and pain-killing drugs, the strains on our social, political and economic systems. And perhaps most of all, what all of these sea changes are doing to our mental health. Stella's idea of FreeGT is going to create a revolution in the health industry."

"I don't know what that is," I said. "What is this free idea of hers?"

"Ah, she's never mentioned it to you?"

"No."

"That's my doing," he admitted. "I've asked her to keep it a secret. I'm sorry. You're in her inner circle and for you not to know about it is a mistake on my part."

At that moment, the door opened and a secretary brought in our roast beef sandwiches, cole slaw, drinks and linen napkins and silverware on a silver tray. When she left, Gene continued...

"FreeGT is a livestream internet site. GT stands for Group Therapy. People can sign in using a handle to join a group discussion of a particular mental health issue from a bulletin board of specific health topics and the time they begin that day. There's a licensed therapist heading each group and perhaps 5 or 6 participants on a Skypescape or Zoom platform who can remain anonymous by masking themselves or placing an inanimate object in front of their cameras. And for all those who can't join in the live group, they can audit and just watch and listen in and can write back questions and comments."

"And it's Free?" I asked incredulously. "Who pays for the therapist? The production costs?"

"We're looking at philanthropic organizations and individual donations. You know, we handle many high-profile clients who would love to be involved behind-the-scenes in some beneficial way for a sponsor credit. And, of course, there are legal ramifications which we're looking at right now. It's completely unscripted and spontaneous, so maybe there'll be a 5-second transmission delay. It's all being worked on as we speak."

Gene dipped his sandwich edge into the accompanying cup of dressing. "This is somewhat hot. So be careful," he warned.

I did as directed, realizing that a good 15-minutes had passed since we sat down together—and I hadn't even pulled out my notebook with the agenda needed to be discussed. But I could see Estelle and Gene forming a union much like I had with Ruthie before we married. And it only made our bond stronger and more enduring, so this cooperative news was wonderful to hear.

But now I wondered just how much Estelle revealed to Gene about my growing up, my career and my marriage and kids—and how little I really knew about him. And yet he seemed quite open to me, so if I was to invade his private life, perhaps he wouldn't mind.

"There's something I must ask you," I began, "And I hope you don't take offense."

"Shoot."

"Is it true that it's your step-dad who's coming to the engagement party and that your real dad died here, where the original WTC building stood on 9/11?"

"True. And not only did my father die in the South Tower on 9/11, but he died on this very floor, the 81st. Leo Erskine and I made sure before its completion in 2014 we would get these offices. But you won't find the name Samuels on the park's memorial wall. Look for Alan Rappaport. When my step-dad married my mother, he adopted both me and my older brother, so we took on his surname, Samuels.

"You were sending a message to the hijackers?"

"That, and what's called closure. I needed to put his death behind me and move on with my life, not in his footsteps, but in his memory, of course. But now let me ask you something since you brought up 9/11," Gene said, perhaps trying to change the subject. "Between 9 and 11 we both had tragic 10's in our pasts. I was 10 when my father died. You had a daughter who died when she was 10, no?"

I was somewhat pissed at his insensitive connection, and abruptly answered: "She was riding her bike when a car hit her and threw her onto the pavement. She died of blunt-force trauma to her head."

"That's horrible," he said. "No helmet?"

"That was before helmets. No kid was wearing a helmet then."

"Where was she..."

"Look," I said, even more peeved at the direction the conversation was taking; "We can leave Rachel's passing for another time. It wasn't my intention to discuss 9/11 or our past tragedies involving the number ten or anything else. I'm sorry for having brought it up. There are more important things on our agenda."

"Well, I know that," he said defensively. "I didn't mean to upset you. I just wanted to get a little background on the family I'll be joining."

"Paul can fill you in. Rachel was his little sister, after all, and he doted on her, protected her. I don't think we realized at the time the full extent her death had on her brother."

"I have an older brother too," Gene said. "So I can relate."

"What's his name?"

"David. You'll meet him at the party. But let me ask you something: An obviously traumatic event, an instantaneous death of a parent or a sibling, say—it's not the same for a child as it is for an adult. My mother was very very sad, but put on a good face to me and my brother. She knew that if she showed how depressed she was, it would rub off on us."

"So true," I concurred. "Ruthie couldn't deal with living any longer on the street where Rachel died and so we moved to New Jersey right after that and consumed ourselves in work. We got a puppy from the pound to keep Ruthie company. Paul was starting High School and had to deal with a whole new environment, new friends, new relationships. I'm only now seeing how much Clara meant to him, how she kept him stable and focused. And why she and Ruthie were so close. In Ruthie's mind, Clara was Rachel all grown up... a daughter and daughter-in-law both."

"I didn't know Clara," Gene said. "I met Stella right after she passed. But Stella told me how much her mother shaped her life and her brother's life... how she 'Clarafied' things for them. Stella is a remarkable person, you must know that," he said, taking another bite of his sandwich.

"As is her brother," I said, wanting to get Peter back into the conversation. It was Peter, after all, who topped the agenda yet to be broached. And here almost a half-hour had gone by... and his name had yet to come up. "They're both remarkable people," I said. "You've met Peter several times already. I think he told me he came in a few weeks ago to talk to you privately about some issues he was having with the utility company he was working for. What did you think of him?"

"Actually, he came to see me for several things while he was at a convention. "He was fearful of being let go for some plans he submitted for a closed-circuit water, gas and electric scheme for flat rooftops. And he wanted to know his options if he were let go."

"He told me this, yes." I said.

"Well he had some interesting ideas. He mailed me the plans before he arrived for our meeting and to see if I could put him in touch with a patent attorney. Well, I looked over the plan and I was impressed with the work he put into the prototype, but I didn't see anything patentable there."

"No?"

"Essentially, it was all natural physical properties like condensation and gravity and solar electric conversion, heating and so forth. All of the devices he configured in like pumps and air conditioners, the photovoltaic solar panels and sodium-ion flow batteries had long been patented already. This was putting various things together in a new closed-circuitry and I didn't think it had much of a chance of patentability—and I told him so. He also needed a certification of potable drinking water."

"Could he lose his job just over an idea he had?"

"Well, he had a working prototype and to be honest, if widely developed, it would put a lot of utility people out of work. Do you know how it worked?"

"Tell me," I said, playing dumb. (If you recall, Peter had left a copy of his plan with me when he stayed over, but I wanted to get Gene's take on it.)

"Distilled water condensation from air conditioners is stored in a sealed cistern and pumped up to a rooftop tanaco, or holding tank, then gravity-fed down to faucets and toilets for drinking, washing and waste removal. A large rooftop photovoltaic panel was rearranged with non-toxic tubing throughout so the sun would be used for hot water as well as for electricity for the entire apartment below. And on cloudy or rainy days, new Chinese sodium vanadium phosphate batteries used to store excess power would automatically take over. And since all appliances would now be electric, heating oil and propane tanks and dangerous underground gas lines could be eliminated for huge cost savings. So electric, water, oil and gas jobs were at stake. In fact, the entire fossil fuel industry would suffer—off-shore drilling to fracking to coal-fed power plants. And I think this was probably behind the apathy and negativity it created. He complained that nobody wanted to hear him out on his ideas. But his ideas, if implemented, would cost millions to lose their jobs."

"So he didn't quit."

"I don't know, Jerry. He sort of gave up after a while I think. He was looking for something of value to do with his life, and the utility job was becoming a dead end for him. I think he began to get really depressed at the way things were going—especially for talented highly educated young people like himself. He was well paid, he said, but his desk job was essentially task masking and could certainly be handled by AI. Then he came under a DOGE-like review, but he was deemed an essential worker; he knew more about their systems than they did—who was doing their job, who was slacking off, which jobs were essential, which jobs were not or could be handled by AI. If he was DOGED he might spill the beans on those company tenure perks, so they decided to keep him on, but made sure he was now outside the loop."

"So in frustration, he started Outfluences?"

"I don't know his motivation. Just that he now had a lot of time on his hands. And these were supposed to be his most creative years. He was pissed at corporate largesse to be sure."

"He told me one of his main complaints was with what he was seeing on social media and the like," I said.

"Well, in some ways the two are connected, you see."

"How?" I asked, now finishing off half of my sandwich.

"You were in advertising. You must know the media considerations that sponsors and advertisers have in targeting their audience. Computer programs—generative AI algorithms—now direct the programming buys instead of ad sales and media execs. They're expendable."

"I see. You seem to know a lot about the subject," I said.

"We have a couple of contingency clients—I can't name them of course—who are now trying to sue their former employers for 'AI infringement'. Which only means their jobs are now being handled by computer programs, utilizing their contributions, their brains and talents, when they had those jobs. So companies are cutting back on staff and the remaining employees have to pick up the slack without being additionally compensated and if they complain, they too can be let go. Unions are impotent and there's nobody willing to defend them."

"Ahh," I said. "This may explain some real nasty social media things going on."

"Yeah," Gene nodded. "It's the young people especially who are feeling this helplessness. And some are very well educated and still have huge student debts to pay off. I feel for them."

"The Z's" I put in. "Your generation."

"Nah, I'm technically a Millennial," Gene said. "But I only paid back Harvard's Law School in full last year," he laughed.

It was past the time I needed to present Peter's firearm defense. And I hadn't gotten to any of my numbered notes I wanted discussed.

So I took out my notebook then, and opened it to the 12-point page. Gene was smirking, eating his pickle.

"You probably know what this is," I said as graciously as I could. "Things I think we need to go over before the party."

"Okay, shoot. Ahhh... forget that expression, stupid of me."

"I have 8 people on my guest list. Some neighborhood friends and of course Paul."

"I think we have you down for 10, but fine."

"The closest bathroom is next to Ruthie's studio off the back porch. I want that bathroom used, and not have people traipsing through the house."

"That's been handled. Doris took pictures. It's fine. We'll supply TP and paper towels. And we're making a sign with an arrow for the porch."

"I already have a sign," I said. "There was one for Ruthie's memorial. It's in the garage."

"All right. I'll let her know."

"In the event of rain, did you plan for a covering of some sort?"

"The caterer has a large canvas tent, and there's the porch."

"Now parking. I'm okay for cars parked in my front yard and down the street. But don't block any of my neighbors' driveways. Even the two to either side of my house who are coming to the party. You have an attendant for that?"

"You've met Robert, my assistant. He's tasked with making sure the cars are properly placed."

"If you have limos for some of the guests will they all fit in the garage driveway?"

"No need for that. The limos will drop off the guests and leave. Then they'll return when the party is over. Drop off is the walkway between the garage and the house, so it should be easy. There's one limo coming with Stella and her girlfriends. And a second with Leo Erskine, his wife and some people from the office. Then I'll be coming by limo with my parents and grandparents from the Marriott so that's three limos in all that I know of. Which reminds me: What are you doing the night before, Friday night?"

"Well, Paul is coming in that night to stay with me and so is Peter…"

"We'll get to Peter in a moment. Paul is staying with you Friday night?"

"That's what we're planning."

"Well, I'd like to invite you two to the dinner I'm having for my people at the Marriott. It starts at six. You'll be able to meet your in-laws before the Saturday event. And it would be great for everyone to get to know you and Paul then."

"And Peter?"

He took a couple of gulps of his Dr. Pepper. "Are we ready to get into this?" he asked.

"Okay, shoot," I said, trying hard to imitate Gene's earlier response. "Forget that expression. Stupid of me."

It was here I had planned to bring in Julie and what she told me over the recent telephone call we had… but I was conflicted about it. Gene and Julie had met at least once before, on his yacht she told me, but I wanted to first feel Gene out about his feelings toward Julie to see if I had any leverage here with her refusal to attend the engagement event if Peter wasn't invited. And so, I had to find out first if he and Estelle had discussed this latest development.

"Do you know Julie Roemer?" I asked.

"Peter's girlfriend?"

"The same."

"Yes, we've met a couple of times," he said. "She's very nice. Very smart."

"She's coming to the engagement party, no?"

"She's been invited," Gene said, "but according to Stella she won't come if Peter isn't there."

"And I guess that's okay with both of you."

"Yes it is." Gene said, now looking defiantly at me, upset for my trying to leverage Julie into the equation. "I think we'd have a dozen or more cancellations, maybe two dozen, if our guests knew there were concealed weapons being brought in."

"I...."

"And there are two couples who want to bring along their kids. This can't be another MM."

"I'm well aware of that," I said. "I...."

"Look," Gene said. "Julie was wise enough to let Stella know about Peter's gun. And she's on the side of rationality in this matter. She doesn't want to be there if Peter is there with his gun. If Peter leaves his gun in California, she'll come. There's no middle ground in Iowa being tilled here. And I believe she's told Peter exactly that. She'd like to see him at the party, but without his firearm. We're all on the same page here, Jerry. Do you want some coffee?"

"Sure."

"How do you take it?"

"Black, no sugar."

Gene pressed a button beneath the table's edge. In seconds, the lady who brought in the sandwiches was at the doorway. "Two coffees, please," he said half-turning. "Both black, no sugar."

"Well," I said, after we were alone again, "I don't want weapons in my house either."

"So, we are all in agreement here. This is really a simple matter. We all want to see your Grandson at the party—but without a weapon of any kind on him."

"I completely go along with you on this, Gene."

"Look. I know where the country stands on this because I've been following this issue closely. It's all about the migrant 'boat people' explosion and gun violence on both coasts, right here in New York—not just on the Southern border."

"Because of antiquated Second Amendment 'rights' and new proposals for banning all guns everywhere, that's scaring people into buying them underground," I said.

"Right. With predictable backlash from licensed concealed carry people, you must know that."

"I know gun sales are skyrocketing and especially unlicensed zirguns," I countered. "The *Times* did a story on this just last month."

"And what did the article end with? It was positive, not negative. With the new devices we have, we can spot these firearms at entrances and turn away anyone who thinks they can get through security. They can actually look inside pagers and walkie-talkies, smartphones and the like for explosive compounds. So security is booming with these ShapeSifters and even newer models that have face recognition programs built into them."

The door then opened, and the familiar lady with our coffees on a tray deposited them before us, and cleared the table of our sandwich plates and drinks. When she had departed, I said, "So if it's not guns it will be something else, like falling from a 7th-storey balcony or being poisoned." Raising my mug, I intoned, "To your health!" caustically enough to further anger Gene.

He smirked at my insolence. "Okay. So what's your point? How do we get around the fact that Peter is testing positive for paranoia?"

"The paranoia is justified," I countered. "He told me he's been actually threatened."

"I don't doubt that," Gene said, taking a considered sip of coffee. "He's put himself in an untenable position with the utility company he worked for, with other companies he's exposed as internet scams, with some Jewish groups who believe he's part of an antisemitic neo-nazi underground. Here, take a look at this..."

He opened the manila folder beside him and took out a photograph of a man wearing a T-shirt with what appeared to be a Z in a circle with a line through the Z going from the 11 o'clock position to the 5 o'clock position. "This is the anti-Z symbol," he said. "Have you seen it?"

"No. But so what?"

Gene took out a second photograph. It appeared to show the back of the same man with the same symbol on the back of his T-shirt but now rotated 90-degrees to the right, so that the Z now became an N. With the line still through it. "Okay," I said. "So what?"

"Do you see the letter N and the letter A formed by the turned about line through the N? And there's the I. And with the Z from the

Getting Past Z

other side, you can't help but see NAZI being spelled out back and front."

I shook my head. "That's quite a stretch," I said. "What are you showing me?"

"This T-shirt is going viral and being sold on some extreme right-wing white supremacist social media sites," he said. "It's thought that Anti-Z's are now being hijacked by the neo-nazi party in the U.S."

I could only shake my head in disbelief. "Look who's being paranoid now," I said in the most sarcastic voice I could muster. "This is complete antisemite bullshit."

"Ask Peter about it," Gene said matter-of-factly, taking another sip of coffee.

"Our family is from old-line German-Jewish stock," I said, trying to control my emotions. "The same people who brought you Marx and Freud and Einstein. My son, Paul, is Jewish and his late wife Clara was Jewish, so Peter is 100% Jewish as you well know. He was actually bar mitzvahed by Rabbi Max and speaks a little Hebrew. My wife was Jewish and actually dragged me to Friday night services. You came with Estelle to Ruthie's memorial so you know all that. Lots of relatives we had were lost in World War II and a distant Israeli cousin in the Gaza War, which, incidentally, Peter was devotedly pro-Israel. And you're accusing him of being a white supremacist and antisemitic, a Nazi? Gene, that's absurd!"

"I'm not accusing anyone of anything," he shot back. "But just telling you what the public perception is, from what we've been hearing and reading lately. Pockets of extremist elements, some headed by former military personnel, are being trained with unregistered weapons coming up from Mexico. Just look at what's happening in the suburbs surrounding San Diego."

I was stunned. I took my pen and wrote in my notes, *'Ask Peter about Nazis taking over anti-Z movement.'*

"If that's true," I said at last, considering who this was coming from, and the implications facing my Grandson, "I'm as upset as you are. But it doesn't make any sense. I simply can't believe it."

"I'm sure of that," Gene said kindly, trying to mollify the tension between us. "Would you like to refresh your cup of coffee? I sure would."

"Yes, I'd like that. Does Estelle know anything about this?"

"Of course."

The door opened, our lady server appeared with a coffee pot and our mugs were topped. Then Gene continued after our attendant left, "Stella is very concerned," he said. "She believes as I do that having Peter at our party could be a liability,"

"So even if he hasn't brought a gun with him, he's not invited."

"Well, I'm trying to be flexible here," Gene said. "I'll have my 2-man security detail at the party, of course. They'll be looking at everything and everyone. I don't expect any problems; there are no political or personal issues with us getting betrothed. No one with a grudge. No Luigi Mangione. No white boy summer. No Hamas or Hezbollah terrorists. No Tenttown migrants. No one in an Anti-Z tee-shirt. At least I hope not. No one can pass through with a weapon of any kind. We recently purchased a ShapeSifter for the law firm's own use. And my security team is made up of World Trade Center guys freelancing on the weekend, so they know their stuff. I hope you don't mind."

"Well, after what you've just told me, why would I have an objection?"

"They won't be in the backyard area, only the pathway between the garage and the house. And once everybody passes through, they'll be invisible and not mingle with the guests."

"Sounds a little like Big Brother, but I get it."

"Well, I'd rather have Big Brother than no brother," Gene quipped.

I had another sip of coffee and considered these new developments. If this security detail was present before the party even began, then Peter, who I figured would be there already from sleeping overnight at the house, could surrender his gun to them that morning in my presence and I could call Gene to let him know Peter was now unarmed and the gun was in their possession. But would Gene and Estelle buy that? Well, I thought, it was worth the trouble to bring up that prospect.

"I'm giving you permission to have your security team at the party," I said, "but I want a concession in return from you."

He nodded, perhaps knowing what was to come.

"What if Peter surrenders his gun to your security people before the party starts, like early in the morning and I'm there to witness it. And either the security people or I call you to tell you he's gun-free."

"He'll still have to pass through security, in any event, to get to the backyard later on. I think you agree with me that we don't want anyone passing through the house."

"Yes," I said. "I think he'd agree to that."

"Well," said Gene, "I think I speak for Stella as well when I say our first desire would be for him to leave his weapon back in California. That would ease everyone's mind."

"I know," I said. "That would be my preference as well. But from everything we've already discussed it appears unlikely he's going to do that. I think he's running scared and realizes the hole he's dug for himself. So I can press that point, but failing to get his okay, could I present this compromise?"

"This is taking a great risk, Jerry," Gene said. "We don't know if he has a second gun, for instance. And here I'm thinking of MM and an arsenal of weapons. We don't know what his thinking is these days, and how far along he is, as you say, of running scared. Stella wants him evaluated as you know."

"Yes. She told me that."

"Tell you what. If he goes to a qualified therapist—one that Stella recommends—and we get a positive report, and here I'm speaking for Stella as well, he can come to our party… with all the other security issues we've discussed in place. We'll even pay for the evaluation."

I wasn't thrilled with Gene's suggestion, but it presented a compromise, and that was what I was after. "Peter seems in relatively decent shape to me, especially since leaving his job, and shutting down Outfluencers," I said, "so he may buy the idea of a licensed therapist to act as an independent arbiter here. But I can also imagine him thinking that as a condition for his invitation it's personally demeaning and unjust."

"Well, let's say it's acceptable to him, with, as I've said, surrendering his gun to my security team if he's brought one, then the next step would be for Peter to call Stella for the therapist's name and number. And then we'd have to wait and see what develops, what the evaluation tells us. If he's staying at your place overnight next Friday, there's only nine days here, so this process has to be started today."

"I'll call him just as soon as I get back to the house. I want this to be face-to-face on a big screen, and my desktop is uploaded with Skypescape."

"And remember, you and Paul are invited out for dinner Friday evening at six, so Peter, if he's coming, should take the earliest flight available out of LAX so he'll be at your place before you leave."

"This could work," I said. "But he may take the idea of first seeing a shrink the wrong way."

"Well, we all want the best for him, and this is the best we can offer at this time."

"Depending entirely on the recommendation of a therapist he's never met before and doesn't know Peter's background or anything else."

"Well, he comes with the highest credentials, works with both prosecutors and defense attorneys that I personally know in L.A. and Stella has great faith in him for being objective and fair. She actually met him at a convention a year or so ago and was very impressed by him."

"And what happens if Peter flunks the examination?"

"You mean, if the therapist determines Peter represents a danger to the community."

"Okay. What then?"

"I sincerely doubt that will happen. I expect a positive assessment. We sat down for nearly an hour lately, remember. I found him completely lucid, calm and even introspective given the stresses he was under. Peter's not even close to being committed to a loony bin for further evaluation. That's not what this is about. We just want to make sure he understands what's expected of him if he comes in, so that we all feel comfortable and safe, that's all."

"And you're sure Estelle is on board here?"

"Actually," Gene said, downing the rest of his coffee, "Stella sold me on the idea. And, after all, I should now be thinking of taking orders from my future wife."

CHAPTER 6

It was only one-thirty in the afternoon so the limo's reversed course back to Upper Montclair took but an hour. Our lunch exceeded the hour I expected Gene reserved for us, but so much was covered I was sure he was pleased with its outcome. As was I. It would now be up to Peter—entirely in his hands—to fulfill the requirements of his invitation. And from the adversarial point of view—those of Estelle, Paul, Gene, Julie and myself—we were all in agreement. And this was very satisfying to me. For it provided for negotiations and concessions I was certain I could handle, now being deemed point man for the group. And sure enough, when I arrived back at the house, there was the PDF transcript of what Gene and I had discussed in my email box. AI had done its thing in what I considered to be record time.

So after Caroline left, with my dinner—lamb stew—all prepared for stove top heating, I had time to go over the transcript before calling Peter, knowing that California time was three hours earlier than my own, and that one o'clock was his usual time to talk with his Dad. So I placed the Skypescape call at precisely 3 o'clock, noon there, and waited for Peter to pick up.

"Grandad?" he asked incredulously, his unshaven face peering into the screen. He was wrapped up in a white terry cloth bathrobe, and I supposed I may have interrupted his showering.

"The very same," I said. "Can we talk?"

"Oh... sure! Nice to hear from you. What's up?"

"Do you still want to be invited to your sister's pre-nup party?"

"Ohhh," he moaned. "Are you now playing *The Godfather* with an offer I can't refuse?"

"No," I countered. "I'm playing The Grandfather with an offer you *can* refuse."

"Let me guess. If I leave my gun in sunny California, the clouds will miraculously part in New Jersey."

"Something like that," I said. "We'd all like to see you here, but the gun part is the sticking point. Can you enlighten me about the reasons you have for carrying a concealed weapon?"

"Well, sure. Let me send you three, no, four emails—all threatening me with bodily harm if I continue blogging. And one is vitriolically antisemitic: *'Boo hoo you dirty jew/ Hitler's coming after you/ Where to hide? Not Oceanside!/ He'll slit your throat, and your girlfriend's too!'* How's that for starters."

I was aghast. "You could turn them over to the police."

"Sure I could, if I was a techie who could reverse their cyberstalking of me and uncover their true names and physical addresses. Not that easy to do when their emails are being sent from public spaces like libraries, internet cafes and the like. And these days I think our local police force may have some larger issues to deal with."

"Well, I want you to consider..."

"Granddad, look. The pistol I own is not a ghost gun or zirgun like you may have imagined since I'm here in San Diego and that the Mexican-zirgun connection is big national news these days. It's an all-metal-composition Smith&Wesson CSX and holds 10 rounds of 9mm caliber bullets. I went to a federally licensed firearms dealer, filled out ATF form 4473, have a certified Bill of Sale for it with my name, address and the pistol's serial number on it, which includes a wallet-sized CCW permit that allows me to carry a concealed weapon. To get that I had to submit to a full background check, a mental evaluation test and had to take 6 hours of weapons training which I passed: Three hours of safety and storing requirements for a Firearm Safety Certificate and three hours on the firing range. I'm duly registered to lawfully own this pistol and I'm not going to give it up. Period, end of official statement."

"Would you give it up for say, three or four hours, to a security team from The World Trade Center—knowing you'd be getting it back—after the party is over and the guests have left?"

"A security team from Gene's office?"

"Exactly."

"I'd have to consider that. I've met with Gene, as you know, and I trust him."

"And what if I said that to sweeten the deal, the security people would turn the gun over to me to put in a safe place while the party was going on. No one but me would know where it is and you have my word on that."

"I'm beginning to see some light here behind the clouds."

"If that's so," I said, "then you'll accept one condition to this compromise."

"Uh-oh."

"Look, Peter. I'm trying to keep a lid on the paranoia here, especially since Madison. This will be a crowd of about 80 people, and even a few neighborhood kids possibly. Sure, it's outside and there are places to take cover, but MM is still on people's minds. No doubt that's the reason why concealed carry is such a big issue these days. Add to that, zirguns. Can't you somehow understand?"

"I do, Granddad." he said solemnly. "The country is going bonkers. And it's no longer just my generation. The country's mindset is changing, and not for the better either. I see a widening division everywhere now on all sorts of issues, not just guns and immigration. There's inflation. Chinese Tariffs. DEI. White boys summer. Growing wealth disparity. DOGE layoffs. People are confused and frustrated that the government is so impotent. It's getting ridiculous… and dangerous. I no longer want to be associated with the Z's or the anti-Z's or anything else. Since the fires and riots, people are now rightfully calling this place *Lost* Angeles. So I need to find myself. I'm looking for a comfort zone. I want out."

Remembering my note to myself during my meeting with Gene, I asked, "Is it true the anti-Z's are conspiring with American neo-nazis?"

"Because of their symbol?"

"Yes."

"Another social media meme-beam," he said. "Pulls in the eyeballs. I've seen the T-shirts, the car stickers, the antisemitic graffiti and swastikas. But the on-going right wing conspiratorial reporting is even more provocative, even more divisive. That's another reason I want out. As I've often said, I think Trump and Vance are humpty-dumpty who together had a great fall and can't be put back together again."

"A lot of people agree with you," I said, thinking this would be as good a time as any to bring up Estelle and Gene's condition that Peter first see a shrink. "So I need to ask a favor of you."

"Well, before you do, let me tell you what's been happening in my life since I was there a couple of weeks ago to see you, because it has some bearing on my future plans."

"Okay."

"A few months ago I presented an idea I had to an Australian rep out here in California for a utility and energy conference..."

"Your rooftop idea."

"No. That was already a dead issue. I could see how politically it wasn't going to work here in the U.S. especially with unions getting into the act. It certainly would put a lot of people out of work and I hadn't thrown that into the equation."

"I see. So you had another idea?"

"I thought if they wouldn't buy the rooftop idea, they may want to give this other idea a shot. I drew up schematics and wrote a detailed proposal, since I had a lot of time on my hands at work, but I was already quite disillusioned with my job and had put out my resume for back East."

"Where Julie was?"

"Yeah. Julie had already finished her fellowship work at CalTech and was offered a good job back in Connecticut so I was left here basically alone. And then I started Outfluences, which I now realize was a mistake."

"A mistake?"

"It was really a diversion to find my way out of boredom at work and sadness after Mom's and Grandma's passing, Julie's leaving and then the fires and the riots. I wouldn't have started it if I knew what the downside risks would be," he admitted.

"Maybe you should get some professional help," I said, thinking this would be another opportune time to insert Estelle's condition to Peter's presence at the party. "Estelle knows of a good therapist in your neck of the woods."

"Well, Granddad, I actually considered that at the time. But by then I had gotten myself in trouble—email threats that were telling me they knew who I was and where I lived—and the first thing I thought about was protecting myself, not seeing a shrink. A shrink can't be with you 24/7 defending you, but a pistol can. So I grew a beard, moved into a new apartment, took a gun course and qualified for a concealed pistol permit like everyone else was doing. Or so it seemed. And the upshot—if you'll permit me using that expression—is that I feel in control again: It's become part of me."

"Nonsense," I countered. "You're acting out what you perceive to be what the nation is thinking and doing since Madison. This protection racket has become a national obsession and only the gun lobby and extreme MAGA Republicans are profiting from it."

"I know it's now a fashionable political football, that much is clear. But I live in California," he went on, "and California, Texas and parts of Arizona are experiencing more extreme violence levels than anywhere else in the U.S. They're reviving a fictional trope of The Wild, Wild West."

I didn't want to go further into the political ramifications of gun ownership and especially concealed carry. There would be no end to the discussion, so I tried to get us back on track.

"Well, what was this other idea besides the rooftop idea you had?"

"I was reading a lot about rising sea levels flooding low-lying coastal areas due to rising temperatures melting both Arctic glacial ice shelves and the vast West Antarctic Ice Sheet. So my idea was essentially building desalination plants along a coastline, taking in the rise of ocean seawater and converting it to potable water for use in those coastal cities and then pumping the excess water through pipelines to arid drought-stricken interiors for irrigation use. In other words, literally turning the tide on climate change."

"Desalination plants? You mean, turning seawater into drinking water."

"Yes, by having reverse osmosis water treatment plants attached to the desalination plants. And to power the plants, using recently developed flexible-lensed photovoltaic solar panels and AI-controlled optimal panel rotationals. Some of these ideas are part of what is known as the Jordanian protocols. If we had used those innovations back five years ago we could have mitigated what happened in New Orleans when the Mississippi River dried up, their water treatment plants failed, and they had to truck in 35 million gallons of fresh water a day to help keep the population afloat."

"I see."

"And the salt extracted, essentially sodium chloride, works well with zirconium and a couple of other elements to form a diamond-hard grainy white surface impervious to water, stays cool under intense sunlight, perfect for outdoor construction projects. So you could say goodbye to coal and oil products like tar and asphalt for paving, roofing, pipefitting, rebar coating and so many other environmentally damaging fossil fuel uses."

"Nice!" I exclaimed. "It sounds like a great idea. But it's just an idea. You need a working model, a prototype."

"Exactly. It works on paper, but it has to work in real life. And so I gave my proposal to this fellow, also a hydro engineer like myself, who works out of a Perth utility company in Australia. He put in some cost figures and presented them to his superiors. They wanted to personally meet me and maybe go further with the idea. When I visited you, Julie and I had already been invited to speak before a delegation at the Australian Consulate in New York later that week. And the two of us presented before more than a dozen people from various political, business and scientific circles. It was a blast!"

"Why Julie?"

"She's a biochemist, you know. She put together the extracted salt part of the proposal and had with her actual samples of these new saline compounds that could be safely used in building, roofing, road construction, and many other applications. The audience came away quite impressed, I think."

"I would imagine," I said, remembering Julie's call to me and her description of Peter's 'interview' which now it appeared she participated in and covered up quite nicely.

"Well, we're a working team, and have been for so many years. And I have some news that only she and I just learned about a couple of days ago, so I need you to keep a confidence."

"All right."

"We're going to Australia! They accepted the proposal and want us to develop the prototype in Perth"

"My God!" I said. "That's incredible news! And I think Australia is now off Trump's hit list."

"For the moment at least. But even if it was, I'm happy to report this isn't a scam. Unless this utility company is in the business of losing their advance for our first-class airfares and moving expenses, and even the security money for an apartment for us when we arrive. And our salaries are outasight. It's all written into a contract that I want to put under Gene's nose."

"Wow! Sounds fantastic!"

"So Julie has to give notice to the chemical company she works for and get out of her lease. And I have to wrap up things here. And then we hope to be off by the beginning of October or so. We have a lot of loose ends to take care of. And dear Granddad, I was wondering if you wouldn't mind me staying over at your place from time to time and storing some things. Julie's apartment in Connecticut is really tiny. The bedroom is so small—as the old joke goes—we have to take turns making love."

Old joke was right, but we both laughed. "I think that would be fine."

"Great. So now getting back to the reason for your call..."

"Well..."

"You had one condition, some favor you needed from me."

"Uhhh... you want to see Julie at Estelle's party, right?"

"Yes, I know what you're about to say: Julie won't come to the party if I'm not there. And I won't be invited unless I leave my gun back here or take it with me and hand it over to Gene's security detail or you before the party begins."

"Yes... that's part of it... and another condition I was about to mention."

"Oh, right. And what's that condition?"

"Hummm... I don't know how to put it. You still want me to keep your Australian plans secret, right?"

"Yeah," Peter said. "You know how close Stella and Julie are. Julie doesn't want to upstage Stella on this betrothal party of hers. So we decided we'll tell everyone well after the party is over and let Gene and Stella have their day."

"That's a wonderful gift you're giving them," I acknowledged. "And I think you're right: It should be their day, all of it."

"And so, what is this other condition?"

"It's not important, now that I think about it. Julie should be with Estelle and you should be there, too. Everybody should feel comfortable and safe being there. Your promise to give your gun to me to hold for the afternoon should be enough to satisfy everyone. Gene included."

"You have my word on that, Granddad. So, I'll have a formal invitation sent to me?"

"My invitation says I can bring along a guest," I said. "So if an invitation is mailed to you and doesn't arrive in time, you're my guest. Does that work for you?"

"I'd really like it to personally come from Stella. Or Gene. That makes a big difference to me. Otherwise, it feels like I'm crashing their affair."

"Okay. I'll get on that immediately. And I'll keep Australia 'down under'".

He laughed along with me. "Hope this all works out."

"It will," I said. "Come early Friday, the day before the party. Take the earliest flight you can to Newark because I'm going out Friday night with Dad to meet Gene's family, so I'd like you to be settled in the house well before six in the evening. We'll have time for a get-together drink then."

"Lots of flights from LAX to Newark during the weekdays. I'll catch the earliest one I can."

"Fine. Let me know when you do. And tell Julie 'hi' for me when you talk with her."

Well, I thought, that certainly was news! And I realized now how Julie could be so flip with Estelle. Her future was with Peter and their escape to Australia, not whether she would be at Gene and Estelle's engagement party. And of course the pressure was now off Peter to attend as well. If he came in, he would be staying at my place during party time, but if he wouldn't drop his request for a formal invitation to the festivities, maybe the one cinema remaining in Montclair would be his entertainment for the afternoon. I needed to talk with Estelle about this. But even more than that, it all seemed so churlish, so insulting to require his seeing a therapist as a condition for his presence there. To my mind, at least, that condition was now off the table.

And yet....

He might still be bringing his firearm. If so, I would have to sit him down sometime after he arrived on Friday and lay out the reasons for handing his pistol over to me for safekeeping. I didn't want any weapons in the house, ever, as I've mentioned. But I was willing to bend in this case. Once Gene and Estelle knew it was in my possession and safely hidden, everyone could relax and do their party thing.

There's a wall safe behind one of Ruthie's oils in the master bedroom and I was certain there was room for a pistol and a holster. If I could get Peter to give his gun to me Friday when he arrived, I could tell Gene in private later when I would be seeing him for dinner. Problem solved.

And that Peter had done all this legally—that it wasn't a 3-D printed zirgun made by some Mexican cartel stooge—but an American-made brand name registered handgun was somehow reassuring given my overall objection to having guns in the house. My greatest fear, I can tell you now, was that Peter had gone off the deep end in depression and had purchased an illegal firearm that he could somehow slip through airport security and conceal carry around with him. So I took it upon myself to go to the four major airline sites to see the latest requirements for transporting a legal handgun. I found out that by first showing the proper documentation at LAX, Peter would be allowed to put his unloaded firearm into his checked baggage but not allowed to carry it aboard in hand luggage to be placed in the passenger cabin's overhead compartments. Every major airline had signed onto this obviously practical safety regulation. By following this procedure to the letter, he was totally within his 2nd amendment constitutional rights, drawn up over 200 years ago when pistols had but one round in them, airplanes were flights of fancy, and ceramic zirguns, three-dimensionally constructed by an artificially intelligent algorithm, right out of some futuristic science fiction fantasy.

And that explained how he got his gun from California to New Jersey when I saw him last. So during his Uber ride to my place did he take his holster containing his firearm from out of his backpack and strap it beneath his sports jacket?... for, come to think of it—that evening and the next morning over breakfast he never removed his jacket. And putting on a little weight? Was he wearing a kevlar vest, now a Vanity Fair fashion item, besides? And was this the reason he couldn't or wouldn't pass inspection at the World Trade Center and Julie had to deliver his updated roof plans to Gene's office? And was all this defensive-protective gear and the AI means of identifying same, now considered part of acceptable social dress and behavior?

Or was I making something up out of nothing... he had left his gun in California on that trip after all. (At that time I actually never saw a gun so to this day I really have no idea.) Either way, I was falling into the drama pit fueling the evening news—feeling both unease for my own personal safety, but more profoundly, disgust and helplessness at what I recognized was happening all about me.

For I could now easily see the growing paranoia America was facing over firearms, legit or otherwise. The country, now having access to a range of weapons of every magnitude and material imaginable, was holding its collective breath anticipating another MM or something even worse. And as time passed, it most certainly would be worse as more and more marginalized people defensively armed themselves. What was needed, of course, was some constructive way to ease the tension, the anxiety—(is *fear* too strong a word here?)—that now permeated our gun-obsessed society. Some way to create physical and legal barriers to transporting guns around, as the airlines had done. Some way to verbalize public distaste for the excesses of these right-wing self-styled vigilantes and restore some sanity into polarized generational, societal and political circles.

For clearly, this was fast becoming a national mental health crisis. Estelle's idea of FreeGT could literally become a life-saver if it could ever get off the ground. Maybe that was the opening to a conversation I knew we had to have. But now that most of the invitational pressure for Peter, which now also affected Julie, had miraculously been released, I was greatly relieved.

That Peter and Julie had been invited to work in Australia, a world away, was the best news I had received for many weeks now. Sure, they were giving up a lot—their friends, families, jobs, and a rising American optimism based mainly on aspirations of the lingering recession being reined in with Trump finally being forced to make the tariff and tax concessions needed to restart the economy. But at least Peter and Julie could make a life for themselves in a society not yet ready to defensively arm themselves, not yet ready to lie down on a therapist's couch, be deemed a community threat and committed to a mental health facility, aka 'loony bin', for further evaluation.

And then my phone rang. It was Estelle, so I transferred over to Skypescape to get a fuller picture, literally and figuratively.

"First off, Grandpa, I want to say 'thank you' because I received a letter from Vassar today saying that my debt was formally all paid off. So this is great because I didn't want Gene to know I still had some student loans laying around. Thank you so much."

"Well, it was your Grandma's idea, really, way before your Mom got sick. Your Grandma hated debt, any kind of debt. She even hated the 15-year mortgage we took out to buy our house. 'Bankers going bonkers' was how she put it."

"I remember her saying that, Grandpa. She's in my prayers tonight. But I need to talk to you about something else. I made a terrible mistake, and hope you haven't spoken to Peter about it."

"Well, tell me what the mistake was."

"I had told Gene I thought it would be a good idea to have Peter evaluated as a condition for inviting him to the party and he told you this, no?"

"Yes, he told me that, dear—and that Peter should call you for the therapist's number out in L.A. for a consultation."

"And did you tell Peter about this yet?"

"No, because I thought it was a lousy idea."

"Oh, thank goodness, Grandpa! You're absolutely right! It was more than a lousy idea; it was the worst idea I think I ever had. I don't know what I was thinking—by creating another layer to our many-layered cancel cake."

"Well, it certainly was half-baked," I agreed, expounding on her graphic image, "and I didn't want to be put in the position of delivery boy."

"So I went on-line," Estelle continued, "and found out that Peter must have already passed a psychological test to get his permit. And then I discussed this with my supervisor and she said no therapist in the world would go along with it, make a judgment call for a one-time consultation especially where no reported incident or crime had been committed, no verifiable threat received, no police involved, nothing but idle speculation and Madison on my mind. And when I told her what security precautions we were taking, she said that *I* was the one who needed intervention. She said it jokingly but made sure I knew I was completely out of line here, and I feel so bad about it. Put it down to inexperience."

"Well, don't beat yourself up over this, dear. You have great potential for success in your line of work. Your FreeGT idea, I believe, is a winner. Gene told me its general outline when we had lunch together."

"I know. And thank you. I wish it was up and running so I would have had some input before paranoia set in. But I want you to know that after my consultation with my supervisor, Gene and I had a long talk and I think I convinced him we were putting undue pressure on Peter to get cleared for takeoff."

"Then there is a way out of this," I said.

"Please tell me."

"Personally send Peter an invitation to the party, put your own note in it saying you and Gene would love him to be there, and send it off overnight by FedEx so he gets it tomorrow and signs for it. He never received a formal invitation. He needs to feel he won't be crashing the party."

"Oh yes, Grandpa! That's a great idea! Gene still has some reservations, as you know, but after our talk I think he'll back me up on this."

"And one more thing, love. Call Julie and tell her you've sent an invitation to Peter. She needs to hear it from you directly, not me."

"I'll do that, Grandpa. Oh, thank you so much for everything you've done. Especially keeping this idiotic idea of mine to yourself and not telling Peter."

"It's what we of The Silent Generation are known for," said I.

CHAPTER 7

I spent Saturday watching an amicable young Latino on an electric mower trim the grass oval in front of the house, the back lawn, and even use an outdated gas-powered leaf blower to clear away debris along the boundary to the wooded area beyond. His company had already been paid by Gene, but he did such a good job with his weed-whacker around the flower beds, I tipped him $60. But even this, I felt, was nowhere near the amount I wanted to contribute to the celebration. A week to go, and I was still considering all sorts of gifts, although I realized whatever I came up with would pale to what Gene was laying out.

Sunday was a morning of tennis doubles and an afternoon of rest, but that Monday I had on my phone's calendar an appointment at ten in the morning with Doris, the party coordinator, to go over the final details of that Saturday's event. I would let her decide for me what kind of meaningful gift I could add to the celebration. She obviously knew preferential details about everybody involved, and how everything supposedly would come together at appropriate times and venues—a job I wouldn't take whatever payment presented itself.

But even before she arrived I got a call from Julie.

"Hi, Jerry," she said. "I'm calling from work so I can't talk much."

"Okay," I said, "what's up?"

"Just wanted to thank you for arranging a personal invitation for Peter. It arrived Saturday by FedEx and he was thrilled to get it, because it was signed by both Stella and Gene."

"Oh, that's great!" I exclaimed, realizing what Estelle must have gone through to get Gene's okay.

"So everything is all set to go. I can't wait!"

"But he's going to bring his gun, right?"

"We talked about that. He'll give it to you when he arrives Friday afternoon. You can do whatever you want with it except throw it out."

"Well, I'll agree to that," I said, "but you have to convince him before your trip to Australia that he will part ways with it. I'm sure the people in Perth would blow a fuse if they knew he was coming with a weapon of any kind. You want to start out on the right foot."

"I know. And you're right. I'll work on it."

We said our goodbyes then and our anticipations of seeing each other at the celebration. And then it was close to the time I was to meet with party coordinator Doris something-or-other, now positively identified on my calendar as Doris Nottingham.

A 2027 cream-colored EV Nova pulled up into the garage driveway promptly at 10AM. Nottingham, an impeccably dressed curly blonde in her early '50s, presented me with her business card again (the first one, given to me a couple months before when she took pictures of my place, somehow misplaced) with the greeting, "Please call me Doris. And I'll call you Jerry, if that's alright with you."

"Sure," I said, extending my hand. "Do you want some coffee?"

"Just had some," she said, adjusting her shoulder tote, and observing the oval. "I see that the grass has been cut. Did that go okay?"

"Yup. Everything looks great, front and back."

"Well, I now have a better picture on how many cars will be here. We're figuring about 25 cars in all, give or take one or two. I think we can put a dozen or so in the oval and some on the grassy areas to either side and have 10 park on one side of the *cul-de-sac*. I know, Jerry—without blocking driveways."

"I see you've been talking with Gene."

"Well, he's the boss, after all."

"He says he's now taking orders from Estelle," I cracked.

She joined me in laughter. "Smart man," she said. "But seriously, some of the crew will park in the oval but the caterer's truck and the DJ's van need to be parked where my car is now, right in front of the garage. They have a lot of heavy stuff to set up."

"I'll tell Caroline, my guest, to park on the street. She'll be arriving early."

"Fine. Some guests are ridesharing from Manhattan, so that's also good, and we have an Uber van to pick up 9 people at the Montclair train station at 11:43."

"How many people do you now expect?" I asked.

"Around 100 including the crew," she said, now looking down at her notebook.

"Wow!" I exclaimed. "That's a lot more than your first estimate."

"Well, about 20 from Gene's side with their guest—couples mainly but some stags and maybe a kid or two, including Leo Erskine and wife... and 5 couples from Stella's side—that's 50 give or take. Then 9 more by train including Gene's brother David. Then Gene, his Mom and Dad, and Grandparents from Florida—that's 5. Then Stella and 4 girlfriends by limo, another 5. Then you and Caroline, and Stella's Dad and brother Peter, and two more couples you invited from the neighborhood are coming—so that's 8. The Rabbi makes 9. And little ole me—10."

"And the staff?"

"We have 2 security guards, 1 parking attendant, 7 on the catering team including the servers, bartender, table and chair set-up and cleanup crew, a photographer, a 4-person string quartet and a DJ. That's 16 in all. So everything considered, somewhere around 100 people."

"Wow. And so this must be a large party for you."

"Oh, medium-sized. If it were any larger, I'd have my assistant Joan with me. This is outdoors too so there's plenty of space to move around. It won't look crowded at all. In fact, it will all seem very open and informal. And that's the way Stella and Gene want it."

"Just for a betrothal. I can't imagine what the wedding will be like."

"Well, you know, that's not in my hands at all. I'm not conducting the ceremony."

"Well, of course I realize that. Rabbi Max is. But I'm just wondering... whether this is a pre-nup party or the real thing."

Doris laughed. "If it's in Hebrew, I won't know any more than you."

There was still a lot of work to be done, and this time instead of a camera Doris had a retractable tape measure on her. Her first measurement was the space between the garage and the house—the flagstone walkway leading to the back porch's side staircase. It was 10' wide.

"That's just about what we figured," she said. "The security team will set up two chairs and two folding tray tables here. All guests will be scanned here before entering the backyard."

"Scanned. You mean ShapeSifted."

"Yes. Takes but a few seconds."

"And what if some threatening shape is found?" I asked.

"One of the two guards will request that person to open their purse or empty their pocket where the shape was found and put the contents on the tray. They'll let small knives pass through but if it's a firearm the guest will have to provide ID like a driver's license and then the ID along with the gun will be photoed by smartphone and the gun surrendered to the guard. Then the guest can go into the back yard. They'll get their gun back when they leave the party by showing their ID again."

"And if the guest won't surrender the weapon?"

"He or she will be turned away. If they take the gun back to their car and leave it there, they can return, be scanned again, and go on in. Robert, Gene's assistant, is monitoring the parking and will tell guests arriving by car that if they're carrying a concealed weapon they will be scanned and turned away. So we don't expect any problems."

"And you're okay with this, I assume," I said.

"This is now becoming S.O.P.," she said. "Even for small wedding parties like 25 or 30 people, I'm getting requests for a security person to be present. Things have greatly changed, Jerry, in the past few years."

"So it seems."

"I'll tell you a story before I leave today that may change your mind about all this. But right now I have some more measurements to take."

I followed her down the flagstone path and up the side steps to the porch. "Friday morning a truck from Culture Caterers will deliver the folding tables and guest's chairs and leave them here on the porch," she said, "for a Saturday morning set-up."

I nodded my approval.

"I see you have a couple of electrical outlets on the porch. Do they work?"

"I suppose so," I said. "We used them for fans and violet light bug catchers."

We then walked across the porch to the other staircase and the rear entrance to the house.

"You have a bathroom sign?" she asked.

We went inside to Ruthie's studio and I brought out the *BATHROOM* sign—actually a ONE WAY arrow street sign Ruthie had bought at a flea market and lovingly painted over with flowers and butterflies in her last days. I had told her we would have a memorial for her in the backyard, and she set about making the sign, knowing her private bathroom would be used for the guests.

Doris was greatly impressed. "That's a lovely sign," she said. "If you would, this week affix it to one of the posts leading up the porch staircase."

"There's already a support," I said.

"The caterer will also drop off a packet of paper towels and some rolls of toilet paper," Doris said, examining the bathroom, flushing the toilet, and turning on a spigot in the basin. "Looks fine to me. Throughout the party the catering staff will check the bathroom and keep it spotless."

We left the house, down the porch staircase, and walked across the lawn. "Stella will be taking this route to the chuppa at the edge of the woods."

"In heels? I hope she can manage that," I said.

"Well, we first considered a roll of carpeting but she'll be supported by her Dad."

"Does Paul know this?"

"Of course," Doris said. "He'll be as sober as a judge," she laughed.

"Then you know of his drinking problem."

"A wedding coordinator knows everything about everybody," she laughed again. "Paul is going to be fine, I can assure you. The food tables and bar get set up *after* the ceremony. But we'll have water and soft drinks when guests arrive. They'll be set up over there," she pointed to the right, a spot close to the property's boundary fence. "No smoke. No bar-be-cue. The caterers are preparing food for hot trays that are heated by Sterno."

"Don't worry about smoke. The Franklins next door are coming as my guests," I said. "And don't worry about the caterers taking any leftover food back with them. They can dump leftovers in the woods for the deer to have. But no plastic. No paper. Just food."

We continued towards the wooded area. "Here's where the chairs will be placed," Doris said. "There'll be an aisle down the middle here to the chuppa where we're walking, and then 6 rows of 8 chairs to each side in a kind of curved amphitheater way. You're sitting in the first row on the Myer side of the aisle."

I did a quick calculation in my head. "Ninety-six chairs." I said.

"Well," she said, "I ordered 100. Some of the people will already be seated. Like the string quartet. They'll be playing off to the left side."

We came to the end of the lawn and the beginning of the wooded area. "The chuppa will be here," Doris said, taking out her tape measure. "On a 10'x10' platform." Then she took from her shoulder tote a small can of red spray paint. "Will you hold this for a moment," she asked of me.

Doris then pulled open the rule to the 10-foot mark, placed it on the ground, and sprayed a dot of red paint at both ends. She did the same for the other two ends 10 feet to the very edge of the woods, exactly the area that had been mowed and leaf-blown cleared. I was amazed that the area she laid out was almost perfectly square. Then she took a picture with her phone.

"The platform," she went on, "will be pre-cut. It just needs to be assembled on Friday and set here. It will have nice wood tongue-and-groove flooring on the top. The chuppa will be screwed in as well. Bill Young, my florist, is doing the chuppa. Then after the ceremony, and the photography shots, the chuppa will be removed from the platform. The catering staff will clear the aisle of chairs and carry the platform back to maybe fifteen or twenty feet in front of the porch where the DJ will be stationed. That chuppa platform then becomes the dance floor."

"Can I keep it? Maybe it can serve as a pickleball court, too."

She didn't catch my sarcasm. "Absolutely. Oh, and incidentally, the DJ whose name is Frank, will also be here on Friday to look over the electrical outlets you have on the porch. He may need to get into the basement and do some amplification work. But since this is during the day, and not at night, I don't think you'll be blowing fuses here. But let Frank do his thing, okay?"

"Sure," I said. "Do I get to hear my records?"

"From the Fifties? Sixties?" she laughingly inquired.

"Well, you said you knew everything about everyone. Do you know who my favorite group was from that period?"

"The Beatles."

"No," I said, "The Sweetmeats."

"Never heard of them," she laughed again. "But bring Frank the records or 8-tracks or cassettes or whatever you have and I'm sure he'll accommodate you."

Officially our meeting was over and I accompanied Doris back to her car. She had my email address and said she would send Friday's events on a schedule with the names and email addresses of all the support people. She thanked me for my time and my venue contribution. But I somehow felt it wasn't enough; I wanted to add something tangible to the festivities and I told her so. "Is the chuppa decorated with flowers?" I asked.

"Yes, it is," she said. "Just the front archway. It will be decorated early Saturday morning, so the flowers are fresh."

"And who is paying the florist?"

"Gene. Gene is picking up the tab for most everything."

"Well, suppose I pay for the flowers on the chuppa. What are we talking about here? Five hundred, perhaps seven hundred dollars?"

"I don't know," she said. "It's the cost of the flowers and the person doing the decorating which should take about an hour at most. Your figure seems in the ballpark."

"Could you ask Gene when you next speak with him if it's all right that I pay for the chuppa floral decorating? I know the invitation said not to bring gifts, but flowers are technically not gifts and I think many people will be bringing flowers."

"Yes, I think you're right, which reminds me to have the caterer bring some vases for the food tables. And yes, I can ask him about you paying for the chuppa flowers and I'll call you or email you back with his answer if you don't want to talk with him directly about it."

"I don't want to get in his face. He has enough on his mind right now and I've taken too much of his time already."

"Yes. He told me about your meeting last week. So I know all about your Grandson and the gun issue. Actually, that's what I wanted to mention to you before I left. Do you have a minute?"

"Sure. Do you want to sit on the front stoop?"

We walked over to the small patio in front of the house and sat on the marble step threshold. "You have a beautiful house, Jerry. When Gene first saw it, he was struck by how lovingly you and your wife cared for it."

"Well, we always had help, y'know. And even now I have Caroline making sure of its upkeep."

"You're approaching ninety I found out. You don't look it, but taking care of this property must take a lot out of you. Have you ever thought of downsizing to a smaller place in the neighborhood so you can keep socializing with your friends and not wear yourself down?"

"I thought you were a party coordinator, not a real estate agent," I said, perhaps a bit too caustically.

"I've done both," she said, gently taking in my retort. "But that's not what I wanted to talk to you about. I wanted you to know Gene is having his security guards carry mace, not pistols... "

"What!?"

"He respects your objection to having guns on the property. The security guards are trained to carry concealed weapons in shoulder holsters beneath their jackets. But their holsters will be carrying pressurized cans of mace, not pistols."

"He never mentioned this at all to me. If I knew the security team was carrying guns I certainly would have raised an objection!"

"It only means less safety here."

"What are you saying, Doris? That the security team should have loaded guns on them?"

"Practically every event I oversee now asks for security, and wants that security person or team to carry a concealed weapon, a gun—not a taser or mace or bear spray or anything else. That goes for betrothals, weddings, birthdays, bar mitzvahs, anniversaries, graduations, bridal showers, even bachelor parties. I know it sounds terrifying but that's the new reality. I've been in this business for over twenty years now. It wasn't anything like this when I started, obviously. But with a burgeoning Tenttown zirgun-carrying population this is what's happening today."

"So let's be clear about this. You wanted the security agents moonlighting from the WTC to carry their usual concealed arsenal, and Gene decided to allow them to carry mace instead?"

"Yes. It's against his better judgment as well as mine. But he wants to make sure you are going to be all right with having security there in the first place. And so, we came up with this compromise. But I'm now going to tell you a factual story that I hope will change your mind and allow the agents to carry guns..."

"Don't bother," I interrupted. "I've gotten a promise from my Grandson to... "

"This isn't about Peter," she said. "This is about Madison."

"I've heard all the stories," I said, now somewhat annoyed by this turn in our conversation.

"Have you? I'm a dues-paying member of an events society," she went on, oblivious to my reaction—"The American Association of Certified Party Planners. It's on my card, the AACPP. We hold several conventions a year in different parts of the U.S. and we have speakers and round-tables and all the rest. We want to perform as best we can to make sure every event we handle comes out great for all concerned. And we try to learn from others' mistakes on many things that can go wrong with planning events of every kind."

Seeing what Gene's party involved, I knew she was basically right, so I backed down a bit. "I can imagine," I said.

"In April I went to our exposition in New York and heard from the event coordinator for the Madison wedding. A Black lady, she survived by being in the last pew and playing dead. She told us the bride-to-be's ex-boyfriend, Michael Hammond, got his idea for shooting up the wedding party from following the Hamas terrorists who killed so many in Gaza back in 2023. He wasn't a Palestinian or even a Muslim—he was a Southern Baptist, a Harvard Fellow and strictly conservative.

Yet, he headed one of the thirty student group signatories on that infamous pro-Palistinian letter Harvard put out. The Gaza War and its horrific conclusion somehow fascinated him."

"He wasn't the only one," I interjected. "It was an atrocious tragedy from every perspective."

"So this wedding planner was asked by the committee investigating MM to testify about what she knew," Doris went on, "and she revealed that the bride-to-be had told her weeks before her wedding about Hammond's obsession with the Hamas terrorists. It was never reported out of committee or leaked to the press, out of fear of copycats trying to out-do him. But it was time, she told AACPP members, to set the record straight: We needed to do more investigative security work to ensure safer events in the future."

This was news I hadn't heard before and truthfully, I was primed to hear more.

"So Hammond's deranged interest in identifying with the Hamas terrorists was one of the things that turned his lady friend off," Doris continued. "She saw something in his warped personality that frightened her. So she kept involvement with him at a minimum and then met her husband-to-be at the hospital she worked at. She tried to break things off at that point, and thought that she had, but Hammond was now insane with jealousy. She had no idea Hammond was cyberstalking her and so when he planned his assault on the wedding party he even knew a security guard was posing as an usher and had a concealed gun on him—and shot him first, before the guard could even get his pistol out of his holster, yelling '*allahu akbar*' as he was uploading the next magazine after each round of shooting."

"I think I read that," I said. "But this was a Catholic wedding. It had nothing to do with Hamas or revenge against Jews, or anything like that."

"Exactly. He was going to show the world Islamic radicalization wasn't based only on religious differences or territorial aggression. His bigger theme was the deprived, the rejected, the ill-forsaken. He wanted to become a certified terrorist and do an unspeakable act of violence because a terrorist gets world-wide front page attention, acknowledgement of grievances against those who exploit the marginalized, and even sympathy. His manifesto, remember, was modeled after the Unibomber's and Luigi Mangione's, and even alluded to Trump's 80th birthday party the same Sunday as the wedding as well as the 250th Declaration of Independence Anniversary coming up exactly two weeks later, put together by a bunch of 'Grifters and Oligarchs'—his take on Trump's '250/GO' taskforce."

Doris had made a convincing argument. "Agreed," I said. "And he certainly proved his point."

"So you see," she went on, "this wasn't just a case of some guy flipping out because his girlfriend rejected him for someone else—as the media would like you to believe. There was that of course, but something much larger, something much more insidious. Hammond was following a blueprint on the making of the modern terrorist—all the planning and preparation work, the secrecy, every possible scenario and backup contingencies. His jealousy morphed into something more—it became all-consuming hatred for those in power, in control, those who take advantage of defenseless, weaker peoples. And he wanted martyrdom, because 'to die a martyr is better than to live a slave' as he told his pals. To say this atrocity was a one-off case of personal jealousy and rejection is a whitewash of what Madison was really about."

"I see."

"And Hammond had been a corporate techie, recently put out of work, replaced by AI or doxxed by the revelation of his Harvard days, who really knows? Freelancing now, he was still technically very savvy. He could go behind the scenes at will. He had the advantage of knowing in detail the wedding plans and how to overcome any obstacles put in his way."

"Like the usher."

"A minor inconvenience. Especially since it's so easy to break into people's email and phones and know their every movement, their every thought these days. Or, on the other hand, using social media to plan and instantly bring together hundreds, even thousands, for some cause with a drumbeat march or traffic blockade. Nothing is truly safe these days, and it's not just paranoia that's driving the concealed carry movement. There are truly disadvantaged people doing stupid, unlawful things and no one to tell them it's just plain wrong. Just look at the 'mob n' rob' kids overwhelming security at stores these days—to see things are getting out of hand."

"Well," I said, trying to take this all in, "the guests and staff at this party are well known to all."

"I'm sure," she replied. "And Hammond got into the side door of the church by tipping the elderly watchman who knew him as a photographer because he had been there on several occasions before the wedding pretending to take photos."

"Like you."

"Yup," she said, "just like me. You don't know me from a hole in the wall. I could be another Mike Hammond in a dress for all you know. But things have radically changed since MM. And that's why investigative security today is so important. Security with teeth as we say."

I knew where this discussion was heading—a quick change from Michael Hammond to Peter Myer—and I was the naive side door watchman who got faked out. But the cases were in no way similar—and the firearm in question would already be safely locked away. Moreover, Peter wasn't homicidal, much less suicidal, had only love for his sister, respect for her husband-to-be, a loving girlfriend and a great future before him. That he carried a concealed weapon was only because he feared for *his* safety—a purely *defensive* position—and I felt certain that he would never use his gun like insane Mike Hammond did for *offensive* reasons. No, I knew my Grandson well enough to say to Ms. Nottingham as we parted ways...

"You can stick to your guns, but I'm not. I'm more of a mace-minded stubborn old octogenarian who has seen enough in my lifetime to discern derangement from engagement."

"At least be willing to temporarily install a camera over the front door so I can better monitor the parking situation. When the party's over we'll remove the camera. I'll take care of it."

"Everything else is prisonized these days, so why not?" I caustically agreed.

CHAPTER 8

I realized my meeting with Doris Nottingham would be quickly brought to Gene's attention. It was obvious to me, since he was paying her way and everyone else's, they all reported to him directly, withholding nothing from him. Estelle had indeed found a powerful, wealthy man to cohabitate with, but now I was seeing for myself the psychological control he commanded—and the first feelings of negativity towards him began to creep in. Once the nuptials were over, I was sure we would grow further, not closer, apart with time.

Money and power did not impress me now, although at one time, I will admit, it had its effects. That was when Ruthie and I started Myer & Co.—an advertising and promotion agency focused on fashion, home decorating and furnishings. We had, as our first and only client, my father's business, Myer & Sons—imported textiles—and now with his in-house agency, business really began to take off.

I had met Ruthie at The Art Student's League on 57th Street in New York City. She was in a drawing class and I was taking a course in advertising graphics to better acquaint myself with what I expected to be my career: Creative Director at some large Madison Avenue agency. My father wanted me and my brother to take over his textile business—and in fact, officially changed his last name from Myers to Myer, dropping the 's', because Myers & Sons sounded a bit confusing linguistically. I wasn't interested in inheriting his business but my younger brother was. And when my father died in the mid-70's, my younger brother Carl took over the business.

My father did exceptionally well during World War II, supplying the Army with camouflage material for fatigue outfits. I lived an upper middle class childhood in a Chelsea brownstone my father bought so he could be close to his business on West 22nd Street—in the heart of what was then the textile capital of the world. And I was talented as well—getting into the prestigious High School of Music and Art, then located next to the City College of New York on 135th street in Harlem. I was an Art Major, of course, but many of my close friends went into music, onto Broadway and Hollywood, and had wonderful careers. I stayed in New York, went to the downtown branch of New York University in The Village for my B.A. in English, then taught remedial English at a Bronx high school working for my M.A. while also taking a graduate course in graphic design at the Art Student's League where I met Ruth—known to her friends as Ruthie Goldberg—and the rest is history.

Ruthie had had a traumatic upbringing. Her father Paul, though recently married with a kid and so might have qualified escaping the draft, volunteered into the Army during World War II because he so hated the Nazis for what they were doing to the Jews. He was shot dead during The Battle of the Bulge leaving his wife and daughter to Fate. Ruthie's grandparents were poor immigrants from Romania, and couldn't help their daughter and granddaughter much financially, so Ruthie's mother then went to work as a dental assistant, leaving her daughter to essentially be brought up by grandparents who doted on her.

When she met me at ASL, she was a couple of years out of high school, very talented in art and drawing but struggling to find a job and paying for her coursework. Her beauty knocked me out. Long black hair, beautiful dark eyes and eyebrows, a wonderful smile encompassing a terrific set of teeth (owing to the fact, I later found out, of her mother's affair with the dentist she worked for). In fact, Ruthie Goldberg was the most attractive woman at ASL by a long shot—and there were many guys looking her way, especially when she applied as a nude model for the live posing class to satisfy payment for her other courses. I simply had to take the class.

That sealed the deal for me. And for some reason—still unknown to me—she accepted my invitation, first for coffee after classes, then dinner, then center orchestra seats to Bernstein's *West Side Story*, then... Well, you get the drift. I was in love and she wasn't playing hard to get. A little research on her part told her I came from a well-off family, could support her comfortably, and let her develop her art talents. Besides which, we shared many things in common. We began to talk of a working life together, an Advertising Agency with her as Executive Art Director and me as Executive Creative Director—with my father's company as in-house client to start the ball rolling. My Dad looked our proposal over and said 'yes' on the spot. We were in business, and business started to boom. And so did our love life.

It wasn't but a half-year later that we proposed to each other, not with an engagement party, but with signing a lease agreement with my Dad for a house in Forest Hills. He had bought the house for investment purposes, but now, seeing that Ruthie and I were seriously in love, leased it to us for $1 a year. He didn't care if we were married or not, but knew living together would motivate us to greater things. Smart man. The week we moved in, we secretly went down to City Hall and signed the papers. We were so busy with work our honeymoon was a cruise around Manhattan Island on Washington's Birthday when offices were closed. Then the next day we were both back at work, but now commuting from our new home in Forest Hills.

Those early and mid-60s years were golden times for us. Our ads appeared in all the highly read women's magazines and caught the eye of many advertisers who wanted us to produce ads for them. My Dad, seeing that we were becoming overstressed in a one-room office, agreed to release us from our contract as his in-house agency, so we could move out, get larger offices of our own, hire more people to work for us, and most importantly, add non-competitive clients to our roster.

It all happened in a flash. We found office space in a six-storey building—420 Madison Avenue—perfect for a small expanding agency. We hired an Associate Art Director and Senior Copywriter and then a receptionist/bookkeeper. We took on more clients in home furnishings and women's clothing and added a junior copywriter and a boardman to the team. Then an Account Executive with retail experience to free up more of my time for presentations. Then a Media Director for the media buys. And with a nice write-up in *Advertising Age*, business really began to take off. By the end of the decade Myer & Co. had 18 people on full-time staff—and several freelancers we could call on for photoshoots, retouching, creative writing, pasteup assignments and TV production.

In that golden period of growth, Ruthie and I decided it was time to grow a family. Ruthie stopped taking birth control pills and soon after became pregnant with Paul, named after her late father, and three years later with a little luck and some planning on sexual preference, with a baby girl, Rachel, named after my grandmother on my mother's side. She continued to work from home caring for the kids, now with a fax machine—and me as messenger boy—to keep in daily touch with her Art Director, while I commuted into work each day. We were making lots of money, so we began paying off our Forest Hills home to my Dad each month, as his health was declining and uncle Carl was taking on more and more day-to-day responsibility running the business. I wanted my parents to move to Florida and enjoy the sunshine and the growing community of elderly Jews down there. But he was stubborn and insisted his home would always be in Chelsea, in the same old brownstone in which I was brought up... and in which he died in 1972, never fully enjoying the two grandchildren Ruthie and I produced as his legacy. And my mother died there as well, a heart attack, three years after my Dad.

History, they say, repeats itself in mysterious ways.

I was expecting Peter's call when his travel plans were confirmed and it came around noon on Tuesday.

"Hi Granddad, how are you?"

"I'm fine, Peter. Do you have some news?"

"Yes. I got the invitation to the party on Saturday from FedEx. Both Stella and Gene wrote that they would like me to be there. I suppose that was your doing."

"Well, I gave them the conditions we talked about regarding the gun and they were satisfied it would be locked away during the party. And they were happy to extend an invitation to you."

"Dad and I also talked yesterday and I told him the latest and he was so pleased he choked up."

"Well, it's a big relief for everyone."

"So I wanted you to know I'll be there Friday as planned. I got a non-stop United ticket for 8:30 in the morning to Newark... so with the time difference and my Uber from Newark, I should be at your place around 4 in the afternoon. Does that work for you?"

"That's great," I said. "I'll tell your Dad and we can have some time together before he and I leave for dinner with Gene. I'll have Caroline put something for you in the refrig and you can heat it up for dinner. I'm sorry you're not coming with us, but I think it's just his parents and grandparents—the minimum age for guests is 65."

"I'm okay with that," he laughed. "I'll be bringing a lot of my stuff, like two suitcases and a couple of boxes, so I hope I can store them for a few weeks at your house."

"No problem," I said. "You can leave them in one of the upstairs bedrooms."

"So I'll see you Friday."

"Looking forward to it," I said.

I asked Caroline to make up the bed in the guest room for Peter as his Dad would be staying in his boyhood room which already had the bed made from his last stay-over a week before. I contemplated the three generations of Myer males together for the first time in more than five years—grandfather, father, son—this time without the female halves of ourselves to oversee our lives and make sure we were acting out our male marital and familial roles to their fullest extent. To say that both Paul and myself were missing that other half would be a gross understatement: The double tragedy happened so quickly and so closely in time we still were a bit traumatized—of being alone, without intimate companionship, without so much as a laugh to share or a tear to wipe away.

And I think Paul and I instinctively knew to keep those feelings from Peter, sensitive as he was, and perhaps even a bit neurotic. But his life's purpose and direction had suddenly been cast before him now—and I remember clearly what my life was like at 27, and my son's life at 27—and how wonderfully optimistic the future was for both of us in our late twenties. I only wished him the same—that his life with Julie in Australia would become a turning point for both of them, and that they'd thrive and grow together, the bond of love between them only becoming stronger with each passing day. And perhaps start again to plan for a family that had been so cruelly canceled a decade earlier.

As far as Estelle and Gene were concerned I had no illusions about their relationship: Gene was late in finding love, not because he was distracted by building his law firm, or being the playboy, but because women these days were not going to give in to any man who didn't take them seriously enough. It took Gene years to discover this with Estelle. But his triumph was to discover in Estelle *his* better half—in her intelligence, her beauty, her calming, charming nature, compassion and yes, fallibility—all the things Gene wanted to find in himself. He recognized they had to combine forces to succeed in their expectations of themselves and one another. Apparently that's what happened when Estelle moved in with him right after Ruthie's passing. Even so, it took another five years for them to work out the details of their life together. So I had great hopes for them both succeeding, and was happy to host their pledges to each other.

Wednesday was cloudy with a good chance of rain in the afternoon, the east coast weather report showed, opening my phone after waking to its alluring alarm clock lady: *"Time to rise and shine,"* was today's singsong greeting. But the one I liked best, but AI hardly ever randomly summoned, was my sexy-voiced lady, now a scold, informing me: *"It's nine already! Get the hell out of bed!"*

For sure, AI had a way about it.

And there was Doris's email to read:

Gene is okay with you taking care of the chuppah flowers. I'm having Bill Young, the florist, give you a call today. He's done many chuppahs and will do the setting up on Friday as we discussed. Attached are email addresses and phone #'s of all the vendors.
If you have any questions, call or write them directly. Best, Doris

I considered that a small, but significant, victory. Ruthie would have insisted on it. She knew her flowers, and considered the flower beds along the front of the house her private domain. Occasionally a deer would manage to evade our increasingly hard-of-hearing Spot at night to find its way from the back woods to the front lawn and munch on the wild strawberry bushes or whatever, and Ruthie would have a fit the next morning.

And yet, she so loved living in that isolated house and surrounding property at #1 Lois Lane: Its privacy, tranquility, its unspoiled woods behind, its inquisitive deer, skunks, raccoons, possums, rabbits, chipmunks, owls, birds and butterflies—and all the creatures who made their homes there. They were now family to her: Rachel was, thankfully, becoming more and more a distant memory. Our move was therapeutic, almost curative at first for both of us, but nothing lasts for long with a fast-growing *nouveau riche* upwardly mobile human population...

When the developers planned to line our *cul-de-sac* with new homes two years after moving in, Ruthie tried her best to purchase the land and keep the area green, but couldn't manage the political aspects and payoffs. But she somehow cut a deal to allow for three houses on either side, rather than four. The compromise allowed for larger, more expensive homes on larger plots. And those families lining the sides—our Welcome Wagon monied guests—we got to know and often invited to backyard bar-be-cues to tummify with us. Add to that, Ruthie's joke she reveled in—"And look," she'd laugh privately to me: "Jews gracing the head of the table!"

Caroline arrived around ten with the dry-cleaned suit I would be wearing for Saturday's event. She, like myself, was nervous about the weather and that alternate plans had not been made in case of a long-lasting heavy downpour. On the other hand, I said that if we got the rain out of the way on Wednesday and Thursday, chances would be better for dryer weather on the weekend. The good news—it wasn't particularly hot and humid. I remembered Ruthie's rejoinder: "It's not the heat, it's the humanity."

But then a call came in from Bill Young, the florist who would be supplying the chuppa. Montclair had several florists so I wasn't acquainted with his shop, but he assured me he had done many Jewish weddings, knew Rabbi Max personally, and the structure with the frontal floral archway would be perfectly assembled on Friday after the flooring was complete, the floral branches from his own tree and shrub nursery, attached early Saturday morning for freshness and fragrance. Cost: $750. But the bill would be coming after the event, since I was the property owner and a member of the community. He was savvy in building goodwill with a satisfied customer who might use him again in the future.

And then around noon it started to lightning and thunder with drizzle which quickly turned into a steady rain by one o'clock. Caroline busied herself cleaning and vacuuming the diningroom and livingroom area while I went on-line to see what was expected of me for Saturday, for Doris had mentioned I would bring forth the symbolic champagne glass that the couple would stomp on to finalize the ceremony.

There were only three people in the history of the world who called me by my given name, Jerome—and two of them had passed—my mother and father. The third was Rabbi Max who delighted in calling everyone in his flock by their given first names, not to belittle them in

Getting Past Z

any sense but said in a kind of paternalistic way, as a father or father figure might do. This was especially true of the many bar and bat mitzvahs he performed, even when the tween's father was present.

And so, when I picked up a call on my cellphone's chat line without first reading the caller's name, the male voice asked, "Jerome?" I knew immediately who I was speaking to without even having to first acknowledge the call or anything else. Since Ruthie's memorial I had stopped going to Shabbat services, even on the High Holy Days, yet still contributed to their annual fund drive. Estelle was keen on having Rabbi Max officiate the betrothal ceremony and he was just as keen to bring me back into his fold. (Would he, I wondered, do a birthday celebration for a 90-year-old?—himself well into his 80's—but that's getting ahead of the story.)

"Rabbi Max," I exclaimed; "the one and only!"

"And how is the world treating you, Jerome? Good, I hope."

"Very good," I said, lying—looking out the bedroom window at the downpour. "Since you're closer to God than me, perhaps you can ask Him what the weather will be like for Saturday."

"If God would let me accurately predict the weather I could easily double the congregation. But praying a little couldn't hurt."

"That's a good idea," I said. "I'll do that before I go to sleep tonight,"

"But seriously," he said, "Estelle and Eugene were out to see me last Sunday and we did some paperwork, and put some finishing touches on their participation. It should be a wonderful day and things seem to be moving along nicely. But I want to talk to you personally about something they brought up... "

"Peter's gun," I broke in.

"Well... no. We actually talked about security. You know, of course, the Temple now has a security guard for Shabbat services. They wanted me to tell you that if you didn't know already. Since the Madison affair, this is now what we have to do. If we didn't, and something happened, I would be responsible... and the Temple would suffer greatly. So this is a reasonable precaution. They just wanted me to tell you that."

"I appreciate that, Rabbi. I agreed to the two security agents Gene is bringing in to scan everyone for weapons. I'm sure that is more than fair."

"Yes. And the guard we have here has a concealed pistol, not mace or a taser or anything else."

"Ahhh," I said, now understanding the purpose of the call. "So Gene is still concerned that the guards at the party won't be able to function adequately unless they have loaded weapons on them. Is that it?"

"It's entirely in your hands," Rabbi Max said. "It's your call, because it's your house. Like it's my call because the synagogue is my congregation's house. Actually," he corrected himself, "it's God's house, but I'm its caretaker."

"Rabbi," I said, "I thank you for your concern. My Grandson is the only one who will be bringing a weapon of any kind with him that I know of. No threats have been made; no mentally disturbed suitors; no antisemitic rightwing nutjobs. Everyone wants this union to happen, especially Peter's dad. You know Paul as well as anyone: he took Hebrew classes from you when we moved in; you bar mitzvahed him and Peter as well. He's now spoken to Peter about surrendering the gun before any of the guests arrive, and has gotten Peter's promise on that.

Everyone's on board. So this will be a peaceful and safe celebration I can assure you."

"We all want *Bracha B'Hatzlacha* and pray that you're right, Jerome. Y'know, we miss you at Friday services. You're one of the very strong support foundations of the Temple and I miss seeing you there."

"I don't like to drive by myself at night," I said weakly.

"Well, we can arrange a pick-up," he said. "We have ride-sharing, y'know. Lots of people ask about you. I mean, you've been in the congregation since when? The late Seventies? That's just about when I arrived. That's almost 50 years!"

"We moved here in 1978. Exactly 50 years."

"I know. A half-century of Rabbi-ing. There's no such word—but I'm going to let you in on an open secret: I'm retiring this fall. I'm going to do the Holidays, Yom Kippur, and then announce my retirement. I'm training my replacement, Rabbi Raymond Horowitz, to take over. So this celebration is going to be one of my last private functions. After 50 years, I think it's time to turn things over."

"I'm honored," I said. "But let me ask you honestly, is this a betrothal like an engagement celebration, or an official wedding?"

"I'm sworn to secrecy," he laughed. "Let's just say that the *ketubah* and all the civic parts of the ceremony have been handled; the reason why Eugene and Estelle were out to see me Sunday. But in the eyes of God, they have to be blessed into a holy union, into the Hebrew temple of faith, something only a *Hazzan* can do."

"They're going to miss you when you retire," I said. "They've told me after you conducted Ruthie's memorial you were one of the reasons for holding their ceremony at my place."

"Which reminds me," he said, "At the end of the ceremony I'm going to call on you to bring the wrapped-up glass up to the chuppa and then they will break it. You know the reason for that bit of theatrics, don't you?"

"Yes," I said. "And Doris Nottingham already mentioned that to me. I'll be pleased to do that."

"You have a *kippah?*"

"Certainly."

"Good. Then let's pray for good weather."

"From my lips to God's ear," I replied.

It rained on and off throughout the night, but Thursday morning things began to clear: my kneeling prayers at bedside possibly being heard. The tennis courts would still be wet and so I received a text message that our game would be canceled. By the time Caroline arrived, the sun was out and I was overjoyed to learn on the Weather Channel that the East Coast would be free of rain until at least Sunday...with pleasantly warm—but not too hot—days to come. I looked skyward and gave thanks where thanks were due.

I determined this would be an uneventful day for me because tomorrow, Friday, would be busy with platform carpenters, chuppa constructors and furniture deliveries. Then in the late afternoon the arrival of Paul and Peter, and later, going out to dinner with Gene and his family. It would be a long day tomorrow and I decided to dismiss Caroline early Thursday and give her a half-day Friday—so I could take a longer afternoon nap and also give her more time to prepare for the two hectic days to follow.

I went out to the woods to feed the deer with bird feeder seeds—something they came to appreciate, especially during winter with no greenery. The new development on the other side of my wooded acreage was overcrowded with houses now, and the habitat for deer greatly reduced, but they found safety on my property and were no way alarmed if I entered their leafy domain to feed them. And because Spot was no longer my companion in my walks, the deer were even more trusting to see me and be fed. But the wild strawberries, blackberry, raspberry and blueberry bushes were in season—so my previous piles of bird seeds, now soaked by last night's rain, were left for the other animals to consume. If I were to move, where would I find such a wonderfully natural landscape? Where would I find such peace and tranquility, such unfeigned, inquisitive 4-legged friends?

For that had been on my mind for the past year or so—giving up the house and moving to where? Sunny Florida where I knew only a handful of friends still kicking? Peddling a bike in golf cart traffic or on overcrowded electric bike lanes? Playing pickleball instead of tennis? Doing a lot of reading and some writing to pass the time? Until when? My first heart attack or stroke? A debilitating hernia or crippling arthritis? A digestive problem or even cancer to send me to an 'attendant facility,'—the first step in a lingering process of endgame decay? Yet I was only following orders put down by Mother Nature and Father Time: To pass away after the maturation of our prodigy. Well, not in Rachel's case where Ruthie and I witnessed the untimely death of our 10-year-old, but Paul would certainly outlive me; and Peter and

Estelle most certainly would outlive their father. Wasn't that the way Nature intended it to be—that the kids we produced would somehow manage to stick around to, at the very least, bury their parents?

For I was in excellent health, according to Dr. Francona, my physician for all of these years in Upper Montclair. He was fifteen years younger than I, but already showing signs of strain. He had been a smoker in his youth, and now that activity was catching up with him for he recently had a minor ischemic stroke which somewhat affected his gait. At my last annual physical in April, I noticed he was now walking slowly with a noticeable limp. He was somewhat bemused at my overall physicality, eyes and ears and teeth, bloodwork, urine and feces samples.

"Whatever you're doing, keep doing it," he said. "You'll probably outlive me."

Well, I had to take his advice seriously. Any significant change to my regular activities would, I surmised, have a negative effect on my overall health. Including moving from this old fading colonial and downsizing to a smaller house or apartment in Montclair as Doris had proposed. But why do that now? I had the money to delay the inevitable—to go out in style—but exactly *what was that style*? Ending up like Clara's mother, Dinah, in an assisted living compound in central Florida? Or taking a leisurely year-long Royal Caribbean cruise around the world? But I had already done that with Ruthie for our 50th Anniversary. So what was left?

And while I was gone, who would watch the house? Feed the deer? Seed and weed Ruthie's flower beds? And Caroline? She would have to find another, and possibly more difficult and complex employment solution. For Paul had made his point: She was trained as a hospice nurse, not as an off-site daily companion for an elderly man. And yes, I was overpaying her. But this half decade since Ruthie's passing was a blessing for us both. She was mainly the reason I was still independent, still fully functioning and could laughingly share with Dr. Francona my fatuous comeback...

"The thought of me outliving you and finding another doctor like yourself would be more than enough to explain *my* ischemic stroke."

CHAPTER 9

Friday. The platform. The chuppa. The tables and chairs. The electrical inspection by the DJ. The *BATHROOM>* sign. (Actually, I put up the sign early Thursday afternoon believing that one of the workers might need a restroom.) And with a sleeping pill taken at 9PM Thursday I figured I got my nine hours' sleep, enough to put me in a fully awake *apres-cafe* state to greet the vendors as early as 9AM... and if they were finished by noon, say, I could catch a nap before Paul's arrival, expected at about three and Peter an hour later. That would fill my afternoon before dinner with Gene's parents and grandparents at six. Doris Nottingham was now tasked with the scheduling of the vendors as early as 9AM, the time I would be up and about, about the time Caroline was expected to arrive.

I had told Caroline she could have Friday afternoon off so we could both rest up for a full day Saturday so she arrived first, promptly at nine, and I made sure her car was parked at curbside because the carpenters and caterers had heavy equipment to unload and needed the garage driveway to speed their deliveries. Doris had indicated I was to keep the garage driveway clear the entire weekend as well, for the Saturday floral attachments, DJ, and the caterers setting up on Saturday with table and chair removal late Sunday morning. My car would be in the garage and Caroline's car would be curbside, along with Paul's car Saturday night when we got back from the Marriott dinner. Doris had indeed done her homework, and I was truly impressed with her foresight and diligence.

A pair of carpenters arrived in a small panel truck soon after and unloaded a bunch of 2"x4"'s and enough tongue-and-groove flooring for several back and forth trips to the spray-painted area at the edge of the woods. It looked to me like they had done the same platform many times before, for they laid everything out quickly and powertooled their way into a sturdy finished product in about an hour. It looked great!

Before they had completely finished, they called Bill Young, the florist, who would be installing the chuppa. His assistant—actually his college-aged daughter I found out—arrived just as the carpenters were leaving. She had, tied to the top of her station wagon, a smaller, more intimate version of the metal pole-and-frame components mainly used for portable domed canopies at street fairs and community get-togethers. I helped her carry the pieces to the platform. She went back and returned with her battery-operated drill and a step ladder, assembling and screwing in the canopy frame in about twenty minutes. Then on the step ladder she tied down the chuppa's white nylon covering to the four corners. Finally, she stapled white plastic netting around the front two poles and the covering, making an archway to hold the flowers which were to come. All told, she was there for about three-quarters of an hour. I could only marvel at the practiced operation I was witnessing.

I offered her some coffee, but she had to get back to her Dad, for they had another wedding, this time a Christian church affair, on the other side of Montclair on Sunday—a busy time for the florist. I found out that her Dad and her Uncle owned a tree and floral bush nursery as well, close by, so everything was cut and delivered fresh the day of the event. She would be back the following day at 9AM to finish attaching flowers to the chuppa's archway. She knew the platform would be used for a dance floor after the ceremony and the chuppa would be unscrewed by the catering team. The chuppa itself, she assured me, would be broken down and taken away on Monday, because of the Sunday church wedding. All this was certainly worth $750 for everything. What a bargain, I thought. And my contribution would not go unnoticed.

Next up, the tables and chairs—but no, I was wrong. Doris had scheduled Frank, the DJ, to arrive beforehand since the furniture would probably be blocking the electrical outlets on the porch Frank needed to test.

He arrived at around 11, in his late model Chevy Malibu, a big guy, graying, maybe 50 or so, handed me his card and thanked me for choosing him as DJ for the event. It wasn't my doing, of course, but I didn't try to correct him. He had done many Jewish weddings and knew the repertoire he assured me, as if to say his music selection would be especially pleasing to Jewish ears. And he knew about the tradition of raising circling chairs for the newly-wedded couple on the dance platform, although I told him this was an engagement party, not a wedding. He looked somewhat bewildered but went about his business testing the electrical outlets with a metered gadget I had seen electricians use. Both outlets on the porch passed inspection, so he didn't have to up the amperage, or voltage, or whatever needed to be done in the basement.

"And you have some particular music you want me to play?" Frank asked as we walked back to his car, obviously having spoken to Doris sometime during the week.

"It's on a LP," I said.

"No problem," said Frank. "My turntable takes 33's, 45's and 78's. And I have players for 8-tracks, cassettes, CDs, whatever you got.

"It's an album by The Sweetmeats titled, *'Parnassus'*"

"Okay..."

"You've heard of them?"

"No, but that's all right. You want the entire album played?"

"No, just the track, *'The Power of Love.'*"

"That's a Celine Dion tune," he said. "I have her album somewhere if you want her version."

"No. She lifted the title. It's a different tune and lyrics entirely. The Sweetmeats recorded this back in 1966 before Dion was even born."

"Well, bring the album to me during the party and tell me when you want it played and I'll be more than pleased to accommodate you."

"Good enough," I said, shaking hands. "See you tomorrow."

Frank Pendleton's car had hardly left the driveway's oval when I spotted a large panel truck turning into the *cul-de-sac*. And sure enough, it was the caterers with their delivery of the chairs and tables. I motioned for them to pass the oval, then back the truck up the driveway's gravel path to the garage. That way, the rear of the truck would be closest to the house and the back porch, saving them some time unloading.

There were three workers, two Black guys and one Latino-looking guy all wearing the same dark blue Culture Caterers insignia uniform so that I would know now, and tomorrow, exactly who I was dealing with. They busied themselves without a word unloading 100 padded folding chairs, 4 folding tables, two brand new plastic trash cans and several black plastic bags with ties containing, I imagined, the tablecloths, plates, dinnerware, glasses and various other items for tomorrow's event. They knew the side way to the back porch, and for the next half hour or so, stacked everything against the porch's wall. Then they ran a thick yellow plastic ribbon which read continuously, MONITORED SECURITY AREA around all they had deposited there and stapled the ribbon securely to the house.

"Just a precaution," said one of the workers. "We know you don't have a camera back here."

"Sorry about that," I said apologetically, although I didn't know exactly why.

"Just don't let anyone break through the tape or we're in trouble. We'll be back tomorrow morning and do the setting up. We'll be here at ten o'clock."

"I'll be sure your stuff is secure," I said, shaking their hands. "You can back your truck up to the garage like you did today. Space for you guys and the DJ."

"And the Rabbi," said another of the workers. "We're supposed to carry his podium down to the... whatever you call it... where he speaks from."

"Oh? Okay. I guess he's coming last and leaving first, so fine. See you guys tomorrow."

And with that, they drove off, I checked my watch. It was a little past noon. I found Caroline upstairs vacuuming the guest rooms. "Leave that for tomorrow," I said. "Go home and relax. It's going to be a busy day tomorrow."

Getting Past Z

And after she departed, I set my alarm clock for 2:30PM—trying to catch a nap before Paul's arrival. I hadn't done hardly a thing that day to tire me out—but as soon as I lay down on my bed, I shut my eyes and...

CHAPTER 10

My whole life has been governed by my alarm clock. It tells me when my dreams must end and when reality begins. At my advanced age, I suppose I could throw the damn thing out, sleeping and dreaming my way into oblivion—and perhaps that would be the smartest thing to do—but I wasn't quite ready, said my mind and body and spirit. The three of them, conferring daily it seemed, wanted me still around, alive and kicking. For what, I asked; what is to come? Silence. Deadly silence.

Certain rituals of basic Western hygiene I could still perform, like daily showering, shaving, defecating and urinating into a toilet, brushing my teeth, dressing and combing what was left of my hair. Others, like tying shoelaces and slipping into underpants were now a bit problematic. For the latter, I no longer could stand on one leg whilst putting the other through a hole the size of a saucer plate, so that I needed to sit on the edge of my bed to get both feet through their assigned under-garment passageways. For the former, there was always Caroline to knot the laces properly.

In today's case, since I had dismissed Caroline early, I would be wearing slip-on loafers to Gene's party. All the other hygienic obstacles I managed to perform before Paul arrived a quarter after three.

He looked sharp in a tan suit, white button-down shirt and yellow-patterned tie. And he had recently gotten a haircut, his hair being somewhat unkempt the last time he was here. He had total access to the house, as my phone buzzed with his thumbprint and I embraced him in the kitchen since he chose to use the side entrance. He was carrying a small duffle and a nylon garment bag with what I assumed contained the clothes he would be wearing for Saturday's event.

"Sorry if I'm a little late. Friday traffic out of the city."

"Nah," I said, "you're fine. Put your bags in your room. Peter will be staying in a guest room."

While he was upstairs I put out a bowl of mixed nuts and brought out a chilled Chilean Sauvignon Blanc from the fridge. Just the thing for a warm summer afternoon. Then I brought out three white wine glasses from the cabinet above the stove.

"Where's Caroline?" he asked, returning, this time without his jacket.

"I gave her the afternoon off. She'll be working overtime tomorrow. Can you uncork this bottle for me?" I asked, handing Paul a corkscrew from the cutlery drawer.

"I don't think we should have too much," he cautioned, removing the cork.

"Oh?" I asked sarcastically, "What happened to my alcoholic son?"

"Well, Dad," he said, "things are changing for me. I thought I'd cut back for a while, and exercise more instead. So I'm running in Riverside Park in the afternoons now."

"And how's that working out, working out?"

"I'm feeling a lot better. Besides, most of my friends are off for the summer and out of town so I have no one to go drinking with. But I have some news for you…"

I poured myself and Paul a quarter glassful and put the bottle back in the fridge. "Better tell me when I'm sitting down," I said, jokingly.

We moved into the living room where it was cooler because of its central air conditioning vents, and sat together on the couch fronting the fireplace. "Okay," I asked, "what's the news?"

"I'm going back into teaching," he said. "The BofE made me an offer to come out of retirement with even a better tenure package than I had."

"Wow, that *is* news!" I marveled. "This Fall semester?"

"Yup. Remedial math. A high school in Dykeman, upper Manhattan. But an easy commute on the IRT."

"Oh, that's fantastic news! Here's to you!" I toasted, clinking our glasses together. "I always thought you going back into teaching would be a smart move. You're too young to retire, especially after what you've been through. This will get your mind and spirit working again."

"I suspect it was one of my drinking buddies who contacted BofE, because they knew the city was short of math teachers and maybe worried about me. But please don't say anything yet to Peter or Estelle. I'll announce it after the party. I don't want to take away from Estelle's day."

"I've heard that before," I said, recalling Peter's Australian venture. "Some other good news I can't share with anyone yet."

"Well," Paul said, "what's left of the Myer family could do with some good news, finally."

"Ah, but you know of your mother's balance theory, don't you?"

"Of course, but I'd like to hear it from you, Dad."

"Your Mom often said that everything eventually balances out. If you're too overweight with good news, bad news will follow and *vice versa* because that's Nature's way of keeping order in the world. You could see this in her even temperament, her comeback after Rachel's passing, her art. That's why she was so successful with our ads. They were all perfectly balanced with drawing and design, photography, type, color, all enticingly presented. Like fine art, you were drawn into the painting and never wanted to leave. And then *she* left *us*."

"I know how much you miss Mom," Paul said, his eyes misting up. "I do too. She told me just after she was diagnosed that she was waiting for the other shoe to drop—that she had had an exceptional life and now it was time to rebalance things. She told me to look after you. You can see what a great job I've done!"

"Don't beat yourself up over that. I have Caroline who can't replace your Mom, of course, but is keeping me going. And," I added, "the pendulum may be swinging back. We have all these good vibes from Estelle and Gene and other stuff I can't talk about now. I think we're in a rebalancing phase—but I'm not taking anything for granted, of course."

"No, and you shouldn't either. But you just reminded me, Dad, of what Mom used to say about the unexpected."

"Oh?"

"She often said, unexpected things happen when our expectations fail us and we refuse to take responsibility for our faulty, unrealistic look into the future."

"Your Mom was a homegrown mystic," I said.

"But seriously, Dad," Paul said, "I've been giving a lot of thought about you being out here alone and..."

"I told you, I have Caroline."

"But not at night. Not on Sundays. And you know of the serious crime waves hitting New York and other major coastal cities with the 'boat people'. Trump threw all his resources onto the Southern border and left the East and West coasts vulnerable to hoards of undocumented aliens coming ashore by boat. And because the City can't take any more in, they're being resettled into suburbs and into surrounding small towns and villages and all hell is breaking loose. It's just a matter of time before they're out here."

"Time to practice my High School Spanish," I laughed.

"It's not a laughing matter, Dad," Paul cautioned. "They're desperate people, and they'll take advantage of any situation that they can. Just look at what happened when Trump became President and locked down Texas, Arizona, New Mexico and California. There was a fucking turf war down there. Just look at San Diego and its suburbs! Scores died."

"They were given every opportunity to return to their home countries, my dear son. We paid for all their transportation, all their travel costs. We tried every peaceful way to move them, to temporarily house them, to give them food allowances, give them health benefits. We gave them enough time to leave peacefully. More than enough time. We extended deadlines everywhere. We bent over backwards for the asylum seekers as they were called then."

"My point exactly, Dad. That wasn't in their plans. They say they have a right to be here until their case is heard. It's so backed up it can take years. With DOGE even decades from lack of personnel and services. And they know it. And in those years they're essentially on their own, left to their own devices and creating havoc. It's not safe being out here alone now, Dad, it really isn't."

"So what are you suggesting? I move somewhere safe?"

"Yes. Why don't you think of moving in with me?"

"With you?"

"Yes. You've seen my place. It has a second bedroom and a second bathroom down the hall. I'll be teaching this fall, so you'll essentially have the place all to yourself for much of the time. And there are many senior centers in the neighborhood where you can meet some new friends. And we can go out in the evenings and have dinner together. I think you'd love being back in the city, you know it so well."

I saw that our glasses were almost empty and this was a good time to put our discussion to rest, so I asked, "You want a refill?"

"Sure, Dad. Just a half like before."

I took our glasses and headed to the fridge, just as my phone buzzed that someone's known fingerprint was at the front door. Peter had arrived.

"Well, I made it!" Peter exclaimed, his luggage still by the oval where his Uber was now pulling away. He was jacket-less but wearing a backpack, and two suitcases and two large cardboard boxes were still in the driveway. We embraced, and I called Paul to help bring Peter's things upstairs. They hugged for a while, not having seen each other when Peter was last here some weeks before. I hadn't noticed until now their close resemblance. Paul looked eerily similar to Peter at Peter's age, and somewhere upstairs was an album of photographs from that period 27 or 28 years before. A pregnant Clara, Paul beaming, Estelle, just two, mugging for the camera. I thought I may just bring those photos down tomorrow after the wedding to give to Paul, although I suspected he had copies of them all.

We each took an item from the driveway and brought them upstairs to put in the spare guest room. Well, not upstairs in my case. Paul went up and came down again to bring up the box I was carrying. And of course I let him, because it was heavily loaded. The boxes contained personal artifacts and books, said Peter.

"Did you bring your gun with you?" I asked.

"Yes, I did, Granddad,"

"Well, how about handing it over to me now," I said, with Paul looking on.

"Wow!" he exclaimed. "That was quick."

"I want to be able to tell Gene later when we meet that the first thing I did when Peter arrived was to ask for his gun and to hide it away in a very safe place. Then he can tell his security team everything is copacetic."

"So how many on this so-called team of his?"

"Two. They're from the WTC with ShapeSifters. I agreed with Gene's safety issues, dear."

"They'll have a field day," Paul put in.

Peter went back upstairs and returned shortly now dressed in a sports jacket and carrying a shoulder holstered gun which he handed off to me. "You want its paperwork, too?"

"No," I said. "That's your business. Mine is to safely hide this somewhere. Why don't you and Dad have some wine and I'll join you in a couple of minutes?"

I took the gun up to the master bedroom and closed the door. Then I took Ruthie's flower vase painting opposite our king-size bed off the wall. Behind was a small wall safe which I dialed, opened and deposited the gun and holster inside. It managed to fit on top of the papers and small money bills I had there. I locked the safe, put the painting back and rejoined Paul and Peter in the living room. Paul was sitting on the couch, Peter in one of the side high back chairs, and I joined them sitting on the other after picking up my wine glass from the kitchen table and slinging my jacket over a chair.

"Whew," said Peter, jokingly, "we can all breathe easier now."

"Do you think I'm being paranoid?"

"Just overly conservative, Granddad," Peter replied. "It's no big thing these days to have a gun in the house, or even carry one around with you, crime being what it is today."

"If you're caught with a gun in school," Paul objected, "you're expelled, no questions asked. And that goes for teachers as well."

"Well, I agree with that. Licenses shouldn't be issued to anyone 21 years or younger."

"So if you're a senior in college, and over 21, it's all right, is it?" I asked.

"Well, there should be a prohibition for that as well," Peter replied. "No one in any institution of higher learning should have a gun on them, regardless of age."

"Look who's being conservative now," I laughed. "Half the country wants no restrictions on guns, any age, any place, any time..."

"Not half the country," Paul put in. "I read the same *New Yorker* piece you did, Dad. The Quinnipiac poll said it's more like 30%."

"Right," I said, "in total. But in the 18-30 age group it was over 50% and many of them are kids still in school. They were brought up with guns in the family, with firing ranges, with gun shows."

"Well," said Peter, half-mockingly, "here we are. Three generations battling it out: Granddad of the Silent Generation, Dad of the X Generation and me of the Z Generation. And none of us can agree on anything these days."

"I'll agree to that," laughed Paul.

"You have some answer on why that is?" I asked Peter.

"Wish I did," he said. "But you can see it's at the tipping point. Everything is in gridlock and it's just not social issues like abortion, race and immigration. It's inflation, foreign relations, tariffs, economic stagnation, class division, unemployment, taxes, personal debt, the environment and too many other things to mention. Nobody is sleeping well these days. Maybe that's why gun sales are going through the roof."

"Yeah, but people aren't sleeping well, my son." Paul argued, "not because of abstract social issues: It's because of personal safety issues. Crime statistics have never been higher. Burglaries, robberies, shoplifting, carjackings, assaults, murders, assassinations. And we elected a President who said he would do something about it. He had four years to put us back on the right track, pull us together. More cops on the beat, remember? Instead he had Musk put in DOGE which quickly retired experienced cops for raw recruits. And then to top it off, a market meltdown because of idiotic tariffs. Double digit unemployment. Stagnation, A total economic disaster. And yet, you have to eat. You have to put food on the table for the kids..."

"Well," I said, "maybe things will turn around this fall. Just look at the latest unemployment numbers. Falling back to single digits. And the electorate is excited again to end this crap with a fresh presidential election. This time we finally have some Millennials and Z's running for office. New blood and new ideas. Last time around we didn't have that choice."

"Yes we did," Paul objected. "We had No Labels. And I would have voted for Kennedy, the independent, before he did his pirouette and threw himself and his people over to Trump. So I didn't vote— in protest of this turncoat. I joined the SHIT party—Staying Home in Terror. Remember their ditty?... *'The Democrats want me woke... the Republicans want me broke... so on Election Day I'll just stay away... and light my only toke.'*"

I wasn't amused. "I'm voting for Newsom," I put in, "being the lifelong Jewish Liberal Democrat that I am. What's the alternative? Same old RINO bullshit from mid-America? JD Vance and Nikki Haley? Trumpophiles? Musky MAGAgots? At least Newsom is a known factor."

"Known for what?" asked Paul. "More Californication as Trump tries to turn it into a red state?"

"The polls are leaning towards Vance only because of the concealed carry issue," Peter put in. "And as you can probably guess I'm for that. But when you look at the Trump/Vance record over these past four years, sure, they may have gotten us through a horrible recession, but at what cost? Everything else, especially internationally with his goddamn tariffs, was put on hold."

"I'm not upset by that," I said. "Trump had to set down domestic priorities first. There were people, kids, starving in our largest cities all across the country. Food riots, mob 'n robs. And the ill-conceived DOGE forced hundreds of thousand civil servants into unemployment.

So there was no one left to help the millions more homeless or deranged -- defecating between moving subway cars because of locked toilets in the stations—indignities too humiliating to mention. The country was losing its way. Thank goodness he finally got rid of Musk and that muskrat cabinet of his and began to look first after our people, dear."

"Bullshit," Peter snickered, turning away in disgust.

"I'll give you that, Dad," Paul said. "Meanwhile the Ukraine war with Russia and the Israeli wars with Hamas and Hezbollah dragged on from ceasefire to ceasefire with nothing to show for it but more dead bodies and flattened cities. And they're still at it! An inextinguible bonfire."

"These are very complicated issues," I said. "They involve countries who've been at war for decades, if not centuries. Even ceasefires are something positive in the scheme of things."

"Ahhh... but taking ceasefires to the next step is the tough part. You'd agree with me that Harris's 2-state proposal between Israel and The PLO was a disaster politically for her. She had no business messing around in an area she had no first-hand knowledge of, to pick up a few votes by trying to show some international expertise. Which backfired nicely for her."

"At least her Middle East proposal was passed out to the public for debate, not hidden away because they might offend some voting block or another."

"Or the plan's originator dismissed out of hand as 'mentally impaired'," Paul sarcastically put in, looking directly at me.

"That wasn't addressed to me," I countered. "That was Trump's rant directed at Harris after she allowed her peace proposal to be published to upstage his so-called secret one."

"Yes. But Harris's proposal was basically yours."

"Nonsense," I said. "I had six very specific points. All interconnected. She had four, all vague generalizations. More like a wish list."

"Wait!" Peter cried. "Slow down. Whose two-state proposal are we talking about? Harris's?"

"Harris, or someone on her staff, took it almost word for word from Grandpa's Letter to The Editor of *The New York Times*."

"She did? When was that?"

"Oh," I blithely put in, "ancient history—about a decade or so ago. I wrote that letter many years before the Gaza War. Harris or her researchers somehow found it, and used it as the basis for her 2-state proposal prior to the 2024 election. But they didn't bother to credit its originator, thank God!"

"Thank God is right," Paul muttered.

"Then who called you mentally impaired?" Peter wanted to know.

"Trump, indirectly, by inference," I replied. "Days before the election he wrote on his Truth Social blog that Harris was quote *mentally impaired* unquote for coming up with her quote *grossly incompetent* unquote two-state Middle East Blunder as he put it. His concept, revealed right after his inauguration, remember, was much better: Get America to take Gaza over, resettle two and a half million Palestinians into Egypt and Jordan, then rebuild Gaza from scratch as "the Riviera of the Middle East"— an upscale seaside resort community to be jointly managed with the Israelis. Two weeks into his 2nd term he invited Bibi to the White House to work out the details. Problem solved."

"Except Bibi was having none of it," Paul broke in. "When told about Trump's ingenious plan for ending the war and handing over

Gaza to the Americans after more than a year of fighting, the murders of most of the hostages, not to mention the 1,200 killed at the rave, Netanyahu was reported as saying, 'I know a country that doesn't have an extradition treaty with the U.S., Donald. Come over when you can.'"

"I remember that now," Peter said laughing along, "but I had no idea that Harris's two-state solution was taken from a letter Granddad wrote to *The Times*. What provoked you in writing *The Times*? When was that? What was in your plan?"

I turned away. "It doesn't matter. Pre-recorded history. Somewhere between T-Rex and T-Rump."

But Paul stepped in: "In 2018 while you were in school," he said, "your Grandpa and Grandma sold off their advertising business and with some of that money took a luxury cruise around the world, you must remember that. Grandpa wrote the letter to *The Times* right after they returned."

"I recall their trip," Peter said. "But I also remember that just as soon as they returned everything got shut down by the pandemic, Dad. You were going to throw a surprise party for their 50th anniversary but it never happened. I never got to see the films they made or the photos or anything!"

"They're in the basement," I said. "When Grandma passed I put everything about the trip into boxes and put them in the basement. Take what you want. I have no interest in them anymore."

"I'm interested only in your letter," Peter said. "This is the first I'm hearing about it."

"I'm sure you can find it in *The Times* archives. It's signed JM, New York. And I sent it without a return address or telephone number.

It went against their policy, but they published it anyway. I didn't want to be hounded by those replying to it."

"Because," Paul put in, "it was very controversial. I was very upset by it after your Grandma told me JM was Jerome Myer. It was best left unsaid, unread, if you must know the truth."

"What was so controversial about it? What made you send it to *The Times?* Peter persisted.

"Your father knows the story," I said. "I..."

"I'm not going to be the one who tells Peter," Paul snapped. "If you want to tell Peter, tell him yourself. You know my feelings about this. I'm not going there."

All of a sudden the three of us were at loggerheads. A peaceful enjoyable reunion was turning into something ugly.

"So let's drop the subject." I said.

But Peter went on: "Well, at least Harris put out some ideas for trying to solve this conflict during the runup to the election while Trump said it was too premature to reveal specific plans and wouldn't. She was purposely ambiguous so as not to offend any of her splinter groups."

"Trump solving conflicts?" his father asked contemptuously. "When are visiting hours?"

"Actually, I voted for Trump," Peter revealed (although he had already admitted that to me when last he visited), "because only KrazyKat would bring things to a head and that's what the Anti-Z's wanted then: Revolution. And had we had that Revolution back in '25 or '26 before midterms, we wouldn't be in this mess today. Everything would have been sorted out by now. Instead..."

"Ten times as bad," I sniffed.

"If Vance had switched places with Trump on the ballot, they would've had a fabulous ticket," Paul interjected. "Vance calmly and rationally taking on domestic issues; mad dog Trump untethered for international interventions because of his threatening, insulting, unpredictable nuttiness."

"Instead, Kamala tried to placate all sides and tolerated the dissent," Peter continued. "Everyone knows she lost the election by ducking tough domestic issues like soaring inflation, immigration and the national debt with soothing rhetoric while kicking the can down the road."

"Wrong," I put in. "Kicking the *cane* down the road. The Silents, what's left of us, and Boomers are the ones most hurting from the effects of DOGE, world-wide tariffs, and the economic downturn that followed. We have nothing left to give our kids, inheritance money they were counting on for *their* retirement, or paying off *their* kids' debts. It's a trickle-down disaster caused by The Donald and the inhumane programs of his former faithful companion, Elon."

"The Lone Ranger and Scout," Peter put in.

"The Lone Ranger and *Tonto*," I corrected him. "Scout was Tonto's horse."

"Tonto? Couldn't be. Tonto is 'fool' in Spanish."

Paul laughed. "But Dad's right. That was long before the woke mind virus, years before the Washington Redskins. Remember the tomahawk chop?"

"Anyway," I continued, "Trump's tariffs, real or threatened, put Powell and The Fed in an awkward position trying to continually manipulate prime rates for an impossible soft landing. Who could make money in the market when Fed insiders tipped off their banking friends first, when the country with the reserve currency is 40 trillion in debt? A house of cards the Fed had been constructing since long before the pandemic. Building walls between classes only leads to resentment and overt hostility."

"But it was Harris's constant extolling of DEI that really pissed me off," Paul interjected, "without truly understanding what was behind the class warfare. "She had no idea of what working class and middle class families were going through then. Squeezed by higher prices for everything—to pay for some CEO's addition to their mansion. Squeezed by new taxes to pay for the care and preservation of the 'newcomers' as she put it. Squeezed…"

"You should have been in San Diego," Peter put in. "Class warfare with live ammo."

"So everything tanked," his father went on, "and the so-called working and middle classes were—are—in revolt and Trump knows it. Once he took office he needed to put in price controls, rent controls, tax credits for healthcare, for childcare, for eldercare, caps on fuel and utilities, on drugs and insurance, along with financial aid packages for higher education with loan rates that you don't have to spend half your life paying back. Instead he listened to Musk and his Department of Grifter Entitlement. DOGE was their federal employee headline-making distraction used to counter Democratic-led DEI programs empowering private industry's working classes."

"Trump's DEI diversionary strategy: Divisiveness, Extremism, Inhumanity," Peter cracked.

"He had his chance back in '25," I argued, "when the Republicans held the Senate and the House, but lost both majorities in the '26 midterms. You can't do much with an opposing Congress: The House holds the pursestrings, the Senate has the filibuster. Moreover, you still have all these pissed-off vengeful Republicans and MAGA-ga-gas to deal with. They still believe Trump will somehow return for a 3rd term as FDR managed to do as 'War President'. Then the question becomes, where can we find a winnable war? Hmmm. Ah-ha, Panama!"

"FDR? Nah." Peter laughed. "We're dealing with a messiah complex here. Mystically parting locks for his yachting buddies, walking on water, that sort of thing. More like Moses or Jesus."

"Don't think I'm not hanging around to see that," I instinctively punned. "It's on my centennial to-do list."

"I think you may just make it, Granddad."

"Just a little more than a decade away," I said, now reclining on the couch. "And luckily, I have this house and some savings. Technically, I'm a Have so I'm not complaining. Otherwise, I'd be rummaging through some landfill near some Boomer Tenttown as they're called, as a Have-not."

"You should sell the house," said Paul, "and take that money and travel."

"Oh? And where should I travel at my age? I'll be ninety in less than a month. Where does a person ninety travel to, when they won't even renew my Honda's registration in New Jersey anymore without paying an arm and a leg insurance premium, more than the car is worth! And I have a clean record, besides, so I really ought to be getting a discount. It's all age discrimination and corporate greed. Welcome to getting old!"

"Take a cruise," said Peter. "See the world… or what's left of it."

"Did that with your Grandmother years ago for our 50th, remember?" I said, "when we were both fit and could do the guided excursions in a 20-person Sprinter. The pyramids, the great wall, the wailing wall, Florence, Machu Picchu, the Taj... I'm not so sure I could even leave the boat now. So you'd have me enjoying solitary confinement in my stateroom? Besides, these new cruise ships are way more than floating hotels now. They're small cities. You no longer get the sense of adventure and discovery; you get the sense of being stuck in traffic.

"Come live with me," Paul offered again. "Manhattan has so many things to offer: Museums and shows and cultural events. Better than being out here alone with the deer. And suppose you have a medical emergency, Dad?"

"I have 911 built into my phone, and automatic dialing to Dr. Francona and full medical insurance coverage. And so long as Caroline is here, I'm perfectly content. Have you ever heard me say otherwise?"

They both shook their heads.

"City living? Socializing?" I went on, "Five years ago they called it a 'social recession,' remember? Now it's being called a 'social depression.' People aren't communicating with one another and when they do, it's not directly face-to-face anymore. As you've often said, Peter, we're talking through filters and screens... and y'know something? The more I think about it, the more I'm inclined to agree."

Peter was flattered. "The Prophet from the West comes home to roost," he beamed.

"Well," said his Dad, "this is just tantalizing technology doing its thing. You can't blame smartphone manufacturers for making devices that give you instant access to the entire world in the palm of your hand. And you can't blame platforms like TikTok for providing instant access to news and information..."

"Or disinformation," Peter put in.

"Or disinformation, misinformation whatever," Paul went on. "No one wants to learn anything from reading newspapers or books anymore, much less sitting in a classroom. That's too much time wasted. Today, it's all visual stimulus crap. And subjects like math are too boring to even put out. So this is more than social depression: It's intellectual depression. And we're becoming stupider and stupider... if there is such a word."

I got up off the couch and went to the fridge for the chilled Sauvignon. "Since we're all in agreement on something, time to refill," I said, returning with the remaining half-bottle.

"A toast," Paul offered, now standing, as I poured the wine around. "To the three remaining Myers who are less stupider than most non-Myers."

We all laughed and clinked glasses. "At least you qualified non-Myers with *most*." I said. "I take it you've conducted a survey of some kind."

"Certainly," Paul responded. "Public opinion is manufactured now by anonymous surveys and polls tabulated by AI. That's the only way to construct a lie without being caught. Polls get our Presidents elected. Polls set our priorities straight. Polls tell us what to buy, what to sell, where to live, what other people are doing with their lives and what to do with our own. If the poll says it's most cool to be in a Boomer Tenttown, that's where I'd want to be with my pollster gun."

"No you wouldn't," I put in. "I would have taken it away from you and hidden it somewhere."

We all laughed again.

"No laughing matter," Peter said. "I bet at least 5 guns will be found tomorrow by Gene's Secret Service."

"How much do you wanna bet?" I asked, not really expecting a response.

"My round-trip airfare and Uber here this weekend," Peter responded quickly. "A thousand bucks."

"Just a grand?" I said in mock surprise. "You're on!"

"And you, Dad?" Peter asked.

"Naw," Paul replied, "I'm hoping we forget about this bet by tomorrow. It smells of a TikTok dare."

There were a couple of gulps left in my glass, but I stopped drinking at that point. Chances were good I'd be driving, not only to the Marriott, but back in darkness which, on a Friday night, was even a bit more problematic for me. I really wanted Paul to do the driving both ways, and while I was excited by his pronouncements of sobering up and returning to teaching, I had no way yet of verifying either.

"Well," I said at that point, "We don't want to be late for dinner with the Samuels and ... .eh, Rappaport family, whatever..." reminding myself of Gene's name change upon being adopted by his step-father.

"Grandfather and Grandmother's name is Rappaport, right?" Paul asked.

"Right. Mother and Step-Father are Samuels."

"Got it," Paul said. "Like you were Myers at one time."

"Until your Grandfather changed it by dropping the 's'. Everything changes with time..."

"And balances out," Paul teased.

"And balances out," I confirmed, pouring what was left of my wine into Peter's glass. Surprisingly, Paul followed suit. Our eyes met, and he smiled: He had read my mind.

Then to Peter I said: "Caroline left you some of her delicious meatloaf in the fridge so you can make some dinner for yourself, and I think there are some veggies there too in the bottom cooler. Be sure the doors are locked before you get to bed. We'll be back around 9:30 I imagine."

"If you don't mind, I'm going to try bringing up your letter," Peter said, taking out his phone.

"It's time to leave," said Paul, looking at me. I nodded my agreement.

"Don't want to be late," I said, putting on my jacket. And to Peter: "Get some sleep. It's going to be a full day tomorrow."

And with that, Paul and I left the house at about 5:30 for a ten minute trip to the Marriott Montclair. He would do the driving in his EV Kia, he told me, because it would be dark by the time we left to come home. Couldn't have said it any better myself.

CHAPTER 11

We had some extra time, so we decided to park in the hotel's basement parking lot instead of dropping Paul's car off at the entrance to be parked by attendants. But once we got to the private dining space off the main dining room, we discovered that the Samuels and the Rappaports had already assembled and were well into their first drink.

"So glad you're arriving early," said Gene, extending his hand to both of us. "I said six, and they took it to mean, serving dinner at six. I wanted some time before to socialize."

"Glad to see you," I said.

"Let me introduce you," Gene said, the others gathering around us. "First off, this is Jerry Myer and his son, Paul Myer, Stella's Dad. This is my Grandmother, Pamala Rappaport and my Grandfather, Ralph Rappaport."

They were both carrying canes to steady themselves, but switched hands to shake ours.

"And this is my Mom and Step-Dad, Richard and Andria Samuels."

They were suntanned and in great-looking shape, I thought, thinking that compared to Paul they looked ten years younger than he. We all shook hands again.

"What do you want to drink?" Gene asked, motioning for the waiter to come over.

"A glass of white wine," I said. Paul asked for the same.

I remembered what I first wanted to do upon seeing Gene, and so I said to him: "Can I see you for a moment?"

We walked away a few steps from the others. "I just want to tell you before I forget, that Peter *did* bring his gun and gave it to me for safekeeping. And I hid it safely away."

"Thank you for telling me, Jerry," he said. "I don't expect any problems tomorrow."

Then we rejoined the group. The waiter was there with our white wines. Gene proposed a toast: "To all of our families. Families always come first. If it wasn't for families we all wouldn't be here. So I'm so pleased to be joining our families together."

"And we're so pleased to have you in ours," I put in.

"*L'chiam*," said his father, and we all clinked our glasses with one another.

Then there was some small talk among ourselves about the fine weather we would have for tomorrow's ceremony, which, both the Samuels and Rappaports believed was a wedding, not an engagement party. I guess Gene had made it clear to his side of the family, while Estelle was still being coy. But upon thinking about it, I realized Gene had to be perfectly candid to get both his grandparents from Florida and his parents from South Carolina to make the arduous trip. And of course Rabbi Max had indicated to me all the *ketubah* and civic paperwork had been completed. Indeed, Estelle and Eugene were already married in New York's eyes; and soon would be in God's.

The seating arrangement around a circular table was intriguing. Gene had placed me between his grandparents, and had placed Paul between his parents—while Gene had placed himself between his mother and grandmother. The table could accommodate at least 8 people so there was plenty of space between all of us, but we were grouped generationally. I guessed he had figured that in this way we would have some commonality, but from the moment we sat down, I realized that the Rappaports and I would have little rapport.

Gene and I helped with the chairs sitting his grandparents first, then he helped sit me between them. I started with a joke about our seat assignments. Noting their canes hung on the backs of their chairs, I wisely cracked, "An Abel between two Cains" I said, sitting down. This didn't go over too well. I got no response.

"You live in Upper Montclair my grandson tells me," Pamala started off. "Why do they call it *Upper* Montclair? Is it on a hillside?"

"You need to take uppers to live there," I joked, and an ancient joke at that. Again, no response. This wasn't going well.

"We live in The Villages," said Ralph. "In central Florida. Ever hear of that?"

"Yes," I said. "It's an over-55 resort community."

"I built it," said Ralph, commandingly. "Back in the Seventies. There's close to 100,000 people living there now. It's the largest retirement community in the world. My company constructed the first housing units there when it was just marshland. We drained it and damned it up. They thought it couldn't be done."

"And they're still there," Pamala added. "We moved in when they changed the charter for only over-55 people. That's living in the same house for almost forty years now and as you see we're still going strong."

"You can visit if you're under 55," Ralph clarified, "But only for a month at a time. So you'll see our children and our grandchildren there, usually in the summer months when schools are out, but only for visits."

"So it's actually very quiet there," Pamala added. "And all the carts and cars we use to get around have to be electrified now. Even delivery trucks from outside. They won't let any gas-driven cars through the gates now. The air is so clean it's amazing!"

"Okay," said Gene, breaking in, "It's time to order. There are only two entree choices tonight in the private dining room. You can either have baked salmon, or a rack of lamb."

This being Friday night, I ordered the baked salmon. The Rappaport's both ordered the lamb. I looked over at Paul and he caught my eye. *Salmon* he mouthed to me. The Samuels team was split and Gene ordered salmon as well. The head waiter took the order and the table was then loaded down with warm buns and butter balls, fancy wooden salad bowls and preferred wine glasses. This was going to be a feast.

"Now," said Gene, "who is drinking what? We have a lovely white vouvray or a chardonnay and we have both a merlot and a red burgundy." A vouvray, I thought. Gene had to have gotten my favorite wine from his betrothed. I smiled at him then and he nodded back. He knew my order.

The dinner, the service, the ambiance, the wine—everything was first class that evening. Even the company was entertaining when I could get a word in edgewise. The Rappaports were keen on having me visit them so that I could see for myself that even at ninety, there were many activities I'd be interested in, even tennis. I could think of renting an apartment if buying something at my age seemed too large an investment to make. There were many health care clinics just a short golf cart ride away. And, put in Pamela, women outnumbered men over eighty three to two, so maybe I could find someone to partner with. In fact, she said, she had a couple of widowed 'girlfriends' who would love to meet me.

It was clear to me, as our plates were being cleared for a delicious strawberry tart dessert, Gene was behind the Rappaport's selling me on The Villages. But why, I wondered. What could I possibly find down there, except possibly better weather in the winter, than where I was now. And romance? Erections, I was afraid to say (and thankfully didn't) were a piss from the past.

"And now," Gene said, taking some sealed envelopes from his sports jacket and laying them face down at the table's center, "are the sacred blessings Rabbi Max wants you, as our closest relatives, to confer on us at tomorrow's wedding. There are seven all together, but the Rabbi will say his blessing last, so there are six here, one for each of you. Each has a number inside, and Rabbi Max will call out the blessing number and you'll stand up and recite it from the card inside. So there's no way of knowing who gets to say what blessing."

"In English?" asked Ralph, "because I don't remember my Hebrew any more."

"Definitely In English," Gene laughed. "And someone with a microphone will be before you so you don't have to shout."

Everyone laughed and reached in for their envelope. It was a sweet ending to a surprisingly upbeat dinner. But Gene wasn't through yet.

"And I have one final surprise," he said. "Remember on your invitation I wrote not to make plans until after Labor Day? You know that Erskine & Samuels leases a yacht out of Westport, Connecticut, don't you? And Leo and his wife Valerie are celebrating their 25th anniversary Labor Day weekend. So we put our heads together and came up with the idea of treating all of you to a honeymoon and silver anniversary celebration cruise, first to Hilton Head and then down to Ft. Lauderdale. It's going to be just one big party and we want all of you to be with us. We leave from here to Westport this Sunday afternoon, the day after tomorrow's wedding."

We broke up at around 8:30, somewhat earlier than I expected. Everyone wanted to get a good night's sleep before tomorrow's event, now positively confirmed as a wedding. Paul and I said our goodbyes and our good wishes, thanked our host profusely and took the elevator down to the basement parking lot. Once on the road Paul breathed a noticeable sigh of relief.

"How did it go for you, Dad?" he asked.

"I was being propositioned on The Villages throughout the meal," I said. "But I didn't commit to visiting the Rappaports, even though their guest room overlooks a gorgeous man-made lake," I laughed. "And I'm really not up for taking the cruise either. And you?"

"For the next couple of weeks I'm in various curriculum meetings to bring me up to speed. School starts right after Labor Day. So I'll have to bow out of the cruise too, I'm afraid."

"And how did you like Gene's folks?"

"I found out more about Gene's older brother from his parents than I ever wanted to know," Paul said.

"David?"

"Yeah, David. I don't remember how we got on that subject, but David is the Black Sheep of the family. And he's coming tomorrow as Gene's Best Man. Ahhhh…" Paul recalled, "that's how we got on the subject. I asked Richard Samuels if he was Best Man and he said, 'No, David is performing that duty. He's carrying the ring, unless he's already pawned it.'"

"Black Sheep? Why?"

"A very long and convoluted story, Dad. I'm not sure of all the details because Gene somehow didn't want his mom and stepdad talking about David and tried to interrupt and change the subject often."

"Well, what's the outline?"

"David worked for his stepdad's construction company out of college but then went into commercial real estate in New York City because it was way more lucrative. And he was doing very well all through his twenty-teens, got married to a lovely actress, bought into that pencil condo on Central Park South and started a family. His real estate company put him in charge of the Times Square area when he expressed an interest in Broadway, via his wife's prodding. But one of his first projects was to tear down a dilapidated old theatre his company had bought. They had a client who wanted to erect a migrant hotel on the site.

"Well," I said, "you have to tear things down if you want to build things up, right?"

"True. But then the covid pandemic hit. Commercial real estate took a heavy hit as WFH took off. The market for office space collapsed. Broadway theatres went dark."

"WFH? Don't you mean WTF?"

Paul laughed. "I mean Working From Home, Dad, but also WTF. That could have been David's response to his boss, because they put him in charge of tearing down The Rialto—that old stage theatre on 46th off Broadway. At one time it was Leonard Bernstein's favorite theatre because of its huge orchestra pit and he produced *West Side Story* there. But it also had a long history of code violations and during the pandemic it was closed, and no one was being paid much to keep it operational. The rusted out water pipes had burst in the basement backstage and it appeared like a sinkhole had developed which affected the integrity of the entire structure. That's how David's real estate company got it so cheaply. Even so, it had been designated by the City's preservation committee as a cultural landmark and they wanted to rename it after Bernstein so David saw some possibilities here for restoration. There was this back and forth and David got Gene and his law firm involved to sort it out."

"Ahhh," I said. "Let me guess. This pissed off the real estate people."

"To put it mildly. They had bought the property for a song and had a signed contract from a developer for putting up a migrant hotel on the site. A lawsuit against the City would push back those plans for months, if not for years. The developer threatened to back out. So you know what they did?"

"Fired David."

"Not quite. They put all the data they had, the entire history of the theatre, the structural engineer's report, the code violations, objections from NIMBY people against migrants flooding the area, the preservation board's expectations, the costs of renovation, reconstruction, the various benefits to the City in terms of receipts, taxes, employment opportunities, tourist dollars—they threw every detail they could find into their computer and let AI's algorithm sort it out.

"Oh boy!" I exclaimed. "This is getting good."

"And with those results, they could fire David with impunity... but not before they made him an offer he couldn't refuse. They would sell him the property for $1 in lieu of severance and other company benefits he had accrued. If he could reopen the theatre with a hit show he'd instantly become Mr. Broadway. After more prodding from his wife he took up their offer."

"Yeah," I said, "but what a risky undertaking. He had to raise some money first to get the theatre into shape."

"Exactly," Paul said. "The preservation people put some seed money in, but it was just a drop in the basement bucket. The structural engineer's report indicated it needed nearly a million just to bring the theatre up to code. He should have quit right there, but I don't have to tell you the Samuels and the Rappaports are loaded. And his wife was a former actress and was excited that her husband was now a Broadway producer. She convinced her parents to put some money in the pot as well. He and his wife also had some friends and business associates he could touch as "pre-angels" for a yet-to-be-announced production. So he hit up Gene and his parents and grandparents and his wife's family before even attempting to get bank loans. And he was offering 7-½%

annual interest on the investment, paid out monthly, a couple of points more than a savings bank back then. His perseverance and cocktail parties paid off. In just two months he had raised enough to begin restoration work."

"This was when?"

"Early 2024. The pandemic was officially over. Broadway was coming back. He was figuring to open the theatre that Fall."

We were close to home now, but I wanted to hear the rest of the story without disturbing Peter. So we parked curbside in front of the house and Paul continued with this fascinating tale....

"Well, what his friends and family didn't know was that David had already invested heavily in crypto and with a company called Alameda Research that went bankrupt when 'Uncle Sam' Bankman was charged with fraud. David, it seems, had lost virtually everything in that scam—a secret he kept even from his wife. But because he was gainfully employed and had great credit he had taken out personal loans from several banks to pay for condo expenses and food and clothes, private schools and summer camp for his two kids, trips to Hilton Head to see his parents, vacations to Florida etc. And with this new money coming in for the Broadway project, he first paid off his credit card and bank loans, then with what he had remaining, began restoration on the theatre."

"Sounds like a plan," I said.

"Except he now didn't have enough cash to go very far with it. So he created a production company that was going to put on the first show, hoping to attract more "angels" to begin paying off original investors and their 7-1/2% monthly income."

"Oh-oh," I said. "Sounds a bit like a Ponzi scheme."

"Made Bernie Madoff seem like an *angel*," Paul quipped.

"So did he launch a show?"

"Yeah. He shored up the back wall and somehow bribed the inspectors to re-open the theatre, and had just enough to do some social media promotion for… and this was its actual name… *Y'Never Know*. David's wife came up with the name."

"What?!"

"*Y'Never Know*. Amateur talent looking for a break into show biz."

"It sounds a lot like Leonard Sillman's *New Faces of '52*." I said. "That's how Eartha Kitt got her start. I was in my mid-teens at Music & Art, so the music majors were mainly into seeing it. But I remember *New Faces* was like a review, a showcase for new talent."

"Right. And David thought he had even a better idea. Very cheap tickets for just over an hour of showtime. He was only charging $10 a ticket for matinee performances at 1PM & 3:30PM geared more to kids and $20 a ticket for evening performances at 7PM & 9:30PM geared to a more adult audience."

"Wow," I said. "That *is* cheap."

"Well, he realized that after the pandemic Broadway was hurting, and to make up the loss producers were charging more than ever for seats. People, especially tourists, just couldn't afford the cost, even if they went to TIX to get ½ price seats the day of the performance. Even prices for those tickets were outta sight. So the basic idea itself was good…"

"But were the acts any good?"

"Well, he tapped his wife to do morning auditions, and she managed to pull in some decent talent. You were guaranteed to see three acts of some kind at every performance, different kinds of acts, plus a comedian MC. So maybe a rock or rap band of some sort, a pop singer-songwriter trying out new material, ventriloquist, acrobats, jugglers, a dance set, a magician, an illusionist… *Y'Never Knew*,"

"But no star."

"Definitely all amateurs starting out, looking to become stars. Some of them just kids really. But the reviews were mostly favorable, mainly because of the ticket prices. It was something to do in New York for less than the price of a double Big Mac. Tourists caught on to it quickly because seeing a Broadway show is a must for a visitor, and positive write-ups in *Variety* and *New York Magazine* added to the buzz. David had full houses from the start with lines forming for the next show. He managed to sneak Gene and Estelle in to see an evening performance and even *they* were impressed. By early 2025 his improbable new enterprise was booming. Standing room only."

"But what about costs?"

"David was paying his acts virtually nothing, a small food allowance, maybe parking outlay. The idea being, someone in the audience would be a producer or a director or a talent scout or having an event of some kind and would see the act and hire them."

"And what about the lighting, the sound, props, ticket sellers, ushers, cleaning?"

"He managed to find some retired stagehands and unemployed migrants who needed work off the books. They were working for peanuts. But they saw full houses, and thought David was taking advantage so he had to raise their salaries somewhat, but nowhere near union wages."

"Oh-oh. So did the unions get involved?"

"Well, that's what David's mother claimed. But it wasn't just salaries. Other productions were hurting because *Y'Never Know* was doing so well with such low ticket prices. But the producers who were paying for top talent, casts, wardrobes, scenery, and so forth, didn't want to lower their ticket prices thereby reducing their profits—for what should have been a little off-Broadway production in the first place. So they joined forces and got the unions involved. They found out about the bribes David paid the building inspectors and closed the show down after only half a year because the theatre didn't meet safety requirements and David couldn't raise more funds in time. And so the backers lost most of their money, and David was now seriously in trouble. And, according to his stepfather, he doesn't intend to repay those investors, claiming that angels always take a lending risk when they sign up for such a highly speculative venture."

"I see."

"And to make matters worse," Paul went on, "when he couldn't pay his mortgage and the monthly maintenance fees he lost his condo, had to declare bankruptcy, and his wife left with the kids to her parent's home in Boston where they're living now and she's lately filed for divorce."

"Ohhh... not good!"

"So David is somehow surviving in his theatre, in one of the dressing rooms, and is waiting for someone to buy the property from him so it can be restored or torn down as originally planned and he can reopen *Y'Never Know* somewhere off-Broadway, maybe in The East Village, where it should have been in the first place. Some backers are threatening to press fraud charges and he could wind up in jail for this. He went to Gene to defend him, but his brother couldn't help him much. Conflict of interest since Gene was an original investor. Moral to the story: If AI tells you to do something, you'd better do it!" he quipped.

We got out of Paul's car and walked towards the house. I still had a question or two. "I don't get it," I said. "Why did the Samuels go into such detail with you with such an involved story? Sure, they and Gene lost some money, but that's really no business of ours."

"I think they were trying to warn us about investing."

"Ah, I see."

"His parents still love David, they say, they know what he and his brother went through as kids, but he has to start working again, making a decent living. He's been buried in his dressing room for years now, working for a pittance as Rialto's Custodian from preservation committee funds, trying to figure out how to bring it up to code or sell it. Any decent offer would be accepted since he only paid $1 for it."

"Well," I said, "they'd have to already know the theatre is a literal and physical sinkhole."

"Right, Dad. David has to just walk away from it and rejoin the real world. My guess is that's Gene's position as well."

"He'd listen to his brother, right?"

"I think that's behind Gene choosing his older brother as Best Man instead of his stepdad. It's his way of first smoothing the water. His brother needs to come back into the fold; that it's time not just for restitutions but for reconciliations. The family comes first, after all."

"That's Peter's story," I noted. "Maybe Estelle is behind this one as well."

"We shall see," said Paul. "And if Estelle and Gene can make their marriage work, well, *Y'Never Know.*"

Getting Past Z

I expected to go right to bed but it was not to be. Peter was up and about, waiting for us, sitting on the couch before the fireplace with a pencil and pad. He had some questions for me that would only take a few minutes of my time. Paul wisely headed upstairs after saying goodnight to us both.

I had had enough to drink for the evening, so I put a kettle on for some hot water and some caffeine–free tea, offering some to Peter who declined. I noticed that he had finished all the wine left to him, and had some of the meatloaf Caroline had prepared. The kitchen had been cleaned up nicely and I was happy to see that, as I was expecting to take on that chore early the next morning.

While the water was being prepared, I sat down on the couch with Peter. He looked tired from his cross-country trip and I suggested we could have this talk later in the weekend, after the wedding.

"Well, Granddad, I had a chance to read the letter you sent to *The Times*. It's still in their archives after a decade or so. And I then did some research on the six points you proposed. And I discovered that every one of them, at one time or another, had been formally presented by either Israel and the U.S. or by the PLO or Hamas or Hezbollah and Iran, argued over but not one agreed to. It's a stalemate."

"And so, the war goes on and on. Five years now. And it will go on and on until all six points are agreed to by both sides."

"You mean, if only five points are agreed to, the war will go on?"

"Yes, exactly. This is a total package for peace that cannot be achieved piecemeal," I said, not intending the word play. "It's one unified, interconnected plan."

"It sounds to me impossible to achieve, Granddad. How do you know that?"

"That's what I was told."

"By whom?"

"Well, first let me get my tea. And while I'm doing that, let me ask you: Do you have an open mind about the occult, about supernatural, paranormal stuff?"

Peter accompanied me over to the kitchen, while I got out a tea bag and poured boiling water into a mug. "Like what?" he asked. "Ghosts? Like things flying off bookshelves by themselves?"

"Like telepathy from the dead. Mediums, seances, spirits, channeling, that kind of thing."

"Yeah, Granddad, I have a hard time dealing with that stuff."

"Well, so did I," I said, returning to the couch with my steaming mug of tea, "until it happened to me. Even today, I'm not at all sure whether it was all hallucinatory or some kind of trick someone was playing on me. Ever hear of necromancy?"

"Something dead?"

"It means communicating with the dead in order to learn about the future."

"If you must know, I think that's all superstitious bullshit."

"Okay. I'm not here to change your thinking. So I'll just present my bullshit story, and you can then decide what to make of it."

His demeanor suddenly changed. "I'm so sorry for insulting you like that, Granddad," he said, reaching over and rubbing my shoulder. "I want to take that back."

"Apology accepted," I said. "It's very hard to explain what happened to me. But I have nothing to prove here. I'm not out for your vote one way or the other."

"You were given this peace plan by communicating with a dead person?"

"In essence, yes. This was on our 'round the world luxury cruise back in 2018. Your Grandma and I went together to the Wailing Wall in the Old City of Jerusalem. As you know the courtyard is divided: I was on the men's side, and your Grandma was on the women's side. And it was a very hot afternoon, so after praying at the wall, I needed to sit down on one of the wooden folding chairs provided. And I was feeling a bit dizzy if you must know, even though I had brought a water bottle with me and was sitting in the shade. I wanted to get up and leave, but I didn't have the strength to get up, not even the strength to call out for assistance. I just sat there with my pad and pen in my lap, thinking about getting the attention of someone to help me."

"Like this pad and pen?"

"Similar. It was just one of the gifts the cruise gave out. If we wanted to take notes on what we were seeing, we had small calendar-notebooks we could slip into our purses or pockets. I had mine out because I wrote out a prayer to God for good health for the family and slipped the note into a crevice in the Wall as is the custom. Then I felt a little lightheaded and needed to sit down and drink some water from the bottle. I was having a sensory shutdown. I knew I needed help, but I couldn't speak, couldn't move."

"Did you pass out?"

"No, not then. I began hallucinating though. I was wearing sunglasses, of course, but I experienced a blinding flash of light somehow internally produced."

"Sounds like sun stroke to me."

"And then sitting next to me was Rachel."

"Rachel? Dad's little sister?"

"Our departed daughter, dressed in her favorite party dress, the one she was buried in. She had bandages wrapped around her head, like she had when she died. But her voice told me it was her and she said, 'Daddy, open your notebook and write down, word for word, everything I tell you.' And she gave me the six points in my letter. And after I wrote everything down, she took the ballpoint from my hand and placed it in the spiral binder, closed the notebook, placed it on my lap, and gave me a kiss on my temple before just fading away. Then everything went dark. I must have passed out and just slumped down on the chair."

"So someone would have had to see that and try to revive you."

"Certainly. The next thing I remember was laying on a stretcher in an ambulance, your Grandma Ruthie and a nurse beside me, and I had an IV in my arm and we were on our way to the main Jerusalem hospital. And yes, they determined my vertigo was from heat exhaustion. And that I'd be fine after a restful night of fluids in the hospital. Ruthie was given my notebook and while I was at the hospital overnight she had a chance to read it back at the hotel—and see what I had written under the headline: *Peace Proposal for a 2-State Israeli-Palestinian Homeland*. I was released the next morning and we taxied back to the hotel where the group was forming to leave Jerusalem. She never mentioned to me that she had read my latest notebook entry. I only found out after *The Times* decided to publish it after we returned to the States."

"And how did she take it?"

"Not well. 'Please don't tell anyone you're its author. We'll lose all our friends and family,' is how she put it. So I never told her about Rachel, of course. That would have really set her off. I think she would have claimed I was in touch, not with Rachel, but with Satan. That's how strongly she felt about necromancy. The work of the Devil. But after she died I revealed to your Dad about encountering Rachel because your Grandma Ruthie, in her final hours, revealed my letter to him—'that cursed pro-Palestinian *Times* letter' as she put it. I thought it was time for him to know my side of the story."

Peter shook his head: "It doesn't seem particularly evil or even delusional. I think you wrote it, Granddad, and don't remember. You must have been very spacy at the time."

"Well, I was, but I rested up the next day on the boat. We did the Suez canal, so it was a quiet day. No excursions. I had time to review what I had written, and it seemed all very complex. But I quite remember the visitation from Rachel, and how she dictated the six points of the plan to me. It couldn't have come from her. No ten-year-old would be sophisticated enough to come up with the complexities and nuances of that solution. So she must have been channeling someone."

"Granddad, you're scaring me," Peter said, "when you put it in those terms. That's way out stuff."

"Well, I know that. And I realized I better not tell anyone at that point about what actually went on because there would go my credibility, right out the window. I had always valued my intellectual and reasoning acuity and while there were parts of the plan that made absolute sense to me, there were parts that seemed quite unworkable. But even so, if all six points were carried out as a unified whole, it seemed to me that this proposal was quite possibly the only way to have permanent peace between the Israeli side and the Palestinian side, existing as they were on the same patch of ground claimed by both parties."

"But you told me before that all six points had to be agreed to. Five wouldn't work."

"Rachel made it clear that nothing could be changed. All points were interconnected and balanced perfectly. I was not to add or subtract anything from the text."

"And that's the text you sent to *The Times*?"

"Word for word from my notebook. I only added *JM New York* at the end," I said, sipping my tea.

"Do you think we could go over the points? A couple of them make some sense to me as well.

I know it's late but I'd like to hear your thoughts on what you wrote. I promise to just hear you out and not make any arguments."

"Peter, we have a busy day tomorrow..."

"Please, Granddad, it would mean so much to me. Be as brief as you want."

"Well, read the letter from the beginning, and I'll briefly comment on it."

An integrated Israeli-Palestinian single state solution is not possible given the vast differences in culture, language, religion, lifestyle, and general mistrust of the others' future intentions. Here's a 6-point peace plan that provides a N/S 2-state solution based on the N/S Korean truce, (armistice) still in effect for over 60 years.

1. Palestinians give up claims to Gaza and the West Bank territory to Israel.

"Hamas has nothing to lose if they cede Gaza back to Israel. Gaza today is a ruined battleground that's uninhabitable. Two million innocents displaced. The territory needs to be completely rebuilt from scratch. And you can see that even ceasefires don't work. Sure, some hostages and some prisoners are released, but then it's back to the fighting. It's been five years of non-stop suffering.

And so far as those few Palestinian families living on the West Bank, they're being harassed and killed daily by Jewish settlers who want their land. There would be some displacement but better they move out before they are annihilated."

2. Israel cedes the Golan Heights back to Syria, becoming a demilitarized buffer zone under U.N. auspices.

"This is a tit-for-tat to the first point. Israel has to show willingness to give up some territory to gain some territory. So they might as well give back the Golan Heights which they took from Syria in the '67 6-day war, as well as placating Lebanon and, of course, Iran, but let the U.N. patrol a buffer zone to keep the parties apart."

3. A U.N "no man's land" or "dmz" is created at approx. 31.2-degree latitude running from the Philadelphi Corridor to just below Be'er Sheva, Arad, Masada and ending at the Dead Sea. North of this boundary line is all Israeli...South is all Palestinian including the resort city and port of Eilat with access to the Gulf of Aqaba and the Red Sea.

"Believe it or not, I visited all of the places mentioned in my letter. Jerusalem was the high point, of course, saved for the last. But a week before that, beginning in Tel Aviv, the tour included trips to West Bank kibbutzim, Gaza city, the Egyptian boundary fence, Be'er Sheva, Arad, of course Masada, and an afternoon and overnight stay in Eilat before returning to Jerusalem. The tour was now sort of infiltrated by overly-friendly Israeli propagandists, posing as guides, who wanted to make sure their message of peace and prosperity for a single state living in harmony with the Palestinians was ingrained in our minds. But if you looked closely, you saw the overbearing control and suffocating living conditions they wielded over an alien and angry population. It was a textbook definition of the word, 'occupier.'"

4. Palestinians have all of the Negev – much more territory than they presently occupy – to develop as their own independent autonomous country, with allies Jordan and Egypt providing water and other resources. The Negev can be converted to a giant wind and solar energy field with photovoltaic solar panels, AI-controlled rotationals and vanadium storage batteries. Sale of electricity throughout the Middle East could easily support the Palestinians, pay for imported resources, and develop new clean-energy dependent industries.

"By dividing the country north and south with a DMZ patrolled by the U.N., the Palestinians can live safely in their own autonomous country with allies on both sides and no fear of invasion by Israeli forces. If they turn the Negev into a huge solar energy plant, they can supply their Arab neighbors with enough power to challenge Iran, the Emirates, and other outmoded fossil fuel exporters in the Middle East region. With U.S. funding and technology, they can be self-supporting within five years I would imagine."

5. A high-speed monorail train, U.N. patrolled, safely connects Palestinians to their Holy Temple Mount and al-Aska Mosque in Old Jerusalem's walled city.

"One of the concerns is how to allow Palestinians below the DMZ, that essentially cuts Israel in half, to worship freely in Jerusalem. A very important condition. A Japanese-designed high-speed elevated monorail could place Palestinians at the Arab gate of Jerusalem in less than 20 minutes."

6. Jerusalem becomes a U.N.-protected International City, open 24/7 to all who use it for peaceful religious purposes. Tourism tax pays for U.N. protection. As such, Tel Aviv, not Jerusalem, then becomes Israel's capital.

"Probably the most controversial point of the six. But Jerusalem must be open freely to all religions and not owned or governed by a single national entity. It must be owned and governed by the free world and the free world's elective institution, the U.N.—because the world looks to it as its most important religious gateway, its religious essence, its heart and soul, if you wish. Therefore, Israel's government has to give it up to the world, make it a safe international destination for worshippers of three major world religions and anyone else who seeks spiritual refuge there."

These 6 points are non-negotiable and all must be included in any comprehensive Peace Plan for Israel, the PLO/Hamas/Hezbollah and all parties living in the Middle East. (signed JM/ New York City)

"That's from 2018 remember, Peter. So much has changed in the following decade it sounds perfectly archaic today. But that's how I received it, word for word, as I told you before."

"Granddad, in 2018 there weren't photovoltaic solar panels or vanadium batteries. We used mirrors to concentrate the sun's rays for electricity with steam-driven turbines. So how would you or Rachel possibly know about these advances? Have you ever thought you were being used? That someone or some political entity was controlling you to write this for their benefit?"

"How?"

"Electronically. Some signaling device under your chair. Just look at all sorts of nasty remote listening and directive devices being designed today."

"Peter, as you say, this was a decade ago. You're saying this electronic rigging was going on then?"

"I don't know, Granddad. But it's certainly becoming a problem today. It seems no one is immune from being bugged or mind-controlled or blown to bits from remote implants no larger than a toonie."

"Well, anything's possible, dear. What is clear to me is that we both need our sleep. It's now almost 10:30. And tomorrow is a full day. So let's say goodnight, and sleep on it. Maybe we can dream up a better peace plan."

"Night, Granddad," Peter said, rising and embracing me. "I'm so glad you explained your thinking to me. I believe this could be part of a really wonderful memoir from a literate and worldly Granddad, that people would want to read," he mused, embracing me again and quickly disappearing up the stairs.

A memoir, I thought. It would have to be believable, relatable. And the consensus out there was once you reached the age of 90, even much earlier for some, you were over the hill. Yet, we were still electing aged leaders whose mental acuities were in doubt to begin with, now tested daily as their terms wound down. It only added to the overall anxieties about the widening divisions the nation was facing.

So, I considered adding *age* and the agility for climbing stairs to the mix. The latter being achingly accomplished, I'd sleep on it.

CHAPTER 12

I set the alarm for eight, giving myself enough time to shit, shower, and shave before putting on Bermuda shorts, a light short-sleeved shirt and loafers. There was also enough time to put on a percolator of coffee before Caroline's arrival at 9.00. But at around 8:45 I noticed through the kitchen's backdoor curtain, two large men by the garage setting up folding chairs and two folding tables with a double-drawer file cabinet between. They were both dressed all in black, black jackets, black shirts and ties, black pants, black shoes. And one of the men was Black as well. They had to be security, I figured. I wondered too if Peter had seen them arrive since his bedroom was over the kitchen facing the garage. Maybe it was best not to interfere, but, after all, they had arrived earlier than expected. Maybe they'd like some coffee.

So I opened the door, anyway, and said, "Good morning. Beautiful day."

"Good morning. We're looking for Mr. Jeremiah," said the White guard.

"I think you'll find him in the Old Testament," I replied. They looked perplexed.

"How about Peter Myer?" asked the Black guard now peering into his phone.

"Yes," he's staying here, but I don't think he's up yet."

"And you are... ?" asked the White guard.

"Jer*y* Myer, emphasizing the '*y*' in my first name."

"Ahh," he said, "I thought our boss said Jeremiah. Sorry."

"No problem," I responded. "Happens all the time. You two want to come in for a cup of coffee?"

They looked at each other, checked their watches, and said in unison, "Sure!"

The coffee had perked and there was plenty to go around. I motioned that they sit at the kitchen table and put out three mugs of coffee, spoons, cream and the sugar bowl.

"We're from WTC security," the Black guard started off as we all sat down. "We're here to check out the guests before they enter the backyard where the ceremony is taking place."

"Right, I said. "And what you have with you is a scanner?"

"It's a nonbiologicalphotoid scanner," said the White guard. "Better known as a ShapeSifter."

I was impressed that they knew its formal technical name. Then again, I thought, why shouldn't they?

"I'm Rick," said the White guard, extending his hand.

"And I'm Joseph," said the Black guard, extending his hand, "but you can call me Joe."

"You guys work at The World Trade Center?"

"Yeah," said Rick, "but they don't mind if we freelance on weekends. WTC is almost empty then and security is done by guys just starting out. I've been with WTC for 12 years."

"And I've been with WTC for 10," said Joe.

"I'm glad to have two experienced security guards here," I said. "There will be about 100 people passing through."

"But not through the house," said Joe. "Only on the path past the garage, right?"

"Right," I said. "I have two guests staying here now, my son and my grandson. And I have an aide, Caroline, who'll be here shortly to assist me. Other than them, all guests are to go past your scanner outside by the garage. There's also a bathroom guests can use in a small studio apartment looking out over the back porch, but its door to the living room has a thumbprint reader like the kitchen door."

"Whose thumbprints are in the database?" asked Rick.

"Mine and Caroline's and my son Paul and his son, my grandson, Peter. And his sister, my granddaughter, Estelle or Stella as she's called, who's getting engaged today. And two neighbors to either side of me. I don't think anyone else is keyed in."

"Just seven?" asked Rick.

"I can't think of anyone else," I said. "I don't have my phone on me, but pretty sure that's it."

Joe looked at his phone again. "How about Eugene Samuels?"

"No," I said. "I know he's throwing this party, but he's not yet part of the household."

"Okay," Joe nodded.

"We're to check a firearm before the guests arrive," said Rick. "Do you know about it?"

"Yes," I said. "It belongs to my grandson and I've hidden it away safely."

"In the house?" Joe asked, stirring some sugar into his coffee.

"Yes. It's in the house. It's in a very safe place. No one with access to the house knows where it is."

"Thumbprint access?" asked Rick.

"No one but myself knows where it is," I said for emphasis.

Joe looked at his phone once more. "It's a Smith & Wesson CRX, last four serial digits 4238, right?"

"I didn't inspect it for its serial number," I said. "But I believe it's what you're looking for."

"Well, that's the firearm we're supposed to check out," Rick said. "We don't touch it. You can read its serial number off to us. If its number matches the one we have on file, it's then entirely your responsibility for safe keeping."

"How do you know its model and serial number?" I asked, somewhat perturbed at them for having what I thought to be confidential information. Of course I was wrong.

"All legitimate California sales are in a database made available to law enforcement agencies in other states," said Rick. "Technically, we're not cops, but we work very closely with the NYPD and they provide the information we need."

"We have a listing for a Peter Myer in Anaheim, California," Joe added, "who's taken out a legitimate state license for this particular weapon."

"And if it doesn't check out?" I asked.

"If there is some discrepancy, we'll have to secure it until after the party is over. And then we'll have to keep it at WTC headquarters until we can verify its registered owner."

I was beginning to feel some unease. "There could be many Peter Myers in Anaheim. How do you know my grandson is the one attached to this gun?"

"Is his father's name Paul Myer living at 737 Riverside Drive in New York City?" asked Joe, looking down at his phone.

I nodded. "Yup, I think you have the right Peter Myer. So if the model and serial number match up, you'll return it to me for safekeeping?"

"Yes." said Joe. "Since it's a weapon already registered, and is to be kept in the house and not brought outside, it's the homeowner's responsibility or whoever is taking charge of securing it. We just have to make sure the firearm is the one listed with us."

That sounded reasonable enough to me, although I realized Gene hadn't informed these agents of the fact that I now had the gun and it was safely stored away.

"I get it," I said. "So you need to check the model and the serial number now?"

"If you would," said Rick. "And bring some ID like a driver's license with you."

I finished most of my coffee and headed upstairs. In the master bedroom I took Ruthie's flower vase painting off the wall, opened the safe and fetched the gun and holster. I didn't close the safe because I knew I'd be coming right back after the gun checked out. Then I pulled out my driver's license from my wallet and headed back.

On the way out I encountered Peter in slippers, bathrobe and pajamas. "Good morning, Granddad. All that wine, our talk and the time change really knocked me out. How you feeling?"

Before I could answer, Peter asked in a more concerning tone, "Is that my gun?"

"Yeah. The security guards are here and need to check out the model and serial number."

"Check it out? Against what?"

"They have your license information from California. They need to see it's the same gun you have registered."

"Oh," he said. "No problem. I can assure them it's the same gun. I brought all its papers with me."

"Then get them, and bring some ID with you like your driver's license. And put some clothes on, please. Once it's checked out they'll give it back to me to lock up."

Peter went back to his room and I headed downstairs where the two guards were now chatting with Caroline who had let herself in via the kitchen entrance. I had forgotten to put paper napkins out, a social gaff which Caroline was quick to redress, and was duly doing kitchen duty by refilling the agents' coffee mugs and putting out plates and donuts. "Pour another cup for Peter, please," I said. "He'll be joining us in a minute or two."

I placed the holster and gun in the middle of the kitchen table, put my driver's license in my shirt pocket and sat down. "You won't need me for the inspection. The gun's owner will be here shortly."

"Peter Myer," said Joe.

"Yes, my grandson from California. He's brought all the necessary gun documents with him."

"Good," Rick put in. "That will expedite things."

We talked about the good weather that day and how many people were expected to come by car and train and other topics related to that day's event. "After everyone arrives, what do you guys do?" I asked.

"Well," said Joe, "one of us will stay stationed outside, and one of us will get some food," he laughed.

"Then we'll switch," laughed Rick. "We're really here for the food. Mmmm... great donuts."

Caroline and I laughed along. I was pleased that these guys had a good sense of humor despite their stressful professional roles. I thought to myself their presence here today would add—not subtract—from the smooth running of the party. Maybe I had been too concerned.

But then I could hear Peter on the stairs, and was before us at the kitchen table before I knew it with a #10 envelope in his hands. He had put on a pair of cargo shorts and a white T-shirt and was wearing what looked like slip-on tennis sneakers without socks. "This is my grandson Peter," I said. "And this is Rick and this is Joe." They all shook hands and Peter sat down. "Want some coffee?" I asked.

Caroline broke in: "We're near empty. I've put some more up."

"That's all right," Peter said. "I'm fine." Then, reversing suddenly: "This gun shouldn't be sitting here," he said, looking angrily at me. "It was to be locked up until after the party."

"We just need to check out its ID and your ID and if they match, we'll let you lock it up," said Rick.

"What do you mean, 'we'll let you'," Peter asked defiantly. "This is a private residence. You have no say about what we do here. Who gave you permission to tell us what we can and cannot do here."

"It's *my* residence," I interjected, looking as sternly as I could at Peter. "And *I* gave permission."

"Granddad..."

"It's all right, son," Joe said, paternalistically, to calm Peter down. "We're not here to take the gun away from you."

"You want my ID? The gun's ID?"

"Yes," said Rick. "That's all. I'm sure they'll match up."

"And what about *your* ID?" Peter asked with a certain amount of disdain that didn't escape the guards.

Simultaneously, they unbuttoned their jackets to reveal laminated photo ID badges hanging from braided cords around their necks. The initials WTC were clearly obvious to me, but Peter, sitting next to Joe, reached for the badge for a closer look. Joe quickly took his badge off from around his neck and handed it to Peter who studied it, front and back, for what seemed to be a half-minute or so. While this was going on, Rick also took off his badge and passed it along the table. Peter studied it as well. The authentications on the ID's seemed to satisfy him.

"Okay," he said, sliding the badges back. "But I don't think you realize that I also have a concealed carry license and that license can be revoked if I display the gun without some kind of serious threat or provocation to me personally."

"Understood," said Rick, nodding, putting his badge back around his neck.

"So, it's not to be shown around in the open like this under any circumstances. It could be considered too dangerous, just like the guns you conceal carry. Same conditions apply."

"We're not carrying guns," Rick said, reaching into his shoulder holster and withdrawing an unmarked slim spray can of what I took to be pressurized mace."

"You don't carry firearms?" asked Peter, sounding completely dumbfounded.

"Not this time around," said Rick. "As you say, it could be considered too dangerous."

"Speaking of which, is this gun loaded?" asked Joe, pointing to Peter's holstered gun in the middle of the table.

"I've emptied out the magazine," Peter said, "but there's one round left in the chamber."

Caroline was there then and poured a mug of coffee for Peter, and then topped off the mugs for the agents and myself. I caught her eye, her tightened expression and the almost unperceived shaking of her head in contemptuous disgust.

"I have all its pedigree with me," Peter went on. "It's all here," he said, sliding the white #10 envelope over to Joe. Joe opened up the envelope which produced three different documents. One looked like a Bill of Sale, one had some kind of Certificate border to it, one seemed to be a license of some kind, reduced down to wallet size. Peter then produced his California driver's license, placing it before him. He smirked slightly in my direction, while taking a sip of coffee.

Joe and Rick looked over the documents casually and nodded to each other. Everything seemed to be in order. Rick checked some information on one of the documents with the information he had on his phone. Again, all seemed to be in order.

Then they looked at Peter's driver's license.

"You grew a beard since this photo was taken?" asked Rick.

"Yup."

"Would you mind signing your name somewhere so we can check your signature?"

"Sure," said Peter. "You guys have a pen on you?"

Joe produced a pen from his shirt pocket and Peter signed his name on the #10 envelope. It matched perfectly with the one on his driver's license. He was smirking even more now.

I got up from the table figuring the interrogation was over and took my mug over to the sink to empty before handing it to Caroline who was stacking last night's plates and glasses in the dishwasher. I was a bit annoyed with Peter's attitude towards the agents who were just doing their job so I was also hoping my getting up from the table would clue the agents to head outside to their station and not be subjected to more of Peter's antics. But they weren't finished yet.

"So," said Rick, "this gun before us is the one on this Bill of Sale receipt, right?"

"Right," Peter said.

"So what we have here is a Smith&Wesson CRX," said Rick, reading from the document.

"Correct."

"Can you take it out of its holster so we can confirm its serial number?"

"I'd rather not," said Peter. "You guys have your phones on you and if I handle my gun and you take a photo of that, I could lose my license. Give me your phones and I'll give you my gun."

Rick and Joe looked at each other and nodded some unspoken reaction to take, as if they had gone through this performance before. "Tell you what," said Rick, "let's compromise. We'll put our phones next to the gun and have the gun identified while you watch our phones. Okay?"

Peter thought that through for a minute and nodded, "Okay."

The guards slid their phones to the middle of the table.

"But before we look over your gun," said Rick, "we need you to unload it. You said the magazine was empty but there was still one round in the chamber. We're not allowed to inspect loaded weapons. So we're asking you to please first physically remove that round and then we'll read off the serial number if you still don't want to."

Peter took another considered sip of coffee. "When you're outside at your station and someone comes through with a gun, you can't tell if it's loaded or not, can you?"

"We assume it's loaded," said Joe, "but we have no way of knowing for sure, and it doesn't matter once we take possession: It's safely locked up. Even if the owner tells us it's unloaded we're not authorized to touch the gun."

"How do you take possession if you can't handle it yourselves?"

"We take a picture of it with some ID from its owner, like a driver's license," said Joe. "We take out a metal container from our file cabinet and they deposit their gun in the container. The containers are numbered, and we give a matching numbered tag to the depositor. When they leave the party they present us with their ID and the tag and we get the container, open it, and let them take away their gun. We never touch the gun."

"So why can't I do that in this case?" Peter asked, shooting me an angry glance. "Did you know I could hand the gun over to these gentlemen for safekeeping, Granddad?"

"I didn't know the procedure the security team had," I said. "When I asked you for your gun when you arrived it was to make sure it would be safe while your Dad and I were out for the evening. It was just one less thing I didn't want to be concerned about."

"And so you could tell Gene, I had brought the gun from California but you had it safely locked away."

"That was the idea," I said.

"And did you when you saw him?"

"Yes. First thing I did."

Peter considered my answer for a few seconds and had a sip of coffee. "I think I'll go through security," he said, "rather than give it up to you, Granddad. I know you had the best intentions at heart, but I don't want to be treated like some kind of special case here. Once the party starts, I'll pass through security and these guys can secure the gun like everyone else's."

Both Joe and Rick shook their heads. "You have access to other ways to the back," said Joe. "Maybe it's better to go through with the first plan, so we can have your Grandfather read its serial number off to us and then let your Grandfather put it safely away."

"I agree, Peter," I said, looking him straight in the eye. "Let's just stick to the plan we had."

"The plan never called for you to take the gun from its hiding place and bring it down here to have it inspected," Peter shot back. "If I had known that, I wouldn't have turned it over to you."

"This is a special case," Rick put in. "We already have you associated with this particular weapon, We just need confirmation...."

"Exactly," Peter interrupted. "Anyone else passing through security outside is an unknown. You did an investigation on me long before I ever arrived from California, like I'm another Mike Hammond or something."

"Look," said Rick somewhat irritated now, "there's nothing incriminating here. Nobody is accusing anyone of anything. We did a background check, that's all. Nothing personal here."

"And," Joe added, "everything checks out so far. You're in compliance. You did everything right. We just need to confirm the weapon we have in our database matches the one you've brought. It's as simple as that."

"But you don't have a database for anyone else who passes through security later today, do you?" Peter argued. "They just have to show you an ID and surrender their weapon. You're not looking for a particular weapon with a particular serial number, are you?"

"No, we're not," said Rick, "so yes, this is a special case where we knew beforehand you might be bringing a registered weapon with you. And that's what we're here to check out."

"Look, son," said Joe again in his paternal voice attempting to tone down the rhetoric, "It's not complicated: If the gun matches the one on the documents you've shown us, game over. This is a private residence so the gun and the responsibility for handling it safely is all yours. Then you have every right to do with it what you want so long as it's kept in the house. And we—Rick and I—did our job and are off the hook."

"We believe that this is the same firearm we've been asked to check out, Rick added, "but we just have to make sure."

Peter thought that through for a few seconds and finished his coffee. Then he gathered up his papers and put them back in the envelope.

"Let them do their work," I said, taking his coffee mug and heading towards the dishwasher with Caroline silently shaking her head, sharing my annoyance at Peter's intractableness.

"Granddad...."

"Just read...," Rick started to say.

"No!" Peter interrupted, "I've made up my mind. I'll go through security outside later. Then you can put my gun in your file cabinet like everyone else's. No one touches my gun but me."

"Can't do that now," Rick said. "We see there are back entrances to the..."

Peter suddenly stood up, reached across the table and grabbed the holster with the gun still within. But now it was slipping out and Joe made a move to catch it falling. Peter grabbed Joe's hand with his other hand and they struggled for its possession....

And then its only round was fired.

Part II

CHAPTER 13

It was loud, blinding and explosive. I thought I had been shot in the head. But no, the pain was somewhere else, somewhere below. And it wasn't just pain now, it was excruciating pain, deep, internal pain I had never experienced before, coming from my right leg. And I was falling, yelling at the same time, perhaps shrieking is a better word, trying to grab my right leg which was crumpling under my weight. Things were out of focus, darker now. I was falling... everything spinning about... passing out.

Luckily Caroline was right there and caught me around my chest as I was slumping halfway down. I heard her cry, "Get a chair over here!" And Peter, closest to me, quickly surrendered his chair for me to sit down on. "Hold his leg up," Caroline commanded while she rolled up my shorts and went back for the roll of paper towels over the sink. She wrapped my bleeding right knee, threading the paper towel roll around my leg for a dozen or more wraps. Even so, a small amount of blood was still soaking through.

"Can you hear me, Jerry?"

"Yes."

Then she went for her shoulder tote and took from it a small ampule of some liquid and a syringe into which she locked a needle. "This won't hurt," she said, as she filled the syringe. "It will stop the pain."

She pulled down some of the toweling and injected my lower thigh with half the liquid, and injected my upper calf with the remaining liquid. "It will take a minute or two. Try to relax, Jerry. breathe deeply."

I closed my eyes trying to block out the physical and mental anguish I was experiencing but at that moment Paul was before me in a bathrobe. "Dad! What the hell happened here?"

Caroline ignored him. "Give me your bathrobe cord," she ordered and Paul obliged. Then Caroline wrapped the tie around my lower thigh, just above my knee several times and made a knot. Then while she was making a second knot above the first, she asked Paul to get her a wooden spoon from out of the cutlery drawer. He brought one over and she placed it between the two knots. "This will serve as a tourniquet," she said, "until we can get Jerry to the hospital. Will one of you guys bring another chair over for Jerry's leg?"

Rick had reached for his phone and was dialing a number. "What are you doing?" Caroline demanded to know.

"Calling 911," said Rick, "for an ambulance."

"We don't have time for that," said Caroline. "We have to get Jerry to the hospital *now*. An ambulance will take fifteen minutes or more. We'll use my car. It's right outside."

The painkiller was working. A trickle of blood was still working its way through the paper roll, but the shock of being shot in the knee was receding. My body was sweating head to toe but my mind was clearing. I looked at Rick and Joe who were just standing by, shock on their faces at what just occurred, the gun along with the holster innocently, inanimately, laying on the table beside them.

"I'll need you two to get him carried down to my car," Caroline said. "And Peter, I'll need you to hold your Granddad's leg up and keep the tourniquet tight, but not too tight. Don't let his leg down. How are you doing, Jerry?"

"Pain is subsiding," I said weakly.

Caroline motioned to the guards, "I need some things from the refrigerator. Will you guys get me a couple of bottles of sparkling water and I also need some tablecloths from the pantry next to the fridge. As many as you can find. Can you guys get that now?"

"Dad..." Paul was starting to say something as he leaned over my chair, but I cut him off and whispered to him, "When I leave, lock the door. Get the gun, put it in the safe in my room, lock the safe, put the picture back."

"Will do," he whispered back.

The guards then returned with the water and a couple of tablecloths. "Okay," she said, stuffing the bottles and tablecloths in her tote. "I think we're ready."

"Listen everyone," I said with all the voice I could muster; "Let's get our stories straight. I tripped and fell, okay. I tripped on the stairs coming down. That's what happened, right?"

The guards looked at each other in disbelief. It took them a moment to nod their approval.

"Right?" I asked more aggressively again, looking directly at Peter now."

"Right," he said, his voice cracking.

"Okay," said Caroline, "let's go. You guys carry the chair. Peter, you keep Jerry's leg up."

The guards hoisted the sides of the seat to their waists, I put my arms around their shoulders for support and with Peter leading the way, my bloodied foot in his hands, we carefully made our way to the front door Paul had already opened, down the threshold step and slowly across the oval to Caroline's car.

She had already opened the rear doors and was tucking the table clothes across the backseat when we got there. "Remember," I said, "I tripped and fell down the stairs. Right?"

"Right," said Rick, bear hugging me from behind the chair as he and Peter carefully lifted and unloaded me to the back seat of the car, laying me gently on the table clothes.

"Tripped and fell, Joe?"

"Right." Joe said, pulling me by my good leg further along the rear seat from the opposite doorway so I could lay down fully supine.

"Peter," said Caroline, "I'll need you back there to hold your Granddad's leg as high as you can. Put it on your shoulder, that high. I'll tell you when to make the tourniquet tighter."

I folded my working left leg so Peter could sit in the back and so he could raise my right leg to his shoulder. I felt nothing. The blood seemed to be coagulating somewhat and the pain had almost ceased.

"Thanks guys," said Caroline to the two guards as she climbed into the driver's seat. "We're at Montclair Memorial in case anyone asks. "But remember to say, Jerry had a fall down the stairs this morning."

"And I'll be here for the ceremony," I tried to say with some authority. "So not to worry."

"Hope to see you later," said Rick, shutting the driver's side rear door.

"Greatly appreciate what you're doing" said Joe, closing the other. I knew exactly what he meant.

We were heading out of Lois Lane when Caroline held up a water bottle from her tote for Peter to grab. "Give some water to Jerry," she said, and loosen the tourniquet a little." Then she opened up the car phone and informed Montclair Memorial we were on our way to the emergency room entrance and to have a wheelchair ready for... "an elderly patient who fell this morning with a knee injury."

"That story won't hold up," she said after hanging up. "They'll take X-rays first to see the damage."

I drank some water. My knee was feeling better upon Peter's shoulder. He looked down at me, and said, "I'm so sorry, Granddad. I don't know how..."

"Don't worry," I said. "Caroline? Can you get Dr. Francona to meet us there?"

"I'll try," she said. She punched in Francona's name on her console which connected to his office phone and got a voice recording to leave a message: "Dr. Francona, this is Caroline Hamilton, Jerry Myer's aide. He's had a major accident this morning and we're on our way to Montclair Memorial's emergency room. If you could meet us there it would be a blessing. Thanks."

"It's Saturday," I said. "What are the chances?"

"Keep hydrating," she said. "And tighten Granddad's tourniquet a bit now, Peter," she said. "How are you doing, Jerry?"

"Whatever you injected me with," I said, "stopped most of the pain. My knee just feels numb. What was that stuff?"

"I don't know," she said. "Some guy was selling vials on the corner." It made Peter and I laugh. Maybe this accident wasn't as bad as it looked. Maybe...

But now we were turning the corner for the emergency room entrance to Montclair Memorial. An attendant opened the rear door and a wheelchair was waiting. I checked my watch: it was now 9:50.

"Caroline," I said, "call Paul and tell him we've arrived. We'll call again when I find out more. But tell him to stay in the house and not to come down here. I want to have someone in the house while I'm gone, but I need you to stay with me. You too, Peter."

And then a masked attendant and Peter gently pulled me from the backseat and placed me in the wheelchair, raised and locked the right foot carrier to a fully parallel level. I had never sat in a wheelchair before, but now I realized, I could experience what Ruthie had to endure in her final weeks. But in the balance of things, it made little sense.

Caroline was told to park her car in one of the visitors' spaces while the attendant wheeled me into the emergency room, Peter right behind. But he couldn't enter. It wasn't because he wasn't wearing a mask like everyone else in the room was. It was simply their policy that only doctors, nurses, attendants were allowed in. Peter would have to look through the circular door windows. We exchanged glances and I raised up my right hand's thumb before I was examined.

"I'm doctor Richard Winslow," said a young man, about Peter's age, in a white lab coat and mask. "I'm talking to... ?

"Jerry Myer," I said, as a mask was placed around my face by the attending nurse.

"Jerry, did you bring some I.D. with you?"

"No, I... " but then realized I had my driver's license on me in my shirt pocket. "Yes, here's my driver's license."

Dr. Winslow quickly looked it over and handed it back to me. "Okay, Jerry, so tell me what happened to you?"

"I tripped and fell coming down my stairs this morning."

He looked at my knee all wrapped in bloodied paper toweling and the wooden spoon tourniquet Caroline made. "Did you fall on something sharp?"

"I may have," I said. "It started to bleed."

Winslow undid the tourniquet above my right knee and pulled away some of the toweling while removing my tennis shoes. "That's a pretty bad wound you have here. Can you lift your leg a bit?"

I tried, but no go.

"We'll need to take an X-ray of your knee."

"Okay," I said.

The nurse standing by and the attendant who took me from Caroline's car, helped me out of the wheelchair and carefully placed me on a gurney that had been lowered almost to the floor. Then they raised the gurney and rolled me into the X-ray room adjoining the emergency room. The X-ray technician there placed a plate under my right knee, adjusted the overhead camera and stepped away behind a wall. Then he helped lay me on my left side, put another plate beneath my knee and took another shot. Then repeated those steps from my right side and took yet another X-ray. The procedure being completed now, I was rolled back into the emergency room and was overjoyed to see Caroline, now in a white smock and mask, standing next to Dr. Winslow.

"I have good news, Jerry," she said. "Dr. Francona is on his way. He'll be here in just a few minutes. How are you feeling?"

"Not too bad," I said. I wondered what she had told Dr. Winslow about what happened to me, but now the nurse was removing all the paper towels and I was feeling some pain around the wound. The bleeding had mostly stopped and some antiseptic she was applying after washing the area stung for a moment but dulled the pain somewhat. I tried to rise up on my elbows to see what she was doing, but Dr. Winslow told me to lay back and relax, as he took my blood pressure, blood oxygen level and heartbeat. I would have sips of water through a straw and wait for Dr. Francona to arrive.

"Peter still here?" I asked Caroline, not seeing his face in the window.

"Yes. I think he's down the hallway doing some paperwork. I'll keep him posted."

Soon the X-rays were ready and the technician posted them on a backlit screen behind me so I couldn't see them. Dr. Winslow looked them over carefully, then stood before me."

"Mr. Myer," he said, changing the 'Jerry' address he used earlier, "you said you tripped and fell coming down your stairs. And you fell on something sharp?"

I knew the X-rays may have told a different story. Even so, I said, "I may have."

"Could that something sharp be a bullet?"

"I was carrying my gun. When I fell I thought it may have gone off," I said. "I don't know. I may have blacked out for a minute or two. Caroline caught me falling."

"So you didn't fall on something," said the Doctor. "You shot yourself in the knee?"

"I guess so," I said. "I may have."

Winslow was wearing a mask so I couldn't see what his mouth was doing, but his eyes gave away his expression of doubt. "Your blood pressure is a little high. And you've lost some blood. I'm going to put you on an I.V. for a while to help stabilize you. We have an orthopedic surgeon in the neighborhood, the best in the business. His name is Dr. Gilbert Stone. Dr. Francona knows him well. I don't know if Dr. Stone is available, but he would be the one to do the operation."

"Operation?" I asked, while the nurse dabbed my right arm with alcohol and a needle inserted and taped so I would be getting some fluid from the I.V. bag now on a pole above me.

"We'll let Dr. Francona take over when he gets here," said Dr. Winslow. I'm not the one who makes the decisions. I'm just here to stabilize you and take the X-rays needed for Dr. Francona's diagnosis."

"I understand," I said, "but I... "

And at that moment a masked Dr. Francona limped through the emergency room doors, and my physical health mentor—the Doc who told me to keep doing what I was doing, who had said that I would probably outlive him—now was standing over me, looking down at me, visibly shaking his head in disbelief.

"Jerry," Francona said after examining the X-rays, "there's a pea-sized bullet lodged just behind your kneecap. You want to tell me what happened?"

"I was carrying the gun downstairs. I tripped, the gun fell out of my hand when I tried to hold on to the bannister and the next thing I knew I heard it go off."

"So it fell on the stairs and it discharged?"

"I don't know. I guess so," I said weakly.

"An accident."

"Completely," I said. "Do you think I purposely shot myself?"

"No," said Francona, "but let me show you something." He and Dr. Winslow turned the guernsey and the I.V. stand around and the nurse put a pillow under my head so I could better view the X-rays on the backlit screen. "See here? This white dot is the bullet. And the bullet wasn't directly fired at your knee, or from above your knee. If that were the case your patella or kneecap would have been shattered, so the bullet rather came from below. Did it ricochet off the floor?"

"Probably," I said. "I have marble floors in the kitchen."

"And when it went off, about how far away were you?"

"I don't know. Maybe five feet away."

"Certainly not fifteen feet or more. Because the reason I'm asking is that a bullet—even a ricochet bullet—from just five feet away would have passed through your leg. This bullet lodged in your knee. It had to have been fired from a much greater distance to impact your leg like that."

"I tripped and fell," was my response. "I heard the gun fire. That's all I remember because the pain was intense and that's all I could think about. I might have blacked out for a moment."

Caroline, who was listening to that scenario, was quick to put in, "Jerry did black out then."

"Did you see what happened?"

"No," she said. "I turned to Jerry when the shot rang out, ran over and held him up from falling."

"Well, we have to remove the bullet. That's the first thing. I don't know how much internal damage has been done from viewing these X-rays. We'll leave that for Dr. Stone. But we can't leave the bullet there. It's probably lead, and lead poisoning is very very serious. Bacteria can spread very quickly and then major complications would develop. So we're going to have to operate and get the bullet out first and then see about restorative surgery."

"Doc," I said, "I'm due to attend a wedding in a couple of hours at my house. My Granddaughter's wedding. I'm part of the ceremony. I can't…"

"Jerry, this is serious. It's not like you have a choice here."

"I have to be at the wedding, Doc."

"And lose your lower leg?"

"Lose it?"

"Have it amputated because of a bacterial infection?"

"I won't be gone long. I promise to be back here before two."

Francona looked at his wristwatch, then at the now half-full I.V. bag, then at Dr. Winslow, then at Caroline. "We're talking three hours here, give or take," he said, shaking his head. "This is not a surface injury where we can simply apply an antiseptic, wrap it up with a bandage and let you go do your thing. These X-rays indicate a lead bullet deep inside your knee. This means a very involved operation, Jerry, which will require you to be anesthetized. Dr. Stone would definitely agree. It's too risky to let you leave the hospital now. I won't authorize it."

I thought carefully about what to say next. The I.V. solution was working well; I was thinking more clearly, feeling stronger, and the pain was manageable, like a lower backache. True, I had no sensation in my leg from the knee down, but I thought, perhaps this was due to Caroline's injections. I didn't want to overrule Dr. Francona—after all, I realized he was acting in my best interest—but I still had the last word about my own health, my own destiny, I assured myself before saying: "Okay, don't authorize it. I'll take all the responsibility from here on out. Just tell me what I need to do in the interim between my release from the hospital and my return here before 2PM."

Francona was pissed. "That's your final decision, Jerry? Because we're going to ask you to sign some release forms when you return re-confirming that decision. It can affect your SS insurance, after care and everything else."

"Yes."

"All right. Richard," Dr. Francona was now addressing Dr. Winslow, "Call Stone and tell him the patient will now be prepped no later than 2:15PM for the knee operation."

"Right," said Winslow, hurriedly leaving the operating room, passing Peter who was once again anxiously peering through one of the round windows. Then Francona addressed Caroline who now realized she had my life in her hands for the next three hours.

"We'll wait until the I.V. is finished and in the meantime, we'll disinfect the wound as best we can and wrap it up tightly. Jerry will be taken back home by ambulance in a wheelchair and is not to get out of the wheelchair at any time. In fact, instead of a splint, we'll strap his leg to the rise just to be sure. Is that clear?"

"Absolutely," she said.

"And then at 1:45 we'll have the ambulance back at the house. The ambulance has a lift for wheelchairs, so the attendant will take over. We'll diaper Jerry so if he needs to go, he can just do whatever in the wheelchair. He can't get out of the chair at any time for anything, I don't care what it is. His leg has to be immobile and elevated until he's back here."

"Understood," Caroline said.

"Keep him out of direct sun, plenty of hydration, but only water. No food, no liquor. Keep an ice pack handy for his neck and forehead, but no more injections. We'll give him something for pain that should last at least three hours."

"Okay."

"Jerry," said Francona looking at me now, "is that your Grandson at the window?"

"Yes," I said.

"I'll get permission for him to ride with the driver back because he knows the way, right?"

"Of course."

"Okay. I need to talk with Dr. Winslow for a moment, then I'll see you promptly at 2PM here."

"Thanks, Doc," I said, "for everything."

"Much too early for that," said Francona. "You may not be thanking me when this is all over."

CHAPTER 14

So there were really two weddings I would be attending early that afternoon: The one between Estelle and Gene and the one between me and my wheelchair: Intimate, comforting, compatible, inseparable. At least for a two-and-a-half-hour honeymoon.

And when we got back to the house at about 11:30, guests were already arriving by car and being directed where to park on the oval by Robert, Gene's assistant. The gravel driveway that encircled the oval was still free of cars and Caroline, who had preceded us and had already parked her car at curbside, was waiting by the front door, water bottle in hand. The attendant now tightly strapped me to the wheelchair, itself anchored securely to the lift, then lowered pneumatically to the gravel. Once on the ground, he released the anchoring mechanism and then tilted the chair up onto the flagstone pathway lining the house before repositioning the strap around my chest. I could breathe freely again and thanked him profusely for his care. "Couldn't have done this without you, Steve," I tried to joke.

"We'll see you right here at 1:45," Caroline instructed the driver, and with that, he and the attendant drove off.

Caroline waved Peter off and began pushing the wheelchair along the bumpy flagstones towards the garage. I noticed the garage driveway had the caterer's panel truck parked facing the street, the DJ's car behind it facing the garage, and a third car now pulling out. It was the florist's daughter and I assumed she was now leaving, having completed the chuppa's archway. She saw me in the wheelchair as she passed by and her mouth dropped open. I waved to her, she sort of waved back, and disappeared down Lois Lane.

I told Caroline to stop then. I figured the security detail would have noticed the ambulance's departure and I needed to talk to Peter before we turned the corner and the security table.

I said to Peter: "Go in the front and tell your father we're here. I need him to bring me my wallet on the desk in my bedroom, and my phone, and the jacket that's just been dry cleaned hanging in the closet. And also my yarmulke and sunglasses on the desk. And the envelope with my blessing #5 in it. Come back through the kitchen and be checked out by security so we don't have a problem."

"And," added Caroline, "bring down a small blanket of some kind we'll drape over Jerry's legs. I think there's one in the upstairs linen closet."

"Oh, please.... I have a great set of legs," I tried to joke. "Women always tell me that."

She was not impressed at my forced levity. "Let's just hope you can say that tomorrow," she intoned.

And yet, I realized I had to keep things light, had to keep telling the lie about my injury—at least until after the party was over. I would be long gone by then back to the hospital and, hopefully, forgotten as even being there that day. I knew I couldn't let the trauma, the drama of that morning interfere with the meticulous planning and the overall purpose of the event. And as we wheeled past Rick and Joe at their station, I made sure they were still on board.

"Morning, guys," I said. "You'll never guess what happened to me this morning."

"You tripped and fell," said Rick.

"Absolutely. That's exactly what happened. But as you can tell, no big deal."

"Glad to see you," said Joe. "You too, Caroline."

"You want to scan us?" she said, somewhat sarcastically.

"Nope," said Rick. "You get a free pass."

"Thanks, guys," I said. "You have a great and uneventful day."

They checked us off against the guest list they had and with that, Caroline wheeled me along the flagstone path into the back lawn. But I hardly recognized it.

The chairs had already been set up in their amphitheater curvature, the caterers had set up the tablecloth tables and the bar from which they were now offering cups of ice water and soft drinks, the photographer was figuring lens depths on the porch, the DJ setting up some wireless sound system with a couple of small speakers to either side of the chuppa, its archway now colorfully decorated with boughs of fresh summer flowers. A box full of colorful Japanese hand-folding fans reading *Gene* on one side and *Stella* on the other with a 'Take One' sign above was displayed on the kitchen entrance stoop.

And overseeing all this activity was Doris Nottingham, dressed beautifully in a splashy floral summer dress. When she first saw me rounding the porch area after picking up my fan, I was looking away so she had the first glance. I can only imagine what she was thinking.

Caroline noticed her first and turned the wheelchair in her direction and we met almost halfway. "I tried calling you this morning," Doris said, "and your son picked up and said you had had an accident falling on the staircase and had been taken to the hospital. I hope it's not serious."

"It's not," I said. "But they have to do more work on it this afternoon. So I can only stay for the ceremony and then go back. Lovely fans."

"How are you getting back?" she asked with some concern.

"They're sending an ambulance to pick me up at 1:45. I figure the ceremony will be finished by then."

"Does Robert know?"

"I don't think so," I said. "I saw him when we drove up but he was directing other cars so I didn't want to interfere."

"I'll tell him," Doris said, "to be sure to leave the circular drive open for the ambulance."

"The ceremony will definitely be finished by 1:45?" Caroline pressed.

"It starts at 1:00 and Rabbi Max can easily wrap it up in fifteen or twenty minutes. No one wants to sit under a summer sun for longer than that."

I looked up at the sky. There was a gentle breeze and some nice puffy clouds to occasionally dull the sunlight. It was, indeed, a perfect weather day for an outdoor wedding. "Jerry needs to sit in the shade," Caroline continued. "Can we find a spot that's shady?"

Doris looked at me, the leg, and the wheelchair. "Do you still want to present the wrapped champagne glass at the end?" she asked.

"Absolutely," I said. "It's my *raison d'etre* for being here."

"Okay," said Doris. "We'll rearrange the seating. The Samuels' contingent will now be seated on the left flank, the Myers' on the right. And since you need to be in the front row, Jerry, that works out because you'll be under some tree cover this afternoon. In fact, it's getting shady already."

Paul and Peter then joined us from the kitchen entrance side. They had taken my instruction to come that way because they needed to be scanned like everyone else before entering the backyard and besides, the livingroom's entryway through the studio was interiorally bolted, my son now informed me.

Paul, now attired in a black suit and tie, had with him my wallet, phone, sunglasses, scullcap, and Peter, dressed in a dark gray suit but tieless was carrying my jacket, the all-important envelope containing my blessing #5, and a mermaid blanket Ruthie had used to keep warm in the studio during winter months. I introduced Doris to them both, although Doris had already introduced herself to Paul with that morning's telephone call and Caroline had met Doris during her first photoshoot months ago.

And now, five minutes to noon, Doris led us all to the end of the first row of carded 'reserved' seats to the right of the chuppa. She was correct: The sun was now passing behind low hanging branches on Ruthie's oak. I would have a shaded unobstructed view of the chuppa. But I could also make out the security team in front of the garage. It looked to me like a line was already forming.

Caroline tucked the blanket under me so that both my upraised leg and the folded leg beside it were covered. I turned on my phone and dialed in the camera at the front of the house on one screen and the camera at the kitchen entrance where the security team was on the other. Robert was directing cars to park in the oval but there was already a back up. I showed the screens to Doris.

"Doris," I said, "Paul and Peter are available to help park the cars."

"Oh, excellent!" she exclaimed. "We need to leave two spaces available in the oval for two early departures, and Robert knows that. One for the string quartet, one for Rabbi Max. Everyone else needs to park on the street but not block driveways."

"Let Robert know you're there to help," I said to my son. "Not oversee."

"Got it, Dad," he said. And both he and Peter were off, newly-minted parking attendants.

"A great idea," Doris said. "I was afraid we were going to have a buildup around this time and was thinking of getting some of the catering people to help out."

And now I could see members of the string quartet line up before the security team who were quickly scanning them and their instruments. I showed this to Doris and she too took off to meet them, to guide them to their chairs on the opposite side of the chuppa from where I was sitting. It was the same quartet that played at Ruthie's memorial—performing from memory without sheet music and music stands. Truly devoted musicians and I was greatly impressed—especially when they first came over to say hello and ask about my leg.

"What will you be playing when I deliver the champagne glass to be stomped on?"

"Are you doing the stomping?" the pretty female cellist asked. Everyone guffawed. And then they were off to tune up their instruments.

And then, as if on cue, Rabbi Max was on the phone with Doris to say that he had arrived and needed help in removing his lectern and footstool from the back seat of his car. This had all been pre-planned, of course, and a couple of the caterer's set up people were sent to the garage area to assist. Doris excused herself and went back to meet the Rabbi.

The place was quickly filling up with people. It was now 12:10. The Montclair train was more or less on time from Hoboken and the nine people from the Uber van were let off in front of the house and joined a small line slowly moving to be scanned at the security table. I flipped to the other camera over the front door. There were still a few spaces left for cars to park in the oval, but those would be filled in the minutes to come. I could now see Robert, Paul and Peter discussing where the overflow cars would be parked, now that the gravel semicircle around the oval had to be left open for the ambulance.

But luck was on my side. For now I could see Lewis Franklin, my next door neighbor who I had invited, along with his wife, walking into view and entering into the conversation. I thought he might be telling Robert to keep cars away from his driveway, but a call from Paul a minute later let me know that Lew was letting us use his entire driveway for more parking space. Those bar-be-cues from a far distant past were finally paying off!

Rabbi Max and his briefcase were let through security with but a nod, the caterer helpers carrying his lectern and Doris Nottingham right behind. I now could see them clearly rounding the garage and into the field of chairs. They placed the lectern a foot or so behind the flower arch. Rabbi Max was rather short, about 5'6" or so, thus to have both a commanding physical and religious stature about him, a small footstool was placed behind the lectern so he could be at least equal in height to the couple he was blessing.

From his briefcase he produced a small silver flask, a silver cup, a small lace napkin, a book of some kind and, now looking in my direction, a crystal champagne glass and a large cloth napkin into which he wrapped the glass. Then, with Doris leading the way, they both came over to where I was sitting with Caroline.

"I heard what happened," said Rabbi Max, "and I'm terribly sorry to hear about it. How are you feeling, Jerome?" he asked, shaking my hand.

"Quite all right," I said. "Is that the glass Estelle and Gene break at the end?"

"Yes. Do you think you can still manage to bring it over?"

I looked at Caroline and she nodded. "Of course."

"At least you have one good foot," said the Rabbi. "But I don't want you hopping over there."

"I won't," I said, playing along with his jest. "It might be considered anti-symmetric."

Rabbi Max grinned broadly. "Thank you, Jerome. I will forever credit you with that line."

Caroline made me finish my first bottle of water, then went back to the caterer's table for another. I was feeling somewhat hungry, but knew food of any kind was off the charts. And so I was feeling a bit weak, longing for the energy-supplying I.V. the hospital gave me. And there was now a little over a half-hour before official undertakings began, and the major guests had yet to arrive. I looked through the kitchen's camera at the security table where a line had formed behind the 9-person train contingent who were just now finishing up their inspection. If we started the formal ceremony at 1:00 as planned, it would truly be a miracle.

Looking more closely I noticed a clean-shaven but gaunt young man just passing through security. He seemed all alone and visibly agitated. Caroline returned and I asked her to seek out a young man with short sandy hair in a blue blazer and gray slacks who had just passed security. I thought it might be David, Gene's brother, who according to Doris was coming in by train. And sure enough it was. For, after grabbing a Coke at the caterer's bar, he was now seated beside me, introducing himself.

"I'm David Samuels, Gene's brother. You must be Jerry Myer, Stella's grandfather."

"That I am," I said, shaking his hand, noticing a trace of liquor on his breath. "We haven't met, but I've heard a lot of good things about you."

"What happened to your leg?"

"I tripped and fell coming down my stairs," I said. "A bit of a hangover. Nothing serious."

"Too much to drink last night?"

"Yeah," I said. "But it was a nice get-together. You have a lovely family, David."

"I really haven't any business being here," he replied. "Gene wanted me as his Best Man when he should have chosen our stepfather who really wanted to do the honors. At the time I told Gene that. But he's stubborn as you probably are aware of by now. Then later he's all apologetic. He's always been like that. I know Stella is trying to turn him around."

"Well, she's a bright gal," I said. "They seem like a good team."

"Yeah. Gene found himself a real catch. She's terrific. He's very lucky."

"And you?" I asked. "What's going on in your life?"

"Well, you probably got the story from my parents last night. Probably not the whole story but the gist of it. I made some bad investments, then rolled them over to other bad investments, and I owe some investors their money back, mainly my family. They're pissed, of course, but I'm trying to work things out. I think that's why Gene wanted me as his Best Man. To bring me back into the fold so to speak. At least he hasn't given up on me. He's always been a decent brother to me because we've both been through so much together."

"You're three years older than him?"

"Yeah, less than that. My 40th birthday is coming up this Labor Day weekend."

"So," I said, "you were only thirteen or so when your father died on 9/11"

"I had my 13th birthday party a few days before. Gene's birthday is in January. He was ten at the time."

"And your mom?"

"She was in shock of course. She immediately went into private therapy. I think that saved her. And maybe that's what Gene sees in Stella, I don't really know. But he's into mental health, for sure. In fact, he's paying for my therapist."

Was I talking to David or Peter? I couldn't help but see parallel stories here.

"And what are you doing these days to keep busy?"

"I'm writing. And I'm keeping busy trying to work out with the City's preservation committee how we're going to handle the Rialto. If we can fix it up and sell it, instead of tearing it down, I can pay back most of the money I owe my family and the other investors. They've put the project on hold for years now because they're so divided but they're supposed to give me their final answer by the end of this month."

"Well," I said, "money is not the same as family. My son Paul got the impression talking to your mom and stepdad last night that you're more important to them than their lost investment."

"I wish they'd tell me that in person," he winced. "I get just the opposite feeling; they feel betrayed, fleeced is the word. And my grandparents, too. Not to mention my wife's family, or I should say my former in-laws after the divorce goes through. Gene is the only one who's stood by me all this time, taken me under his wing. He wanted me as Best Man so naturally I couldn't say no. But I think he's thinking that over right now because when he called this morning he told me he definitely wanted me to be here for the wedding and then tomorrow take the honeymoon cruise he's putting together, but would I mind if our stepdad stepped in as Best Man in my stead."

"And what did you say?"

"I said, it's your call: Whatever you want is fine with me. I'll find out when he gets here."

"Well, David," I said, seeing Caroline returning with an ice pack for my forehead, "it's been nice meeting you. I hope things work out."

"For you as well," he said, shaking my hand. "Take care of that leg. I know what life is like with my grandparents and their canes and walkers and golf carts: It's a road less traveled."

The quartet started to play. It sounded Mozartian, though it could have been Mendlesohn or Shubert or Brahms. They took cues from one another, like Mexican mariachi, and probably had in their repertoire hundreds of classical pieces they could call up at will, depending on their sense of the events about them.

And now with an ice-wrapped cloth napkin for my forehead I was feeling a bit better, but quite hungry, wishing I had had another donut for breakfast. But checking the kitchen camera I saw that the line was moving along faster now. And so maybe things would get off on schedule even though the limousines bringing the bride-to-be, the groom with parents and grandparents, and the Erskines hadn't made their entrance. I checked the front door's camera, only to see the oval was filled to capacity with cars, the Franklin's driveway now had 4 cars parked there, and the Lane was being filled on one side with more cars. The lawn was filling up and many went directly to the bar for cold soft drinks. It was exactly 12:30.

And it was then when the most unexplainable part of the day, or maybe second most unexplainable part given the gunshot wound to my knee, was now upon me. At first I couldn't believe what I was seeing, but I was completely rational, I told myself, in spite of the painkillers and anti-inflammatories in me. This couldn't be delusional. Or could it?

Because on the far side of the chuppa, partially hidden in the deep wild grasses and berry bushes, there was ... a deer. A full grown doe since it was without antlers. I could see its head clearly through the low hanging branches from where I was seated. And she was listening with great intent to the quartet, not more than thirty or so feet away. The harmonics probably caught the deer's attention, and it moved closer, but not too close, to get a better view and once safely situated became absolutely rigid in wonder and delight. Because when the quartet ended one selection and was tuning itself for the next, the deer turned its head and we locked eyes for a moment, and when the quartet began its next selection, its head immediately turned back in their direction. Did I know this beautiful creature? Was it my daughter?

I was about to nudge Caroline behind me to confirm what I was seeing, but at that very moment my phone rang. It was Doris who told me Paul and Peter were returning to the party since Robert had mostly everything under control and most, if not all, the cars were now parked.

"But," I said, "where are the principals?"

"On their way," Doris said, "We're going to seat everyone soon. Gene wants his parents and grandparents in the shade where you are, so I'm going to reverse myself again and have the front row on the right side with the Samuels contingent but with you and Caroline on the end of the row. So don't move. You're fine where you are. How are you feeling?"

"All right," I said.

"Because if you're not up to it, David can bring up the champagne glass at the end."

"I'm okay for doing that. At least for now I feel okay."

"Well, there's always a back-up," she said. "Just let me or Gene know."

"All right," I said, turning back to Caroline, "Maybe another cold bottle of water, please, before the principals arrive and they run dry." And when I looked back for the doe, it was gone.

But the Franklins had arrived and Lew and Andria easily passed through security and came directly over to say hello and ask about my leg. With that out of the way, I said, "Thank you for allowing guests to park in your driveway."

"No problem," said Lew. "I thought it might be good publicity."

"Publicity?"

"Well, you know how desirable this neighborhood is, especially the Lane. Someone might ask you if you knew of any sales around here."

"I really don't," I said.

"Well, you do now," said Lew. "We're looking to sell. I'm retiring at the end of the year and we're planning to downsize somewhere. Maybe Medford, Oregon, where our daughter is."

"Wow, that's news!" I exclaimed. "Though I'll hate to lose you as my next-door neighbors and friends for all these years."

"Oh, we'll keep in touch," said Andria. "We remember all the good times with you and Ruthie and you're always in our prayers."

Caroline returned with my water, said hello to the Franklins, who then departed for the cold drink stand.

"They're moving," I said to her, "at the end of the year. Do you and Chris want their house?" I teased.

"What! And integrate the neighborhood? I always wanted to be the next Florence Nightingale, not the next Rosa Parks."

I enjoyed seeing so many people standing around, fanning themselves, taking seats together and chatting, getting soft drinks and cups of ice water. The weather had turned out, a gentle breeze, not too hot, and the section of chairs to the right of the central path, now mostly in the shade. And nobody noticed me in my wheelchair at the end of the first row. Or if they did, they didn't know it was my lovely property they were partying on, enjoying themselves this early afternoon.

But now, I suddenly had to urinate and I realized I better do it sooner than later when the official party was to begin.

"Caroline," I said in a mock-fearful tone, "I have to go pee."

"Well, you have your Depends."

"But that *depends* on whether it's an emergency or not," was my clever comeback. "We still have time for me to take a leak in the woods."

"In the woods? You're strapped into a wheelchair, remember."

"I mean, help push the chair into the woods, maybe ten feet or so, just for some privacy and I'll do it in the cup."

She looked at the underbrush surrounding us. "I don't think there's a way in," she said.

"There's a small path a few rows back, next to the large oak tree," I said. "Take a look."

She returned seconds later. "It's very narrow, just a footpath. But we'll see."

I emptied the rest of the water from the cup, put the wrapped champagne glass on Caroline's chair while she turned the wheelchair about and we made it over to the footpath. "Maybe it's possible," she said. "Hold on to your skullcap, it's going to get bumpy."

And with that, using all of her strength, she managed to push, raise and lower the sides of the wheelchair around sticks and rocky moss past Ruthie's Oak to about ten feet into the dense underbrush. There was just enough clearing there so that the wheelchair could be turned around. "We're here in God's country!" she laughed. "Go do your thing. Or do you need some help."

"I think I can manage."

"Call me when you're finished," she said, stepping back to where the woods began.

I unbuttoned my jacket, pulled down the blanket and released the tie and zipper on my shorts. The diaper was now visible but almost impossible to pull down, strapped tightly as it was around my hips. It took some effort to rip open one side of the velcro fastening—and now I really needed to go! And badly!

It was all I could do to get the cup beneath my penis before a cascade of urine flowed from it. And of course my hand was not steady enough to catch it all, so while I managed to fill the cup almost to its brim, some urine leaked into the diaper and onto my sports jacket, Bermudas and onto the seat. In short, and in shorts, I was an octogenarian mess.

I tossed away the urine from the cup, yet kept the now empty cup by my side, zipped up my Bermudas, tied its closure, pulled up the blanket and called for Caroline. "How did it go?" she asked in her sometimes sarcastic way.

"A dream of a stream," I said. "I can't wait to wake up. Please get us out of here."

She managed to turn the wheelchair around in the small clearing, pushing and tugging it out of the woods and back to our end station in the front row. I gave the plastic cup to Caroline to dispose of and now she could see the damp situation I was sitting in. "I'll get some napkins," she said.

But I realized then, mainly through the sensory perception of my nose, I was not fit to bring the champagne glass over for its ceremonial ending. Or to be ten feet in close proximity to another human being. Moreover, my knee was beginning to hurt again and paranoia was rearing its ugly head. Maybe some urine had entered the wound. Could urine cause an infection? Now at 12:45, perhaps it was time to call the ambulance and remove myself before the ceremonies began. In exactly another hour they'd be here for certain, but by that time...

Caroline returned just then with some paper napkins and clean water and saw my distress. From her tote she pulled out a bubble pack of pills and gave me one.

"Don't worry. This has been okayed by the doctors."

"I'm feeling a bit woozy."

"Do you still want to do the champagne glass?" she asked, mopping around the chair seat.

"I don't think I'm up to it," I said, downing the pill. "If you can find Doris or David, give the glass to them."

"Yeah. I smell like an outhouse."

But Doris was now standing before the chuppa, a pencil-thin microphone in her hand. "Ladies and Gentlemen, everyone, please find a seat," she said. "The honored guests are about to arrive."

CHAPTER 15

"This might help," Caroline said, removing the blanket, then reaching into her shoulder tote and producing a small can of Lysol disinfectant, spraying the chair, my shorts, my jacket, my hands and then the blanket itself. It did the trick. I smelled like a hospital waiting room but at least it masked the previous offending odor.

"Ah, much, much better," I said. "I now know the derivation of the verb, 'pissed off'."

"Do you still want me to see Doris?"

"Yeah, if you would. I think David should do the champagne bit."

Caroline managed to flag down Doris as she left the chuppa and I could see her handing off the wrapped champagne glass to her. Doris looked with concern in my direction and I nodded my approval of the change. So I really had nothing to do with the ceremony, or even being there that afternoon. I was risking losing a limb for a ceremonial bit of nonsense that no one could ever agree upon what its purpose was. And now David was approaching with the wrapped glass, just to make sure it was my decision to relinquish the wedding's closing argument.

"Yes," I said, "I'm not feeling particularly well right now."

"Because I just found out from Doris that my stepdad has been tapped as Best Man."

"I didn't know that," I said. "I wasn't asked to turn this ceremonial function over to you."

"I want to believe that," he said.

"In fact, David, why don't you sit right beside me. I need a buffer now that the Rappaports and Samuels are sitting in this row. Will you sit next to me? I don't want them to catch my riff on Descartes: *I stink, therefore I am.*"

He laughed. "It would be my pleasure," he said, his lightly liquored breath mixing well with the Lysol and urine. And curiously, we both felt a strong bond with one another just then, after only our first encounter a few minutes earlier. I easily could have been his real father, and he could easily be another child replacing Rachel, but one we would never have after Ruthie's early menopause. And now I was recalling my meeting with Gene and our WTC lunch where I wanted to skip over our related tragedies. And while there was something about Gene that made me wary of his probing, his older brother who, no doubt, was even more traumatized by his father's death, seemed more open and compassionate in his disclosures. He was the flip side to Gene's conservative biases, contrasting traits found in most sibling rivalries, my own family included.

"Don't get me wrong," I said. "I think you have a wonderful family. Our families will mix nicely. We have a lot of parallels. Pleasure and pain parallels, as I'm sure you know."

"Oh, yes," he sighed, "and they're still going on."

An older couple arrived just then at the security table with three of four younger people behind. "Do you know who just arrived?" I asked David, and he turned around to look.

"I think that's Leo Erskine and his wife whose name I forget. And those other people may be from the E&S law offices, but I'm not sure."

"Did you ever think of going into law like your brother?"

"Oh, I had a lot of opportunities. My stepdad wanted me in construction and summers I would work for him like Gene did, but I knew I wasn't cut out for it. In college I got interested in real estate for some reason because it was a hot commodity. And after Cornell I got my New York license and started selling. And it was very profitable for many years. The City was bursting at its seams and I connected with [a real estate firm] which had a large commercial portfolio and I had more money than I ever dreamed I would earn. But like everything else, you just want more and more."

"Is that when you started to invest in crypto?"

He sighed again. "Not a lot at first. I was very skeptical. It looked like an off-shore scam, but the figures didn't lie, at least not in the beginning. I had some extra money to gamble with and crypto was even hotter than real estate. And you could cash in and out 24/7 and Signature Bank was FDIC insured so everything looked kosher. I got into the largest funds I could because I figured they wouldn't go under if anything happened. And I still had my six-figure job."

"And Gene never knew? Do you think he would have approved?"

"Gene is very conservative... and of course he wouldn't have approved. But I don't need my younger and wiser brother's okay for anything I do...."

"And speaking of the Devil," I said, "I do believe his entourage has arrived."

Because now parading by the security table and being lightly, if at all, scanned were his grandparents, matching canes in hand, his parents guiding them along the flagstones and across the lawn to their front row seats next to David… along with me, my wheelchair and Caroline behind, handing me yet another bottle of water.

And finally, bringing up the rear, but veering to the left, Gene himself—in a dark blue tuxedo-looking suit, but tieless and open-throated—joining now with Rabbi Max at the back porch steps who handed him his tallit and yarmulke.

Now the string quartet was full throated, playing a theme from a movement in a Brahms symphony I recall from Music & Art days as their Alma Mater: *Now upward in wonder our distant glance is turning…*

Rabbi Max was in full bloom himself, walking solemnly and self-consciously to the chuppa, acknowledging the crowd with light waves, taking his position behind his lectern and the various accouterments he had placed there earlier: *Where brightly through ages an immortal light is burning…*

The crowd hushed and mostly all the seats on both sides of the central aisle seemed full. With Rabbi Max now enthroned, he signaled for Gene and his best man to make their entrance.

Having made sure his wife's parents and his wife were comfortable, Gene's stepdad, Richard, moved over to David and me.

"Hello David, glad you could make it," he said, shaking hands with his stepson as a sign of cordiality, although David had arisen to pursue a physical embrace.

"Hello, Dad," David said flatly. "Hi, Mom, Grandpa, Grandma," he waved to little verbal response but their waving fans.

Then turning to me, Richard asked, "What happened to you?" his suntanned nose taking in the fragrantly foul aroma of deceit.

"Tripped and fell this morning," I replied. "Nothing serious."

"Oh, that's good. We were wondering where you were."

"Front row, side," I said. "More expensive seats in the shade."

"Well, here's to a fast recovery," Richard said, ignoring my sarcasm, and quickly headed back along the lawn to join his favored stepson at the base of the porch steps to share the news.

I looked at David, visibly depressed that his stepfather had hardly acknowledged him.

"Not a man of many words," I said, trying to lighten his mood.

"I've often wondered what words he used on my Mom to get her to marry him," he replied.

***

The betrothal choreography which seemed flawless up to that point, now had a bit of a hitch to it. I couldn't tell what was happening from where I was seated, but Estelle's contingent was being delayed at the security table.

Paul was supposed to walk his daughter down the aisle and was seated in the front row seats on the Myer's side along with Peter next to him. I tried to get his attention as to what was holding up the procession as he was much closer than I was, but Peter shot me a look of bewilderment as well. And now, Doris, who was on the porch directing traffic, came down the steps and turned the kitchen corner towards security. Had something or someone in the ladies-in-waiting group been negatively scanned?

Whatever it was, the line of five women, led by Estelle in white, followed by Julie and three other young ladies all beautifully attired in different colored flowing summer dresses, began to move again and Doris went back to her perch on the porch. Then she gave the signal for Rabbi Max to invite the Groom and his Best Man to the chuppa, which he was all too happy to oblige with his pencil microphone and in his best ancient Hebrew quickly followed by his best translation into modern English.

Gene and Richard walked solemnly down the center aisle trying to keep in stately step with what sounded like a Shubert march. And while all eyes were on them, the five women with Doris at their head, climbed the porch stairs and disappeared into Ruthie's studio to freshen up. Paul was watching all this intently knowing that his role as Estelle's ring bearer was about to play out. But not before the four ladies-in-waiting accompanying Estelle, soon emerged two-by-two out of the studio, and, grasping the side rails for support, down the porch stairs and onto the lawn to take their front row seats. And with all heads and cameras now following this fascinating display of beauty and grace, Paul quickly found his way to the mid-stair level of the porch, waiting anxiously for his nervous daughter, probably now being calmed by Doris the Director of this wedding extravaganza, to make her entrance. I could only marvel at the planning and timing all this took, without a rehearsal, without so much as a broken heel or a twisted ankle. But for the bullet lodged in my right knee, starting to pain me once again, all was going to plan.

And then, after what seemed to be an eternity, a tall, lightly veiled bride suddenly appeared on the porch, her light brown hair tied in a tight bun, enveloped in a beautiful flowing white silk dress with covered shoulders and elbow-length fingerless white gloves holding a bouquet of pink flowers. Her father quickly went to meet her, and she clung tightly to his arm as he used a side rail to safely guide them down the porch steps and onto solid ground. Then a slow processional walk down the center aisle, managing smiles for the smartphone fanatics to either side, Estelle still clinging tightly to her father's arm, perhaps concerned about the grass obstacle course in 3" stilettos, as they acknowledged the special guests along the front row of chairs and were now standing beside Gene and his stepfather, backdropped by a fragrant floral chuppa and a smiling footstooled Rabbi Max. I checked the time. It was exactly 1:08PM.

The music died down. Rabbi Max indicated that the ring bearers step to either side of the chuppa and for the bride and groom to step up on the platform facing one another and at arm's length from one another so that Rabbi Max was centered perfectly between them. Then the Rabbi, text in hand, was ready for his initial Hebrew chant, his deep voice displaying his cantorial prowess.

"*Baruch atah Adonai Eloheinu melech ha-olam, asher bara sason v'simcha chatan v'kallah, gilah rinah ditzah v'chedvah, ahavah v'achavah v'shalom v'reut. M'hera Adonai Eloheinu yishammah b'arei Yhudah uv-chutzot Y'rushalayim kol sason v'kol simcha, kol chatan v'kol kalah, kol mitzhalot chatanim meichupatam u-n'arim mimishte n'ginatam. Baruch ata Adonai, m'sameiach chatan im hakalah.* Blessed are You, LORD, our God, sovereign of the universe, who created joy and gladness, groom and bride, mirth, song, delight and rejoicing, love and harmony and peace and companionship."

And now he was ready to pray over the wine poured from a silver flask into a silver cup on the lectern:

"*Baruch atah Adonai Eloheinu melech ha-olam, borei p'ri hagafen.*"

And after giving Eugene and Estelle a sip, then covering the cup with a silver lid, he was ready to address the congregation with his pencil microphone: "Ladies and Gentlemen, I am Rabbi Maximilian Shulman from the Montclair Central Reform Temple, here in beautiful Upper Montclair, New Jersey. On this lovely summer afternoon it gives me great pleasure to officiate the betrothal and wedding of Estelle Rachel Myer to Eugene Alan Samuels. I have before me their *ketubah,* or wedding vows, and a New York State civil marriage certificate which becomes effective with witness signatures after this religious ceremony. So if there are no objections to the proceedings, we will move on." A rustling of hand fans but silence. A good omen.

"And now each of the betrothed will present their symbolic dowry to the other," said the Rabbi.

It was now time for the ring transfer and Gene's turn to ask his father Richard to present the velvet box that held the golden band. Once Gene opened and removed it he looked steadily at Estelle and said into the microphone held before him by Rabbi Max: "Behold, you are consecrated to me with this ring according to the law of Moses and Israel." He then slipped the ring on Estelle's right hand ring finger.

And then it was Estelle's turn to ask her father Paul to present the case that held her golden band, and slipping it on Gene's right ring finger said in response: "I am my beloved's and my beloved is mine."

Spontaneous applause in the audience and Rabbi Max then passed the wine to Estelle who had a sip, passing it over to Gene for his sip to complete the ritual. At that point Rabbi Max motioned to Richard and Paul to take their seats.

For now it was the Seven Blessings part of the affair—one which held a hint of dread for me. All of us with cards would be asked to stand one by one to recite what was on the card—as D.J. Frank came around with his pencil microphone to amplify for posterity our enfeebled prayers for the couple's future. There was no way I could stand, and those from last night's gala would be looking at my wheelchair, wondering what really had happened to me from the previous evening to this afternoon. For my falling and tripping explanation was as threadbear as the blanket covering my knee. Caroline was reluctant to give me yet another painkiller pill. And to make matters worse, extremely worse, I had randomly picked card #5 entitled... 'Health'!

The quartet was now into a softly played Haydn sonata.

Card #1 belonged to Pamala Rappaport, and supported by her cane in one hand and a trembling card in the other, she waited for the mic to be put before her and then read off '*May you be blessed with a loving home filled with warmth, humor and compassion. May you create a family together that honors traditions old and new. May you teach your children to have equal respect for themselves and others, and instill in them the value of learning and making the world a better place.*' Pamala then sat down to applause for her effort.

Card #2 was Paul's turn. He rose, waited for Frank to deliver the mic before reading: *'May you be best friends and work together to build a relationship of substance and quality. May your sense of humor and playful spirit continue to enliven your relationship. May you respect each other's individual personality and perspective, and give each other room to grow in fulfilling your dreams.'* Again, instant applause.

Card #3 belonged to Kaye Samuels. She rose vigorously, a beautiful smile encompassing her face, waiting for the mic to be placed before her before reading: *'May you be blessed with wisdom. May you continually learn from one another and from the world. Together, may you grow, deepening your knowledge and understanding of each other and of your journey through life'.* Heavy applause.

And then it was Ralph's turn with Card #4. Like Pamala, he had to find his balance with his cane first, but rose steadily and, once the mic was before him, read off vigorously: *'May your life be blessed with the art and beauty of this world. May your creative aspirations and experiences find expression, inspire you and bring you joy and fulfillment. May you find happiness together in adventures big and small, and something to celebrate each day of your lives.'* Great applause for this display of stamina.

Now it was my turn reading Card #5. I felt all eyes on me as Frank moved over to the end of the row of chairs and dropped down on his knees to hold the mic beside my wheelchair. I knew I had to deliver, so I put it out in as strong and expressive a voice as I could muster: *'May you be blessed with health. May life bring you wholeness of mind, body and spirit. May you keep each other well-balanced and grounded, and live long enough that you may share many happy years together.'* Did the audience sense some irony here? Did they think we chose the cards we were reading or traded them so that I would be reading the 'Health' card, obviously incapacitated as I was? For the applause was tepid at best. Shaking my head, I could only grin in embarrassment and self-consciousness at Estelle, Gene and Rabbi Max who were grinning back at me from the chuppa. I'm sure they didn't realize the intense pain I was feeling again in my knee.

And now Frank was moving down the aisle to Richard Samuels and his reading of Card #6:

'May you be blessed with community. May you always be blessed with the awareness that you are an essential part of a circle of family and friends. May there always be within this group love, trust, support and laughter, and may there be many future occasions for rejoicing in their company.' Thankfully, the applause was back up to speed as Richard took his seat.

And finally, it was time for Rabbi Max's reading of Card #7 which was the culmination of all the prayers and blessings for the couple—and the Rabbi knew how to milk it to the Max. He didn't need a card, for in fact he had memorized the script, having delivered it so many times before. Nor did he need Frank to move to the chuppa with his mic, since the Rabbi had his own. He could say the prayer in Hebrew first, looking directly at the couple before him and then, with great delight, translate what he had just said into English, speaking now to the wider audience. *'May you be blessed with love. May your admiration, appreciation and understanding of each other foster a love that is passionate, tranquil and real. May this love between you be strong and enduring, and bring peace into your lives.'* A tremendous ovation as one might expect. The string quartet dutifully raised its volume as the silver wine cup was passed between the couple ending the third part of the ceremony. There was only one more event on my ceremonial timesheet. I checked my watch: it was 1:28 and we were running just a little late. But this would go fast and furious; the Breaking of the Glass, or *simchah*. Upon Rabbi Max's command David strode to the chuppa with his fragile gift securely wrapped in a large linen napkin, and placed it directly in front of the podium quickly returning to his seat beside me. "Incomprehensible ritual" he whispered to me.

So some word of explanation about this controversial closing was needed, and Rabbi Max was right there with the Hebrew prayer and English translation: "***Baruch atah Adonai Eloheinu melech ha-olam, shehakol bara likhvodo.* Blessed are You, LORD, our God, sovereign of the universe,** who created all things for His glory."

The Rabbi went on with his interpretation: "There will be times in life when things break down, break apart, and no amount of cement can be used to repair the damage. It is during those times we reflect on the happiness we received from God for this object's existence before it was taken from us. We feel the strength in our commitment to rebuild anew, to start afresh, secure in the joy of knowing that everything in life is transitory, even life itself. Breaking this fragile item is showing love and respect for our Creator and all that He does for us each and every day of *our* existence."

At that point Gene raised his right foot and smashed down on the champagne glass and Estelle followed with her own stomp, furthering the glass's timely demise. The audience responded with a cry of *Mazel Tov*, Good Luck. And the quartet dutifully jumped in with a major theme from *Fiddler on The Roof.*

Not to be undone, Rabbi Max then handed a flat golden-foiled wrapped present to Gene who handed it off to Estelle which, I assumed contained her newly-framed *ketubah* and then a smaller envelope to Gene, containing, I would guess, the civil wedding certificate to be duly notarized (together with the Rabbi's bill?). The wedding ceremony now complete, the couple embraced, Gene raising Estelle's veil, and after briefly kissing, making their way down the center aisle for *yichud,* a few minutes alone in private to unwind, in Ruthie's studio.

"Well done," I said to David, and he laughed. But my watch now told me it was 1:35 and the ambulance would be out front waiting for me in less than ten minutes. "Time for Act Two" I said to Caroline, and she knew exactly what I meant. I was to be at Montclair Memorial Hospital at precisely 2 PM and both she and David grabbed a handle of my wheelchair and, waving to the various Samuels and Rappaports, across the lawn we went, slowly rolling past the chuppa and Rabbi Max gathering up his paraphernalia. I shouted to him, "Wonderful!" to which he replied, '*L'Chaim*!'"

CHAPTER 16

There have been loads of coincidences in my narrative but none so spacy as getting to the oval at exactly the time the ambulance pulled up in front of the house. We both arrived at precisely 1:43 according to my watch and its attendant was already preparing to lower the back lift to allow my wheelchair to be securely fastened to it. I told Caroline and David to go back to the party and enjoy themselves; that I was in good hands now and everything would go smoothly from here on out. But Caroline was adamant in taking her car to the hospital and meeting me there, and upon hearing that, David asked for a lift to the Montclair Transit Station, a mere two blocks away.

As I was being lashed in, I said to David, "Stay here with Gene and the family. Everyone is in a good mood. It's going to be a fun party. I think everyone wants to put this Broadway thing behind them and help you move forward with your life."

"Thanks, Jerry, for your encouragement, but I feel more like the champagne glass I brought up to the chuppa. I don't think my being here this afternoon is going to repair the cracks."

"Y'never know," I said, acknowledging to David I knew the basic storyline of his past adventures of being a producer.

"But sometimes you *do* know, Jerry. My being here just doesn't feel right to me."

I wasn't about to change his mind. "Can you take him to the station, Caroline?"

"Of course."

"I just have to get my gun back from security, Caroline," David said matter-of-factly, waving goodbye to me, now heading towards Joe at the security table. David was also 'packing'? I was lost for words.

Steve, the attendant, had now raised the platform and I was wheeled into the ambulance and anchored again. "See you at the hospital," I said to Caroline below. The rear doors swung shut and we were off.

I was passing in and out of consciousness, the pain in my knee pulsing in feverish rhythm to the ambulances' tires passing over the roadways' tar interstices. But at last we came to a halt. The rear doors were opened. We were there. Still securely tied to my wheelchair, still sitting upright, I was wheeled past the emergency room, into a cool, dimly lit operating room, somewhere beneath the center of the hospital's ground floor.

"Glad you could make it back, Jerry," said Dr. Francona, looking down at me from behind a sky blue facemask. "Hope the wedding went smoothly."

"I'm feeling spacy, Doc."

"Doesn't surprise me," said Francona. "Ummm, that a new cologne you're wearing?"

I wasn't in the mood for Francona's wisecracks. But now Francona turned serious as he took a clipboard he was holding and placed it in my lap. "We have some forms we want you to sign before we start things, Jerry. I told you when you left this morning there would be some release forms to sign when you returned. Do you remember that?"

"Yes."

"Good."

"Let me turn on this overhead so you can read them better. Did you bring glasses with you?"

"My sunglasses are bi-focals," I replied, taking them out of my jacket's breast pocket. I quickly scanned the three pages before me. The first page had the precise time of earlier that day such-and-such a doctor or a nurse took x-rays or otherwise examined me, the result of the examination, the exact time Dr. Francona was called, Dr. Stone was called, and other various interactions relating to the wheelchair all signed off by the principals involved. The second page was an affidavit of Informed Consent attesting to the fact I had been told about the seriousness of my injury, my options, and that I denied having services performed at that time for the removal of the bullet in my knee. The third page had all the ambulance time references, the return to my home, the pick up return to the hospital, and other various activities performed by hospital attendants who signed off on the timesheet. There was a fourth page that was to be signed by Caroline Hamilton upon arrival, attesting to the painkillers given to me, and other services she performed while I was in her care.

I didn't read the pages thoroughly, but they looked accurate to me, and I realized that by signing these forms I was releasing the hospital of any responsibility regarding the operation they were to perform on my knee since I had refused their initial evaluation for immediate remedy earlier that day. But I wanted to hear that from Dr. Francona.

"What if I don't sign these papers," I asked.

"Then, Jerry, we'll take you upstairs to the main entrance, cut you loose from the hospital's wheelchair, and call a cab for you. You'll be on your own from then on. Montclair Memorial won't take you back."

"I guess I better sign," I said.

"Up to you," said the good doctor.

I signed the forms and looking at my watch, entered the necessary time of my signing. Francona then witnessed the forms as my personal physician. And with his clipboard he quickly exited the room by saying, "We're going to do everything possible to save your leg, Jerry, but we're not miracle-makers."

I'm not going into detail about the prep work and the operation itself. Those of you who have had major surgery for one thing or other know what's involved. Some of it is embarrassing, some downright ugly. But once Dr. Stone, the orthopedic surgeon, arrived on the scene I felt more serene, more confident this operation would turn out okay. And now Caroline dressed in scrubs and masked also joined the team. Knowing she was there during the operation, if only to lend moral support, further enhanced my optimism. When the anesthesiologist applied my breathing mask I gave her a thumb's up, the last thing I remember.

The prep work took about a half hour, the operation took about three hours, and I was unconscious for a half-hour beyond that while they moved me upstairs to a private room. I opened my eyes to see the setting sun cutting through the venetian blinds and Caroline sitting in a chair in the corner, reading a book. I was hooked up to an I.V. and a heart monitor by the side of the bed. My legs were slightly raised and I was lightly covered with a sheet and blanket but other than that I felt so comfortable my first thought upon awakening was I was back in my bed at home. (Wishful thinking for it would be a while before I could return to my upstairs bedroom.)

"Hello," I said somewhat groggily.

"Well, hello stranger!" said Caroline, putting down her book, moving her chair closer to the bed. "Would you like me to raise your upper body somewhat?"

"Yes," I said. "Where am I?"

"Top floor, Montclair Memorial," she said, pushing a button that raised the top half of the bed a bit. "How are you feeling?"

"Not too bad. How did it go?"

"Take a look down at your feet. You still got two of them. Wiggle your toes on your right foot?"

My right leg felt numb but I could wiggle my toes a little under the blanket. Caroline was delighted.

"I need to let some people know you're awake," she said. "Be right back."

And with that she quickly left the room, not to return for a good five minutes. I could feel that my right leg, from mid-thigh to mid-calf was wrapped in some kind of cast that kept it stable, but I could rotate my ankle a bit and wiggle my toes. I had sensation down there. The operation, I felt, had been completely successful. I would be back to my usual self in no time.

My cognitive functions were coming back. I tried to remember the order in which things happened that fateful Saturday; of getting up and dressed, meeting the security team, going upstairs and getting the gun from the safe, meeting Peter in the hallway, our second contentious meeting, getting shot, giving Paul instructions, being carried to Caroline's car, arriving at the hospital, being X-rayed, Dr. Francona's arrival, being strapped to a wheelchair, returning home in an ambulance, meeting David, the deer, the wedding, reading my blessing, returning to the hospital by ambulance, signing the release forms, the prep work, Dr. Stone's examination and impression that sepsis hadn't spread, my lights out... all in a day! I was hungry and thirsty but enough was enough! It was time to get some sleep. What a foolish notion!

Caroline was back and unhooked me from the I.V. drip. "I let Dr. Francona know you're awake and can move your toes. He'll be here tomorrow early to check on you."

"Oh, good," I said. "What time is it?"

"It's a little past 7 o'clock. I know it's been a long stressful day," she said, "but there are a few people very concerned about you. Are you up for seeing them and just saying hello?"

"Isn't it past visiting hours?"

"Well, that's being taken care of. It's really up to you whether you feel strong enough to see them, see them all at once so they're not parading in and out. Just for ten minutes or so, no more, because everyone knows you need to get your rest."

"Are they here?"

"Yeah, they're waiting for word downstairs."

"Okay, send them up."

And in a minute or so, the room was crowded with Paul, Peter, Julie, Estelle, Gene, and Caroline.

Estelle, still dazzling in her wedding dress, began: "Grandpa, we brought you some food from the reception. We didn't have any deep-fried matzoh balls left, but there's some salad here and some chicken with rice and some salmon croquettes. It's still warm."

"Deep-fried matzoh balls?"

"A big hit," Peter said. "They ran out."

I tried to laugh. I had never heard of such a thing.

"How are you feeling, Dad?" Paul asked.

"Not bad," I said. "I seem to have all feeling restored. I'm going to be fine."

"We also brought some wine," Julie said. "There are glasses in the styrofoam container."

"I wouldn't mind having a taste now," I said.

The ingenious container's lid was raised and there were three plastic stem glasses in the deep holders within. The salmon smelled delicious, but I thought I would wait to eat until everyone left before I indulged myself. But wine? That needed to be downed now. Caroline?

She nodded her approval, but made a 'tiny amount' indication with her thumb and forefinger. Of course, if she said 'no', wine would have to wait. I was under strict orders to rely on her now; the hospital, short staffed as it was on a weekend, was delighted I was being attended to by a private registered nurse. She had a notebook with her that listed all of my meds; the times they were taken and would need to be taken. All under Dr. Francona's auspices. Apparently, a small bit of alcohol would be just the thing to put me soundly to sleep so the bottle of Merlot was opened and three glasses poured.

"A toast," Gene proclaimed. "To my new Grandfather-in-law's full recovery."

I raised my glass in response: "And I thank everyone for coming over this evening after a long day. Congratulations all around!" And then added: "And to a wonderful honeymoon cruise."

"Sorry you and Paul can't be with us," said Gene. "But I'm happy to announce Julie and Peter have offered to take your places."

"We didn't offer," Julie laughed. "We begged."

"Oh, that's terrific!," I laughed along with the rest.

The other two glasses of wine were passed about and everyone had their fill. But I could see they were all exhausted as was I, and ready to knock off. "So, everyone," I said, "it's going to be a busy day tomorrow. Let's all get some rest now."

"Love you, Grandpa," Estelle said, coming over and kissing me on the temple. "We'll drop by to see you before we leave."

"I'm staying at the house," Paul said, "with Peter and Julie. So we'll also be back early tomorrow to look in on you."

"Oh, wonderful," I said. "Goodnight. And thanks again for coming."

And then they were off. All except Caroline who, after the crowd had left the room, reached for the remains in the wine bottle and together with the salmon croquettes, we did them both justice.

I think I should put in here how fortunate I felt to have not only the support of family, but of Caroline who was indeed part of the Myer family now. She was more than an aide to me, I realized. She was my housekeeper, my confidant, my dear friend. She was one of the central reasons I had for maintaining the lifestyle I led in Upper Montclair, and her loss, either by my moving or her leaving for some reason or other would have a serious impact on my emotional, if not my physical health. I was determined to maintain this relationship for as long as possible. And now, with this infirmity, it seemed I was more indebted to her staying on at whatever cost, whatever sacrifice.

CHAPTER 17

I slept like the proverbial bear in a cave, awakening from a winter's hibernation. Caroline had left at around 7:30 or so and I awoke at around 7:30 the next morning. A full twelve hours of deep, uninterrupted sleep. My heart monitor must have told the attending nurses on the floor not to bother me, that I was fine the way I was. And I could only marvel at how refreshed I felt after such a strenuous day. Even my knee felt better, although I realized it would be days if not weeks before everything was back to normal.

But those realizations were wishful thinking ones. For after breakfast, and other urinary and defecationary matters, as promised, a masked Dr. Francona limped by.

"How's it going?" he asked, shaking my hand.

"I slept great," I said.

"Must've been the wine," he cracked. "I'll have to remember that."

He pulled down the cover and the sheet, and raised my gown to expose my knee, now in a coffin-like cast. "Wiggle your toes for me," he said, and I did. "And now rotate your foot a bit," and I performed that act to a T. The good doctor was pleased.

"How is your knee feeling?"

"I don't feel much," I said. "No pain, just some pressure."

"Well, that's normal. You'll be in this cast for a few days yet. And then you'll be fitted for a brace and we can start physical therapy."

"How long will I be here?"

"Well, if everything goes to plan, we're hoping to release you on Wednesday. So this is Sunday. So three more days."

"How did the operation go?"

"About as expected. Luckily, Dr. Stone found no sepsis. But the bullet smashed into some medial bone matter causing a serious meniscus tear and some collateral ligament injury so some reconstruction work was needed. You won't be able to put any weight on your knee for some time. No deep knee bends. We'll know more when physical therapy starts."

"You mean I won't be able to walk?"

"Yeah, you'll be able to walk, but you'll need a walker to take the weight off your right leg. And then if everything goes well, and you can put some weight on your leg, you can graduate to a metal crutch or a cane for balance and support. But some activities won't be coming back."

"Like what? I'll still be able to drive, right?"

"Yeah, you'll be able to drive. And we'll get a disabled driver sticker for you, too."

"Like what then?"

"Like climbing stairs. Riding a bike. Playing tennis. Climbing into a bathtub. But they have bathtubs with door panels built in now, so you can get in and out easily to bathe or to shower. And you're going to need a raised toilet seat. But you can get those anywhere."

"Climbing stairs," I moaned. "I have my bedroom on the second storey of my house."

"Well, there are two possibilities: You can install a lift, like an elevator, or a motorized chair-on-a-rail that you sit in and carries you up and down stairs. I can bring some material for you to look at when I see you next time."

"Or I could make a bedroom for myself downstairs," I said, thinking of Ruthie's studio.

"Certainly. That's an option too."

Francona covered my leg with my gown, the sheet and blanket and said his goodbyes. "I'll look in on you tomorrow," he said. "Today is a quiet day, but tomorrow X-rays will be taken." And he was off.

As this was Sunday, Caroline would be off as well. I rang for the nurses' desk and asked if they could bring me my phone, taken from me when I arrived along with my wallet and keys, sunglasses, clothes, loafers and other items presumably locked up in a safe place. And minutes later my phone was delivered, but with very little charge left. I tried calling Paul but got no answer on his phone. And then my phone went dead due to lack of power. Newer double screen 3D phones had built in slide-out prongs so an adapter or charger wasn't ever needed, but this was last year's model. Without a charge I couldn't even take a selfie!

And just as I was beginning to worry no one in the world would give up their Sunday to look in on me, there was a knock on the door, and in walked Peter and Julie, carrying three or four flower branches in a vase I figured must have come from the chuppa. They had left Paul behind to guard the house while the caterers picked up their tables, chairs and other items and cleaned up the backyard.

"So I really never got the story yesterday," I started off. "What was the party like after the ceremony?"

"Oh, how I wish you were there, Granddad," Peter started off. It was amazing. The food was wonderful and so was the wine and the champagne. I ate my head off."

"And the music was great also," Julie added. "A super DJ that seemed to know everyone's favorite artist. He didn't see you leave so he called your name out for some LP you wanted to have played."

"Oh yes, I asked him to play a favorite of mine when he was setting up on Friday."

"And then he had some Israeli music for when Gene and Stella were lifted up on chairs. It was hilarious! I took some pictures on my phone that I can send you. Do you want to see?"

"Of course." And truly, the photos Julie showed me of Gene and Estelle being paraded around each other on chairs high above the platform trying to feed each other wedding cake were deliciously funny. Peter, in fact, held one of the four chair legs lifting Gene to new heights. I was thrilled Peter and Gene had buried their hatchets and that Gene had invited them both on their honeymoon cruise.

"Did you tell Estelle and Gene about your plans for Australia?" I asked.

"Not yet," Peter said. "After the cruise is over. We don't want to take away from their honeymoon and Erskine's anniversary celebration. When we get back there'll be time. We now have a date for leaving: September 30th. It's already the 1st of October in Australia—and we move into our new apartment later that day. It will be all ready for us."

"I bet you're both thrilled," I said.

"Can't wait," said Julie. "After these last few years in the States, this is like an angel coming down and touching us. And if everything goes to plan, maybe I can get my folks to emigrate. It's so hard now in almost every way to be elderly in America."

"And scary," Peter put in. "For years now, it's been getting rougher out there with the past recession and crime against older people getting out of hand. And especially for you now, Granddad, with that accident it will make it doubly hard to feel independent and safe in that big house. I feel so bad for you and what happened, I can't tell you, Granddad."

Peter's eyes were tearing up and I felt badly for him as well. I suspected he had kept secret, even from Julie, his participation in the shooting—and would be carrying this burden with him to his grave, or mine, whichever came first.

"It's not as bad as you might imagine," I said. "My foot is intact, just a question of diligent rehabilitation and some physical therapy. I'm out of here on Wednesday, back to the house, says my doc. And I'll have Caroline. And I found out something just yesterday about her partner, Chris. After all these years, she let me know what he does for a living. You'll never guess."

"Knowing Caroline, he's a Zen Master," Peter proffered.

"Close," I said. "He's a licensed physical therapist. For professional reasons, Caroline and Chris never work together as a team. They don't want to give conflicting advice on cases they handle. But maybe my case can be the exception.

Peter and Julie had to return to the house to pack for an 11:00 pick up by the luxury van which was to carry them, Gene and Estelle, Gene's parents and grandparents up to Westport, Connecticut and the chartered yacht that would take them, first to Hilton Head South Carolina to drop off his parents, and then to Ft. Lauderdale Florida to drop off his grandparents.

Peter had brought plenty of clothes with him from California, but Julie had brought only a couple of change of clothes with her for the wedding. Luckily, she said, she was exactly the same size as Estelle, and throughout their lives together they were always trading clothes. So it wouldn't be necessary to first go back to her apartment in New Haven for outfits; she could just wear Estelle's.

No sooner had they left than Gene and Estelle arrived to say their goodbyes. Estelle brought some wedding cake for me and I told them that Julie's photos of them trying to feed each other from the held chairs they were revolving on had been sent to my phone.

"Can't wait to see the dry cleaning bills," she laughed, as they both sat down.

"Wish you could have been there," Gene said. "How's the knee?"

"Coming along," I said. "Not much for it to do when I'm lying in bed like this."

"When are you getting out?" he asked.

"They think Wednesday if everything checks out. You'll be on the yacht then I take it."

"We'll be away through the Labor Day weekend. The boat gets back to Connecticut that Labor Day Monday."

"That's a nice ten-day honeymoon," I said.

"And a nice getaway for the Erskines too," said Gene. "But then it's back to work, and I expect a very busy fall."

"How is FreeGT coming?" I asked Estelle.

"Ready to launch," she said. "We're putting together staff now. The InterInn people made us a very generous offer to use their platform. I think we have enough backing to start sessions around the end of September."

"Hmmm," I said, taking that in. And then, like a lightning bolt, a fantastic thought crossed my mind. But I figured, rather than Estelle, I needed to talk to Gene about it first, in private. And yet sitting before me now was a married team. This was indeed a sticky wicket. "Estelle, would you mind terribly if I had a word with Gene alone," was the way I phrased it.

She furrowed her eyebrows somewhat. "Do you want me to wait outside, Grandpa?"

"If you would," I said. "It will only be a minute or two."

After Estelle had left I motioned to Gene "Sit on the side of my bed," I said. "There's an urgent matter that I need to discuss with you."

He did so, and showed some compassion as he cupped my right hand into both of his, probably thinking he would be hearing something about meeting estimated hospital bills.

"This isn't about me," I said. "I'm worried about David. He seems very depressed."

Gene looked annoyed that I would bring up his brother. "I'm paying for him to see a therapist, y' know."

"Then see if his concern mirrors mine. At least you'll have some..."

Gene cut me off. "Jerry," he said, looking straight into my eyes, "I'm not my brother's keeper. He's old enough to know what's best for him. Second guessing him is not in either of our best interests here. He'll just claim I'm interfering in his life."

"Then that's what you have to do. By the way, you *are* your brother's keeper in case you've forgotten. He's in no way capable of making his own decisions now. But he'll still listen to you. You have to step in and take charge. We had a long talk yesterday. Other than you, he feels abandoned by the family, his wife and kids, by almost everyone."

"Jerry. I talked to him briefly before the wedding. I invited him to join us on the yacht. He'd have his own stateroom. Time to talk to our mom, Richard, his grandparents. Time to patch things up. And he said he didn't want to ruin my honeymoon. So yes, I tried, but he refused my help. What more do you expect of me?"

"Do you have his therapist's number?"

"Yes. What do you want me to say?"

"Tell him of your concern, that you think your brother should be institutionalized and evaluated for his own safety while you're gone."

"I can't do that, Jerry. Even if it were legal—which it's not—half the country would be institutionalized on somebody or other's concern. He hasn't done anything to call for such drastic measures. His shrink wouldn't cut those orders just on my say so."

"Did you know he brought a weapon to the wedding? A pistol."

"Of course. My security team has verified receipts for all six."

"Six?"

"David and two others on the train. One in Stella's wedding entourage. One with Leo's own security. And one from a couple who didn't follow Robert's order about leaving their gun in their car. The wife forgot she had a loaded pistol in her purse, if you'll believe that."

"Six? Amazing!" I had a flash thought about my lost thousand dollar bet.

"Not to mention Peter's gun which I assume is still in the house."

"It's locked away."

"But not before it accidentally fired when you tripped and fell going downstairs with it."

"Right."

Gene shook his head. "That bit of cover up is going to cost you dearly, you know."

"We're not talking about that," I said. "We're talking about David here. And just now I had a brainstorm. Do you think your brother would want to work with Estelle on FreeGT? You must remember how successful he was producing *Y'Never Know*. He may be an ideal Executive Producer for the website. He certainly knows about therapy. And if he starts working again..."

"This is Stella's baby," Gene said, cutting me off again. "She makes the decisions here, not me."

"She doesn't know David like you do," I argued. "I wanted to pass this idea along to you first, because I thought Estelle would be more receptive if it came from you, not me. I hardly know your brother. I just feel he's in deep psychological shit right now and without a support network or some meaningful work he's very vulnerable."

Gene was visibly upset and released his grip on my hand. "It seems to me I've heard that before with your grandson," he said, somewhat angrily. "And It seems a bit ironic to me that you were pissed when Stella talked about getting an evaluation for *her* brother and now you want me to do the same with *my* brother. Maybe you should hang out a shingle, 'amateur psychologist.'"

"Fair enough," I said. "But the circumstances were vastly different."

"Well, let me think about it," Gene said, calming down a bit, now considering my proposal. "Stella and I will have time to discuss it on the boat. Maybe there's something here, maybe not. She already may have filled all the positions she needs. She has to tell me what positions are still open, and if there's something there, I'll mention David to her. I know how impressed she was when we saw *Y'Never Know*."

"It would certainly cheer David up if he had something to look forward to."

"I'll see what I can do."

"If you need me for anything," I said, "I'll be here until Wednesday, it seems. If you want me to talk to David, I can certainly do that. I won't mention anything about FreeGT, but I can try to convince him to go into a psychiatric setting somewhere for his own good for the few days you'll be on your yacht."

"All right," said Gene, bending over and kissing me on my temple. "You know, you're no longer Jerry to me. You've become my other overseeing Grandpa."

After Estelle and Gene said their goodbyes and left, I asked for a cup of hot tea and had the piece of wedding cake Estelle had brought. The more I thought about it, the more similarity I saw between Peter and David's stories—two highly intelligent, well educated but psychologically stressed men—one in his late twenties, the other about to turn forty. Two different generations, but both having the same problems of making a decent, honest living, being second-guessed by AI, finding and holding on to a long-term partner, justifying some meaning to their lives in a ever-widening polarized society splitting apart from intractable political, racial and economic stressors. Especially these past four years of Trump's stewardship. How did we lose our way so quickly, become so isolated and detached? How did so many ordinary citizens load up on weapons of every sort, become so paranoid and homophobic? How did the American Dream become a nightly nightmare of blasting squad car sirens?

I tried to contrast that with the decade of my 30's, the late sixties through the late seventies when Ruthie and I began our partnership in marriage and work and having children. How different that all was, how seemingly normal, how rational, how rewarding—not just monetarily, but having mutual concern for one another's welfare and the underlying sense of wellbeing with a promising future together. And how that embedded belief helped us recover from Rachel's passing as quickly as it did, although not without periods of grieving and depression on anniversaries like her birthday or the evening we told Jamaica Hospital to pull the plug.

Moving to Montclair helped enormously, isolating as it was at first. Initially I objected to the move. It was running away from the tragedy, I remember saying, instead of facing it straight on, with therapy and perhaps even medication. But Ruthie was adamant, and reminded me of the cursed three weeks each September when the U.S. Tennis Championship was then being held in Forest Hills after which we renewed vows to move away from that annual madness but never did. It took losing a precious daughter, purposely riding her bike on the sidewalk, to a mindless, semi-drunk tennis fanatic recklessly backing out of a neighbor's paid-for driveway spot to convince me: Ruthie, Paul and I had to get out of there quickly or collectively lose our minds.

I remember clearly those feelings half a lifetime ago, but now from the setting of a hospital room and the lonely hours I was about to spend alone with some ancient memories—ever more dear to me than the expectations for the next chapter in my life: the struggle to fully recuperate and regain control of my independence.

CHAPTER 18

Even though I couldn't call out, my phone accepted incoming calls with very limited power and sure enough it woke me from a late morning nap: It was Paul informing me that the caterers and the florist had picked up everything, cleaned the yard perfectly, and had just left. Could he come over and visit during afternoon visiting hours? "Of course," I said. "And bring my phone charger you'll find in the socket next to my desk, oh, and a book you'll find on my nightstand."

After lunch Paul arrived with my phone charger and *Quantum Agnostics,* the book I had been reading the night before the wedding. He plugged the charger into the wall socket and attached the phone to the cord. "They wanted to know at the desk if you wanted TV in the room."

"I don't think so," I said. "There's nothing but bad news shows out there. And I can get TV or the Internet off my phone if I want to see something. I'd rather finish my book."

"Everything comfortable for you, Dad?" Paul asked, pulling up a chair to the bedside.

"No problems," I said. "I'll only be here until Wednesday, if everything checks out."

"It was a lovely wedding. So sorry you missed it. But everyone took photos and the photographer must have some wonderful shots. He said the album would be ready when they returned after Labor Day."

"Did you want to go with them? Gene said he asked you, but you have staff meetings next week."

"Well, if it wasn't for that, I'd probably go. I could use a vacation. As it is, it worked out because someone has to look after you when you come home."

"Caroline will be there."

"I know, Dad, but until you get around on your own, I've decided to stay out here. At least through Labor Day. Then when classes start, I'll move back into the City. You're going to need another pair of hands there at the house when Caroline leaves for the day."

"Well, that's wonderful of you," I said. "Back in your old room?"

"Strange, huh?"

"And even stranger—I'm not going to be able to climb stairs any time soon, so I thought I'd convert Mom's studio to my bedroom. I can use her day bed for the moment, but we'll have to get a regular bed put down there. It has a sink and a toilet, but no shower. So we're going to have to build out into the kitchen pantry or onto the porch or something. I haven't figured it all out yet."

"You won't be able to climb stairs?"

"That's what Dr. Francona told me this morning. Putting weight on my right knee is the problem. But I need to get a second opinion on that."

"We can put in a chair-on-a-rail system. It would cost the same as building out a shower from the studio. Let me do some investigating on this."

"Good. And one other thing, They left behind the chuppa platform, right?"

"Yes. Doris said you wanted it for a pickleball court."

I laughed. "I was being facetious. I actually want it as a shelter for the deer in winter."

"What?"

"Yeah, the thought came to me during the wedding. It would need some roofing material to protect the tongue-and-groove slats, but then it could be put on poles and placed in the middle of the woods. It would keep the ground underneath dry. Maybe straw bedding. The deer would love it."

"Dad, that's a crazy idea. There's a word for it: Anthropomorphism. It's giving animals human characteristics."

"How different is that from AI bots I've been reading about that are used as guard dogs?"

Paul laughed. "Okay, Dad, whatever you say. What else?"

"I'll need a raised toilet seat. I'm sure you can find these on the internet."

"Unused, I take it," he said, smirking.

"Yeah, straight from the factory. The last thing I need now is an STD."

"No, the last thing you need now is to see the hospital bill."

"Well, I think I can manage that with accident insurance kicking in."

"What accident insurance?"

"I have Medicare Advantage."

"Dad, they're not going to treat this as an accident. There are X-rays, remember? They have specialists who do nothing all day but look over accident reports and they'll analyze the X-rays. There's no way in hell they'll back up your story of shooting yourself when you tripped on the stairs. Besides, the gun that you claim you were carrying isn't yours. They'll find that out immediately. They're going to ask for the gun..."

"It's in the wall safe, right?"

"Yes, Dad, it is. And you never gave me the combination, so I can't get to it or anything else you may have stored there. And now, *you* won't be able to get into the safe."

"I'll give you the combination. There are some bonds there and a little money and the deed to the house and insurance policies and my will and a few other personal items."

"And Peter's pistol. They're going to want to check that out. What happens then?"

"Well, give them the pistol to check out. I was bringing it downstairs for him to turn over to the security people when..."

"And so you now want to involve Peter? The security team?"

Paul instantly saw the quandary I was in. There was no good answer here, but his logical mathematical mind maybe had a solution I hadn't thought about. "So," I said, "what do you suggest?"

"If you want to keep Peter out of this, as I know you do, and Gene's security team, and Caroline as a witness, and me as a collaborator hiding a weapon to a shooting that was never reported to the police—then you're not going to be able to put in an insurance claim without them investigating the entire sordid mess," he said. "It's called fraud. And defrauding an insurance company can get you in big trouble."

"In other words, pay the bill."

"Pay the bill. But try to negotiate it down. Maybe they have a payment plan, but they'll tack interest onto that."

"How much do you think it will be?"

"Dad, I have no idea. There are ambulance rides, examinations and X-rays, the operation itself, this room, medications, nurses, attendants, dressings, on and on. And that doesn't include follow-up physical therapy and more examinations. Plus all the things you'll need at home."

"I have some savings," I said, "and some Roth IRA mutual funds I can cash in without paying taxes. And I can always take a second mortgage on the house."

"A second mortgage to a non-working 90-year-old? Well, maybe..."

"Sure. The bank loves me."

"Well, use me as a co-signer. I don't want the house, but I think it could bring in a good price if it's sold. And I'd rather sell it than hand it over to the bank. But first things first. We have to make Mom's studio comfortable for you when you get out of here."

"Yes. You're the officiating officer in charge of obtaining a raised toilet seat."

Paul stiffly saluted me. "Yessir!"

"And we'll go on from there."

"We always seem to somehow puddle through, Dad. It's the Mark of The Myer."

With one exception, there isn't much to report about my time spent at Montclair Memorial between Sunday evening and Wednesday morning when I was finally released. I was seen each day by Dr. Francona who explained in great detail about the work done to my knee, and the impact the operation would have on my physical therapy and beyond. It seems much of the middle part of the knee was destroyed by the bullet and that an artificial replacement part was inserted to keep the knee functioning. Well, not a part really, but a gel-encased rubber-like mold that would semi-harden like cartilage over that three day period to keep bones in place and allow the passage of blood to flow to my lower leg and foot, while providing a cushion for the weight placed on my right knee. The only problem was that if too much weight was applied, the mold would likely shift its position and I'd be back for yet another procedure.

And so certain activities needed to be curtailed, like climbing stairs, while other activities would need external support for the leg like a walker or a crutch. Bottom line: for the rest of my life I needed to stay off that leg as much as possible. The leg was saved from amputation, but for all intents and purposes, perhaps that was the wisest option, as I could then be fitted for a prosthetic lower leg that I could put my full weight onto. And, Dr. Francona was quick to add: "You can have that amputation done at any time, you know."

Well, I'm sure Dr. Stone and the others doing the operation took into account my age, overall health and my mobility and made the decision not to amputate. But they knew nothing of the layout of my house and the fact my bedroom was on the second storey. Could I somehow navigate climbing and descending without putting weight on my right foot? This would be the first question for the physical therapist who would be visiting me every other day for weeks for rehabilitation after I left Memorial. In the meanwhile Paul would be responsible for making the studio habitable for sleeping. And now, I also tasked him to consult Caroline's partner Chris, for buying me a sturdy foldable walker, as I would no longer be using a wheelchair.

Other than the stairs, and giving up tennis and biking, I saw no real problems. I would still be able to drive a car, or be a passenger in a cab or Uber, go out to the backyard using the kitchen side entrance, go to a restaurant or a movie, put together a meal or dress myself, slip into loafers or sneakers. All that really needed to be done was to put in a shower stall somewhere adjoining the studio.

Easier said than done, I quickly realized. The studio was situated above the basement of the house, so in winter hot air from the gas-fed boiler below was blown up through the floor vents keeping the studio and the adjoining bathroom pipes warm. So a shower stall could not be built out onto the porch area unless there was some way to keep the water in the pipes from freezing.

But first things first. X-rays were to be taken Monday morning as promised and I was lifted onto a gurney and wheeled into the X-ray room. Same Dr. Winslow, same three positions, same procedures. I could see the mold had replaced about a third of my knee once the X-rays were placed on the screen. Dr. Stone was pleased and let out a huge sigh of relief when I told him most of the pain had subsided and I was to be taken off anti-inflammatories that day. The plaster cast and stitches would be removed in a week or so, if everything continued to heal.

Tuesday was to be a day of rest. Paul visited in the morning to tell me he had purchased a raised toilet seat from Amazon, spoken to Chris about getting a foldable walker, and received a email from Estelle on the yacht who said she was having a wonderful time and didn't want to call me at the hospital, but would call me tomorrow evening after I returned home.

And then I had the one exception to my routine—an unexpected visitor in the afternoon, right after lunch. But first a nurse wanted to know if I wanted to see this person, not being part of the original contingent who had already signed in and out and known to the staff. His name: David Samuels. I told her, send him up.

David arrived with a small package he placed on my bedside table and bending over, kissed me on the forehead. I didn't smell alcohol, and like my son, realized his diurnal drinking ritual began in late afternoon into the evening. Now, at least, we could have a sober conversation. And I guessed correctly why he wanted to see me personally, not over a smartphone connection.

"I got a call from Gene last night. I think you know what it was about," he said in a nervous tremor.

The game was up, and I realized Gene probably revealed that the David-as-Producer idea was not his or Estelle's, but mine, so I had to be as candid as possible here: "I don't know how much you know about FreeGT, but from what I know about your production expertise with *Y'Never Know* I told Gene I thought you might be interested working on Estelle's project."

He let out a sigh. "As well as being in therapy myself."

"That too," I said. "Actually, that's a positive credential in this case."

"I wish you had first told me about your idea, Jerry. I don't see a fit here."

"No? Why is that?"

"This is all Stella's brainchild. Gene's helped with putting some philanthropic donation players together, but you have to realize that a David Two is exactly what they're *not* looking for now. Gene's deeply in love with Stella, you know, and can't have her fail in this endeavor of hers. My involvement might very well screw things up and endanger the project. And that might put the marriage on the rocks, even before the ship has time to set its sails."

"Why do you think you'd be such a liability?"

"I don't know what I would be, but I come with a lot of lost baggage. I told you only a small part of what went on when I was producing *Y'Never Know*. There's a whole nother episode that just speaks volumes to the bad timing I bring along with me. Gene knows of it, I'm sure Stella doesn't and you don't either."

"Well, tell me."

"I don't want to get into the weeds. It's all there in a chapter called, *Man Weds Bot* in my memoirs. It's finished now and with an agent. There's a copy in the package I brought you."

"Your memoirs? You're too young to be writing memoirs." I said.

"Well, it's just a bunch of actual events that happened to me since graduating Cornell that somehow formed a pattern of self-doubt and insecurity—from some poor decision-making on my part and some outright fraud on the part of others. I thought people my age might benefit from reading about it, that's all."

"Interesting," I said. "What's it called?"

"*Recisions: The Way Back to a New Start.*"

"Recisions. That's a word I'm not acquainted with. Reviewing a decision?"

"Exactly. It unwinds time back to the point where we made choices in life that affect our lives now. It's part autobiographical and part historical and part philosophical and part rubbish."

I laughed. "It sounds a little like the book I've just finished: *Quantum Agnostics*.

"Oh? What's that about?" David asked.

"The author makes the claim that we live our lives over and over again in the same way, born and reborn for all eternity in our own space/time warp—same birth date and year, same parents, same environments, same world events, same hopes, same fears. When we die, there's no such thing as an 'afterlife' to redeem our sins, or look forward to a better life. So we don't get to go to an external heaven or hell. We make a heaven or hell for ourselves living right here on Earth. And it's only through that revelation that we can take responsibility for our present lives to better understand and improve ourselves with every iteration."

"So everything is predestined? Out of our control? Just the opposite of *Recisions*," he laughed.

"Look, I just finished the book. Why don't you take it with you when you leave. We can trade and then meet some day and have a good laugh together."

"Absolutely!" David exclaimed. "Sounds like a great idea!"

"Certainly better than finding you a spot on FreeGT," I replied, not meaning to sound so callous.

So the topic of David spending some time in a psych ward until Gene and Estelle returned was never discussed. As Estelle admitted to me when discussing Peter getting a psychological evaluation, it was a lousy idea, making judgments about others' mental states. (But had we followed Kamala Harris's plea to have Donald Trump's mental competency checked out along with her own after his taking office back in 2025, we might have spared the nation years of what can only be described now as a growing, insipid paranoia by gun owners and other Second Amendment MAGA freaks.)

Nevertheless, David left his *Recisions* manuscript with me. And I also discovered in the package, a *Y'Never Know* cap and tee-shirt, no doubt part of the concession stand overflow he had when the show was unceremoniously closed back in April, 2026. I had the rest of the afternoon to skim over his 'memoirs' and particularly the chapter *Man Weds Bot,* the title of which intrigued me, at first thinking the 'man' was David himself.

Which of course it wasn't, knowing that David had married a lovely showgirl-business partner now separated from him and living in Boston with their two young daughters. No, the chapter dealt with the period right after a City building inspector—taking the side of jealous producers in the area—closed the Rialto Theatre claiming that it was still unsafe, after David had spent more than a half-million to shore up its back wall for a C of O.

David had a friend from Cornell who was best friends with some rich guy who had fallen head over heels with an 'influencer' on a popular internet platform. He had bought virtually everything Roberta was promoting, and was desperate to meet her in person. She was very lovely, very bright of course, but only wanted a business relationship with this man. And try as he might, he couldn't arrange to meet her. This went on for some time, for over a year in fact, which only added to his frustration, now a growing obsession. At the end of his emotional rope, he impulsively proposed to her.

Roberta was Influencing for a corporate giant into all sorts of items geared to Millennial and Gen Z viewers—home furnishings, clothing, personal accessories, toiletries, gifts of all kinds for engagements, weddings, bridal and baby showers etc. Obviously, they were aware of (let's call him Tim) Tim's obsession with her. And some maniac in their public relations department came up with a show-stopper involving their newest, hottest product—a dual-screen twin-lens smartphone that could take 3-D photos and videos. What was this PR brainstorm? Roberta would accept Tim's proposal of marriage.

There was just one tiny drawback: Roberta wasn't a woman or even a person. She was a bot with enough graphics processing units and an embedded algorithm to put tears into the eyes of an on-line chess hustler. She started flirting with Tim on a personal level now, leading him on to a romantic fantasy, all being part of an advertising campaign for their new phone. He was beginning to smell a rat.

And then came the day of reckoning where she announced to Tim she was merely a chatbot, disguised as a human Influencer—but would marry him anyway—live and in person—with the introduction of her corporate sponsor's I-Dphone—I-D standing for In-Depth. It sounded crazy—and it was crazy—but this was back in 2026 and the live Splinternet craziness, replacing going out and spending money in recessionary times, was 'in'.

Much to the amazement of the sponsors (for they had already arranged for a Tim stand-in) the real Tim accepted Roberta's offer. He realized, of course, he had been taken for a ride, but negotiated with the sponsor for a buy back of all the items Roberta had influenced him to purchase. And the sponsor went along with this, because Tim had a story here that could sink the entire promotion. He also asked for a nominal $100,000 for mental/emotional damage their scam caused him and they agreed to that as well.

The sponsor wanted the wedding to be held at their corporate headquarters in California, but Tim was adamant it be held in New York, his hometown, so his family and friends could attend this live idiotic event. The sponsor reluctantly agreed to Tim's request. Now it was just a question of where and when.

And that's where David's part of the story comes in. Tim had been keeping his friend apprised about this forthcoming silliness and his friend knew David well and the problems David was having with the Rialto's closing, just at the time he was beginning to make some real money with *Y'Never Know* and paying back investors, his friend being one of them. And so this was a no-brainer. The sponsor could rent the theatre to perform the wedding and take it streaming live on the sponsor's internet site. And so long as David was not charging an audience, he and the sponsor persuaded (read: bribed) officials to reopen the theatre for this one-time promotional gig.

Of course, David was not doing this out of the goodness of his heart. He asked for $100 grand as the one-day rental fee. The sponsors offered half of that—and they settled for $75,000. That found money would go a long way in fully paying back his wife's family and then temporarily holding off a small group of investors who wanted to put David in jail for fraud.

And so, on the third Saturday in June, 2026, at 1:00 in the afternoon, a *Man Weds Bot* ceremony—the first ever—was performed live with an interdenominational 'minister', flowers, a wedding cake, organ music, a lively audience, and plenty of I-Dphones to spread around and hold up to the camera's eye, showing the amazing three-dimensional effects of a revolutionary new twin-lens smartphone. Roberta radiant in a flowing white gown covering her GPU walking mechanism, Tim magnificent in his tux, and the AI lighting, props and backdrop made the entire production an overflowing 3D success.

Except for one thing.

1:00 in the afternoon in New York was 12:00 noon in Madison, Wisconsin… the exact time another wedding was to begin between a Black orthopedic surgeon and his White operating room nurse fiancee. The carnage that was to happen minutes later would be known as MM because like 9/11, the Madison Massacre was too incomprehensible, too traumatic to fully spell out. And naturally as the news broke, the networks broke into their programming to report the latest from that killing ground. *Man Weds Bot* wasn't even noted by reviewers that afternoon, and its tape didn't even make news that Saturday evening or Sunday's morning news shows to lighten the tension. It was all MM.

And so, when David spoke of the bad timing he brings along with him, well, of course he in no way could have known about these two simultaneous events happening—one of which is still vivid in our memory, the other long forgotten but for the ingenious product it introduced, now part of the visual capturing of our national ennui.

Wednesday morning was to be my first attempt at getting out of bed and using a walker. The cast on my knee had set, I was looking forward to standing upright for the first time in four days, and I needed to use the restroom, raised toilet seat et al.

The attending nurse served me breakfast and then brought in a walker with a potty attached to its frame. No, I said, I was going to go all the way. The potty was removed, and with a little help, I raised myself to a sitting position on the side of my bed, put two bare feet on the floor and gripped the sides of the walker with every ounce in my body. And yes, I'll admit to having some vertigo as I took a few staggered shuffles towards the bathroom, lifting the walker ever so slightly with every step, the nurse just ahead opening and then closing the bathroom door behind me.

But my first attempt to be fully independent in restroom matters was a smashing success. Peeling off my gown, I peed, took a crap, brought the walker into the shower stall, rinsed my hair with a bar of soap found there and took a long-needed relaxing hot shower. I even thought about shaving—except there wasn't a razor or shaving cream on the shelf over the basin. Then after drying myself I put my gown back on, knocked on the door and was let out. I would never again return to the bed; I could now reverse position myself with the walker to be able to sit in a chair, my right leg splayed out like a too-tall passenger on a domestic flight coach section aisle seat. It would take time before I regained enough muscle power in my arms to rise and descend on my own but at least I was up and about.

I was going to be released today at 10AM and picked up by Caroline and Paul but first on the list of to-dos was getting dressed in the clothes I had on me at the wedding. The hospital had nicely washed and folded my underpants and Bermuda shorts, somehow washing out the bloodstains on the right leg side, but I decided to wear the white *Y'Never Know* tee-shirt and cap David had brought me instead of the shirt I wore at the wedding. With some help from the attending nurse all was accomplished, including putting on a new pair of white cotton socks, a gift from the hospital, to go with my loafers.

Next on the list was a check out by Dr. Winslow and my final X-ray, just to be sure the knee insert was where it should be upon my release. And instead of a gurney, I would be using the walker to navigate the hallway to the elevator down to the X-ray room. The nurse packed up all of my personal belongings remaining in the room and assured me they would be added to my other belongings held at the front desk when I checked out. Then a second nurse joined us.

Each step down the hallway to the elevator was putting me into a coordinated rhythm involving forward movement, balance, and visual estimation. And even with nurses on either side of me, I was beginning to feel more confident about using a walker. If this was to be my fate, so be it. I would master this part of my rehabilitation and move on to a cane in no time.

The X-ray was taken and compared to the one taken Monday and it showed a perfect match, meaning the insert hadn't moved. The cast could come off, Dr. Winslow assured me, in about a week and after stitches were removed an elastic velcro-strapped brace would wrap around the knee when I was up and about and could be removed at night. I could then begin physical therapy to regain strength and flexibility, but putting full weight on my right leg was still problematical. My physical therapist would set the timetable for my return to normalcy, obviously depending on my progress working out.

That part being accomplished, the nurses and I returned to the elevator and brought up to the reception area on the ground floor where I was met by Paul and Caroline. Paul had brought my new lightweight aluminum foldable walker and showed me how easy it was to expand and set up and I proudly traded the hospital's walker for my own, saying thanks and goodbye to the nurses for that morning's outing. Now, all that was left was to get my possessions from the front desk—and possibly the bill for my stay at Memorial.

My possessions were all there, shirt, watch, wallet, belt, sunglasses, phone, signed copies of the release forms, David's manuscript—but no bill. That would have to wait until the cast came off, all stitches removed, and only then would those procedures be added to the final accounting and once paid, my relationship with Memorial be officially resolved. So I didn't say my goodbyes. I said, see you again soon. The staff knowingly, silently, smiled back.

Paul had left his car back at the house so we all piled into Caroline's as it had a much larger interior than Paul's and I needed to try out folding and unfolding my walker while sitting in both the front passenger side and in the back. Caroline, after all, would be doing the driving for a while, and if I needed to go somewhere, I would be the passenger with a waist-high contraption that would have to be folded and placed somewhere where it wouldn't interfere with the driver. And so we worked on several scenarios with me getting in and out of the passenger seat and Caroline first assisting with unfolding and folding the walker, then placing it on the back seat and then me trying it alone.

Everything was possible. Everything seemingly going to plan. And in the *Recisions* of things, all perfectly avoidable had I used my eyes in the back of my head to review, or rather preview, the recent past's traumatic events.

We drove home mainly in silence, each of us considering the ramifications of this latest adventure into the unknown. I knew there were changes that would be affecting my lifestyle; mobility probably #1, but also safety and isolation close seconds. Could I still dictate and act on my preferences? I had no idea.

CHAPTER 19

I can't describe just how wonderful it was to be back home. Caroline had stocked the refrigerator and the cupboards with all of my favorites—and Paul had dutifully rearranged the studio so that there was enough room for myself and the walker to traverse it, bringing all of Ruthie's art materials upstairs and into an empty closet, leaving only a chair and a small desk. He even built a clothing rack so I could hang pants and jackets, and brought most of my clothes and shoes from the master bedroom along with a chest of drawers that he and Caroline managed to carry down the winding flight. And lastly, a newly-delivered raised toilet seat for the studio's bathroom!

The one sticking point was a shower stall. It couldn't be built outwardly onto the porch, for the pipes would freeze in winter. And it couldn't be built inwardly since it would jut into the kitchen. The only possibility was to extend the bathroom parallel to the side of the house where a walk-in pantry now existed. Well, I thought, the pantry was hardly used and I could store my wine, beer, soda, pickles, olives, various condiments, cans, plastic items and bar–be-cue accessories down in the basement. How I would manage the basement stairs was quite another matter. It was more important to have my daily shower, maybe two, especially in summer. I'd have a contractor look the situation over later in the week.

The three of us had lunch together on the porch. I noticed the chuppa platform was now just a few yards away, fully exposed to the elements which would damage the tongue-and-groove flooring. I told Paul to find a tarp in the garage and cover the platform. Then maybe Saturday he and Caroline, and Peter if he was available, could clear out a space in the woods for its eventual use as a winter shelter for the deer. Paul merely shook his head and rolled his eyes.

Caroline had given up her 'off' day Sunday for the wedding on Saturday, so I told her to take off the following day, Thursday, as a make-up day as well as Labor Day coming up the following week. I brought up the fact of my knee cast coming off around that time, and that I'd be looking for a physical therapist. Would Chris be interested? Perhaps they had already discussed it, and I knew of their non-competing agreement with each other, but she was non-committal.

After Caroline left, Paul and I retired to the living room couch. The next day, I found out then, was an all-day meeting Paul was required to attend in the City and so he would stay with me that night but would be heading to the City before I awoke. I would be all alone in the house for that day. I wasn't concerned in the least. And, I assured him that after Labor Day and the start of classes, I'd be fine being alone as well. Besides, Peter and Julie would be returning from their trip and perhaps Peter would stay for a while at the house instead of heading straight back to California.

I knew the anxiety I was causing in my newly limiting condition but I felt confident I could manage running the household as before the accident. Handling the walker was getting easier with every step. And living only on the ground floor of the house wouldn't be a problem as everything I needed was there, and if there was something I needed Caroline could get it for me. Things would go on as before, I assured Paul, in much the same way. And I would walk all by myself, even climb stairs, with time and practice.

"Dad, you really need to give some thought about what you want the end-game to look like. You're turning ninety in a couple of weeks. It's time to think about that."

"I hear The Rappaports in your voice, dear.

"It doesn't have to be The Villages. There are lots of other places, some even around here."

"Then why move at all?"

"You'd have 'round-the-clock care and be able to socialize with people your age. Out here you're all alone with nobody..."

"I have Caroline, remember."

"I'm sure she's a very stimulating conversationalist," he said snidely. "I'm talking about your mind, and your spirit, not your physical condition. I know how she helps you survive here, but surviving and living are two different things. Your mind needs stimulation, Dad, to live fully, to be part of what's going on beyond Lois Lane."

"I've lost a lot of friends in the past few years, dear. They were intellectual companions to me. So, really, what's left? Painting classes? Chess? Writing my memoirs, like David? I've already been around the world with your mother. Everything I ever wanted to do has been done. And now, mastering a raised toilet seat will be icing on the cake."

"David? You mean Gene's older brother?"

"The same."

"Writing his memoirs? He's too young to be writing memoirs."

"That's exactly what I told him."

"You spoke to him?"

"He visited me in the hospital yesterday afternoon and dropped off the manuscript. And we chatted for a while. He's a bright guy who's made some bad decisions along the way."

"I know. Remember, I related to you what his parents told me at the Marriott dinner. They never mentioned he was writing his memoirs. And why would they? He has to do something *meaningful* to keep busy. He just can't hole up in that theatre of his."

"The City Council is going to tell him this Friday what they want done with the Rialto," I said. "The theatre people in the neighborhood and the preservation committee want to restore it and rename it after Leonard Bernstein, and the City wants to condemn the building and put up a 40-storey migrant hotel."

"Would the City pay David something for it? Then he could finally pay off his debts."

"He's paid back a lot of people already. Just not his family. I would think they're all rooting for the City to take the space off David's hands and get a little something back."

"And Goliath?"

"Goliath? Who's he?" I asked

"David's younger but wiser brother," Paul quipped.

"I don't know where Gene stands on this," I said. "He's very protective of David, but realizes David has to do some meaningful work as you say. Gene's not much of a theatre buff."

"And David?"

"I think he wants to restore the theatre and produce shows there. He's caught the producer bug. And the 75th anniversary of *West Side*

Story is coming up. He'd love to produce that. And that would be fine with his wife, he told me, because she loved the time they were doing *Y'Never Know* together. They never divorced, you know, they only separated. And he told me that after he repaid his debt to her family, they did a 180 over him. They're now hoping their daughter reconciles with him for the sake of their two young daughters who greatly miss their Dad."

"Quite a dilemma for David."

"Yeah, it's spelled out at the very end of his memoir as unfinished business."

"Does he have a name for it?"

"It's called *Recisions*."

"I think that's some kind of legal or financial term."

"Well, in David's definition it's a return to the time of decision-making and looking at all the possible consequences of our choices."

"Were that only possible, Dad. Hindsight is always 20/20. I remember how you kept berating yourself for not locking up Rachel's bike during tennis week. You had a meltdown."

Paul had struck a nerve; I hadn't the words to go on. I felt my eyes swelling with tears.

"Sorry for that, Dad," Paul managed to say, with genuine contriteness in his voice.

"It's okay." I said. "And you're basically right. We can't know with any certainty how things will turn out; we can only go by our best instincts at the time. And we can't keep beating ourselves up for the bad choices we make. And there's always Mom's balance theory."

"Let's have some wine," Paul proffered to change the subject. While he was in the kitchen opening a bottle, my phone rang. It was

Estelle, all nicely suntanned calling from the yacht, now moored in Palm Beach, Florida.

"Gene's gone with his grandparents to take them back home," she said, "and I'm here with Peter and Julie and they want to talk with you first."

"Put them on," I said. "I'm here with your Dad and he probably wants to say 'hi' too."

A long distance virtual family reunion—on a twin-screen double lens smartphone with a Skypescape video conferencing platform—made possible with Peter and Julie on one end and Paul and I on the other all talking over each other. Which is exactly what happened. From the yacht we heard of nightly celebrations of one kind or another—Erskine's Silver Anniversary being the biggest and best. The weather was warm and mild, the crew exceptionally talented for talent night, the food superb, the sunsets unbelievable. It sounded wonderful to a couple of lonely men in the middle of nowhere, with only raised toilet seats on their minds.

After restocking the boat the next day, the three couples and the Erskine's two daughters would be coming back to Westport and be there on Labor Day, with Peter and Julie returning to Julie's apartment for the night and then perhaps coming out to stay with me for a few days, after which Peter would return to California. I got from what they were saying that maybe they hadn't announced their Australian plans yet, but that they probably intended to before their trip was over.

Getting Past Z

Having them stay with me, knowing that Paul was to begin classes later that week, was a blessing.

But then Estelle wanted to speak to me in private, and so I instructed Paul to then get a tarp from the garage and to cover the chuppa platform with it.

"Gene mentioned to me that David might be interested in doing some production work on FreeGT," she began. "I think he would be qualified with some training but I've staffed up everything but for one position, and I don't think David would want it in any event."

"What is it?"

"Well, you know FreeGT is running seven days a week. We've filled the producer slot for the weekdays, but we're looking around for a producer for Saturday and Sunday. It's really a part-time gig job, and the pay reflects that. We can offer $1,000 for the two days, about 5 hours each day from 3PM to 8PM. So that's four grand a month, maybe fifty grand a year before taxes. Down to the core when you're living in the Big Apple. But at least he'd be working again."

"What does Gene think?"

"Well, he says it's my baby, so he's leaving it up to me. But he reminded me of David's drinking problem and maybe I should talk to David's therapist first to get his opinion."

"We could just as well be talking about Peter," I said. "I'm having a *deja vu* all over again."

"Somehow Peter moderated greatly on this trip," Estelle said. "He's like his old self. He has half a glass of wine, if that, with meals. Never hard liquor. It's quite amazing. Something's up."

"Maybe something's down... down under," I hinted, enjoying my role as Australian secret keeper.

"Grandpa, stop it!" she laughed. "You're the worst!" I got the immediate impression she had talked with Julie and knew all about the couple's upcoming plans.

"Well, what about David? Do you think he could handle the job if he's committed and sober?"

"I'm going to leave that until after we get back. I first need to talk to David about it and see if he's interested. And if he is, Gene's idea is a good one and I'll try to get hold of his therapist for an appointment, but the guy takes most of August off each year so I can't reach him until after Labor Day in any event."

"You should call David before you get back. Just to feel him out."

"I thought I'd do that on his birthday. It's just a couple of days from now. Gene is going to call him with birthday wishes and then I could mention the job opening, see if he might be interested and then get his okay about talking to his therapist because the job really requires that. Everyone on the staff, especially the weekday producer I hired had to go through a rigorous mental evaluation. We looked at support people who are interested in psychology, maybe were psychology majors in college or have a master's degree in psychology and are counselors themselves, who understand all aspects of cognitive therapy, maybe who have been in therapy themselves, so they can better interface with the licensed therapists we'll have moderating the discussions on the site."

"That's really a mixed message. Just like in Peter's case, suppose the therapist has reservations about David's drinking. Would you go along with his evaluation?"

"Of course."

"You later thought it was a crazy idea to have Peter evaluated."

"Grandpa, this is a different, much different situation. Peter wasn't in therapy and didn't know the therapist I was going to recommend. David has been in therapy with the same doctor for over a decade so he understands the process and wouldn't feel hurt or humiliated. There's much more at stake bringing David aboard FreeGT than Peter bringing a gun to our wedding."

"How so?"

"The role of producer would be critical in a life or death situation. He would have to work hand in hand with the therapist in charge for each of those five hours and be super rational throughout. I know David can relate to the therapist part in all of this but he'd have to be absolutely sober for the technical part. If something unexpected happened on the set or even remotely he'd have to make an instantaneous decision on what to do. We'll have a seven-second transmission delay, but even so, this is live as you know, with possibly some unstable, in-crisis people needing immediate help and I can't afford a mistake or poor judgment here."

"Your Dad and I were just discussing thinking things through before making decisions. There are no guarantees here, love. All the training in the world can't predict the unexpected."

"Well, that is my one condition. Complete sobriety—no opiates or alcohol—before coming on the set and being on the set. If he can go along with that, we can start training immediately and I can offer him that weekend job when we open in October."

"I don't know what he'll say about it."

"Neither do I, Grandpa, but sobriety is the by-word here."

We said our goodbyes just as Paul returned after tarping over the platform. It was dinner time and we found some fresh shrimp salad Caroline had made to go with our white wine. I told Paul about Estelle's offer to David but Paul was skeptical. "As you see, drinking is still on the menu for me, Dad, in spite of cutting back. It's tough to do by yourself. Maybe David should get into AA. I was thinking of doing that, but then the job offer came along and I knew I had to greatly moderate. Breaking an addiction is a lot of just plain willpower. I don't know how much willpower David has."

"A new job, new goals, new responsibility. He might be able to do it on his own like you did."

"Well, Estelle will know what to do if he falls off the wagon. She's always been very steady, very conscientious. And she's making all the tough decisions on this project of hers."

"You know what she once said to me about your drinking?"

"No, tell me."

"She said, if you don't hurt anyone and it adds to your sociability it's probably all right. But for how long could that go on; that was the question."

"It's like anything else, Dad. You shape up or ship out. If you're surrounded by good people who only want the best for you, you shape up for them because you don't want to lose their friendship, their companionship. And so you look out for them and they look out for you."

"So this may be a real break for David and he'll give up his drinking because of the good people surrounding him, wanting him to succeed. Put in those terms, it only makes sense."

Getting Past Z

True to his word, Paul was up and out of the house before I awoke in the studio, Ruthie's day bed not exactly the most comfortable way to get a good night's sleep. The leg was not bothering me, but using the walker everywhere was fatiguing. With Caroline off that Thursday I would be by myself until Paul returned in the late afternoon. Then, I thought, we might want to go out to a restaurant for dinner. I needed to see how the walker behaved.

The thought came to me then, after reading a little of David's *Recisions*—and finding some of it, but not all of it by any means—enlightening—that maybe I should start a memoir, but begin the timeline not with college days or even during my marriage to Ruthie, but perhaps four or five years in the past when the first nationwide uprisings against the government took place. Exactly when and where? Spring of 2024 and the student rebellion at Columbia, Harvard and other elite ivy-league schools with their pro-Palestine, antisemitic protests over the Gaza War. Or later that June with Biden's disastrous debate with Trump, showcasing his age and verbal gaffes, then pulling out of the Presidential race and placing V.P. Kamala Harris in his stead. And then later in the summer, the assassination attempts on Trump's life. Or days before the November election and Trump's refusal to condemn the Puerto Rican racial insults of an unvetted warm-up comedian at one of his rallies, leading to the surprising 'toss-up state' win of Pennsylvania's 19 electoral votes, handing the Presidential election to Trump with his installation in January, 2025 along with a Republican Senate and a Republican House. Jigsaw pieces resulting in more, not less, nervousness and anxiety about the National state of affairs that Trump's 'conservative' administration was unable to contain with forward-looking rhetoric and backward-looking excuses.

It was beginning to line up—social disorders of every kind that was daily fodder for the tabloid press. Add to that, tariffs and the dollar-based debt crises throughout the world, the dollar finally giving way as the world's 'reserve currency' to China's yuan, resulting in a beastly recession and stock market crash. Not to mention the alien incursions along the coastal states, proliferation of undetectable Zirguns, drugs and MM. Yes, these past five years or so were the most traumatic and difficult to comprehend—in my lifetime anyway. And at 90, I had seen some pretty traumatic rough stuff throughout my life. Maybe other people would be interested in my look back. David, at least, thought so. And now everyone was writing their memoirs, right? At the very least, a drawn out rationale for not rolling over and playing dead.

Personally, I was economically in good shape. I hadn't made many poor choices regarding investments as David had, and in fact had made a little money with my utility mutual funds, pulling out everything with Trump's 2024 election win. So I didn't have a market meltdown story or a fraudulent crypto investment scheme to tell. But I could see the handwriting on the wall by mid-2024 and the divide over the economy, immigration, guns and abortion—the issues that were to propel Trump to the presidency.

These were tough division-makers for the nation, but especially for Republicans who took hard-line stances on most issues and made Trump, already a saint in many people's eyes, the Massiah. He was cognitively on his way out, spending his days wandering through the sand traps of his mind—yet every so often (like every day) on his Truth Social blog, his inspired message directly from the top of Mt.

Sinai, inciting his ragged MAGA base (now renamed Make America Gag Again) to even greater displays of antagonism and hatred (not to mention his GoFundMe-like TIP appeal for his legal bills). It was time to put him away, the convicted felon that he was, but everyone realized the martyred downside to that scenario. The Democrats, smartly, didn't go near the subject—neither a Presidential pardon nor incarceration—letting the courts very slowly, very deliberately, hang Trump out to dry.

Perhaps a memoir of what was happening in my life around that time would be valuable to some younger readers who found themselves perplexed by the divisions about them, then and now. Peter had laid it out for me early on, though I didn't get it at the time. Then, there were the Z's and there were the Not Z's, one side wishing to evolve, one side wishing to revolt. And now, four years later, they were trying to reconcile seeing that extremes were killing them off, literally and figuratively. It was sad to see our children and grandchildren bewildered at the lawless chaos about them, not having any guidance on what to do about this breakdown in order, responsibility and civility. And it was tragic to see how many bright, well-educated Millennials and Z's were succumbing to escapism in any form available, even moving halfway around the globe to settle in a country without friends or family. For the more I thought about it, the more I was convinced that Peter and Julie had given up on Americanization, and the nightmare aspects of the American Dream, as much as they saw new opportunities in Australia. They chose to abandon their friends and family to make a new reality for themselves, believing that there was no way to breach the oligarchy of America and the limitations to their freedoms such ingrained supplication to wealth and power laid upon them. Better to cut and run before even that option was closed.

My advice would have been to try to work through the system and gradually change it as Estelle outlined to me when she differentiated her long term goals against those of Peter. I felt with Trump finally out of the way, and a more compassionate President, the country could now move forward rationally and optimistically, knowing too well where we had been, unable to commit to stability and innovation, justice and reform. We were stuck in an 'old man's' past, the world whizzing past us, scientifically, culturally, politically and now economically. And so four more years were wasted in recession and economic stagnation. Perhaps this was to be America's new approach to upward mobility—ingrained now as Americanization or The New American Dream: Either somehow work two jobs and struggle to keep up, inherit your parents' life savings, win the lottery, or fall by the wayside on an air mattress and a leaky tent. The Middle Class be Damned!

Would anyone read the memoir, the ramblings of a 90-year-old semi-hermit unable to fully care for himself? It was something to think about as I pushed open the kitchen door with my walker, and bobbled into the back yard with a backpack holding a bagful of dog kibbles for the deer.

Paul returned around 5 PM after a full day of BofE meetings discussing topics not only of curricula, but of student behavior and new security measures in and out of the classrooms. I wanted to hear more and suggested we go out to dinner, my first venture in a social situation with my walker in hand.

We ate at a Mexican restaurant with a wheelchair ramp at its entrance so I could easily navigate into its colorful dining room. I knew about their enchiladas because occasionally I would have them deliver, and we ordered a couple of plates. Over Corona beers I asked Paul what he thought about my idea of starting a memoir spanning this past decade, but more closely focused on the Trump Presidency, and the failed possibilities of his second term.

"You and a million others," he said. "Many Washington insiders and Bidump chatbots. What could you add to their despair?"

"Simply perspective. I've always been non-political, really, at least outwardly. It was bad for business, so I rarely let my feelings known. I had my views but never expressed them publicly, everything welling up inside of me. Maybe some people would be interested in reading about a guy who kept his mouth shut until the very end and then let it all pour forth."

"Well, at least it would give you something to do," he said, tossing off my idea.

"Something to do...." I shot back, his flip comment angering me somewhat.

"I hate to think about you in the house all day, wasting away, unable to fully get around like you used to. You really should be thinking of expanding outwardly, not withdrawing inwardly writing a memoir."

I took a long sip of beer. "This is beginning to sound like a conspiracy," I said. "Everyone in the family is telling me I have to give up my place and move to The Villages."

"They have programs you'd really enjoy. And it's safe there and you'd have people your age to converse and interact with.

But it doesn't have to be The Villages. There are places here in Jersey..."

"Do you want this house?" I broke in.

"I've told you before, Dad, no. I'm fine where I am."

"When I die it's willed to you, you know."

"So change your will. Will it to Estelle or Peter. Or sell it now. I don't care what you do with the house. I care about you, not the house. At least before the accident you had your tennis buddies and had some friends you bicycled and played chess in the park with. Now all of that is off the table. You have Caroline and that's it. And I don't think she appreciates being put in the role of chauffeur."

"She gets paid for it."

"Believe me, Dad, I know! You think she wouldn't find such a cushy job if you moved away? As a hospice registered nurse she's in great demand, and probably would make even more in that capacity. She's under-utilized. And you probably realize that."

I had to think about what my son was telling me because deep down I knew he was right. With my leg the way it was, a lot of activities I used to do and found great pleasure doing now had vanished overnight. He had made his point; I was essentially alone, with curtailed mobility, and I could see myself getting depressed over it, a steady decline to finality.

"Tell you what," I said as our dishes arrived, "For Thanksgiving, I'll speak to Gene about going down to Florida and visiting with The Rappaports. No promises. Just a look about for a couple of days or so. Just scoping it out."

Paul was ecstatic. "That would be great, Dad! I'm so glad to hear that!"

"Caroline can check on the house and make sure the pipes don't freeze."

"Your first full venture away from home in what? Six, seven years?"

"But if I find it's not for me, I'll be coming home to stay, so don't get your hopes up."

"Of course not. But dinner's on me, Dad! Woo-hoo!

CHAPTER 20

My visiting The Villages was in no way a commitment to move I kept telling myself on the way home and I didn't want it to spread around so I got Paul to swear an oath of secrecy for the time being. I needed time to look at all the ramifications of that decision—the three or four steps outlined in *Recisions.* David had made a point in the book that the prime factors involved in decision-making had to be written down and dated; they couldn't just be memorized or revised in one's head. That way, you had a tangible record of the choices available to you and when they were made -- a timeline—most valuable when circumstances changed that altered your final course of action. It could be as simple as taking some friend's advice, or as complicated as trying to meet a newly revised business deadline—but whatever the case, the pros and cons of what went into your thinking at the time was essential. And it was *your* thinking—not some impersonal algorithm that did the computation. In fact, he changed the 'A' in AI from *Artificial* Intelligence to *Applied* Intelligence, meaning that human brains were designed to control the brains of our creations—and would always be so.

As I've said, I felt a visceral connection towards David from the time I met him at the wedding. He would be finding out tomorrow, Friday, about what the City Council's plans were for the Rialto—whether to restore it, or demolish it—and my heart went out to him. I'm sure, after reading *Recisions* he had a Plan "A" and a Plan "B" for whichever way the Council voted. But there was really no good outcome here. He wanted to remain as Preservation Committee custodian and see the theatre's restoration to its conclusion, which would mean raising even more money before the first show could be produced. And if they voted to demolish for a 40-storey migrant hotel, he would have but two weeks to relocate. Which only meant that Estelle's proposal—to find sobriety and a part-time job as a FreeGT producer—might be his best and only option, a Plan "C"—C for Compromise or maybe, Cornered.

And to top it all off, the following day, Saturday, September 3rd, was David's 40th birthday. But no one in his family would be around to make some kind of celebration for him. They would still be on the yacht coming back from Florida and wouldn't be returning to New York until Monday, Labor Day. And from everything I could gather, his wife, kids and in-laws would be in Boston. He would be alone, not good for someone turning over a milestone year.

And so, I thought, maybe it was up to me to at least have a drink and dinner with him. If he had finished *Quantum Agnostics* we could then re-exchange books and have that good laugh as promised. He would have already talked to Estelle about the FreeGT spot so we could parse that out as well. I'd call him the next day to find out the Council's decision and to invite him out to dinner on Saturday, perhaps with Paul driving, because getting into the City now by myself was out of the question. I was sure Paul and David would have a lot in common so it would be a fine evening in the City.

Friday morning Paul was busy with paperwork, preparing for the following Wednesday's public school opening in New York City. He could stay until Sunday afternoon, he said, but then wanted to get back to his place to avoid the Labor Day traffic. And as I had already given Caroline the entire holiday weekend off, I would be alone once more. It was all so curious to me: I had never experienced aloneness, isolation, until after being crippled by my bad knee. Now I was beginning to understand not only the limitations to my movements, but the helplessness that might arise were I to lose my balance, fall and injure myself, be without my phone for assistance. Maybe I could get one of those #911 pendants... and maybe the Florida trip would flip the coin.

Caroline served Paul and I lunch out on the porch, it being a beautiful late summer day... and then around 1PM, alone in the studio, I placed a Skypescape call to David.

"Hi, David," I said, now looking at a new haircut on a radiant face.

"Hi, Jerry," he responded, "How's country life treating you?"

"Not bad. It's a beautiful day out here. Did you get an answer from the Council?"

"Yes, this morning. They had invited me to attend their meeting in person and I did."

"And?"

"West Side Story buried. Forty Migrant Storeys in the clouds," he cracked.

"Oh, I'm so sorry, I was thinking it would go your way,"

"Well, in a way it did go my way. I got almost as much as I asked for in compensation for the work already done on the wall, and other expenses I had."

"Oh, that's better."

"Yup. I asked for half a million, and I knew they wouldn't go for that, so they countered at a quarter million and they knew I wouldn't go for that. In fact, they knew I would probably drag these negotiations into the courts and that would tie them up for months. So then they offered me three hundred thousand and I countered for three twenty-five and they accepted! They wrote out a check to me on the spot. I have until September 15th to vacate."

"You're happy with that?"

"It means I can pay back my Grandparents, Stepdad, and Gene. Each put in 100 g's, y'know

"No, I didn't know."

"Well, that's what I owe them. And so my debts to the family are all now taken care of. Which leaves me twenty-five grand to get drunk on."

"I have a better idea," I said. "Don't get drunk now. Get drunk tomorrow night, on your birthday with me and my son Paul. We'd like to come in and celebrate with you."

"Ahhh, Jerry... so nice of you to think of me like that. But I've made other plans, I'm afraid. I'll be unavailable."

"Really?"

"Yes. really. You won't even be able to reach me. I can't tell you how relieved I feel, like the feeling I had when I was producing *Y'Never Know* and saw lines stretched down 46th waiting for the next showing. Exhilarating doesn't even describe it."

"Well, all I can say is, Happy Birthday!"

"Thank you, Jerry. When I get back, we'll get together, I promise."

"Don't get too drunk."

"Nah. I'm too high to get drunk," he laughed. And for reasons still a mystery to me, I laughed along.

Paul and I divided the delicious meatloaf Caroline had made for us before leaving for the day. She would be taking Saturday off without pay so that she and Chris could have the 3-day Labor Day weekend all to themselves and a small holiday with friends at the Jersey Shore. I had indirectly brought up physical therapy as being the next step for full recovery for me after the cast was removed later that next week or early in the week following. I wanted to get some idea of Chris's rates but as Paul noted, once Caroline left, I still hadn't received the hospital bill. Would I even have any money in my account left? I might have to get a bank loan, or even a second mortgage to pay that off. I could forget about any insurance coming through if I wasn't going to be perfectly honest about the shooting.

"No bank will give second mortgages or any mortgage to a retired, somewhat incapacitated 90-year-old. They know they'd have to foreclose and they just would rather not get involved. The loan manager will laugh you out of the bank, Dad."

"Well, you don't want the house. And Peter doesn't either. But maybe Estelle and Gene might be interested in buying it, renting it out for investment purposes."

"That's a thought, Dad. Maybe you could sell the house to Estelle and Gene, then rent it back so you could still live here."

"Wow, dear! Now, *that's* an interesting idea. Grandpa as tenant. Just the flip side of what kids out of school are doing these days, renting their rooms back from their parents."

"Nah, those rooms are already rented out to migrants. Their kids live in the basement. I'll be trying to teach them basic math in a week or so, so they can add two plus two, get a job, do something useful and finally move out."

"It's that bad?"

"Worse than I expected. TikTok doesn't teach math. Doesn't teach anything. The kids today have the world in the palm of their hand, but no palm of a teacher's hand to slap them silly into learning something of value. As if I was even allowed to do that."

"There are free on-line teaching courses, dear. You must know that, certainly."

"Sure, Dad. But it's not one-on-one in a classroom setting. There's no substitute for that. That's why they wanted me back. The kids were failing because their attention span had deserted them. That's what our meetings were all about last week. How to get their attention back when a pocket screen is ever so more enticing than a teacher lecturing up front."

"They banned phones in Public School classes years ago."

"Well, it hasn't worked. The kids have figured out ways around it. A phone represents independence. It's the idea of being on your own, the freedom to control your own destiny, your own lifestyle. Even before you know anything, before you have the skills to succeed in life."

"They're looking for easy answers. For some authority figure to clear the way for them."

"No, Dad, that's not it. The kids hate authority, adult supervision, they always have. They're looking at celebrities and Influencers and how to beat the system. And social media is now their escape route because it has so many rebellious pathways to explore. Pathways that lead to dead ends. They need to rethink the whole idea of social media. It's causing kids to drop out. It's *anti*-social media, really."

"Peter said the exact same thing to me when he stayed with me a few weeks ago."

"Well, there are exceptions. Peter, I'm proud to say, was always an 'A+' student. He loved being taught math and physics from me. And Estelle loved her Mom teaching her all about social studies. Clara and I often thought about taking the kids out of school and home-schooling them. But then, they wouldn't be with their friends, and wouldn't be able to socialize like they did. We wanted them to have normal teenage lives. And, remember, this was before the popularization of smartphones. Smart as in cunning. They're now so addictive you can't be without them. Even in the shower."

"I think you'll have an interesting return to teaching," I said.

He laughed. "Wake me up when class is over."

Getting Past Z

I didn't have to wait that long. I was awakened by a call around 9AM Saturday morning. It was from Estelle and Gene. I could see they were on the yacht and they looked concerned.

"Hello, Grandpa," Estelle said. "I hope I didn't wake you."

I used an updated gag line, "No, I had to see who was on the phone."

"We're here off Virginia Beach. The weather has been perfect."

"That's good, dear. Everything okay?"

"Well, that's what we're calling about," she said. "We can't seem to reach David. Have you talked with him lately?"

"As a matter of fact, yes I have. I called him yesterday to see if he'd go out with me and your Dad tonight for his birthday since you guys were still on the boat."

"And what did he say?"

"He had made other plans for tonight."

"Did you mention what we talked about, about becoming a FreeGT producer?"

"No, because you said you'd speak to him about it on his birthday, today sometime."

Gene interrupted at that point. "We tried calling him just before we called you. He's disconnected his phone and there's no GPS so we can't tell where he is."

"I wouldn't be too concerned," I said. "He sounded very upbeat to me. You know, he settled with the City Council yesterday."

"Yes," said Gene. "I knew about their decision for a few days now."

"You did?"

"I have some contacts on the Council," Gene said. "It wasn't going to go in David's favor. They just wanted to end the process without litigation so they can quickly build their damn hotel."

"Well, David thought the settlement was fair."

"He said that to you?"

"Well, not in those words, exactly, but he seemed pleased with it."

"Did he tell you what it was?"

"Yes. But I don't think I should be the one to tell you. Let him speak for himself."

"You said he thought the settlement was fair?"

"Yes."

"And he was upbeat?"

"I got that impression, yes."

Now it was Estelle's turn: "Grandpa, we're very concerned about him. Maybe he's still asleep or turned his phone off. We'll try again to reach him later."

"I told him a few days ago we'd be calling him on his birthday," Gene put in. "So he knew to expect a call from us. If he's not picking up because he's angry with us, remember, we invited him to come along with us on the cruise. We would be celebrating his 40th here with us."

"I think he wanted to be at the Council meeting yesterday. There was that conflict to deal with."

"Bad timing," Gene said, putting his hands up to his face and shaking his head.

"We'll try him again," said Estelle, "and we'll call you back if we hear from him."

"I'll be here with your Dad all day," I said with goodbyes.

Over breakfast I told Paul of Estelle and Gene's call to me earlier from Virginia Beach.

"Guilt trip," he said, buttering his toast. "You said Gene had known about the Council's decision days earlier? Why didn't he say something to David?"

"It was probably told to him in confidence," I proffered.

"Most surely it was," Paul said. "and that's why it's a guilt trip. Gene was the only one in the family looking out for his brother you told me once. And this time he was conflicted and couldn't help, so he's feeling rather guilty about it, I would think."

"He's really worried about his brother," I said. "You could hear it in his voice."

"Nice way to end a honeymoon," said Paul. "Glad I had those meetings."

"Maybe we could check on David. Maybe he's just not taking calls from his brother. It wouldn't hurt if I called just to say Happy Birthday."

"You did that already, Dad."

"Well, I could just tell him about Gene's concern about not reaching him on his birthday and to please take his call, or call him back, something like that," I said, finishing my coffee.

"You wanna bet he doesn't take your call either?"

"I don't do too well with bets," I said, remembering the thousand I now owed my Grandson.

"Okay, a gentleman's bet. Do you have your phone on you?"

"It's my Siamese Twin."

"So go ahead, call David."

I tried but a female-voiced bot came on after several rings to inform me that the phone had been temporarily disconnected.

"So now," said my son half-smirking, "join the guilt trip. It's somewhere off Virginia Beach."

Paul remained upstairs to complete his curricula for the Fall term that needed to be submitted by Tuesday, the day after Labor Day and the day before classes began in the New York City Public School system. It was a formality, but needed to be handed in for record keeping. Curious, since this could now be handled by AI, but apparently the system wasn't up and running yet.

And I thought this would be as good a time as any to begin my memoirs, alone as I was in the studio with nothing else to occupy my time. At first, I thought I'd begin them at the start of the decade, the curtain rising on the beginning of a pandemic, Clara's passing and the agonizing breakdown of a closely-knit family. But that was too depressing an opening. Then there was the political turnover of Trump 45 to Biden in 2021, the Capitol insurrection and the beginning of the MAGgot infestation. But that was also too depressing an opening. Same with Ruthie's cancer a year later. I needed to begin with some controversy in its infancy—a breakdown in civility—still unresolved by the end of the decade for both continuity and drama. And there were two or three issues that were bubbling up at the beginning of the decade, now taking over the nightly news and our collective consciousness, especially in the political arena with 2028 elections coming up in

November: Democrats Gavin Newsom and Grethen Whitmer vs. JD Vance and Nikki Haley for the Republicans.

First on the list was the lingering recession caused by Trump's tariff disaster, now hailed by Trump as 'behind us' though clearly, for most Muddle Class Americans, still evident in every way imaginable—from the price of food staples to gasoline to housing. Next, the effects of immigration, legal and illegal, tamping down reported wages, (unreported under-the-table wages not worthy of a comment), and what had happened in the span of a decade to divide the nation into strident racial and ethnic segments—not just along the Southern border, but all up and down the East and West coastlines where "illegal boat people" were now being smuggled into the country. A close third was gun ownership, which was connected directly to the second. Moving down the list were issues such as the effect of social media and smartphone addiction, AI and persistent unemployment among young educated Americans, widening income and wealth disparity, unwinnable involvement in the Middle East wars, widespread opioid drug use, and the Z generation's cultural, social, and political split. Perhaps I could find a time when these ugly intrusions to our relatively sane democracy began to raise their heads from their Gaza-like underground tunnels—like Peter's visit to me in mid July 2024 when many issues were brought to my attention, somewhat unaware as I was about current events going on about me.

So, I began typing on my laptop…

Caroline, my aide, was just leaving for the day when Peter's Uber pulled up. Perfect timing I thought. It would be just the two of us for a couple of days. Now, at last, I'd be able to hear his side of the story. That is, if he was willing to share it with me.

Part III

CHAPTER 21

Estelle never called me back that day meaning that they hadn't contacted David. In fact, later that evening I placed another call to him, only to get the same bot message of a temporary disconnection. It was obvious to me he wanted to spend his turning-point birthday his way, free of family concerns, free of congratulations—for what? Managing to get to the ripe old age of 40 still in one piece with the help of his brother's generous support to his mental health?

And now that debt could be largely erased with the sale of the Rialto. I wondered just how much Gene knew about the transaction, but for obvious reasons couldn't reveal the details. But the Council must have considered that if their settlement offer was too meager, Erskine & Samuels would handle the litigation, or if that was a conflict of interest for them, another powerful law firm would gladly step in on behalf of the preservation committee and other NIMBY theatre producers in the area. It was a dynamite NYC front-page issue—the ever-rising overflow of migrants into coastal cities—that could well affect the political outcome of November's Presidential election.

But this was Labor Day weekend, with more than two months left to reverse Eric Adam's disastrous automatic monthly migrant income—put in place more than 4 years earlier to clear the streets of tents and panhandlers, crooks and hustlers. Of course, the program was taken advantage of; that was a given. But the backlash among the tax-paying public was startling. It culminated with a sit-in during the Macy's Thanksgiving Day Parade of 2025 that was in revolt to both the Adam's 'gifts' scandal and Harris's failure to be elected. The city voted heavily for Harris who had job training as her major campaign pledge for solving the migrant crisis. In sharp contrast, Trump promised that on Day One of his Presidency, he would begin to export 14 million "illegals" to their home countries. And if he couldn't get the Congress behind him, he would do it with executive order. Which began the "uncivil war" as *The New York Times* Editorial Board put it, firmly behind Harris and against Trump—which caused the paper massive subscription losses, both the physical and on-line editions after Trump's election.

But that ancient history pales behind the unsolved Labor Day 2028 mystery of what happened to David Samuels which slid into the following day, Sunday, a day before Estelle and Gene's yacht was supposed to dock early morning in Westport, Connecticut. Unknownst to me, Gene had ordered the captain to greatly increase the speed of the boat because he feared for his brother's wellbeing. The yacht actually anchored Sunday late afternoon in Westport. Julie and Peter left for Julie's apartment in New Haven; the Erskines remained on the boat with their daughters for another evening of partying; and Gene and Estelle's limo was awaiting them when they debarked, rushing them to midtown Manhattan in less than an hour, just as the sun was setting.

Gene had a duplicate key to the side entrance of the Rialto which David had given him in case of an emergency, and Gene considered not having a response from his brother as such an emergency. As Estelle told me later: "It was worse than paranoia. He spent all of Saturday pacing the deck, contemplating David's demise, accidental or intentional; he was in shock." Nothing she could say or do could alleviate his helplessness, his foregone conclusion that David, on his 40th birthday, committed suicide either by gun or alcohol mixed with fentanyl in the squalid Rialto dressing room he called home.

But of course the dressing room was totally empty, nothing of David's remained. He had left it spotless; even the bed was nicely made. And on top of his desk was a small package labeled '*For Gene Samuels*'—anticipating the fact that his brother would be first to enter the premises. Inside the package, as Estelle later related, was a copy of David's *Recisions* and the receipts for three registered letters sent on Friday to The Rappaports, The Samuels, and to Gene. Along with copies of the checks sent with each letter, each check for $100,000.00. David's reverse birthday presents fully paying back debts owed to his Grandparents, Parents, and Younger Brother.

But where was birthday boy? A note to Gene in the package answered the question. David had rented a car, filled it with clothes, books and other items from his stay in the Rialto dressing room and had driven to Boston to be with his wife, daughters, and in-laws. And he would be there for all of the Labor Day weekend and a couple of days after that on holiday with his wife and kids on the Cape. Don't try to reach him, said his note; he was starting a new life, one which he wanted for all of these past two years of separation and depression. He was making a break with the past and had thought through every aspect of his decision. And if it meant giving up all that he had in New York, then this was to be his destiny. The action of the City Council was the right one, for it confirmed his decision. And even his therapist—the one paid for by his brother—applauded his move. David had somehow found a slingshot for a controlling Goliath—and struck with uncanny accuracy. Gene was visibly shaking with relief, actually weeping on his wife's shoulder she later recounted.

"I guess David was taking a chapter from his book," I said to Paul, about to leave for the City after I had spoken by phone with a relieved Estelle, calling from their Battery Park condo Sunday morning.

"Maybe I should have a look at it," he said. And so I got *Recisions* from the studio and gave the manuscript to my son.

"There's a chapter on Focusing," I said. "Maybe it can help teach your kids to be part of, and enjoy, the classroom experience."

"Dad, the only thing that's worked over all my years of teaching is the pizza connection."

"What's that? Hillary Clinton's pedophile ring?"

"I'm teaching percentages, see? So I've pre-ordered a large pizza and in front of the class I begin cutting it up. With each division I ask a student for their answer on the percentage of pieces already cut and how many more cuts do I need to make before everyone in the class has an equal share to consume. Before lunch, it certainly focuses their attention."

"Goodbye, dear," I laughed. "You've given me the answer to what I'm having for dinner tonight." And that's exactly what I had delivered later in the afternoon. With mushrooms and anchovies.

And then it was Gene's turn to call around sunset time. What was I doing for tomorrow, Labor Day? He wanted to know.

"Nothing, really," I said. "Caroline is off and I'm practicing a dance routine with my walker."

"You want some company?" he asked. "We took some extra food off the boat and it will just go to waste if it's not eaten."

And that's how it happened that Estelle and Gene and I met the following day, Labor Day Monday, for lunch on the back porch, but how they chose at that opportune time *not* to outline how I could transfer the house I had lived in for nearly half a century, to them.

You see, Gene had an inkling of what my hospital bill would be and what the follow-up physical therapy would cost. How he got this information is still a mystery to me, but nevertheless he was very close to the amazing figure presented to me on Wednesday of that week when I had the cast removed, yet another X-ray taken, stitches to the patella cut away and a flexible velcro knee brace-wrap applied.

The amount was so staggering that I thought he was kidding at first. It would have eaten up all of my savings and some of my Roth IRA funds, intended for a rainy day, or my end-of-life hospice care, whichever came first.

But now that there was a competent lawyer in the family, that figure could be lowered somewhat, even though various insurance plans I had—home, car, health, accident—couldn't be tapped without an investigation. And here Gene couldn't help me. He also had an inkling that his security guards were involved in the shooting, and this would not only be a conflict of interest in representing me, but also an outright crime if it was determined we were trying to defraud the insurance company. It wasn't worth his disbarment, or in my case, a serious fine. So I was stuck with the bill to come.

"Grandpa," Estelle put in, as she set the table on the porch, "we have some found money as you must know. David repaid his entire debt to Gene with the sale of the Rialto, and so there is a check for $100,000 waiting for us which we never thought we'd see again."

"And," Gene added, "I had a few $75 dividend payments David made besides, so we really came out ahead. I was ready to write the whole damn thing off."

"Not to mention the fact, that he's still alive and kicking, somewhere on the Cape," I said, with all the sardonic wit I could muster, that Gene had overreacted with unfounded thoughts of his brother's birthday/suicide.

"And he never told you when you talked with him about his plans?" Gene asked in his lawyerly voice.

"No. But I told you he sounded upbeat, relieved that he got the settlement he wanted."

"Apparently he wanted me to believe he was going to harm himself."

"Nonsense," I countered. "That's your paranoia coming through. He wanted to make a statement, it's true, but the statement wasn't about doing harm to himself. He was telling you he needed to be free of your overprotection, your brotherly advice on how to handle his life, your criticisms when he failed to live up to your expectations. He needed to make his own life for himself and take responsibility for it. It's all in his memoir, if you have time to read it," I said with a noticeable dose of sarcasm in my voice.

Gene was taken aback that I should be speaking out like I had. But I was more than twice his age, infirm, apparently now destitute and deserving of the empathy that comes with that. So he held his tongue. And Estelle, mortified though she was with our back-and-forth, busied herself with setting the table, unable or unwilling to defend her husband. Had I seen something in Gene that she had herself over the long period of their togetherness, but was able to put aside in order to marry him? And now once married, could she live with this overriding desire of his, this wanting for power and control?

I had really stepped on a bee-hive. But I still had a card up my sleeve to resolve our now in-law dispute. And over lunch of a delicious chicken salad, I carefully and craftily let it unfold.

"I've been thinking a lot about the winter," I said. "Even if I can get rid of my walker for a cane, it's going to be a challenge out here."

"No kidding," said Gene, still annoyed with me.

Estelle needed to quiet things down and her professional instincts kicked in just then. "Grandpa, your welfare is first on our minds. We know you have Caroline to assist you, but the thought of you alone in the house at night, now with limited mobility, is scary to say the least."

"I understand your concern," I continued, "and so I'm giving Florida a second look."

Suddenly, Gene's face calmed down and he nodded in agreement.

"Would you take up the Rappaport's offer to show you what The Villages have to offer?" Estelle wanted to know.

"That certainly would be one option," I said.

Gene was now nodding enthusiastically. Things were now going back to plan. This, I realized, was the reason for their visit. It had been carefully rehearsed, and I was playing along, knowingly, I should put in here.

"David gave us an unexpected hundred thousand," Estelle said to reemphasize her opening lines before the conversation took that unexpected twist. "It's like found money."

"And, with dividends, like I said," Gene put in, "we're ahead of the game. And so are the Rappaports now. They'd love to have you come down. And we can grease the wheels a little."

"Grease the wheels?"

"We talked to them this morning," Estelle went on. "We wanted to tell them what we found in David's dressing room—and that they should be expecting their check by registered mail tomorrow. They were incredibly happy, to say the least. They want to celebrate. They wanted us to come down and celebrate with them for Thanksgiving. But I'm going to be over my head with FreeGT this Fall as you know, and it's a busy season for Gene. So we didn't commit for Thanksgiving. But then we thought of you, of course. And maybe that would be the perfect time to go down and see them."

"But of course we didn't mention that to them before we talked with you." Gene said. "But if you're serious about Florida, that would be the perfect time."

"Well," I said, "the end of November is a long way off. I have to get myself in shape, trade in this walker for a cane at least. I have physical therapy coming up."

"All the rest of September, all of October and three weeks in November," said Gene. "Physical therapy for this kind of knee wound is about a month, I was told. Three times a week, so maybe a dozen times to get you back, walking steady with a cane. We know you can do it!"

"And," Estelle put in, "we'd lease the plane to take you there. The same one that brought the Rappaport's up from Florida for the wedding. It would be our treat."

"Ahhh," I said, "that's what you meant by greasing the wheels?"

"And a few other perks," Gene was smiling again. "You're part of the Samuels' family now."

I may have let slip before about Gene and Estelle's desire to take over the Montclair house I had called home for nearly half a century. Of course, I would have to be relocated first. And so this initial step had to do with my visiting the Rappaports in Florida and to see if I could be persuaded into moving down there. Then, with that as a 'go', they could bring up the proposition of house transfer. A win-win in their eyes, but so much wishful thinking. They needed to read David's book to accurately record how the dynamics of this project would change in the following ten weeks.

I don't want to bore you with the immediate days to follow. They involve, as I mentioned before, the cast removal on my knee, X-ray, suture removal on my kneecap, and the fitting of a lightweight velcro brace I could manually adjust for support and maneuverability. And finally, a stop off at the discharge station, and the hospital bill for my stay of four days there and that day's follow-up.

If I told you the total amount you would call my memoir complete fiction. To put it mildly, I was stunned. It was for just under $250,000. A quarter million dollars! Which didn't include, of course, outside prescriptions, the physical therapy to come—left entirely in my hands to arrange for, nor the cost of the walker Paul bought, nor the cost of Dr. Francona's daily visits which I suppose he'd be billing me for later. Once everything was paid for, my checking and savings account with Montclair Chase would be emptied. And I would be tapping into my tax-free Roth IRA, as my last resort—in other words, a hospice somewhere—and burial next to Ruthie and Rachel, leaving my surviving son Paul a pittance of inheritance. I had a few other endowment-type beneficiaries like The Nature Conservatory, but these were nominal amounts. I wouldn't go out a pauper by any means—for I still had the Montclair property and only minor credit card debts paid off monthly—but leaving decent amounts of money to my grandchildren Peter and Estelle was now problematic.

I had 30 days to pay the bill, and then daily interest would be added. But Gene had told me, without knowing the exact amount of the hospital bill, that I was to put everything on hold for the moment. He first wanted to talk to the hospital staff—as my attorney—to see if there were adjustments that could be made, knowing I wouldn't be using insurance to soften the blow.

So I was actually trembling as Caroline and I left the hospital, the bill in an envelope grasped along with the walker. Once in her car with only the wrinkled envelope before me, I brought up the idea of her partner Chris doing some physical therapy on me.

"Jerry," she said, "I told you already that Chris and I don't work together; he has his clients and I have mine. We have different ideas on healing and we don't want it to get in the way of our relationship."

I couldn't very well tell Caroline at that point that once my hospital bill was paid, I might have to cut back on her services. It was something I didn't want to face, although I suspected she knew that was a possibility. Could we work out a part-time plan? Would she agree to a cut in salary? And Florida? Maybe that was the way to broach the subject of our eventual disengagement. For the words 'fire' or 'dismiss' was not in my vocabulary, certainly not with Caroline who truly was principally responsible for my independence and good health. Moreover, I had come to believe she would be my hospice nurse, and that, when the time came to say *adieu*, she would be the one by bedside to make that transition as comfortable as possible as she had for Clara and Ruthie.

And yet, now looking at the sweaty, wrinkled envelope on my lap, I knew some tough ugly decisions would have to be made, and soon. Maybe there was a way she could begin working with another client while Chris took over, and when she was with me, Chris would be with another client. That way, they wouldn't cross paths. And she'd have other employment to fall back on. But there were no good answers here except continuing the way things had been before the accident, now made improbable with a quarter-million-dollar hospital bill.

"Suppose," I said, "you work with me on Monday, Wednesday and Friday, and Chris works with me Tuesday, Thursday and Saturday. Just until physical therapy is over, and I'm walking with a cane. Maybe a month. Until things return to normal."

She let out a long sigh as we approached the house. But she didn't say 'no'. "I'll talk to Chris about it this evening," she said. "Maybe the three of us can figure something out."

I had to go on the assumption that Gene—my new attorney it seemed—wouldn't get my bill reduced much, if at all. I remember all the forms I signed when I returned to the hospital after the wedding which he probably hadn't yet seen. The doctors would be billing me for the time I had left the hospital to attend the wedding, since I had left on my own against their advice. If something adverse had happened, they would be in big trouble, no doubt, with their insurance companies. So they piled it on.

[Note to Readers: if you want to change hospitals, or even doctors, after signing in—know beforehand the consequences of what you're doing!]

I spent the rest of the day in the studio with my laptop going over the various money market accounts held with a variety of brokerage firms. I had luckily closed out most of my risky investments in mutual funds back in mid-2025 and early 2026 before the bulk of the recession hit and the markets crashed. They had recovered somewhat since then, but nowhere near their peaks in 2024. Those who stayed fully invested in the stock market through the early turmoil of the Trump presidency, literally lost their shirts. I wasn't one of them, owing not to some great insight into the market, but rather the idea of putting enough safely away to afford Caroline and the house costs through the next five to eight years. For I never thought I would live past 85—and here I was already 90 tomorrow, Saturday the 9th of September, with all my faculties more or less in place. I recall Estelle's questioning of her Dad's drinking problem: How long could it go on like this? In that case it all worked out. In my case, your guess is as good as mine.

My accounts showed that indeed I could pay off the hospital bills without dipping deeply into my Roth IRA and the safety net I had created for myself with that tax-free asset and the value of the Montclair property which I believed could fetch about a million dollars, give or take a hundred grand or so before needed repairs and capital gains. And if I wanted to keep Caroline on fully, I could do that for about four-five more years. As Paul noted, she didn't come cheaply. I was paying her $50 an hour for a six-hour day, or $300. Times 5-½ because she only worked a half-day on Saturday. Which came to $1,650 a week, times 52 and that, with a paid Christmas/summer vacation bonus, was in the neighborhood of $90,000 a year. And I was to find out later that day, if you'll allow me to jump around a bit (but not for joy), her partner Chris earned more than twice her salary as a licensed physical therapist and dietician. His regular rate was $125 an hour, but I would get a deal. More on that in a minute.

The upshot was my initial worry about not being able to afford Caroline after the hospital bill was paid off was overblown. With her salary kept at the same rate (although I realized that she would be due for a raise of some kind soon), household expenses—including food and wine, utilities, but not home repairs—kept in the range of roughly $2,500 a month, and giving up driving a car, I could maintain living conditions in about the same way as before the accident for, as I've said, at least four to five more years, or until I was 95. After that, the house would have to be sold for I would have exhausted all other sources of income. And if the house were sold, both Caroline and I would need to find other living and working conditions. But maybe she'd be close to retirement by then, had saved enough, and decided her working days were over. As for me, some Last Resort; a TikTok-like hospice with the emphasis on *spice*.

These were some of the thoughts buzzing around my head as Caroline was leaving for the day, a hefty salad and a cheese ravioli plate for me to microwave as dinner.

"Jerry," she said upon leaving, "your plan to alternate days with Chris would cut my salary in about half—or were you thinking of paying me the same whether I came in or not?"

"No reduction," I said.

"You know he charges $125 an hour, don't you?"

"I do now."

"So adding my salary to his for the month or so he's working with you is okay with you?"

"If he can show me how to climb stairs so I can take a shower, it will all be worth it," said I.

Saturday, September 9th. A dull, cloudy day outside but a red-letter day on my calendar—the day I turned Ninety. And yet, not one card of birthday congratulation in my mailbox that morning, just Bill Young's invoice for the chuppa flowers. Not a single call. No one stopping by, no one sending me an email, or even an e-card. Nothing. Not even from Paul who had to know it was his father's birthday, even if others didn't. Although I realized Paul, Ruthie and I had an unspoken agreement about my birthday after Rachel's passing, coming as it did, the very day before her accident. For years after that we used my birthday as our Memorial Day to visit the Myer plot and Rachel's gravesite in Woodside Cemetery out on Long Island and where Ruthie was now interred, as I would be someday. So maybe Paul, out of respect, allowed me space to mourn my daughter's death on our Memorial Day—and yet, this was a milestone birthday for me, one which I wanted somehow to be acknowledged. To have another milestone birthday, even a five-year one, was beyond improbability.

I sponge bathed myself, shaved and awaited Caroline who surely knew from all the years working with the family that September 9th was her employer's special day. Last year she baked a birthday cake but this year, there was no cake when she arrived, although she had some "good news" to tell me.

"I talked with Chris last night. He's willing to take you on at a somewhat reduced rate for his 'hour of power' as he likes to say. And he'll throw in a complementary evaluation tomorrow morning at around 10:30—to tell you what he thinks can be done and how long it might take. I'd be making my same salary for three days of work a week and Chris would be working three times a week for $100 a treatment—$300 a week. All told, $1,950 a week until therapy ends."

"Sounds like a deal," I replied, although Caroline saw through my faux enthusiasm. But what the hell! At Ninety you're supposed to be taken advantage of. You're more senile than Biden and Trump put together, remember? Or have you forgotten already? Besides which, Ninety gives you certain social considerations—like having people give up their seat on the subway or bus—providing you're still getting around on those modes of transportation. And if you're using a walker or a cane or even a crutch or two, even pickpockets and purse snatchers are polite and respectful in their violation of you, even saying *"lo siento"* as they disappear into the crowd.

I went back to the studio whilst Caroline busied herself cleaning the upstairs bedrooms and continued working on my memoir. I was doing pretty well with it, there being no interruptions for hours at a time. I could produce 5-7 single spaced pages in a day; and my mind was sharp enough, with some caffeine thrown in, to keep me going all through Caroline's Saturday morning tenure there.

"Remember," she said, popping her head into the studio, "there's a salmon filet for dinner and Chris will be here tomorrow at ten to do an evaluation. You don't have to dress for him, in fact, he wants you in your underwear."

"Thanks, dear," I said. "I'll be waiting, walker in hand."

Caroline had prepared my favorite dinner of a thick fresh salmon filet, steamed kale and mashed potatoes—and with the opening of a bottle of a deliciously smooth French Chardonnay the day wouldn't be a complete loss. But there would be no acknowledgment of my birthday, not even from Paul. I realized he had just started teaching that week and was probably already over his head. And there was our Memorial Day consideration, of course. But a phone call from him would have been greatly appreciated. Anger wasn't the word. I was disappointed, despondent and resentful. I needed to strip down, smoke a blunt—saved from Ruthie's last days—to calm me down for an afternoon nap.

And sleep I did! Beyond REM, beyond the bounds of consciousness, into some other world of ageless dissociation from reality. For in my dream I was made to understand what it is to lose one's mind, becoming so detached as not being able to distinguish faces, or places or even the need to relieve oneself. I recalled the fatuous adage, 'If you can manage to get through your Eighties, it's all downhill from there.' To a newly crowned nonagenarian, this would be the decade of decay, until time itself ultimately, finally, wore itself out, stopped working, collapsed into itself—a black hole. Even a memoir wouldn't be enough to save its memory. A family's Memorial Day would eventually disappear with its last descendant. But first, a buzzer on my phone would jar me awake.

It was, of all people, Chris at the front door at exactly 2PM, a large satchel in his left hand, his right hand extended to have me shake it and welcome him inside.

"I first need to bring in the massage table," he explained.

"I thought Caroline said you'd be here tomorrow, Sunday."

"Well, I had a cancellation, and thought we'd get the initial assessment over with. It's complimentary, of course. I need to know more about your physical condition."

From the rear of his station wagon parked in the oval, he pulled out a foldable metal table, rolled inch-thick foam pad and a freshly folded fitted sheet. Chris was a large man, powerfully built and agile. What would take a couple of men to carry in, he could do on his own. I would be in good hands.

I stripped off my bathrobe as he set up the table, the pad covering and the sheet in the middle of the living room. He spent a minute looking me over front and back in only my skivvies as I clutched the walker for support. He nodded his approval.

"Carrie tells me you're celebrating your ninetieth birthday," he said, putting on a pair of disposable rubber gloves. "You have the body of a man ten years younger, you know."

"Until the accident I played a lot of tennis and rode my bike everywhere. Even did a little swimming at the Y. That's no longer possible, I understand."

"No, but there are ways to compensate for that. But you've never had a stroke, never had a heart attack, correct?"

"Right."

"Do you mind if I take your blood pressure and measure your oxygen level?"

"Do what you do," I said.

He lifted me from the walker onto the table effortlessly. From his satchel he pulled out a blood pressure cuff and stethoscope and took my pressure. Then he took my blood oxygen level with a finger monitor. He seemed pleased at the results. "Looking good," he said.

Then he asked me to lie back on the table, and undid the velcro straps and cuff around my right knee. "Lift your left leg up as high as you can," he asked of me, and saw that I could almost lift it a couple of feet off the table. "Now bend your knee so your foot is on the table." No problem doing that. Then he asked me to do that with my right leg which I could barely move a couple of inches off the table. "Can you keep your right leg raised?" he asked. I tried but it was a strain and it quickly fell back. He then placed his fingers along various parts of my right leg and foot top to bottom and asked if I could feel them. I could in every case, even around the knee area.

"They did a pretty good job," he commented. "What were you told about putting weight on your right leg?"

"Not to put any significant weight on my right leg, because it might dislodge the insert they put in. If that happened, they'd have to go in again and readjust it."

He nodded. "Well, we'll have to strengthen that right leg of yours. I can't promise you'll be able to walk normally again, but if you're supported by a cane you'll be up and running in a month or so. Well, not running, but hopefully caneing."

"Driving a car?"

"Once strength in your leg is back."

"And steps," I asked, pointing to the stairs leading to the upstairs bedrooms.

"With a Cain, all things are Abel," he laughed at his Biblical play on words and I joined in, an ironic gag now, knowing I had used that very line with the Rappaports a week or more earlier.

"Really?"

"I know you need to get upstairs because the bathrooms have bathtubs and showers," he said.

"Caroline is a good reporter."

"No, she's just nosey." His sardonic wit was embarrassing to say the least, but accurate.

"I smell to high heaven and heaven is an upstairs hot shower," I said, countering.

"Well, maybe we can do something about that now," Chris said. "Let me first bring up your walker. Which bathroom would you like to use?"

"The one in the master bedroom. First room on the right."

He disappeared with the walker and returned a minute later. "Okay, it's in the tub. Now, do you know anything about a fireman's carry?"

"No."

"I'm going to lift you up by your mid section and carry you on my right shoulder. You put your two arms out before you and I'm going to grab one to carry you upstairs and into the bathroom. Then when I set you down in the bathtub you grip on to the walker for support, got it?"

"You're going to carry me up a flight of stairs?" I asked in amazement.

"Actually, that will be easier than me carrying you back down," he said.

And that's how the rest of the hour went—like clockwork. I took my first hot steaming soapy shower in days and enjoyed every minute of it, then dried myself off, shaved, and called for Chris to assist me again. He said I needed to put on some decent clothes so we reversed the procedure, but instead of landing me back in the living room, we landed in the master bedroom where I had fresh underwear and some newly washed Bermuda shorts and sport shirts. He placed me on the day bed, went back for the walker, then gave me the privacy of dressing myself. Of course, everything I was now putting on was too large, seeing as how my aging body had produced its own shrinkflation these past years. Maybe it was time for a new wardrobe I figured, thinking of Florida and peering into the full length mirror backing the bathroom door. Even so, I felt like a new man.

While I was dressing there was some hammering on the porch; it sounded like someone putting in nails into the overhang above the staircase. But I couldn't see from where I was. It had to be Chris, but when I finally dressed myself and managed to slip into a pair of loafers, turning around was—amazingly—Caroline! "What happened to Chris?" I asked.

"He's outside packing up. You look great!" she exclaimed. "How was your shower?"

"I got carried away by it," I laughed. "He's pretty strong."

"You're telling me! Are you ready for Chris to carry you back downstairs?"

"Sure," I said.

Chris then carried me piggyback down the stairs. "Jerry, I need to put your knee brace back on. Sit down on a kitchen chair and I'll do that for you now" While he was adjusting the cuff he asked, "Can you get hold of the carpenters who did the platform for the wedding?"

"I think so," I said. "I just need to call the wedding coordinator. Why?"

"I'd like them to install a handrail on the left side of the stairs leading to the second floor. So there's a handrail on both sides of the stairwell. You're going to need that when you begin climbing and descending stairs again."

"I can call them on Monday," I said.

"Well, no rush. We won't be tackling that for another couple of weeks or so."

"So you think that's possible?"

"Yes. Next week we'll be doing exercises to increase strength and flexibility in both your legs. And then we'll graduate to a metal crutch before we get to a cane. I think we're looking at 4-5 weeks all told. Certainly by mid-October. How does that sound?"

"Fireman's carry on Saturdays?"

"Absolutely."

"You're on," I said.

And then there was a buzz on my phone and someone with a finger entry to the kitchen entrance was standing there behind the curtain. Who, I wondered, would be coming to see me at 3PM? It was *Paul* and he was with a woman I had never met before. My knee all wrapped now, I got back on the walker and shuffled over to the door to greet them.

"Hi, Dad," he said, awkwardly hugging me on the threshold over the walker's metal bar. "This is Jean. Jean knew Clara years ago; classmates at Queen's Teacher's College. Jean's teaching remedial English to the new Spanish-speaking arrivals at my school this semester."

I shook hands with a tall, slender and elegant looking woman in her late 50s. "Glad to meet you, and Happy Birthday," she said, handing me a small wrapped present of some kind. Paul hadn't forgotten.

"Come in," I said, "and meet Chris who's doing physical therapy on my leg."

Caroline and Chris said hello to Paul and Jean in the kitchen and were about to enter the dining area when there was another buzz on my phone and another couple at the kitchen doorstep. It was the suntanned duo of Estelle and Gene with wrapped presents and a Happy Birthday greeting—and now I knew something was up. Because as I was about to bring them into the circle, yet another buzz and yet another suntanned duo at the kitchen doorway: Peter and Julie... with yet another, larger present, and a Happy Birthday.

And yes, a surprise party for my birthday was in the making, and indeed I was to be *more* than surprised. I was to be amazed. For not long after, coming up the oval, and parking before the main entrance, a sky-blue Honda honking away. And now departing from its interior were David and a woman with a beautiful smile, thickly lashed blue eyes and dark black curly hair I assumed to be his wife, both carrying wrapped presents for me.

"Jerry," David said, "this is my wife Abby."

"Happy Birthday," she gushed, shaking my hand, both she and David now quickly passing by my walker and introducing themselves around.

"It's getting a little crowded in here," said Gene. "Let's go into the back yard."

The crowd moved from the living room through the studio, but because of the walker I needed to take the kitchen's side entrance. And rounding the porch I was now looking at Chris's massage table placed on the chuppa platform, decked out with a tablecloth and a vase of flowers and above the stairs, a skillfully painted plywood sign he had presumably nailed up earlier...

> 90th on 9/9 <
CONGRATULATIONS, JERRY!

And now, a rousing chorus of *'Happy Birthday To You!'*

I caught Gene's practiced smirk at my surprised expression as he passed by and headed towards the garage with Chris. They returned a minute later with cartons of food, drinks, plastic plates and glasses, and dinnerware which Caroline and Chris laid out.

But there were more guests to arrive. For someone had sent invitations to five of the six families lining Lois Lane, with the date and a 3PM arrival time, requesting no presents but only secrecy for my surprise party. The 6th family—the O'Briens—were not invited—and only later was I to discover why.

Of my Lois Lane neighbors, only the Franklins and the Bakers came. Doug Baker was one of my doubles partners and sometime-opponent on tennis days. Lew and Debbie Franklin came over to talk with anyone interested in buying the house directly next to mine. But priced at a million for a finished basement ranch with a quarter-acre lot and a 15'x30' in-ground swimming pool seemed pretty high to me. If he could get a million for his place, think of what I could get for my 2-storey Victorian with a finished basement and an acre and a half surrounding it. The problem was, I had no intention of leaving. Turning ninety didn't mean less options in life. For many, it meant more options. I wasn't going to let a bum knee set me back; if anything it restored my desire to live out the rest of my life the way I wanted to. It would take more than money at this point to change my mind. But what that 'more' was was still vague and undefined, maybe even non-existent. And I wasn't going to seek it out; it would have to come to me, a revelation, a message from Rabbi Max's 'SpaceX wavelength', as he put it. Or maybe, taking David's point, writing down all the *Recisions* options so that I had a visual representation of the choices before me. I'd have to ask Paul for the manuscript back.

The massage table was now full of salads and various drinks, napkin-wrapped utensils, glass flutes, vases of flowers and presents galore. Gene took it upon himself to be M.C. since we were all standing about looking somewhat bewildered, not having made formal introductions with those newly baptized into the circle.

"Let's present ourselves to each other and any news to share—good news, that is—and then we can dig into the wonderful food. And just look at the huge cake that Caroline baked! I'll let Caroline and Chris start it off."

"I've known Jerry for about a decade now," Caroline began, "and in all truth, he looks younger today than ever. So there are nine candles to blow out, one for each decade. I'll bet he has the breath capacity to do it in one blow. But my partner Chris can better fill you in on how Jerry is doing with the therapy on his leg."

"After next week," Chris piped in, "Jerry's walker will be a thing of the past. We'll be using an adjustable metal crutch to get around, and seeing how that goes, we'll graduate to a cane. And Jerry will be able to manage stairs. So his Studio apartment days will be coming to an end."

A round of applause. Peter and Julie were next.

"I'm Peter, Jerry's grandson and this is Julie, my best friend. We know the house well and when Jerry returns to his back bedroom upstairs at night, there will be no one to guard the front of the house. So we brought this present for you, Jerry," Peter said, awkwardly placing the box on the walker, then seeing that I wouldn't be able to open it like that, he repositioned the box on the table and opened it himself. "They were out of DogBots, but instead we got you a Puss'n'Bots to set on the windowsill next to the front door."

Peter pulled out a yellow striped cat-like doll and everyone laughed. "We named it Rayitas, Spanish for little stripes. And Rayitas can see in the dark and report any movement by sending a loud meow to Jerry's phone upstairs."

Again, applause, and now it was Julie's turn.

"Peter and I have been offered a fantastic opportunity to build inexpensive solar housing and desalination plants in Perth, Australia and we're leaving on September 29th so we can begin work at the beginning of October. We'll miss this year's eclipse but we expect to be there for the 2030 eclipse so we'll send back video to all those who send us their email address."

"And," Peter added, "as a bonus, we'll be emailing out a quarterly report on our progress. So you'll be hearing from us regularly."

Applause, and then Paul took over. "I'm Paul, Jerry's son and Peter's Dad, and this is Jean, my new friend who's teaching remedial English at the High School where I'm presently teaching math. We want to follow up on Peter and Julie's present. Here's a pendant, Dad, you can wear all the time. even when showering. If there's an emergency of some kind, just press the button in the middle and a red light will come on. It means your call went through 911 and your GPS is automatically sent to the nearest police car in the area. We've already registered the pendent's call letters with 1 Lois Lane. You'll have help in minutes."

"If Rayitas sees a squad car he'll go *cat*atonic," I punned to much laughter.

"I'm Lew Franklin and this is my wife, Debbie. We live right next door, over there, and if we see a squad car outside we can let them in the house because Jerry has been kind enough to put our thumbprints into the reader for just this kind of unexpected emergency. Also I want to say that our house is up for sale and if anyone here wants to come over and take a quick look this afternoon, we're happy to show it." No applause, but Doug Baker quickly filled in the vacuum.

"I'm Doug Baker and this is my wife, Marilyn, and we live on the opposite side of the Lane next to Jerry's house and I also have my thumbprint in the database. I hope someday, Jerry, you'll be able to play tennis with us again; you were a tough opponent."

Not a chance, I thought, but a nice gesture. And now, it was David's turn.

"Hi, I'm David Samuels, Gene's older but wiser brother. And this is my wife, Abby, an extraordinary mother to our two daughters. We've driven all the way from Boston today to return a book to Jerry and to make some announcements. Here's *Quantum Agnostics* back, Jerry. Thanks for lending it to me," he said, placing the book on the table. "And now, the announcements: I've been made Creative Administrator at Boston Playhouse in charge of all productions for this Fall and beyond. And two, many of you are aware that while I was in charge of the Rialto restoration, I was writing a book called *Recisions*. Well, Fireside Paperbacks will be publishing it, paid me a decent advance, and it will be out later this Fall."

Now, a full round of applause. This indeed was good news. And I could see Abby was thrilled by these new developments as she passionately kissed her husband on the lips.

"And I'm Estelle or Stella as my friends call me, including my dear husband Gene who married me on this very platform a month or so ago. So we brought with us our wedding album as proof. And for Grandpa, a set of earbuds for his new phone."

"Thank you," I said, not quite knowing how or why to use them.

"And for those of you who don't follow the latest shotgun news," Estelle went on, "I'm four months pregnant, thankfully past SCOTUS abortion limits—and expecting in late February."

This to much applause. "And before I forget, my website is www.FreeGT.com, Estelle went on, "now up and running and doing fantastically well. So tune in, turn on and drop out, as Tim Leary liked to say. But before you do, we invite you to partake in all the goodies we brought with us and share in my Grandfather's birthday celebration with a toast of champagne."

Gene had opened a bottle of Moet and was pouring out glass flutes. "To Jerry," he pronounced, handing me a glass; "If he can manage to reach 90 without drugs for extended telomeres, imagine how old we'll get to be, surviving in centennial tenttowns, thanks to our geriatricians and pharmaceutical companies." And with that, I blew out all 9 candles on the cake with a single breath.

A wonderful surprise party! It lasted well into the early evening and so I invited David and Abby Samuels to stay the night in the master bedroom instead of driving in darkness back to Boston. Their girls were staying at Abby's parent's house so a telephone call was all that was needed to complete the deal. And after Abby retired for the night, I wanted to talk more to David about his *Recisions* book which I found fascinating in parts.

For instance, the book's last chapter is called "*Ken*"—the full-length movie that won Best Picture award for the 100th anniversary of the Academy Awards, back on Sunday, March 5th. *Ken* was the first full-length feature completely programmed by AI. The algorithm was only informed that Ken, in a flashback, was married to Barbie in 2025 and now she is pregnant. Ken gets himself into deep financial trouble during the stagflation period, somehow gets himself out of trouble and the climax of the movie is Barbie has a daughter she names Emoji.

Somehow *Ken*, besides getting Best Picture, took away 6 awards for its script, musical score, settings and special effects—all done by computer. So the Academy had no one to receive their Oscars but the programmers, who refused acceptance, because the algorithm made all the creative decisions, not them. The broadcast was both panned and praised by the reviewers, adding a cultural division to the motion picture entertainment industry not previously seen.

"I wrote that chapter," said David, "just before the sale. I think it may have sold the book."

"What I think you're implying," I said, "is that American culture, in general, is now being shaped by generative AI or that part of social media addictively driven by AI."

"Well, I use the initials AI not as *Artificial* Intelligence, but *Augmented* Intelligence—a term that came up during the recent recession. And I wanted to express the thought that introducing Augmented Intelligence to present-day human decision-making capabilities presents a conflict, not a resolution."

"The programmers walking out."

"Exactly. They realized, somewhere along the way, the algorithm was the star, not them. And they weren't going to be hypocritical about it. They weren't pissed, by the way, if you heard their press conference later. They had decided long before the Awards that this press conference was going to be *their* moment, not the Awards ceremony. They needed to tell the world, who was watching this Centennial Celebration in great numbers, that human-based creativity was on the fault-line, ready to disappear into the void if not addressed."

"It's too late to give up a computer's programmed creativity, David, you must know that."

"Certainly, Jerry. We can't deprogram what we've done, intentionally or otherwise. But we ignored the bread crumbs all along the trail and went our separate ways. Some of it turned out well, but for the most part we only found ourselves deeper in the woods with busted compasses. We need to regroup. The stagflation we're just getting out of is the first hopeful sign of a path forward. I hope it holds up."

"Do you think Shapiro would have made a better candidate?"

"I'm voting third party. *The Reality U Experience* party. TRUE cuts through all the bullshit and tells it like it is. No celebrity endorsements and Influencers. No PACs. No social media moguls. Just fact-checked print you can read, analyze and decide upon. Just the raw facts about corruption and how the last four years have been a disaster for the economy, for the family, for younger generations."

"You sound an awful lot like my grandson, Peter."

"I wish I had his talent and his genius and could escape to a promised land. We had a long talk this afternoon. I'd trade places with him in a heartbeat. What a great adventure for him and Julie. I know they'll do well there."

"And so will you with the Boston Playhouse and *Recisions*." I said.

Peter had taken a fortuitous escape route not available to David. But in the scope of things, I felt both would do well.

The party ended with sunset, all the guests departed, save David and Abby in the master bedroom upstairs. Exhausted, I went soundly to sleep in the Studio, now with a deep feeling of wellbeing.

It didn't last, for I woke to movement about me. I threw on my bathrobe and used the walker to find David and Abby having coffee in the living room. They smiled broadly when they saw me, half-awake, unshaven, somewhat pissed at being so unexpectedly exposed.

"One last surprise," said David, amused at my plight. "We're taking you to Sunday brunch at the Marriott."

"The hell you are," I said, blindsided by their offer.

"It's all arranged," said Abby. "We've reserved a table on the terrace."

"You have exactly forty-five minutes to get yourself dressed. Our reservation is for 11:00," David added mock-commandingly.

I didn't really have a rejoinder. I didn't want to prepare breakfast, although I knew Abby would do the fixings. And I supposed this was their way of repaying my offer for them to spend the night there. So I turned around and returned to the Studio where I knew I had some decent clothes and time enough to shave and take a crap. I even beat their deadline by five minutes. And with some help from David with the walker, now folded in the back seat with Abby, we made good time to the Marriott, arriving at 10:50, and being escorted by the *maitre 'd* to our reserved table on the terrace where, surprise! *surprise!!,* Gene and Estelle arose from their chairs, welcoming us all.

"I thought you had left for the city last night," I said sitting down, the walker now placed against the dining room wall behind me. "This looks to me like a set-up job."

"Well, yes and no," said Gene, his chair placed next to mine. "Today is 9/10 as you know, and every year I take a day or two off to commemorate our Dad, and leave Battery Park behind because of all the memories there. So being out here in Montclair today with my brother and Abby is fortuitous to say the least. If you hadn't invited

David to stay at your place, we had reserved a suite for them here. And it's so good to see you again, Jerry. Icing on the birthday cake."

~∂∂∂~

So the brothers had completely made up, Gene being paid off, David apparently quite sober and enthusiastic about the future and the sister-in-laws chatting along fabulously. It was a wonderful brunch: Eggs Benedict perfectly done, coffee just right, even chocolate mini-eclairs as a gifted Marriott dessert.

This was to be Gene's gift on this special day, and so by 1:30 David and Abby said their farewells, hugs and kisses all around, and left. Gene would drive me back to the house but first there were a couple of things we needed to discuss. Estelle excused herself for the ladies' room. I knew what was coming, and had thought through various scenarios of what was to follow… but not the one Gene had in mind.

"You know," Gene began, "the 30-day extension on your hospital bill is soon coming due. What were you planning to do about it?"

"You told me not to worry about it, so I haven't given it a thought," I said, a lie too obvious to mention.

Gene smiled. "That was your Grandson-in-law speaking, not your lawyer."

"Well, which side of your mouth should I believe," I said, knowing full well the effect it would have.

But he was having none of it. "Looking back, I think the decision you made not to implicate my guys or Peter was a brave call," he said. "But somewhere along the line you had to know it was going to cost you; without an investigation, insurance wouldn't touch this with a 10-foot pole."

"Of course," I said. "I didn't bother to file a claim."

"Can you pay the bill?"

"I have to dip into some savings, cash out some mutual funds and Roth IRA, but I think I can manage."

"You'll need that money if some other health crisis emerges. There's no way to avoid that at your age, y' know. People your age are looking for a secure community of friendly support and professional health practitioners at the ready."

"Your grandparents, for instance," I said, playing the game.

"Exactly. You'll see what they see at Thanksgiving. I think you'll be impressed. I know *I am* whenever we visit. They believe they can break into centennial years. Their goal is to live dementia-free until nature takes its course. And it will, naturally, but in the meantime they're exercising daily, taking special vitamins and are getting monthly stem cell therapy shots."

"I know," I said. "They told me all about it over dinner when they were here."

"So, you're very much like them," Gene went on. "But my Granddad was instrumental in building The Villages so staying in Florida wasn't a difficult decision. But I can certainly see how the thought of moving to Florida must be for you. Especially after the accident."

"Well, that's coming up over Thanksgiving. I can't say anything more about it until I see it with my own eyes. What's over the Internet is pure promotional fluff. I'm going down with an open mind."

"You know of our interest in your house. And now with a baby on the way, it's even more desirable, for Stella as well as myself. You know, our one-bedroom condo isn't convertible to having a second baby's room. We're planning on keeping it as a *pied d'terre* because there will be times one or both of us will need to stay overnight in the city. We love your place for the escape to the country, for its space and privacy. And keeping it in the family, I know, is what you want as well."

"When is the baby due?" I asked.

"Your great-grandchild is due late February-early March." he responded, emphasizing the relationship we would share. A very lawyerly tactic I thought. He was good, no doubt about it.

"Still five months away."

"True. But we don't want to leave this for the last moment. It wouldn't be fair to Stella who's under a lot of pressure at the moment getting FreeGT off the ground. The sooner you tell us what your plans are, the better. It would be great if we moved in over the Holidays, to give us some time to convert one of the upstairs bedrooms to a nursery and get settled, you understand."

"As I said, there's Florida with the Rappaports. After all, you set that up, remember?"

"I think it's an option you should explore."

"Then I can tell you more right after Thanksgiving."

"We could move up the date, you know. There's nothing special about Thanksgiving."

"No, but that's what was arranged. And I need the time to convert from this walker to a cane to get around. That will take a few weeks more."

"You'll have the Rappaports for friends and they can introduce you to all of their friends. It won't be like you'll be entirely on your own. I know that can set up all sorts of anxieties, but you'll be socially in the crowd from the time you get down there."

"Well, I'll be going down there with an open mind," I said. "We'll see."

I saw that Gene had boxed himself into a very tight schedule, one he never imagined at the time of that dinner party prior to the wedding day. But he went on with his well-rehearsed pitch.

"I had a long talk with Paul recently," he declared. "Did he mention it to you?"

"No."

"He said he had a copy of your Will. After Ruth died you changed your Will and made your son your executor, remember?"

"Of course."

"Among other things," Gene said, finishing his coffee, "you left the house to him."

"Yeah. He can do whatever he wants with it. And he'd probably get a good price for it if he doesn't want to live here."

"He's told you he doesn't care to live out here. He's more of a city guy."

"Yeah, but he's seeing a new lady friend. He may have second thoughts about that."

"Well, we talked about that. And maybe you should, too. He would rather pass the executor title over to his kids and let them decide what to do in the event of your death."

"He said that?" I asked, a bit peeved.

"Scouts honor. Paul and Peter both want Stella to handle the house should you choose to move. But it's up to you to make her your executor and not your son. It needs to be changed in your Will."

"And your law firm can certainly do that," I said with some unbridled sarcasm in my voice.

"Yes, we can. But since there may be some conflict of interest here, I would take it to another attorney of your choice."

"I know of an attorney in Montclair," I said.

"That would be fine."

"And the idea of enlarging the Studio and making it my apartment?"

"Do you really want that?" Gene asked. "Don't you value your privacy, your independence? Look, I have a better plan. Let me pay off the hospital bill in full, and take care of Chris and Caroline. You keep your money, all of it. And if Florida is not for you, find a place here in town to rent so you're with your friends. And come out and visit us and feed the deer and do whatever you were doing before the accident. But change your Will and make Stella, not Paul, your beneficiary for the house. He doesn't want it anyhow, and I don't think Peter does either. But Stella does, and so do I. So if and when you die, it turns over to us. Until then, it's still in your name. In effect we'll be renting it from you. We'll even pay the property taxes. How does that sound?"

"Know of any hit men?"

That crack got to him. His face turned red and I thought for a moment he was going to punch me out. Instead, he took a sip of water from his glass and turned away, trying to get the waiter's attention for the check. Luckily, Estelle was now back at the table and sat down to the other side of me.

"You guys finished your discussion?"

"Yes," Gene said bluntly. And then turning to me, "Can we drive you home?"

"Certainly," I said.

Gene paid the brunch bill, got my walker and helped me navigate back to the car. He was so angry he couldn't make conversation with me. I had it in my power to apologize for that tasteless remark, but I needed him to know I was still in control here, not him. If I was going to move or sign away the house to Estelle, whatever, it would be on my terms, not his.

But I needed to think that through. Stubbornness and ego might be getting in the way of practicality. Gene had presented a very generous package I must admit. And my idea of living in the reconstructed studio was, I could tell, not in anyone's best interest. I would still need Caroline's services—and Gene would probably not be willing to keep her on. I had a few assets left without Gene's offer, and Caroline could be with me for a year, year and a half tops. But what then? Gene, Estelle and their baby would have moved on by that time, and my options would be greatly narrowed.

Gene's offer, as it were, as extortive as I've noted it to be, might be the best option after all. I needed time to think it out, check my bank and mutual funds account, see what was left without Gene's help. And my health, as good as it was, was the determining factor here. For being in good health only extended the time I would have to draw down my funds to nothingness. Were I faced with a terminal disease, or some other infirmity that meant hospice or certain death in a designated time frame, the decision would be far easier to make. An ironic situation to be sure.

"I'll take care of the hospital bill and I'll give you my answer about the house right after I return from Florida," I said to Gene as he and Estelle escorted me to the kitchen entrance.

"Do I have your word on that?"

"Absolutely," I said, realizing as I did he was probably wired and this was as solid a commitment as I was willing to make at this time—that he would get an answer about the house right after Thanksgiving, leaving him and Estelle the Holidays to begin moving in... or not.

"Then we have a deal," he brightened. "And remember, I'll reimburse you for what you're putting out to the hospital if we get the house."

"Deal!" I said, and we shook hands.

"Granddad," Estelle broke in, "I know that Dad would rather not be involved with this house. It brings back all sorts of memories of Mom and Grandma. He would be more than willing to pass the house onto me and Peter. He's very comfortable in his co-op, he said, and loves being in the City as you know."

That coda, well rehearsed I was sure, made Gene smile a bit, knowing his mission had been more or less accomplished. All this on the day before 9/11 as well. His father would have been proud.

The next day, Monday, I contacted the carpenters who did the chuppa platform and told them what I needed in the way of a second handrail for the stairs to the floor above—and also moving the chuppa platform into a clearing in the woods, virtually in the middle of the wooded acre behind the house. They were working on a project, but had free time the following weekend to come out, take the measurements for the handrail and tar paper the chuppa platform before carrying it into the woods.

Tuesday was Chris's hour of power with me. He was pleased with the progress I was making, now that I had mastered getting about with the walker, and gaining strength in my legs. We did the regular muscle exercises on the table. I was almost ready, he said, to graduate to an adjustable titanium crutch that he had that I would be using for the stairs, once the handrail was installed. In the meantime, his fireman's carry would get me to my needed shower upstairs.

The week went quickly by. I moved some money around in my savings and checking account, cashed in some dividend-based mutual funds that had been paying me around 5% interest even through the recent recession, and finally cashed in my Roth IRA and added it to the enormous amount that the bank through my credit card would be paying Montclair General Hospital for the work they did. And then, of course, there was Dr. Francona's bill for looking in on me each day of my stay there. I emailed his office I would pay the $2,000 bill when I saw him for my annual checkup in early October.

Other than those annoyances, I spent most of the time in the Studio continuing to write my memoir on the computer, and enjoying the cooler drier weather. Saturday, Chris was there in the morning and stayed some extra time until the three carpenters showed up and Chris helped them take the measurements for the handrail on the left side of the winding staircase. He wanted it to be a tad lower than the handrail on the right, since my height had shrunk by a couple of inches in the past decade or so. The carpenters took the measurements needed, told us they would install the handrail the following day, Sunday, and Chris left.

Now it was my turn to explain to the men what the chuppa platform would next be used for: not as a dance floor, nor as a platform for food and drink for a birthday party—but for a winter shelter for deer. They were incredulous to say the least. But they were getting paid good money to tarpaper their carefully designed tongue-and-groove creation and then lug it out into the middle of the woods to a small clearing I knew about. Sunday, when they installed the handrail, they'd also have four 4'x4's with them, a ladder, saw, shovel and some cement to anchor the platform to both the ground and a fully grown oak tree for added stability. I also had in the garage a few metal POSTED—NO TRESPASSING signs I wanted replaced high up on tree trunks along the perimeter of my property, bordering the backyards of the housing developments beyond and the hiking trail along the creek.

Since I couldn't accompany them through the woods with my walker, their smartphone cameras and my directions had to capture the exact position where the clearing was. And by luck, we located it on the first try. They were now beginning to see what I had in mind, even suggesting the platform be tilted a little for rain to run off. They spent a half hour discussing the platform's height, how they would lift it into place, screw in metal braces for the load-carrying beams, and the depth of the holes where cement would be poured as the final gesture of support. And, they said, they would need a fourth worker if I didn't mind, but just for the time spent on the platform, and the placement of the signs.

Their estimate: $1,500 for the bannister; $3,000 for the platform installation, $500 for the signs = $5,000 altogether, a nice round figure. I was going through my savings and investments like there was no tomorrow. And in the scope of things, I figured that might be where things were heading.

The rest of September was devoted to using a metal crutch to get around instead of the walker. Chris and I practiced on the three steps that right-angled the second floor's staircase into the dining room and kitchen area. It only had a banister on the left side and just the back of an antique hutch that stored plates and silverware on the right, so this would be a delicate balancing act. At first, Chris supported me, but after a dozen or so back-and-forths, he let me do the stairs on my own, always ready to catch me if I lost my balance. Luckily I passed inspection. But nevertheless I wasn't going to attempt the full flight staircase yet. That was to come just as September was ending.

If you recall, Peter and Julie were leaving on the 29th from Newark to London on their first leg of a marathon flight to Perth, Australia. And they asked me if they could stay the night at my place and Uber to Newark the following day. They'd arrive in Julie's car and Julie's sister Beth would drive it back to Connecticut—for now she was its new owner. I was happy to entertain the three of them for a late lunch that Caroline prepared before she left for the day. And after Beth had left I was feeling somewhat frisky—enough so that I asked Peter to accompany me upstairs, for I had never climbed and descended the full staircase with the crutch. Once on the landing I asked him to stay in the hallway for just a minute. Waiting for him was a Certified check for $1,000, taken from the wall safe holding his gun and holster. He had forgotten about our bet, but I hadn't.

I can't tell you, dear Reader, what a sense of accomplishment I felt as I performed the acrobatics without a misstep. It's perfectly true that Peter was standing beneath me, and Julie was standing behind him, just in case. But slowly and surely I did a 'round trip. And though I gave up the master bedroom that night to the couple, I knew the following morning that my days and nights in the Studio were over; that Chris would never have to perform a fireman's carry with me again. That shitting, showering, and shaving on my own was now firmly on my terms, my time, my way. Frank Sinatra had nothing on me!

And Chris was impressed, arriving as he did just as Peter and Julie were saying their goodbyes as their Uber took off for Newark. Inside now, I led him to the staircase so he could see for himself my ascent and descent, this time even a bit more lively. "It means," he said, "we should be looking at canes now. And I should be looking for another client."

CHAPTER 22

It was now the beginning of October, leaves still on trees, but turning in their autumnal glory. On Friday, October 6, just after Caroline left for the day, I got a call from Gene. He and Estelle would like to drop by on Sunday with lunch and was I available to host them? Of course I said do drop by, as we both knew I wasn't going anywhere on Sundays. It was a day of rest, after a week of crutch handling. And I welcomed the company. For in these intervening weeks I realized, aside from writing these memoirs, there was little I was doing to keep my socializing instincts intact. The thought of going to Rosh Hashanah services the next week crossed my mind, and quickly faded. Gene or Estelle would have to bring it up. There was no way I would join a ride-share to see Rabbi Max's last performance.

And yet, I didn't want to begin shutting down, for aside from the knee, all my other faculties, mental, physical and spiritual, seemed fine, at least from my own observation of the same. To others, it might seem the old man was beginning to lose it, much like we imagined was happening to Joe Biden a few years before. Could there have been something called the 'sympathy vote' at the time? Certainly he got the Boomer-and-Beyond vote, but the concern was there as the demographics and exit polls showed. In our hearts we wanted him to succeed, for we saw ourselves in him, in his final days, our final days. And what we saw was a very slow diminution of faculties, so slow in fact, it was hardly noticeable until it wasn't. And that decline affected young and old alike, for all realized it was something inescapable with the natural passage of time and decay.

So of course, I wanted the company, and was grateful that Gene and Estelle thought of me. I had some idea at the time this get-together, like others before, was indeed pre-planned, rehearsed, responses vetted, but at our luncheon that early October afternoon everything seemed quite benign, quite in place.

They arrived just after noon, still warm out, still delightfully breezy and smelling more woodsy by the day. There was, off in the distance, the faint sound of a chain-saw and closer, some birds squabbling, but other than that, the peace and quietude of the woods. And it was Gene who first made note of it.

"It's always a pleasure to be here, Jerry," he said, carrying a wicker picnic basket, his other arm now around my shoulders as I maneuvered the crutch into the lawn area. Meanwhile, Estelle went inside the house from the kitchen entrance where she knew a folding table and folding padded chairs would be stored away in the pantry. Gene left me to help her bring the three chairs and table into the lawn area.

"What happened to the chuppa platform?" he asked, returning. "I envisioned having lunch on it."

"It's now a shelter for the deer this winter," I said. "I had some workmen put it up in the woods."

Estelle laughed. "I'm sure they'll appreciate that."

"Well, they're pretty domesticated after all. They know when a human is trying to befriend and assist them. In a way, they're as attuned to humans as cats and dogs."

"Speaking of which," Gene put in, "did you ever get Peter's Puss'n'Bots up and running?"

"You mean Rayitas?"

"Is that its name?"

"Yeah, Peter named it; it's Spanish for little stripes. He's sitting on the window sill next to the front door. I get a loud meow on my phone if there is a delivery or a porch pirate or some girl scout selling cookies. It's actually quite handy. And look," I said, unbuttoning my jacket, "my son's 911 gift pendant. So now I'm completely hooked up biometrically. I even feel robotic at times so I must be living in the moment."

"How is your knee," he asked.

"I'm making progress. Chris was here last week and I did the inside staircase using this crutch. I finally gave up the Studio and slept in the master bedroom. Tuesday I begin using a cane. I picked out a sturdy wooden one rather than one made of titanium; I think it looks better on me. And then I'm ready to climb the stairway to the stars."

"So the physical therapy must be working," Estelle concluded, setting the table with a tablecloth they brought with them, fancy ceramic plates, silverware, wine glasses, napkins.

"Yeah, Chris is a pro. Knows his stuff. He and Caroline make a great team. But he told me that while they have a loving relationship, marriage is out of the question. And I found out that Caroline was married once before, early on. She never mentioned it to me and I never pried of course, but it's interesting to find out something about someone after nearly a decade or so."

Gene and Estelle exchanged glances, smiling now at each other.

"Remember, we lived together for almost five years before we got married, Grandpa," Estelle said, "and we're still finding out new stuff about each other."

"All good," Gene added, looking lovingly at Estelle, reaching for her hand across the table.

"Better than good," Estelle countered. "Pregnancy is underrated. I can actually feel the baby move and that's a real turn on. Baby; not *he* or *she*. I don't want to find out its sex beforehand. I want to go full term with woke blinders on."

Had there been some conflict about the pregnancy I hadn't been aware of? Had its confirmation come before or after they decided to tie the knot? Not that it mattered or was any of my business really. But now I surmised they had missed a period and decided then and there it was the time to send out invitations. It only made sense. But had Gene proposed abortion rather than marriage? I leave it to you, dear Reader, to parse that out for whatever it's worth.

"And another small surprise," Gene said, reaching into the picnic basket, withdrawing from it a chilled bottle of Vouvray.

I was delighted and had him corkscrew it open. "To the Samuels," I toasted. "All three of you now."

We dove into our chopped liver sandwiches and potato salads.

"Any word from Peter?" Estelle asked.

"They arrived quite tired but the trip was flawless," I said, quoting from an email Peter sent a few days prior. "He's going to be putting out a quarterly newsletter to all friends and relatives, remember, so everyone will be up to date and they won't be tied up answering correspondence. They'll be much too busy for that, he wrote. So you're on the list and you should be hearing something by year's end."

"And Paul," Gene asked. "Have you talked to him lately?"

"He and Jean are really hitting it off. They took this weekend off to leaf-peep the trees somewhere in Vermont . I'm really happy for him. He says Jean is so much like Clara, they could have been sisters. Y'know, they actually knew each other from years ago."

"I think I knew that," Estelle said. "I'm so happy for Dad."

The wine was taking its effect and I was feeling especially energetic, so before wedges of strawberry shortcake were distributed, I suggested, "Let's take a walk in the woods and come back for dessert. I've only seen the carpenter's video of the deer shelter. Since you're here to grab me if I have any trouble with the crutch, now's a good time to see it in person, since I paid for it sight unseen."

"Great idea," Gene said and we were off across the back lawn and into the woods. I had very little trouble with the crutch, making sure it was planted firmly on the ground and not on some fallen branch or a soft spot before I took my step. I led the way and Estelle and Gene followed, taking in the lovely fall atmosphere. And soon the clearing was before us, the shelter perfectly placed about 8 feet off the ground, perfectly secure with the 4x4's firmly buried in cement bases, with one edge of the platform screwed tightly onto a board and the board deeply bolted into a mature oak at the edge of the clearing.

Gene seemed to be impressed. "Wow!" he exclaimed. "A Waldorf-Astoria in the Woods."

"Bambi's family are going to have to make reservations," Estelle put in. "They'll all want to sleep here."

That was a lovely Sunday, to be sure, but when they left around three to beat the rush-hour weekend crowds back to the City, the loneliness feeling I had been experiencing lately was back. With the crutch I could probably make it to the park and try to pick up a game of chess, then Uber back. Or get to the Senior Center in town and mix it up with a few fellow oldsters still rattling around. But I thought I would wait until I could cane it. The crutch looked menacing; the cane would look more natural, more in the keeping of an elderly image. And image today was everything, wasn't it?

But at least I could make it up and down stairs and so later that afternoon I used the Studio to advance this memoir since the computer table was set against the large window overlooking the porch, the lawn and woods beyond, while there was no such table in the master bedroom. But now I was sleeping and showering upstairs like before. And with Caroline helping me return my clothes to the upstairs closets and with Chris's help, a bureau which held underwear and shirts, I was totally back in business.

And the following Tuesday, Chris arrived with an array of canes, some metal, one lightweight poly-something-or-other, others wood, some with rounded curved tops, others with straight grips. He recommended an adjustable metal cane with a 'T' hand grip. I chose just the opposite: a classic thick wooden cane with a rounded top and a rubber foot. He carefully measured fist-to-floor and promised it would be ready by Thursday when next he would see me. Then a session or two of staircase caning up and down and therapy would be over. All that was left was an annual physical with Dr. Francona, bill payment, and I was free—somewhat impoverished, but free of the ordeal of the past two months.

Which is more or less as it happened that month of October. Chris delivered my cane on Thursday, we practiced the stairs and we wrapped up therapy on Saturday. The following week, Caroline returned for a full 5-1/2 day workweek. And on that Wednesday at 11AM she drove me into town for my physical with Dr. Francona, left me at his office while she did food shopping for the rest of the week.

Francona was happy to see me, of course, because now he would be paid for the services he rendered (whatever they were) with his daily visits to the hospital. And seeing that I was now using only a cane for walking balance, even more pleased. He gave me a thorough physical—blood pressure, oxygen level, lungs, urine and feces samples, bloodwork with PSA and other cancer markers and naturally the right knee which, except for a couple of scars now looked exactly like my left knee. He made notes on his computer and compared them with those of the physical I had last fall. There was one disparity he needed to check out again. And it had to do with my heartbeat. He needed to take an electrocardiogram, standard procedure at my age, but he noticed something with his stethoscope that seemed a bit different this time.

From youth I had a small heart murmur but that wasn't it. The ECG showed something called sinus bradycardia—frequent ectopic ventricular beats. They had gone up about 15% since my last ECG, now a borderline condition given my age. Francona advanced the theory that the stress of the knee condition was possibly causing this rise. Had I ever experienced a pain or a burning in my chest, he asked.

I had to be truthful. "A handful of times, usually in bed at night. But they were not long lasting and I figured it was gas or something I ate."

"Not walking around? Exercising? When you used to play tennis?"

"The pain isn't severe. Just lying in bed, reading or watching TV. Just a couple of seconds, that's all."

"Well, it's something we'll look at again. We'll take another ECG in a couple of months when you've been walking a while with the cane. It could be just stress from the physical workouts... but write down in a notebook or on a calendar when these pains come on and what you were doing that day."

"Will do."

"Otherwise, you're in very good shape, knee notwithstanding. And I'm punning on that," he laughed.

I felt good, good enough to entertain an offer from my son to see his co-op again. For soon after my return home from the accident we had a discussion about my being out in Montclair by myself at night, somewhat incapacitated now and vulnerable to breakins and other misfortunes of the elderly living alone. He proposed the idea that I move in with him, for his was a two-bedroom, two-bath affair, with 2 elevators, 24-hour doorman and underground garage parking space. I'd retain my privacy but with added security.

It was a nice thought, but I blew him off. I was still using the walker at the time and depended on Caroline for most of the daily chores I could no longer accomplish. But I still felt I had some level of independence and self-reliance. The thought of moving back to the city... and selling the house—since Paul had said several times he didn't want it, even as an inheritance—was still off the table. But he persisted: I should take advantage of a tight market and make myself a million dollars in a heartbeat. With money like that I could move anywhere or go into a retirement community. After all, I was in my 90's now. How much longer did I think I had to leave things so undecided?

And then the bullet to the knee, my hospital stay and the now-paid bill, *sans* insurance. Such events have a way of reappraising an opportunity. Thus, a telephone call from Paul midway through October:

"Dad, you've got to see my co-op again. I've done some work on it. It's certainly big enough for both of us. Privacy and a second full bathroom. In the winter you can go down to Florida. I'll help you get you down there. Jean would like to go, too, over the Holidays. And I'll be staying at Jean's place most of the time anyway. It's much closer to the school. You still have some City friends I know, so it's not as if you're a loner here. Why don't you consider moving in with me?"

"Because I have everything I need in Montclair. Caroline takes good care of me and..."

"And most of your old friends have died off. That's what you've said."

"A lot of them have. I still have some friends at the Senior Center and chess in the park."

"And you need Caroline to drive you there now."

"It's what she does. I'm paying top rate for her services."

"After paying off your hospital bill, how long can that last?"

"How long can *I* last? That is the real question."

"Nobody knows the answer to that question, Dad. It's really how do you want these last years to go? You want to be comfortable. You want to continue doing the things that keep you and your mind active. You don't want to be limited in what you can still do without killing yourself in the process. Going out on your terms, not forced to live on someone else's plan for you."

"Exactly, son. So that is Montclair in my scheme of things. I'm still able to make that decision for myself. And that's what I want for myself; my plan, not someone else's."

But I folded after I did a quick accounting in my head. Even with a monthly Social Security check and even with Chris's temporary intervention at an end, future-wise I'd still be laying out around 7 grand a month, times 12—which—with bonuses was now close to $90,000 a year. Adding to that, yearly living expenses and house repairs of roughly $30,000. And since I'd be giving up driving, various transportation costs. I'd be spending somewhere around $120,000 annually just to keep me up and running. Well, not running, but hopefully caneing.

That lifestyle might last a couple of years, penny-pinching my way to Heaven. And what I'd have left is the house, just the house and its valuable acreage. True, with that money I could name my own end-game, find an assisted-living compound somewhere, or even book an extended round-the-world cruise. And, of course, hand it all over to sophisticated thieves just waiting to exploit elderly confusion.

But for the moment, with Caroline back on her usual schedule and my caneing improving daily going up and down from bedroom to studio, with side trips to the deer encampment to see if my dog kibbles had been eaten (they had been, but probably not by deer who still could forage for greenery) I was making great progress on my memoirs, 5-7 pages a day! But then, Paul wanted me to come in for lunch at his place and on the last Sunday in October, just before Halloween and election day the following week, and he was out to pick me up around noon.

"Jean is with her family this weekend," he explained, "so I had no one to talk to, and then I thought of you," he laughed, as I slid into the front seat with my cane by my side. "How's that working out?" he asked.

"All good," I said. "If I turn it upside down, I can use it as a hockey stick."

He laughed. "I'd buy front row seats to see that!"

This being Sunday noon, the highways into the city were clear of traffic and we made good time using the George Washington Bridge and down the West Side Highway to avoid congestion pricing, even discounted as it was on the weekend. My son's place on Riverside Drive and the Seventies was well above the 59th Street demarcation zone, but the program had so enraged the city, it had become a flashpoint for demonstrations, much as Columbia University had become during the Gaza War. It was best to stay away, whatever the cost.

We found a spot to park on the street right in front of his building. So instead of using his underground parking spot, we walked through the front entrance where Paul introduced me as his Dad to the doorman, Juan. "Lots of cabs along Riverside Drive," my son said, "and Juan knows them all. I hardly use my car at all, but I'm glad to have the dedicated garage space as part of my monthly dues."

We elevatored up to the 8th floor and Paul's corner co-op apartment. I hadn't been there for a couple of years now, and was re-impressed at its size and luxuriousness. He had bought some new furniture, new curtains, re-painted the place and added potted plants throughout. "The plants are from Jean," he said, almost apologetically. "Her apartment is filled with them, and these are its babies. Her apartment is actually larger than mine, and sunnier too. In the summer, she sets out cherry tomatoes on stakes by the windows. I have that small balcony off the master bedroom but it only gets late afternoon light, not enough for tomatoes, but some terrific sunsets."

"Clara grew tomatoes when you lived in Edgewater if I remember correctly."

"Yeah, in the little garden we had. Clara and Jean have so much in common, it's frightening. Sometimes I think I'm talking to Clara. They knew each other in teacher's college, did you know that?"

"Yes. You told me that."

Paul led me around the apartment as would a real estate agent, forgetting that I had been up to the apartment years ago. "So here is my bedroom and the balcony and there's a full bathroom behind that door. And across the hallway is the guest bedroom and another full bathroom down the hallway. And you can see how spacious the living room and dining area are. And through the accordion panels is a full electric kitchen with a microwave and dishwasher. There's a garbage chute outside in the hallway and downstairs in the basement is a full laundry with washers and dryers and even ironing boards."

"Sounds like you found the perfect spot, son."

"Well, that's what I want to talk about. I have some deli sandwiches and beer in the refrigerator. It's not too windy today so let's bring them out on the balcony and have a chat."

Paul did all the back-and-forth because with my cane I could only carry a couple of capped Coronas. But finally we were settled in, and on this clear October day I could easily see all up and down the Hudson and New Jersey beyond. A narrow balcony to be sure, hardly a 'terrace', but a spectacular view over Riverside Park's tree line. I was beginning to have the feeling that I was there to take it all in, to begin to see my son's apartment as my own.

And I was right.

"I'm spending more and more time with Jean, as you can imagine, Dad."

"Which Jean are we talking about? Estelle's Gene or your girlfriend Jean."

Paul laughed. "Suppose I said it's about both Jeans and get that out of the way."

"Fair enough," I said, chomping down on my delicious shrimp salad sandwich.

"My Jean has invited me to move in with her and our school is much closer to her apartment than it is to mine. We can get there in ten minutes on the #1 IRT. Here it's closer to a half hour."

"So after talking to Estelle's Gene you've come up with a plan."

"Well, it's no secret that they would love to have the Montclair house. With a baby coming it would be ideal—and who would know that better than I. I thought at first you and Mom were crazy to leave New York, but I realized we couldn't stay in Forest Hills with Rachel's memory on our minds every day. The change of scenery changed my life—for the better. It was the right move at the right time. For you and Mom as well."

"Well, what are you saying? You think a change of scenery is better here in the guest room?"

"Take whatever room you like. I'll be living with Jean. The apartment would be all yours. And if Caroline won't help out, we'll get another aide to look in on you, to do shopping and laundry."

"Caroline has often told me she doesn't want to commute. Her place is with Chris in Jersey."

"So we'll get someone else, just as competent."

"Who is this 'we'll'?"

"Okay, so here's the deal. Change your Will so that Estelle is the primary beneficiary to the Montclair estate if and when you die. I don't want the place and neither does Peter. Estelle does, so give it to her. That's number one."

"I can see doing that. I have no problem with that. Who knows? She may not be with Gene when I die, and the house would be a great inheritance for her, especially with a baby. As for Peter, it seems like he's making his way for now, but you never know. So I would want to give something to him in the Will as well. Maybe whatever I still have in savings and investments."

"Great."

"And you, my son, what do you get from all of this? You're giving up an inheritance that is rightfully yours. Besides, things may not work out with your Jean before I die. Would you move back here? Would we become roommates?"

"Anything's possible, Dad. But I'm in pretty good financial shape at the moment. I don't foresee us becoming roommates. We would look for some nice places for you, some well-known retirement colonies."

"Like the Villages in Florida. You know, I'm going down to see it over Thanksgiving, don't you? I'll be with Gene's grandfolks, The Rappaports."

"I know that."

"So what if I like it there? Suppose I stay on. Suppose I take Gene's offer and trade the Montclair property in lieu of picking up the hospital bill and then paying for all my future expenses if I move to The Villages. What happens to this apartment then?"

"I'll sub-let it. The co-op allows that with some reservations. And if things don't work out with Jean and you're down in Florida, I won't renew the sub-let and take back this apartment."

"Well, first things first. I can change my Will with the lawyer who drew it up in Montclair. And I can go down to Florida on Gene's dime to stay with the Rappaports and see The Villages over Thanksgiving. And only then will I decide what I want for myself in my nonagenarian years. This has to be a rational, not emotional decision. I still have my mind to consider."

CHAPTER 23

Speaking of my mind, it was now focused on completing my memoirs thru the end of October and most of November—until just after Thanksgiving weekend. I'd end it there with my decision on what I was going to do, where I would be living, how I saw my end days: visiting doctors' offices, dodging golf carts, fixated in front of a screen—either at the movies or the TV or the smartphone—for that was the most common ritual for those without wife or partner. Sure, there were Senior Singles Clubs everywhere, but heavily in favor of women, women with very set ways, left adrift after death or divorce of their mate, whichever came first. As for the men, we seemed to have more time on our hands, though time was continually running down faster now with more and more health concerns; a complex and awful reality awaited us.

So I knew I didn't want to keep writing—or couldn't—after some future point of declining cognitivity and awareness. Writing was as much a chore as it was a diversion, I found. It kept me occupied throughout the day, but interfered with sleep—as I tended to mull over and revise that day's work. Yet I was producing 5-7 finished pages a day, depending on how long my breaks were, the revisions made, the intricacies of the subject matter. I figured the final draft would be about 200 pages, and that I would self-publish on the Internet. No publisher in his or her right mind would be interested in my story, after all. Not when every opinion writer in both Republican and Democrat camps had already pocketed their advances on the November election which had occupied the public's mind for the past year or so.

It was that way four years ago, I remember, when it seemed every book published had a political message to convey. Of course, we didn't know then what a Trump win would mean for the next four years—and how the small generational fissures we observed would widen into all-out abysses. The riots of Columbia University, UCLA and dozens of other 'citadels of higher learning' dividing pro-Palestinian activists from pro-Jewish activists was nothing compared to our southern border's 'final solution' (in the words of a *Times* correspondent on the scene). Peter, now happily working in Australia couldn't believe that his Nazi mis-quote was so prescient. The two-sided Z Generation had broken America's back. The Z's—idealists, traditionalists and loyal corporate soldiers—mainly Democrats and beholden to the ideals of Obama, Biden/Harris—vs. the Not-Z's—nihilists, unbridled bigots and gun-toting 'Constitutionalists' —mainly Republicans firmly dedicated to flipping a congressional minority with more of Trump's MAGA madness. It made for some interesting confrontations—but the question of resolving the differences in our polarized society remained. And Trump, try as he might, couldn't quiet the growing dissension by manipulating tariffs and other diversions. It would win the 2028 election for Newsom and the Democrats handily and finally bury Trump's four years of unstructured, unvetted Truth Social turmoil with an overwhelming consensus for peaceful, constructive reconciliation.

November 2028's election, I realized, was most likely to be my last. I had seen it all—from World War II through dozens of mini-wars from demonic dictators to Democratic dreamers. Each of the five generations I witnessed— Silent, Boomers, X's, Millennials, Z's— thought they had the answer to a better way of life, to more healthy lifestyles, to a higher standard of living, to educating populations about the destruction of the environment, to a more secure and productive world, to world peace and prosperity. Each self-righteous generation got it wrong, naive to the wants and needs of the others; and each contributed, unknowingly in most cases, to the depression and growing despair of the past few years. Surely, there had to be a way out of this. Trump didn't have all the answers by eliminating tariffs effectively ending the recession, but knew instinctively that America had had enough: we needed a time to heal, to regrow the economy, to get back our diversified pride, our basic optimism for the common good. Oh, and our sanity, let's not forget that!

Luckily, what was left of the Silent Generation was past a point of decision-making. I'd leave the scene with as little trauma and theatrics as possible. It wasn't fair to the family, after all. What seemed more fair, and what I accomplished somewhere towards the end of October, was revising my Will with Harold Randleman, the lawyer in Montclair who had prepared, then revised my Will after Ruthie's passing. I left the house, not to my son Paul, but to my granddaughter Estelle. Her brother Peter would get whatever was left in my bank account. Paul would inherit what was left in my IRAs. And a couple of environmental conservancies would get set amounts. With copies made and notarized, I placed them all in the wall safe in the bedroom—ironically, right beside Peter's gun, emptied of bullets now—waiting for Paul, the only person with its combination to open it upon my death.

Halloween brought with it a cold spell. The kids were out and running about as Rayitas noted with meows throughout the evening. I had twenty little kits of candy and loose change ready for them, but only half were taken by the shivering hoard, their parents patiently waiting in cars at the end of the Lane.

The cold snap made me leave the Studio for the master bedroom, because even with an electric space heater or two, it was still freezing down there. And it was just as cold, if not colder five days later when the polls were open for voting. The Republicans had hoped the cold would keep people from voting in New Jersey, now heavily converted to the Democratic ticket. But no such luck. Indeed, the country wanted no part of the Trump endowment: Vance and Haley and Trumplicans everywhere fell by the wayside. The United States of America was getting United again, at great pain after a decade of turmoil and division. True, America was now producing again, but now with international supply chain delays, at a significant premium to what was spent before 'our investment in ourselves.' And so, 'Made Solely In America™' tags were disappearing by container ship boatloads: ™ no longer standing for Trademark but rather Trump/Musk. It was a tepid start, but we were finally acknowledging the rest of the world again.

Perhaps, I thought, even the immigration mess could be resolved peacefully somehow—the one unresolved issue even Trump couldn't fix in his second term in office, tariffs be damned.

For the cartel coyotes held the Trump card in their hands even as he was sworn in as President in 2025. The Southern border would be their diversion, even as Trump sent thousands of National Guard and Army personnel down there as the Failing Wall (a play on Wailing Wall by some *Guardian* wit) was being completed. It left the East and West Coasts unprotected, or rather, protected only by local police and the Coast Guard. So while there were symbolic clashes along the Southern border, the main swell of undocumented immigrants were dropped off all along the Eastern and Western coastlines as soon as darkness fell. And no amount of drones or speed boats or explosive buoys were enough for the hoards of passengers on fishing boats, pleasure craft and Chinese submarines by the dozens. It was Cuba's Mariel's Boat People in a massive *deja vu* after 70 years.

Trump had been taken in, completely conned it seemed, by this diversionary tactic. He was committed to finishing the wall, of sending millions back to Mexico and the Latin American countries to its South. But they simply turned around and with the money they had made under the table whilst working in the US, bought their way back via the coastlines.

Even so, now four years later, The Democrats with Gavin Newsom at the helm took the Presidency as well as keeping both houses of Congress. I didn't even stay up past my bedtime to get the West Coast tallies. *Landslide* didn't do it for the Wednesday papers. They called it a *Nationwide Earthquake.* And the aftershocks are still being felt now weeks after the election.

I had been working diligently on my memoirs for about two months now but it was tiring me out. My writing was reflecting that, losing its focus and energy at times, so I figured I was ready for a break and began preparing for my Florida trip. I had Caroline put together some of my better summer clothing, a finely tailored white linen suit, short sleeve shirts, Bermuda and cargo shorts, sandals and so forth—things I imagined retired Floridians wore. Everything was large on me as I had my personal Shrinkflation these past two decades, not bothering to update my wardrobe since Ruthie passed away.

Well, I thought, who was I impressing, really. Certainly not the Rappaports. Their role was to impress *me*. Obviously Gene had told them of the deal: If they could convince me to stay down there in The Villages with their crowd, Gene would repay me for what I laid out for the hospital bills and all other living expenses I would incur down there in Florida—in lieu of Estelle taking over the title to the Montclair house, for she was already the beneficiary to it when I died. This was a trade in Gene's favor, of course, because I estimated the house and land to be worth well over a million. So for me to break even, I'd have to live for another decade or thereabouts. I had better start taking those telomere-extending pills.

And then I started to wonder about a deal Gene could have made with Paul—to have me live in the City in my son's co-op apartment while he and Jean got it on in her rent-stabilized apartment a few blocks North of Columbia. Was there some kind of time limit here, some kind of 'in lieu of' consideration? We never got that far when we had our discussion on the balcony. It was all about my safety, my comfort, the wonderful sunsets. But Gene was a player. Paul had to have known about the deal made to Estelle. And maybe, just maybe, there was another "finder's fee" involved: Have me temporarily live in Paul's co-op apartment. Then have Paul and Jean break up and he'd move back in as father/son roommates. Which would no doubt send me caneing to an old-age home, now that the Montclair estate was no longer mine, nor the master bedroom in Paul's co-op apartment. Privacy, independence, self-reliance, gone in an instant. A deviously spiteful plan which would have pissed me off no end. If you want to know the definition of *paranoia,* friends; I just gave you a stunning example.

Something was happening to my mind; I can't fully describe it, but it had to do with not thinking things through as to what was in *my* best interest, not someone else's. It wasn't Alzheimer's because I could still think rationally, in the moment, lucid and insightful. But there were missing pieces now, events happening about me that I should have known about, but didn't. Or forgot that I did. Or distort with fantastical scenarios like the one above. I didn't want to play games, certainly not at my age. But being taken advantage of—of being robbed of fooled —ah, that was #1 on my list of end-game no-no's. It made me very cautious these days about things I used to do spontaneously without a thought of theft or fraud. Like ordering things off the Internet. Like using my bank's debit card or PayPal for purchases. Like moving money between investment accounts. Like signing over my house to my Granddaughter upon my death. But then again, I wanted to believe I was dealing with people who had my best interest at heart. Who better than family?

Had I just been lucky these last few years without a major loss? (I still considered the bullet to my knee an unlucky accident, not a loss—a one-in-a-million chance trajectory off a marble floor.) Yet, I needed to write things down now, just as *Recisions* advised. Write them down in a kind of time-line, considering as many present and future resulting factors as I could, giving them numerical significance for each major decision to be made. For I sensed I was making rapid, impulsive, reflexive decisions, more and more out of emotion than rationality, or from someone else's influence and trust. That needed fixing... while I still had the impulse to fix it. Once that impulse was gone, I surmised, I wouldn't be able to distinguish the real from the faux, the good deal from the bad, the 'prune from the pit' as my mother liked to say.

So I put my memoirs on hold for the moment (I figured there were approximately 200 pages already written) and concentrated on my trip to Florida, coming up in less than a week's time, the following Wednesday. Gene and Estelle would pick me up and I'd be leaving from Newark on a privately chartered business jet around noon—getting into Orlando in about 3 hours' time. The Rappaports were to meet me there, and we'd all Uber out to The Villages. Nothing planned for that Wednesday evening, except for a light dinner, as I would need my rest before the hectic Thanksgiving Day dinner celebration the following day. Friday and Saturday were to be spent apartment hunting with a licensed real estate broker and evenings devoted to the many fun diversions The Villages offered with the Rappaports as my guides. And Sunday I'd be returning to Orlando for my flight back to Newark where Gene and Estelle would once again be waiting for me, and my ride back to Montclair. I headlined each segment of the weekend into a shirt pocket notebook, with space for additions, corrections and comments as *Recisions* suggested. A sort of calendar of events—but without expectations or preconceived notions of success or failure. And already I was feeling more confident about Thanksgiving weekend to come.

That was the plan, and for the most part it came off like clockwork.

In a minute I'll go into the details of a conversation I had with Gene and Estelle upon my pickup at Newark that Sunday. But let me add here that the Rappaports were terrific hosts and quite to my surprise did not try to influence me into joining them at The Villages. They gave me a guest bedroom on the second storey of their home overlooking a man-made lake and wonderful sunsets beyond. The Thanksgiving meal at the common restaurant was delicious, even though the 4th sitting they originally requested had already been sold out, and so we settled for the 3rd sitting from 4PM to 6PM. Even so, everything was fresh and beautifully prepared and served. And our rides in the AI golf cart they owned was even fun, though I was skeptical at first of being driven around with the Rappaports looking back and often chatting with me as we made corner turns or encountered other carts and electric bikes.

On Friday they turned me over to a Mr. Timothy Otis—a real estate salesman from The Villages main office. A very likable guy but like all RE salesmen, his income was based on the commissions made on his sales. So he had some flesh in the game. The problem was, I realized, I hadn't fully decided on just what I wanted—only it should be a nicely furnished rental apartment, large enough for myself and a visiting guest, preferably on the ground floor with a small garden or patio in the back if possible. I would probably be buying or leasing a golf cart to get around, so it had to have a driveway as no carts were permitted to remain curbside.

And how much was I willing to spend for a furnished rental?

"The sky's the limit," I said, knowing that Gene was picking up the tab.

Otis was a bit disappointed I was looking at rentals, rather than buying something outright, but he had a list of apartments to show me, and so we started out after breakfast on a bright Friday morning, this time me sitting next to Otis in the front seat of his cart.

"So how did the trip go?" Gene wanted to know, Estelle sitting in the back of their EV Charger.

"It was fine," I said. "Everything ran smoothly."

"And did you rapport with the Rappaports?"

"Well, they're rather conservative as you no doubt know. Four years ago they thought Trump's election would somehow unite the country again, the way it used to be. Now, of course, they were having second thoughts about the entire Republican agenda and decided not to vote this time around. We really didn't discuss politics at all while I was there. Thank God!"

"And did you have a nice Thanksgiving?"

"It was lovely, peaceful. And I had some time to watch the Macy's Day Parade in New York on TV. I was gratified that there were no people lying down on the street like back in 2025; instead, this year, catching a glimpse of an unauthorized flatbed float that had a portly blonde-coiffed man dressed like Donald Duck waving a crutch with its foot the shape of a golf club and banners on either side that read: THIS LAME DUCK IS THE *REAL* TURKEY!"

"Yes, I saw that too!" cried Estelle from the back seat. "I couldn't stop laughing."

"And how did you find The Villages?" Gene pressed on.

"It was like summer camp. They had an app for your phone so you could see all the activities planned for that day. Exercise in the morning and crafts in the afternoon. The large central plaza was the main meeting place and you took off from there. If you didn't want to cook, you ate cafeteria-style in mess halls with outdoor backyards and if you had a cane or a walker, they had helpers bring you your food. They even had a Fed Up. It was all very well planned. I was tested to see if I could drive an AI-programmed electric golf cart because that's how most people got around. A few bikes. But in my section cars weren't allowed. Just trucks for deliveries."

"And did you qualify for a golf cart?" Gene asked

"Yeah. But the Rappaports put me in the back of theirs, even though they said you were nervous about them programming the AI controls. It was a gas, if you'll allow me to make a joke about it."

Gene laughed. "Yeah, I had some reservations at first but it sounds like fun."

"Well, I could see it's like an amusement park for many. But it had a serious side, like the 24-hour health services clinic and the security and fire stations they showed me. I have to admit a lot of planning went into building the community."

"And how did you like their home?"

"It was quite nice, actually. A two-storey wood framed house fronting an artificial lake with a small backyard and some nice shade trees. But... that wasn't anything like what was being offered to me. I would be living in an apartment available in a more modest neighborhood."

"And?"

"Otis only showed me a few one storey and two storey cottages with two-bedroom, one-and-a-half-bath ground floor apartments even though I told him I could now manage a flight of stairs. They were all about 800 square feet or so, nice kitchens and bathrooms. All in this fake tile. And the living room and bedroom floors were also in the fake tile. Fake tile on the walls—everywhere. Made for easy clean up, but what a sterile look!"

"You could put down rugs and carpeting, no?" Estelle suggested.

"Sure. You could do anything to make the place liveable. But then, every so often you might get the urge to look out a window. No woods, no wildlife, no lakeside view like the Rappaports had. Just rows of three-storey condos and two-storey cottages with golf carts and electric bikes parked alongside. I guess the idea was, you'd be so bored living in your apartment, you'd go to the square where all the activities for that day were being held. And you'd take a class in something, or work out somewhere, or go on a nature hike or see a movie. As I said, it was like summer camp for Seniors."

"Doesn't sound so bad, Grandpa."

"Well, it wasn't so bad. Just not me, that's all. I took a lot of photos and had Otis send me some more information on my email but made no commitment one way or the other. If I had a wife, maybe this would be a good end-game, but for a single..."

"I'm sure you'd find some nice lady who..."

"C'mon, Estelle. Let's be real. Getting involved with someone at my age puts you on a fast track to cemetery living—and I already have one foot in the grave."

So, while Florida held some appeal to me, The Villages seemed a little too sterile, too programmed, too boring. I began to realize I needed more socialization with people like me who shared my interest in world events, cultural activities and nature. Sure, I could settle back and live a fully relaxing life—Gene's money taking care of the anxiety of running out of mine—but for the cane, and this new heartbeat prognosis, I felt perfectly fit. My basic instinct told me to just stay where I was, keep doing what I was doing, not to make any radical change.

And yet I could see how much transferring my house to Estelle and Gene, especially now with a baby on the way, would be of extreme value to them. They had helped me in so many ways, I felt a debt of gratitude towards them. So maybe there was some kind of compromise that could be reached. But I also knew that time was running out; that I would have to make some kind of final decision before the Holidays.

First off, I would need to talk to Caroline for the day-to-day support for my current existence depended mainly on her. Monday morning, after a good night's sleep, I found she was back in the kitchen making breakfast for me.

"How was your Thanksgiving?" I asked.

"Oh, wonderful," she said. "Chris and I visited friends from the Southern Jersey shore. It was lovely. And how was your Florida trip?"

"First class all the way," I said. "Executive jet down there, put up in a beautiful guest room, shown around the place by golf cart. Had a wonderful Thanksgiving dinner with all the trimmings."

"And the prospects for moving down there?"

"Well, that's the option I have to think about," I said after a sip of coffee. "If I did, what would you do?"

"Oh, don't concern yourself about me," Caroline said. "I have plenty of opportunities around here. In fact, I'd be doing more of what I was trained for. I never really had to use those skills with you, you were always so healthy. Even now with the cane, you're not really a patient of mine; I'm sort of a general caretaker, an aide, not a practical nurse."

"Does that bother you?" I asked, sensing a note of disappointment in her voice.

"Well, of course not. I'd rather see you healthy as a horse. Less stress all around, and I enjoy working here, or I would have moved on long ago, Jerry."

"So you think we could go on like this for a time? I mean, no one knows how long that would be. You might be fully utilized as my hospice nurse at any time."

"Well, all I can say is, you'd be my third Myer over a decade or so. I pretty much know what to expect.

I went back to my memoirs that morning, putting in my observations about The Villages and bringing things up to date. There were three clear options before me, and I needed a fourth, I felt, to clear these other three off the table. Because none of them truly worked for me. One, stay in the house with Caroline as my caretaker, although I sensed she wanted to move on. Two, bite the bullet and move down to the Villages and the Rappaports, all on Gene's dime. Or finally, move in with Paul, have the social and cultural activities the city offered, but lose my independence and self-reliance, something I cherished all these years since Ruthie's passing.

It was easy to write down the pros and cons to each *Recision*—but at the end of that exercise it all became a blur. There was no good answer here. Even so, late on Monday, after Caroline had left for the day, I got a call from Paul. Classes had just wrapped up and he was wondering if he could join me for dinner, just the two of us. I said sure. Caroline had left a hefty meatloaf in the microwave to be warmed up, and I had some brussel sprouts in the vegetable bin that were getting soft and needed to be eaten.

Paul arrived around 5:30 and we relaxed with cocktails before dinner on the couch in the living room. We started off with politics, naturally, since the election of November 7th had been so overwhelmingly Democratic and the Republican answer so shockingly benign. No riots. No Capitol insurrection. Not even protest groups laying down on Broadway to be hauled off by the police. JD Vance was decent and conciliatory in his concession speech to Newcom. Maybe civility was entering mainstream politics again.

"So goodbye and good riddance to MAGA. Make America Grift AGAIN! Vance lost because he couldn't shake off Trump's lingering base of bigots and faked nostalgia for a simpler time, a time of plenty, a time of corruption, power and control. We didn't have to employ illegal aliens or so-called asylum seekers to do the dirty work. We had Blacks. And back then you didn't have to capitalize our imposed inferiority on them." *[Ed. Note: The author says preceding is to be read as sardonic cynicism].*

"Dad, that's being grossly hypocritical. You've often told me you depend on Caroline for your very existence—who's making more money than I ever did as a teacher. What are you saying?"

"Paul, I have very few options now. Everyone wants me to replant myself in Florida and start a new life at ninety. Do you realize how ignorant that sounds? The only thing I have in common with The Senility State is a fondness for chopped liver sandwiches. And Caroline makes the best I've ever had. If she ever decided to open a deli, she'd be making far more than I'm now paying her. She's the reason I'm still around and kicking."

"Maybe there's a way you can stay out here with Gene and Estelle and still have Caroline to assist you."

"Sure. Build a guest house in the back or convert the Studio to a small apartment, something like that."

"Sure. Why not?"

"Because then I'm a guest. A guest in my own home. And that's not the way I want to go out. That's not the way your Mom would want me to go out. We loved the privacy of the place; we loved doing our own thing, of bringing you up, of living independently and free. I know how much Gene and Estelle see in that. They see exactly what your Mom and I saw when we left Queens. So I know the feeling. But I'm not at a point where I can simply turn it all over to them."

"Would you live in New York? In Manhattan? Many people your age live quite comfortably there, even with greater disabilities than you. There are lots of things to do, clubs you can join and socialize. You've often talked about how good the restaurants were, and how you liked the museums and shows."

"Well, it certainly beats The Villages. I was bored... forgive the expression,... *bored to death!*"

Paul wisely let that tasteless quip go by. "I know of a two bedroom, two bath apartment right on Riverside Drive with a terrific view of the park and the river. It has 24-hour doormen, a couple of elevators and a roof garden besides. And of course the park itself is right across the street."

"Sounds like your co-op," I played along, while recalling having this discussion before.

"It *is* my co-op. I'd be moving in with Jean. We're getting that serious y'know."

"You mean, I'd take over your co-op. And what would happen if you and Jean were to break up. I'd have you back as a roommate? You'd get your master bedroom back and I'd get the guest room? This has all the ingredients of some kind of temporary arrangement so that I give this place up and move into the city, then eventually roommate with you."

"I can assure you, Dad, that's not how it is."

"It sounds like you and Gene had a long talk while I was gone."

"Which Jean are we talking about?"

"The lawyerly lawyer."

"Yes, we had a talk but it wasn't that long. He would actually purchase the co-op from me as an investment, and you could live there as long as you'd like and have all your living expenses paid for, even medical and further rehab—everything! There would be a second bedroom if it ever came to hospice. If Caroline wasn't available, we'd get some other help. It could all be put down in a contract."

"The Florida offer brought North."

"Dad, it makes sense. Think it over, won't you? I know the emotional attachment you have with this place, but maybe it's time to let reason take over emotion."

"Follow the money."

"Gene and Estelle are a lot like you and Mom. They want to raise their family here."

"Follow the mommy."

He laughed. "Exactly. You had reservations about moving out here. But Mom won out. And you often said what a smart move that was. History has a way of repeating itself."

"All right, Paul, I'll think it over. I like your co-op, you know. Nice view."

"And it's safe, Dad. Most important at your age. I won't have to worry about you there."

"Like Gene worrying about his grandparents driving around in AI golf carts," I laughed.

Paul had classes the next day so he left right after coffee and dessert. So now I had on the table two outside offers along with the alternative of doing nothing. Everything was coming into focus and some of my paranoia about having to room with my son in the City had evaporated. Indeed, Paul had never lied to me, and I could see his relationship with his Jean was evolving towards permanency. If lawyerly Gene were to purchase the co-op from Paul as an investment, he would do quite well, as high-end real estate prices in Manhattan were only going higher, now that the city had clearly divided between the moguls and the migrants.

True, I hadn't kept up with the real estate market. Since the mid-twenties, and even during the pandemic, it was skyrocketing upward, with both unaffordable rentals and home sales. Increases in insurance, taxes and fuel were forcing landlords to charge their tenants astronomical rents. And mortgage rates back in the 7-8% range were forcing established home owners to sit still and wait it out, even if they needed more space for their growing families.

Where they could, the best option was to enlarge their homes, making attics, basements, and garages living spaces, mostly for family members, like their adult children coming home to roost, but also for desperate newcomers renting anything with four walls and a roof. Which led to all sorts of confrontations with neighbors, HOAs and Town Boards. Builders needed to build smaller affordable units, but they couldn't or wouldn't because prices of raw materials and labor costs were literally going through the roof—given Trump's America First supply chain tariff policies and crackdown on cheaply paid under-the-table undocumented workers, aka illegals, aka migrants, aka asylum seekers, aka boat people, aka newcomers.

All this meant the country was stalemated, paralyzed, unable to lend or to borrow, but heavily in debt, leading to stagflation for the latter part of 2025, all of 2026 (especially noticeable on the July 4th weekend—ironically the 250th Anniversary of the Declaration of Independence—with the final dismissal of more than half a million 'bureaucratic' Federal Government employees) thus heading into 2027 with double-digit unemployment, double-digit inflation. Everyone was telling anyone who would listen: "I told you so."

But in truth, nobody got it right. The middle class had given notice, then unexpectedly retired, heading down South to cheaper, warmer climes, living out of cars, campers and tents in parks and parking lots, eating at the local Fed Up—(a successful new chain of bakeries serving affordable coffee/tea/fruit juices, cupcakes and donuts in a throwback quarters-only Horn & Hardart Automat venue)—or whatever the communal pantry had put out for that day, watching their kids drop out of colleges and fall by the wayside as tuition and living expenses were now only affordable for the elite.

As for the older generations who had saved enough to save themselves from the humiliation of being caught shoplifting or siphoning gas, we were just marking time until some health condition would take all the rest of our savings and relegate us to a "home" of some kind—a euphemism for hospice. And then, in remembrance, pass the unfinished memoir and/or photo album, please.

But of course we had somehow survived into 2028, or at least our smartphones were telling us that: that AI would come to the rescue, new fossilless-fuel industries created, new affordable abodes living off solar panels and flow batteries, new meatless hamburgers and alcohol/opiad-free recreational drinks, new ways to get through homicidal or suicidal impulses with your newly loaded zirgun. Stick with the Program and survive; the new mantra of the young and able and all others refusing to enlist and fight in a foreign war. Stick with the Program of peace and goodwill and of helping others cope. And wait patiently till your parents die and leave you the house and enough inheritance to move upstairs from the damp, roach-infested basement apartment where you've been living this past decade. You deserve it, after all. They brought you into this world; they need to bring you out. Alive if at all possible.

There would always be that fourth option for me, or rather, made for me: Placement in a secure 'old age home' or hospice, but not for a while, not while I still had my wits about me. I gave the other three options plenty of space and time, thinking out several years into the future and what that future would look like. I felt like a space cadet on my way to the planets and beyond to the stars. *Recisions*, and even Elon Musk couldn't help here; it was an irreversible leap into the unknown.

And of the three options—remain where I was, move to Florida, accept Paul's offer of his co-op—Paul's offer, after much soul searching, seemed the best choice. I knew instinctively that he didn't want to share his apartment with me. He seemed serious with Jean and was looking forward to moving in with her. So the co-op would essentially be mine and the adventure of returning to New York City was very attractive. If Gene was picking up the tab, I could Uber around and see some old friends still alive; go to museums and shows; have decent restaurant meals; have the place cleaned once a week. Giving up the Montclair property under these conditions seemed the wisest thing to do.

And so, a couple of days before the end of November, I called Paul to tell him of my decision. I would be moving into his co-op.

"Oh, Dad, that's great! It's what I was hoping for."

"So get packing. I'll be having Caroline do the same for me. Maybe everything I need you can put in your car. Mostly clothes, books and papers. A couple of paintings. Maybe 2 or 3 trips would do it."

"Oh, this is so great, Dad! How did you decide?"

"Well, I liked the idea of a trade: my place for Gene picking up the 'living expenses' tab for as long as I live. It means I can leave something to you and Peter and Estelle. And it means I don't have to worry about money for as long as I have left. He's getting a million dollar estate, but I'm getting a million dollar expense account. We'll see who comes out ahead."

Paul laughed. "Get it in writing."

"Oh, I intend to do that. I'll call him now and tell him of my decision. And like you said, I'll pass the agreement before the eyes of a lawyer I know out here. If it passes the smell test, he can start moving in the middle of December I figure."

"Hannukah. I know they'd like that. That's a great idea!"

"Maybe we could all have a Jewish Welcome Wagon party then. Bring Max out of retirement."

As I'm writing this, 12/1/2028, there are a quarter-million 'newcomers' formerly known as 'asylum seekers' formerly known as 'migrants' formerly known as 'illegals' living, or I should say, existing, in the five boroughs of New York City. It's no longer deemed a Sanctuary City since every hotel is overflowing, every house with a bedroom or basement is rented, every tent in Central Park's ballfield occupied. And with the colder weather now upon us, and with the public shelters full, the Mayor had announced 'relocation orders' to have their overflow move out of the City into the suburbs... sanctuary suburbs. Except few suburbs were accepting them, even with the $1,000/month stipend families were receiving while waiting for their asylum cases to come up in the courts—with the backlog of a year or more—enough money to pay some token rent, enough time to receive automatic citizenship for the anchor baby and probably the same for the mother... and possible father, should one step up and admit to parenthood and future support payments.

But the suburbs weren't buying into the City's scheme. Who would want some stranger in their house, looking at all the things they could pawn which would never be missed? Who would want a child care worker who doesn't speak English, doesn't have an education past grade school, may be selling their bodies or drugs, enjoys drinking and having friends over. Because that's what the City was pitching: licensed free child care, the 'license' being two weeks of training in a converted NYC public school. As for the men, some were being 'licensed' to drive an Uber or Lyft which led to all sorts of road rage incidents with legitimate taxi medallion holders. No vetting but plenty of fretting.

The immigration issue only intensified these past four years—instead of the Biden-Harris bill being 'completely dead on arrival', Trump's immortal words in his acceptance spe...

A RIFLE SHOT!! I distinctly heard a RIFLE SHOT from deep in the woods. Yes, it's hunting season, but not on my property, not with signs all around that this is private property! Too late in the afternoon to explore. I'll go out first thing in the morning, check the shelter and the Posted-sign trees. Hunting season should be banned here in New Jersey. But with the lobbyists in Washington, it wasn't going to happen. In fact, gun sales of all kinds set records last year. And so did murders of all kinds, not to mention suicides. Controlling the deer population was nothing compared to controlling the human population. Both, I would imagine, soon to be on the endangered list.

I didn't sleep well. I was up, showered and dressed well before Caroline was to arrive. Fortunately it was a mild day, a bit cloudy, but not freezing cold outside. I caned my way downstairs, put on my parka, and skipped coffee altogether. I needed to see the deer shelter early on, when I knew the deer would still be in the vicinity. I had a terrible feeling that the rifle shot I heard around sunset the evening before brought down one of my tribe. If that was true, there might be some evidence, some blood, perhaps a spent cartridge or two.

So I left Caroline a note that I had taken a walk in the woods, would be back soon… and headed off with a 20lb. bag of dog vittles in my backpack. Caneing through the underbrush was no longer a problem, the trees all denuded now and the drought-dry Fall had killed mostly everything off. I could clearly see the path before me for a great distance, no foliage to block my view. With nothing green to eat, the deer welcomed the dog vittles. I was now replenishing the various plastic tubs just inside the shelter every three or four days. There were also a couple of pails for rainwater coming off the tilted roof, but these were empty too, no measurable rain falling since before Thanksgiving. If the deer wanted a drink, they would have to go past my property line into a wooded area still owned by the county where ran a creek. Sometime in the past it was wisely determined that streams and creeks and other water tributaries would not be developed, but left in their natural state for wildlife and hiking trails. New Jersey often got things wrong, but this was the right call. And my property neatly bordered that titled 'wilderness area'.

I checked the shelter first and deposited the vittles in the four empty tubs—North, East, South, West. No sign of the deer. I looked around, going down several deer trails but saw nothing out of the ordinary. Only bird chirps, although I knew my presence there would freeze any deer's motion. I figured with the leaves all down, I might see one or two, but no.

Then I went further towards the housing developments now clearly seen through the trees.

And there on the boundary line where my property ended were my yellow metal signs at the beginning of various entryways, high enough so they wouldn't be torn down –

PRIVATE PROPERTY
NO TRESPASSING —tightly screwed, not nailed, into the fattest trees around. The signs were all there, all four of them about 200 feet apart, facing the backyards of the developments. Then after making a sharp left and caneing over towards the wilderness area, one more sign near the hiker's trail. Everything was in order. So what did I hear the evening before? Perhaps some homeowner was testing out his rifle. It was the scenario I most wished to be the likely one.

I returned to the house to find Caroline preparing my breakfast. She didn't know when I'd be back so she began making some scrambled eggs to go with already prepared bacon strips.

"I was in the woods. Last evening I heard a gunshot—probably a rifle—coming from that direction."

"Hunting season," she said. "It's happened before, you know."

"Sure. But now there's a shelter out there and that's where the deer go to get fed. I'm sure hunters have figured that out. Hunters who are trespassing on my property."

"I never thought that was a good idea," she said, spooning out eggs on my plate. "The deer can fend for themselves. This isn't the Animal Rescue League."

"The developments changed all that," I argued. "That used to be virgin woods back there. The deer had plenty of space to thrive. Their habitat was greatly reduced, and with it, their sources of food. They just have my acre and a half now and the strips of land along the creek. And they're sitting ducks for hunters along the creek. Excuse my mixed metaphor."

She laughed. "Maybe you should trade deer for ducks. You'd save a lot on food."

Caroline had touched a sensitive nerve. Since I put Spot down, I paid more attention to the deer as if they were pets. Which, of course, they weren't. But after Caroline would leave for the day, I longed for companionship now—and the deer who I'd often see on the back lawn knew me and didn't bolt away. They weren't pets exactly, but there was some communion there. I put out food and water for them; they returned the favor by letting me see them up close. A buck with antlers, two does, two fawns born that Spring. They didn't have names, but they did have personalities. Anthropomorphism. I knew some of this was neurotic, but so what? When Gene and Estelle moved in, would they continue caring for the deer? I would mention it, but obviously it couldn't be a condition for our trade. I would approach Estelle with the idea, since she would be spending more time there with the baby. And the baby would love to see the deer on the lawn. Real animals, not a Puss'n'Bots, not some kind of wheeled pull-along puppy like the kind I had when I was a toddler.

I returned to my memoir now quickly wrapping up. Caroline was tasked with giving most of my clothes to Goodwill, saving just the finest suits, sportcoats, shirts, pants and shoes for New York City. I had a small library and I wanted to take some books with me, some records and the 3-speed turntable from my youth, some portfolios from my advertising days, also a few paintings Ruthie did. But the local charity got all my ice skate and ski equipment left in the basement including a couple of nice nylon ski jackets and boots, and even a pair of rollerblades from the Seventies. I was leaving my car behind in the garage for Estelle's use, Ruthie's English bike for Gene to use. I certainly wasn't up for driving or pedaling any more, especially on New York City streets. I figured Paul would need to make three trips with the car full of boxes of books, paintings and clothes. And of course this laptop I'm typing on now.

There was nothing more I needed since Paul's co-op was completely furnished, tastefully I should add. And so all that needed to be done was a calendar of events, narrowed down to the second weekend in December when Paul could drive out and make the necessary trips back with my stuff. He could leisurely bring his things to Jean's place. But I could now tell Estelle and Gene that Hanukkah was the due date: the takeover of the Montclair estate. Empty, but for Rayitas at the front window and the deer on the back lawn wondering where I was.

Three days later, actually in the late afternoon of December 7th, I was upstairs writing when I spotted a drift of white smoke above the barren trees in the middle of the property, about where the shelter was. I had been there two days before to put out food for the deer, but limited myself to twice a week now, because of the cane, the 20 pounds of dog kibbles on my back, and with a recent soaking rain and seeing the creek had not run dry, not having to bring a jug of water for the deer to drink. The smoke seemed to be contained, not spreading, but I was alarmed just the same. It needed to be investigated at the very least. A fire in the woods, dry as it was, would be highly problematic. So I put on some boots, a parka, and my binoculars around my neck. Stupidly, I left my phone behind. I had no way of capturing whatever I was about to find on video. Put that down to a bit of senility, or carelessness of thinking my venture through.

I made my way across the lawn, and took a path with many old oaks beside it, trees wide enough so I could hide behind them and use my binoculars for a closer look. And indeed, once deep in the woods, I could now zero in on the deer shelter and the plume of smoke, made by a small campfire in a pit to one side of the shelter.

But that was not what was so disturbing to me. Beneath the shelter were two domed tents facing each other and a third tent just outside the shelter's perimeter. And there were people moving about: two large men in hooded parkas, a woman in a woolen cape and two children, a boy and a girl, around seven or eight years old. There may have been more people in the tents, but I wasn't going to stick around to find out. This was enough to clearly determine strangers camping on my private property. I had enough information to inform the police since I wasn't going to do any confrontational stuff, certainly not with a cane for a weapon in case it was needed. So I reversed course making sure I wasn't seen and made my way back to the lawn and thumbed my way into the house through the kitchen entrance.

By the time I returned it was twilight, and probably too late for the cops to come out and find their way through the forest, even if I were to lead the way. I would wait for tomorrow, a Saturday, and call the police after Caroline had left for the day at noon. Better, I thought, not to involve her at this stage. And I realized then that Paul was coming out later that day to begin moving my things to his place. I didn't want to involve him either. But maybe it was possible the two of us together could ask these people to leave the property. Paul was the diplomat in the family, and maybe the cops didn't have to come out. Maybe it could all be settled with a handshake, without the threat of the police. Surely these trespassers didn't want anything to do with the police.

So I placed a call to Paul. I needed to relate what I witnessed with someone just to make sure I was doing the right thing. The alternative, I realized, was to do nothing and let Gene and Estelle handle it the following week when they would be moving in. But not only was that unfair, but dangerous. So Paul's advice was crucial at that point.

"I have some disturbing news," was my opening line.

"The deal is off."

"No, the deal is still on. Are you coming out tomorrow to move some of my stuff."

"That's what we had planned, no?"

"Yes. That's still on as well. But I just found out this evening there are squatters on the property. They've pitched their tents under the deer shelter. Three tents."

"Squatters?"

"Squatters, trespassers, homeless vagrants, whatever you want to call them. Two men, a woman and a couple of young kids. There may be more, I didn't stick around to find out."

"Did they see you?"

"No. I was a good distance away watching through binoculars."

"Ummmm. I'd call the police first thing tomorrow. Let them handle it."

"Caroline will be here in the morning, finishing packing. I'd rather not have her see what may happen."

"Why not?"

"Because I'm working out a severance package for her that I'll give her next Friday, her last day here. Gene's not paying for it, it's entirely my gift to her. I want to give it to her on a high note, not have this drama as part of her goodbye. She needs to know she left me well taken care of, not going up against squatters on the property."

"She's a strong lady. She can handle it. Remember how she handled the shooting. I don't think this thing about having trespassers and cops on the property is going to affect her one way or the other."

"Well, you're probably right, dear. But I think I'll wait til she leaves. When are you coming out?"

"I thought I'd be there before she leaves tomorrow. I wanted to say goodbye to her too and give her a little present for all the years she's been with us and next weekend she'll be gone. I was planning to move half your stuff tomorrow and the rest out Sunday around noon, because as I understand it, Gene and Estelle want to move in next Saturday."

"Yes, that's the plan. So you'll be here tomorrow late morning?"

"Around 11:30. How does that sound? After Caroline leaves, and we find the people still there in the woods, we can call the cops. And we'll let them handle things. Don't play hero, Dad. Leave them alone. The Montclair cops will take care of them."

Well, Paul and I were in agreement but it wouldn't be the Montclair cops out here, but the *Upper* Montclair cops who would be here. After the building boom and the pandemic, the City Council unanimously voted for a second police force just to monitor Upper Montclair with its own storefront headquarters, squad car and uniforms. It would still be under Montclair's jurisdiction so all court cases would be held there, but like everything else, the force of 4 men and a woman had to be paid for with increased taxes. The population increase from the new developments evened things out somewhat. And the increased security was seen as a plus. Especially to the O'Brien family at the end of Lois Lane who made a deal with the police to use their driveway as a radar roost for catching speeders coming 'round the bend where the speed limit suddenly drops from 35 mph to 20 mph to satisfy the demands of the grade school crossing guards down the road. If you didn't know where the sign was, or ignored it after school hours or on the weekend, you were given a ticket—or not—depending on having the surveilling cop 'pay it off for you.' A little extra money each week kept the force on their toes, and the grade school crossing accident--free. A win-win for Upper Montclair and a total loss for an unsuspecting out-of-towner.

I had a half glass of red wine, some chocolate chip cookies as comfort food, turned off the lights and caned my way upstairs to my waiting warm bedspread quilt and blanket covering my bed. I was feeling fatigued earlier in the evening these past few weeks, not just from Chris's workouts, but the trip to Florida, the stress of moving, and the ever-shortening days. Added to that, the squatters—well, not technically squatters because they weren't occupying a house not theirs—but certainly trespassers and interlopers who were messing up my woods. It made for some disturbing sleep.

CHAPTER 24

I woke to hearing Caroline in the kitchen preparing my breakfast. I had had an unsteady sleep, waking intermittently, wondering if I had turned up the thermostat properly, for the room felt chilly now. I thought about just staying in bed that day like I did on Sundays, but habit and the need to piss got me to the toilet, and to the clothes I had strewn around the room the night before. I would shave and shower and put on better clothes after breakfast, I decided, because of Paul's arrival and possibly the police as well. I wanted to look my best for them, insane as that thought was.

Caroline noticed my lethargy immediately. "Sleep well?" she asked, pouring me some apple juice.

"Not particularly," I said.

"Your knee?"

"No, actually those new collagen capsules are working just fine. A poor night's sleep, that's all."

"Paul's coming out this morning?"

"Yep, he's moving the clothes you packed, a couple of Ruthie's paintings and some boxes up from the basement. Just some books, my ad portfolios and some trip mementos."

"The photos?"

"Well, I was thinking about that. What do you think?"

"Were you thinking about that when you went to bed?"

"It crossed my mind, yes." I said, (and while true, I was mainly thinking of the squatters).

"Probably caused the sleep anxiety. Maybe it's best to leave the photos behind. I remember what a difference it made when you took them off the living room table."

"Just memories," I said, digging into my scrambled eggs.

"Photos are different than memories," Caroline parsed. "Photos are physical evidence. Memories are made-up photos in our mind. When you looked at the living room table, I remember it saddened you, and when they finally went into the basement you lightened up. So my advice would be to leave them behind. Paul probably has some of the same photos at his place anyway."

"Actually, no. He has a very sparse apartment. Some figurines Ruthie did, that's all. And of course a couple of her paintings. I'm only taking the flower vase painting from the bedroom and a couple of others. I'm leaving most of them for Estelle to decide what to do with her grandma's work. Estelle's artwork is a direct result of Ruthie's teaching when Paul and Clara would leave the kids with us every so often. So maybe I'll leave the photos behind as well."

"I think that's best," Caroline said. "And Gene probably has some personal mementos of his own he's bringing as well. Let the newlyweds furnish their home the way they want."

"You're right," I agreed. "I can't get it through my thick skull that after next week this isn't my home any more. It's all theirs. And that's a hard thing to swallow after all these years."

"It certainly makes for some sleepless nights," she laughed. "Finish your decaf!'"

I did as I was told, then headed upstairs again to shower and dress, waiting for Paul to arrive. Caroline had packed all spring, summer and autumn clothing, leaving behind some woolen shirts and pants for the next week and my departure for the City. For indeed, it was feeling more like winter now, a couple of weeks before its official beginning. I even had a woolen cap with ear flaps, woolen socks and arctic wool-lined waterproof boots. But everything else had either been given to charity or packed for the City. I knew I'd never be playing tennis again, the racquet went to charity, but I insisted she pack my tennis shorts and sneakers anyway. I would always have the need to exercise and there was always the remote possibility of trying out pickleball… with a cane. What would that look like, I asked myself, staring into the mirror while shaving. What will anything look like, from a perspective so unknowing I was now an anxiety-ridden mess.

And the squatters. They had to go. Knowing they were probably still there, and now having told my son, there was no way I could hide the fact or claim I knew nothing about their squalid encampment. The sooner we contacted the police, the better.

Paul arrived right around 11:30 as planned. Caroline hadn't finished her food prep for the weekend as was busy in the kitchen so Paul began packing the boxes of clothes and books in his car, then went upstairs and removed Ruthie's vase painting from the master bedroom.

"I'm glad you're taking this, Dad," he said, placing it on the back seat behind a box of 33rpm record albums to hold it in place. "I have a perfect place for it in the apartment."

"I won't be taking the framed photos that were in the living room," I said. "Estelle can do what she wants with them."

"I'm glad you decided that," Paul said. "I have many of those photos in an album I'm leaving behind."

We went back into the house where Caroline was getting her things together before leaving.

"I have a little gift for you," said Paul, "for all the years you've been with us and all the good vibes you've given off."

He took from his parka's side pocket a nicely-wrapped present a little larger than the size of a deck of cards and handed it to Caroline. It was up to her to unwrap it or take it with her to check out later and I hoped for the former, but she only said, "Thank you," and graciously hugged Paul and then me. "See you on Monday," she said, putting the gift in her purse. "Have a good weekend, you two."

And then she was off.

"What did you give her?" I asked Paul.

"One of those new smart health watches. Expensive, but it does all the health monitoring things these smartwatches do and it also has a 911 emergency call feature built in, so you don't have to wear pendants anymore. I bought one for you too, Dad."

I laughed. "Just when I was getting used to your pendant birthday present."

"This is much, much better. You go to a secure site on the Internet and put in all your health history, and the exact map locations of where you mostly live and work. You put in the 4-digit activation code that comes with your watch. If you need 911 assistance for anything, you just press two buttons on either side of the watch simultaneously for three seconds and bingo! Your location for emergency help is dispatched immediately to the nearest hospital or volunteer ambulance corp. Also your doctor, any caretaker you may have and the local police. You'll have help within minutes."

"The police as well?"

"If they're in the area."

"Hang in there, m'boy. Your watch may be needed in a few minutes."

The house and garage now secure, we then planned some strategy on our way across the lawn.

"I just want them to know they're on private property and see if they'll voluntarily move."

"Listen, Dad, you may be dealing with asylum seekers here. They've flooded New York City and the Feds have requested less populated suburbs to help out while their cases move through the courts."

"Fine. But I don't want them in my backyard. I'm 100% NIMBY."

"They don't know from that," Paul cautioned. "They just need a place to hang out now that the City is overpopulated with them. Even Central Park is full and can't take in any more. So they may have been bussed out here.

"I know. Some wit on Interinn ironically named them the BIAS crowd."

"BIAS?"

Getting Past Z

"Bussed Insane Asylum Seekers." The putdown has gone viral as they say."

"Well, don't you dare use that with them."

"Of course not," I said.

"In fact, maybe we should just turn around and let the police handle it."

"Well, I'm not going to threaten them with the cops," I said. "I just want to warn them they're on private property and are trespassing. I want to give them some time to decide to leave voluntarily. And if they don't, then I *will* call the cops."

We reached the edge of the lawn, the woods before us. "How's your Spanish?" Paul asked.

"Not anywhere near yours. You do the talking. I'll back you up with the cane." It was meant as a joke, but as we entered the forest heading towards the encampment my nervousness grew.

"We need a deadline," I said. "Today is Saturday. They have to leave by Wednesday. Remember, Estelle and Gene are moving in next Saturday afternoon after you pick me up. If these migrants are out by Wednesday, I'll have a couple of days with Caroline to clean up any mess they've made."

"Okay," Paul agreed. The word for Wednesday is *miercoles.* And the word for the garbage dump is *el basurero.*"

I didn't bring binoculars along, so we had to make our way almost to the shelter itself to see what was going on. And it was worse than I even imagined. For now there were rolls of toilet paper hanging from branches surrounding us and the three or four tents had grown to seven with pails containing what I supposed to be water everywhere. Charro music was coming from one tent and men were moving about, sitting around a charcoal briquette fire that had a covered pot of something simmering on some grating over the pit. We watched from a distance, taking it all in, until we were noticed by one of the men sitting by the fire. He stared at us but did nothing except exchange glances in our direction with the other man across the pit.

"Hola," said Paul.

"Hola," said the heavyset mustached man I had seen through binoculars the day before.

He arose and we advanced slowly.

"Habla Inglés?"

"No, Senor. Solo Espanol." The man extended his hand, and Paul and I both shook it. "Estoy Paul y mi Papa, Jerry."

"Carlos," the man replied. "Mucho gusto."

"Mucho gusto," Paul echoed. "Ustedes son su propertie privato."

"No, Senor. Compromiso." The man zipped down his parka, carefully took out a card from his flannel shirt and handed it to Paul. Paul looked it over and handed it to me. I was taken aback at first. It read:

> Raymond Collins
> Chief of Police
> Upper Montclair, New Jersey

... and below was listed the police station's address on Elizabeth Street and its telephone number.

I exchanged glances with Paul who merely shook his head. Somehow this trespassing was sanctioned by our own police department. He handed the card back to Carlos.

"Lo siento, no mi promiso," Paul said. "Creo que no."

"Si, Señor. Promiso provisional. Hasta que el nuevo año dia. Entonces estamos quitar a almacén."

"Almacén?"

"Ehh... edificio grande al lado del tren."

I was mystified and was about to ask Paul what that exchange was about, but he was now extending his hand to Carlos. "Cuidese. Adios."

"Adios," Carlos replied, and we turned around and walked back out of the woods.

"What was that all about," I asked Paul.

"They have permission to stay there until New Year's Day. Then they're moving to a large building near a train. I really don't know what he's talking about, but the Chief of Police surely does. I think we ought to pay a visit to him this afternoon."

The car was full of my crap but I managed to slide next to my son for the five-minute ride into Upper Montclair. I would let Paul do the talking with our Chief of Police Collins, since I had never met him personally, and Paul was far more diplomatic in these things. I probably would blow a gasket, and I think Paul recognized that as well.

"Let me do the talking," he offered. "I think I met him once."

"You did? When was that?"

"At the wedding. Somebody filed a complaint about the noise and the music and Collins came out in ordinary clothes, flashed his badge and gave the DJ a warning to keep the music down. You had already left for the hospital."

"This was on a Saturday afternoon? And the music was too loud? What about all the screaming kids in their backyard pools? What idiot would file such a complaint?"

"Beats me. You've made any enemies on Lois Lane?"

"Not that I know of. In fact two of my neighbors were there at the party."

"Maybe from the developments. I'll ask Collins when I speak to him."

"Nah," I said, "Let's just stick with the trespassers. I don't want to confuse the issue."

We reached Elizabeth Street and the storefront for the police department, but there was a sign on the front door CLOSED/CERRADO and below the time the office was open: 8-5 Monday thru Friday, till 12:00 Noon Saturday. Otherwise, the Montclair Police Station was open throughout the weekend, or we could call 911 in an emergency.

"I should be wearing the watch you bought for me," I said sarcastically.

"I'll take you home and then I have to leave," Paul said.

We returned the way we came and Paul left me in the driveway. "Dad," he said sternly, "I don't want you out in the woods. Let these people be until we can get to Collins. Work through him. Evidently they got some kind of permission to be there and only Collins can straighten that out. Don't play hero here."

"You're coming out tomorrow?"

"Yes, a few things I couldn't get in the car. Expect me around noon again. And remember what I said: they're clearly on your property but let the police handle things."

Getting Past Z

~~~~~

Another mostly sleepless night punctuated with those annoying chest pains, probably psychological stress I figured. I didn't want strangers anywhere on the property—I didn't care who they were or what kind of permission they had. It was still my property, my taxes paid for it and paid for Collins as well. And by what right did he have to invite them there, without informing me first, without so much as a telephone call? He probably figured they were so far in the woods I'd never notice. Didn't he realize the shelter wasn't put up for hunters or for people's tents but for deer? I took a couple of anxiety/sleeping pills around one in the morning, and managed to get some rest.

But this being Sunday, Caroline wouldn't be there to grind the beans and brew some strong coffee for me. Or put out some delicious lox and cream cheese bagels. Or some poached eggs. I would have to do all that on my own. I was spoiled, admittedly. But getting an aide for me down at his place was something I needed to talk to Paul about. Gene would be paying for that, since that was obviously 'living expenses' but maybe I could first do some interviewing with an agency to find a Caroline II. She would be missed. So her severance amount, all on my dime, was foremost on my mind. I was thinking $20,000-$25,000, but I needed to keep that parting gift just between Caroline and myself; if Paul found out he'd bust a gut.

I made some watery coffee and a buttered danish for myself, returned upstairs to shower and dress and wait for Paul to show up. And now, looking out the bedroom window, I clearly saw two figures, two men, at the edge of the woods, looking over the lawn and towards the house. I quickly ducked and searched around for my binoculars, which, I realized, was still downstairs. And by the time I caned down there and back up these figures were gone. More anxiety. I took an extra hot shower to calm my nerves, but I realized I was a nervous wreck. On the other side of things, I realized, my move into the City was beautifully timed. I wouldn't have to deal with the insecurity of being by myself, a cane for both my steadiness and defense weapon should it ever come to that.

I put those thoughts into my memoirs which I would be wrapping up this coming week, with my move into my son's co-op. The manuscript was close to 200 pages now, and while not publishable, it might be blog worthy. I would have to ask Estelle, who knew all about these things, whether that was possible—and whether the adventures of a 90-year-old man was interesting to anyone not a contemporary. The entire exercise, I realized, was to give me some emotional outlet now that I wasn't entirely mobile. And I hoped that would change once I got accustomed to City life again, and the advantages it offered to nonagenarians like myself. But continuing these memoirs was self-defeating in a way; they underscored my frailties and vulnerabilities, my anxiety of loneliness and insularity, my fears of being taken advantage of from forgetfulness or carelessness.

And now Paul was here; an hour earlier than expected. I figured, correctly it seems, he was worried I would go into the woods and confront the group. So he got an early start and was out at the house around 11AM, extremely glad to see me dressed and shaved and upstairs writing away on the computer. We both had stories to tell...

"There was a squad car in the O'Brien's driveway, so I stopped the car and walked over to the patrolman, introduced myself and asked him if it was possible to make an appointment with Chief Collins for tomorrow, Monday, around 10AM? He wanted to know why, but I said it wasn't for myself, but for my father who lives at 1 Lois Lane. And it was a personal matter that even I didn't know about, but it had nothing to do with the speed trap."

"He must have loved that," I laughed.

"Well, he just smiled, took out his notebook and made a notation in it. 'I'll let the Chief know' he said."

"Great," I said.

"I can't be there," said Paul. "Wish I could but I have classes this week. Caroline can drive you there and you can deal with Collins for yourself. Just be pleasant, diplomatic. Don't show any outrage or this will backfire, Dad."

"You have my promise on that," I said. "And I have some news for you."

"What?"

"Earlier this morning I saw two men at the edge of the woods, looking directly at the house. I went to get my binoculars downstairs but when I returned they were gone, so I don't know if they were the same guys we saw yesterday or not. But it just makes me nervous, that's all, that this house is being cased."

"Be sure you tell Chief Collins that. He has to see it from your perspective, and be put in your shoes."

"With extra padding on the right sole," I quipped, but Paul wasn't laughing.

Caroline"s final week with me would be hectic, I realized, because I had several things to wrap up in town. I needed to see Harold Randleman, my lawyer, to finalize my agreement with Gene. There were several questions I had regarding the 'living expenses' clause. I realized it didn't include holiday air travel, cruises and so forth, or family gifts or eating out at expensive restaurants—that would still be on my dime. But if I wanted an aide, a Caroline II, to look in on me every day, or even every two days, that needed to be spelled out before I contacted an agency. (As it happened, Gene had already approved that as a living expense.)

Also, what would happen if Estelle and Gene divorced? Estelle would get the house, because it was now deeded to her, but Gene had laid out a lot of money for me to vacate and keep me going—and this, no doubt, needed to be somewhat repaid. And were I to become ill, hospitalized or needed to have further surgery on the knee, would 'living expenses' cover what SS and my policy with United Healthcare didn't, or wouldn't? Or would that be coming out of my pocket? These were some of the questions I emailed Hal, and he had emailed me back saying that everything had been worked out and to come in this week to sign the agreement for notarization. I planned to do that on Tuesday.

Also on Tuesday I needed to say goodbye to Dr. Francona and get a New York City G.P. referral from him, preferably on the West Side of Manhattan. And I would have to transfer all my prescriptions from the Montclair pharmacy to one close by the NYC co-op.

Then on Wednesday or Thursday, I hoped to say goodbye, if it wasn't too cold out, to some of my chess buddies in the park. I really never expected to see them again, but they had my telephone number just in case they found themselves in the City and wanted to have a drink with me somewhere. Or even come up to the co-op and play a game or two.

And lastly, on Friday, my goodbye to Caroline and my severance gift to her—now set firmly in my mind at $25,000. Built into that was all the extra time she was at the hospital with my knee operation and recovery but never billed for. She was there for me when it counted most.

But first would come Monday, and my meeting at 10AM with Captain Raymond Collins, the newly installed head of the *Upper Montclair Police* department. I was vague with Caroline about the reason for the meeting. Instead, I had her drop me off in front of the office while she bought groceries for the rest of the week—and a bottle of decent champagne left in the refrigerator for Estelle and Gene's arrival Saturday afternoon. We agreed she'd pick me up in an hour.

I had never been inside the new police offices on Elizabeth Street, other than to notice its unassuming storefront with its only squad car parked in front. But a lady police officer served as a receptionist in the front area, greeted me warmly and asked for my name. My visit had been registered into the computer, and after I passed through their Shapeshifter archway I was ushered down a hallway to a second office with a sign reading *Capt. Raymond Collins* on the door. Beyond that, I glanced down to the end of the hallway and a steel door with a little window and bars across. The holding pen, I surmised.

Collins was a tall man, in his late forties, early fifties I guessed, with short cropped brown hair and wire rimmed eyeglasses which he removed as we shook hands. "Have a seat" he said, and I took one of two chairs fronting his desk.

"We haven't met," I said, "but my late wife Ruthie knew you when your department broke away from the Montclair force. She attended most of the Montclair Town Board meetings."

"You're at 1 Lois Lane. The large white house at the end of the *cul-de-sac*."

"Yes."

"Well, I've been there recently, as you might know. In August I was called out on a Saturday afternoon where there was a party going on in the backyard. I asked for the owner, but was told you had just been taken to the hospital."

"Yes, that was my Granddaughter's wedding celebration. I wasn't feeling well, so I was taken to Montclair Memorial."

"You fell on some stairs?"

"Yes."

He paused and nodded. "Unfortunate for you. I see you're still using a cane."

"My knee was crushed," I said. "But why were you called out? I just found out about a complaint being made about loud music."

"Well, the music was loud, and there were cars parked in the street blocking driveways so your neighbors couldn't get their cars out."

"I had monitors for that. I was never told about blocked driveways. In fact, two of my neighbors allowed cars to park in their driveways and were there at the party."

"Well," Collins said, "this was a fire access hazard. You didn't have a permit for so many cars and people. We weren't contacted at all. So this was a fineable event. But I let it go. I just told the DJ to lower the volume and then make an announcement to have the owner of a car parked at the end of the Lane to move it to clear the driveway. He could have been fined as well. But I let that go, too. This was a wedding, a Jewish wedding, and I didn't want the department to get involved in what could be interpreted as antisemitic bias. There's been enough of that already."

I was stunned to hear that. "I wasn't told anything about this," I said.

"Well, you were having an operation, I understand. I'm sure such news would have disturbed your recovery. Some things are best left unsaid."

"A neighbor at the end of the Lane?" I questioned. "The O'Briens?"

"I don't remember," said the Chief.

"Who lets you use their driveway for a speed trap? Who puts up a Palestinian flag beneath an American flag on his flagpole?"

"Look, Mr. Myer," said Collins, his voice rising somewhat, "those complaints were resolved peacefully and without problems. Why are you bringing this up? Because you weren't told? Well, the department wasn't told about the number of guests and cars you were having for the wedding. It went well above what's allowed without a permit. So this is all behind us now. Is that why you're here today? Because if it is, you're wasting both of our time."

I was now playing defensive, even before I was to bring up the squatters. I owed him an apology, but I could see this wasn't going well. Paul was right, I had to be diplomatic with the Chief. I had to get him on my side. But how?

"I'm sorry to learn of all this," I said. "I truly owe you an apology. That's not the reason why I'm here today. Some new events are happening on my property, and this time you *are* being informed in advance. I really need your help on this."

"Another wedding?"

"No, quite the opposite," I said. "Trespassers have set up an encampment in the middle of the woods behind my house. I saw it for myself Saturday. It's clearly on my property."

Collins shook his head and put back his spectacles. Then he turned on his desktop computer, did some inputs, and swiveled the screen around halfway so we could both look at it simultaneously. He had zeroed in on Lois Lane and the land about it.

"Here's your house, right? And your property boundary surrounding it, right?"

I looked closely at the schematic. It seemed to be correct. "That looks right," I said.

"And where approximately did you see the encampment?"

I pointed to a spot almost exactly in the middle of the woods. And Collins noted it with a piece of scotch tape and an X.

"Well, it certainly seems to be on your property," he said. "How many people did you observe?"

"Hard to say. They've put up tents around a fire pit. I think five or six tents. So maybe there are a dozen people, kids included."

"You met with them?"

"Me and my son, Paul. He speaks some Spanish and spoke to them. They said they had permission to camp there until the end of the month. Then they would move to some big building by a train."

"You never gave permission, I take it."

"No, sir. Paul made clear they were on private property and we wanted them off the land."

"And what did they say to that?"

"They produced a business card with your name, and the Upper Montclair police department address on it. That's why I'm here today."

"Well, let me fill you in on what's been happening lately, because obviously you're in the dark about this."

"I know about the influx of asylum seekers in New York City. It tops the local news every night. And I know about having the overflow bussed to the surrounding suburbs and anywhere they can find now. Some reports have them at a quarter of a million who can't find decent housing this winter."

"Yes, that's true," said the Chief. "And 2,500 were bussed to Montclair proper. Upper Montclair was tasked with finding space for 500 of those. We're placing mothers and children under 14 in the grade school gymnasium and the Roman Catholic church basement, and a couple of other indoor places but most of these people are going to have to sleep outdoors in their tents. It won't be pleasant if it starts to get really cold or it snows. The Red Cross is donating hundreds of blankets and food vans."

"What about the park across from the school?" I asked. "The park itself could probably hold all their tents. And they'd have the school's cafeteria for food and the use of their bathrooms or put some porta-potties out in the park."

"Exactly. That was the first idea. And the best idea. But the parents objected because if the school gymnasium was going to be used, the park would then be used for PT and the kids play there after school. The Town Board voted it down. There was one other good option, but it wouldn't be ready until after the Holidays."

"A big building near a train."

"If you go down to the end of Elizabeth and make a right on Douglas, you'll come to the old train crossing and a large building to the left. It used to be a Sears warehouse and its loading dock abutted siding track for railcars joining the freight trains. All that's gone now, but the two-storey warehouse is still there, empty and rotting inside, but with plenty of space for all the tents, a communal kitchen, bathrooms, play areas on the rooftop. The Town Board inspected it, approved it, and work was started back in October. And they're working on it 24/7. We expect it will get its C of O right after the Holidays. And then most of the 500 asylum seekers will be housed there."

"Until then, they can camp on my property. Is that it?"

"No. Until then we've put several families along the hiking and biking trail beside the creek that adjoins your property. Look at the map. This is where we placed them because the creek could supply running water, actually boiled drinking water for them. What may have happened is they explored the surrounding area, passed through your property and camped out there thinking it was part of the public space."

"So this is just a misunderstanding, and you'll meet with them and tell them they have to pitch their tents next to the hiking trail?"

"I speak High School Spanish so there should be no misunderstanding. But what's the rush? I'll get to it sometime later this week."

"I want them off the property by Wednesday, this Wednesday. I have some guests coming in over the weekend and I figure me and my aide need a couple of days to clean up their mess."

"Mr. Myer, with all due respect, I take orders only from the Town Board. Your request is noted but I also have many other responsibilities here. I'll have to move some people further up the creek to make way for their return."

"Yeah, up the creek is an apt description," I sneered, completely forgetting Paul's admonition about confronting Collins. I saw his demeanor change. I had overstepped the boundary line of cordiality.

"I think our meeting is over," he said, rising from his chair.

"I just want to make it clear," I said still seated, "that there are POSTED signs everywhere where my property meets the trail. They clearly state PRIVATE PROPERTY-NO TRESPASSING. And this should have been translated to them when you decided to place them there."

"They're not doing any harm there. I think you can put up with them for a few days more."

"They're camping under a shelter I put up for the winter for my deer."

Collins sat back down somewhat bemused. "Let me understand. You've built a shelter for pet deer you have on the property?

"I wouldn't call them pets, but it's a family of deer that live on the property and know me. I put food and water out for them. And the migrants are living under that deer shelter."

Collins took that all in. "And that's the main reason you want them out? Because of the deer on your property?"

"Captain, I've lived here, in the same spot for longer than you've been around. I've had a hundred real estate people, developers, builders come by inquiring if I would sell them the back plot to put up more housing. And I said no. There needs to be some greenery still left around here, the peace and tranquility found in nature. There has to be a sanctuary for all the wild animals still left after the hunters get through. That's why the creek and the hiking trail and the woods beyond were saved. Why Lois Lane has seven homes, not nine. Upper Montclair was going the way of Secaucus. Is that what you want for your kids?"

"It's not a case of what I want," said Collins, "The Town Board makes the decisions here."

"I could see their point if there was a natural disaster like a flood or fire. Then they would have to find housing for the residents of the community. But these migrants, as you put it, are not from here. They've been bussed from New York because there's no space for them there. And you think there's space for them here in a Sanctuary Suburb?"

"Mr. Myer, again, it's not a question of what I think. The Town Board took a vote. I'm just carrying out their orders."

"Get them out of town and put them in the woods somewhere. Anywhere where they can't be seen or heard. In other words, make them disappear."

"As I said, come January 1st or thereabouts, we'll have them living in that abandoned warehouse on Douglas Street."

"And who's paying for this? The Montclair taxpayer. I bet land and school taxes will go up for this."

"I pay taxes too, Mr. Myer, same as you."

"You know, it was my late wife Ruthie who was mainly responsible for breaking off Upper Montclair from Montclair. It was her doing at many, many Town Board meetings. There never would have been an Upper Montclair without her pestering the Board for added green space and security for this then-virgin area. And you were promoted to

Chief of Police by this division. So your mandate is clear: You have to preserve the peace and privacy of this enclave. And its natural wonders like deer and all the other animals that are making their home here."

"My mandate is finding homes for human beings who have no place to go, not deer," said Collins, now a bit angered by my suggestion that Ruthie was responsible for his new Chieftan position when they split the Montclair police department in two. But I continued anyway:

"I want these squatters off my property by this Wednesday."

"So let me ask you a question, Mr. Myer," said Collins, tilting back on his chair; "What's the priority here: The welfare of homeless migrants encamping for a limited time on your property, or a few deer you consider as pets that are not being harmed in any way by them."

"By encamping, do you mean trespassing? Because if you mean trespassing, then that's a prosecutable offense."

"Says who?"

"Look. I have signs on the trail trees that say, POSTED. Big capital letters. And underneath they say, PRIVATE PROPERTY-NO TRESPASSING. A police officer, even not knowing Spanish, would know how to tell Spanish-only speakers to stay off that property."

"Ordinarily, that would be the case. But in this case the Town Board has determined these people have no place to go and has declared a humanitarian emergency. And so until a suitable living arrangement can be made for them, they're allowed to camp out…"

"Even on private property?"

"Even on private property," said Collins. "It's out of my hands. If you have a problem with that, go before the Town Board and state your case. They meet every Wednesday night at 7:00 at Montclair's Town Hall."

"Where are the minutes of that meeting giving them the right to camp out on private property?"

"They're printed in the weekly Essex Examiner on Friday."

"Do you have a copy I can look at?"

"I'm afraid not. You can find a copy in Montclair's public Library."

CHAPTER 25

The meeting lasted not quite an hour and luckily when I caned outside, Caroline was waiting for me. "Wow!" I said, once inside the car, "I'm glad I've had no run-ins with the law these past years. Police Chief Collins is a piece of work."

"Ruthie liked him though."

"She did? She never told me that."

"She was leading the cause for an autonomous Upper Montclair police department which would elevate Collins to Chief. He was just a police sergeant before that."

"Well, that I knew. Actually, I reminded him of that fact."

Caroline shook her head. "Jerry, that's not going to score any points for you. Why did you want to see him anyway?"

"Did you know that Montclair had received 2,500 migrants bussed in from New York City and that 500 of them were placed in Upper Montclair?"

"I think Chris told me something like that. Patterson got 5,000. In fact, almost every town in upper New Jersey got a bus full or two. But what can you do? This was absolute stupidity on the Government's part. It was all a diversion by the cartels. While we were building the wall and playing cowboys and Indians down there, they were playing pirates and coming up the coasts by the boatload. And you want to know who it's hurting the most?"

"Who?"

"People like me who work in the service sector. Especially health care, elder care. I've had all this training and schooling and then some unskilled migrant lady comes along and will care for an elderly patient without knowing what she's doing and getting paid minimum wage for her services. And so then my agency has to lower my fee to match the unlicensed influx just to stay competitive. And on top of that, I pay taxes. These boat people don't even have social security numbers!"

Compared to my objection about having squatters on my property I realized it couldn't hold a candle to Caroline's complaint, so I hoped she wouldn't press me about my Collins meeting.

"You'll have a great referral from me," I said. "And your agency..."

"Which gets a placement commission and checks up on my work from time to time as you well know. These 'asylum seekers' are freelance opportunists who don't report to anyone. Well, maybe the cartel who they owe their life savings to, but for the most part they are taking jobs away from us, and being Black doesn't help the situation any."

We were approaching Lois Lane, no squad car in O'Brien's driveway, only their motley Palestinian flag blowing in the breeze just beneath the Stars and Stripes. I could only be sad for Caroline, my severance little comfort for an intelligent, talented, caring woman who might now be facing the most challenging part of her career.

It was midday, still relatively warm out, but I had no intention of going out to feed the deer or even using my binoculars from the bedroom window. I didn't want to leave the squatter problem for Gene, but maybe that was the best option. He was, after all, a lawyer and probably knew all about private property rights and boundary lines and so forth. But I wanted to get to the source of Collins's rationale for these people being there. So I made it a point to put down on my calendar for the next day, Tuesday, to get to Montclair's public library and see for myself the minutes of the last Town Board meeting in the Essex Examiner. If the Board had made an exception for having these migrants camp out in people's backyards because of a 'humanitarian emergency' I sure as hell needed to know about that. And so would Gene.

A puzzling closure to my memoirs to be sure. But after Friday it was out of my hands, and I was glad for that. In a way, things were working out, because I knew I wouldn't be able to deal with this migrant crisis alone, somewhat incapacitated as I was. The house was as secure as I needed it to be all these years, but this was a more dire situation—strangers living on the property, speaking in a different language, seeing only a vulnerable old man wandering about. Maybe Paul could stay with me at night till the end of the week when I'd turn the place over to Estelle and Gene. Or possibly Chris. But then Caroline would discover the basis of my distress and I didn't want to upset her.

I wrote for a couple of hours, had lunch and caught up with Internet news until Caroline left for the day around three, then wrote some more. I was now practically up to date... and wondering just how to end my manuscript. Confrontation with the squatters was off the table. So was another meeting with Captain Collins, should I find some fault in his interpretation of the Town Board's directive. Perhaps informing Estelle and Gene about all this with a hand-written note left with the champagne was ironical enough to solicit a concluding laugh or two. A happy ending, at least for me, knowing that Gene was now stuck with the problem. At least through the Holidays. Nasty but appealing. But no, Gene was providing me with a soft landing after all. I really had no motive to inflict pain on him or Estelle. They were, after all, looking out for my best interest. I had no ax to grind here. And yet... he would question why he wasn't told about the situation earlier when something could have been legally done to enforce the privacy of the property. I was at a *Recisions* crossroad. So I would let the only other person to know of these recent developments handle the denouement for me: My son Paul. For Paul represented my escape clause; I could always count on him to get me out of an awkward position.

I was thinking of having a snack around four when my phone rang. Paul was looking at me from the interior of his apartment. He had just returned from school.

"How did your meeting with Chief Collins go?" he wanted to know.

"Ehh... " I stumbled, "about what you'd expect. He said the squatters were there because of a vote taken by the Town Board last Wednesday. Upper Montclair got 500 men, women and children. The women and children were housed and the rest were allowed to remain in their tents. And they found space for them along the nature trail by the creek next to our property until permanent housing could be completed. They're converting the old Sears warehouse to house them after the Holidays."

"And the Town Board approved them being on our property?"

"Well, that's what I'm planning to find out tomorrow. Collins said I could find out exactly what the Town Board's directive was in their minutes printed in the Essex Examiner. And I can find a copy at the Montclair public library. And I'll ask Caroline to take me there tomorrow because I also want to say goodbye to Dr. Francona and get a referral to a New York City doctor and change my prescription outlet to one close to your co-op."

"Did you tell him about our meeting with the squatters?"

"Yes, as best as I could. Remember, they showed us his card, so obviously he's been in touch. He said there was nothing he could do. He's under orders from the Town Board."

"Aw, shit! It will all become Gene's problem when he moves in. I didn't want that to happen."

"Neither do I," I said.

"You know, Gene and Collins know each other, don't you?"

"No. But Collins said he was out to their marriage party in August. He said we held the party with too many people and cars and we should have had a permit for this. I didn't know anything about this."

"That wasn't it, or maybe it was, I don't know either. Either way, this permit thing should have been handled by Notingham. That's what Gene was paying her for, after all. She totally screwed up. At any rate, Collins said there were complaints from neighbors about the loud music and cars in their driveways. He was looking for you, owner of the property, but you had already been taken to the hospital."

"So you saw him there?"

"Yeah. He was dressed informally, so I didn't know who he was at first, but a security guy came over to me and said the Chief of Police had arrived with a complaint. And then Gene came over because he naturally was informed as well. And Gene said he would handle it, and for me to rejoin the party. So I did. And the DJ had to turn down the music. And there was a car blocking three inches beyond a driveway's yellow stripe down the Lane, and its owner was asked to move his car. Fortunately the Rabbi was leaving, so an empty space opened up on the oval and the car was placed there."

"The only yellow stripe denoting a driveway belongs to the O'Briens', so this all makes sense."

"But Dad, you haven't heard the most laughable part yet."

"I'm in hysterics already," I said, fuming.

"Gene explained to Collins that in about ten minutes the music had to be turned up for just a couple of minutes and invited Collins to have some food and something to drink and stay to watch the proceedings and then promised the music would be turned down for the rest of the party."

"What?!"

"The Jewish chairlift."

"Ohhhh. This is unbelievable!"

"So the chairlift went along smoothly and the music was extra loud of course, and when Estelle and Gene were put back down on the platform, DJ Frank lowered the music for the rest of the evening to Collins's satisfaction. And Collins left the party."

"A new convert to Judaism no doubt."

"But wait, Dad. Gene told me later that to get Collins off his back with the chair scene he slipped him a couple of Hams."

"Hams? What the hell are hams doing at a Jewish wedding?"

"Hams, Dad, are Hamiltons. Money. Bills."

"Twenty dollars?"

"A Hamilton, Dad, is One Hundred Dollars."

"No, really? A couple of hundred bucks? Paying off the Chief of Police? I can see the speed trap thing for a patrolman, but a Chief of Police is supposed to set an ethical standard for the force."

"It's part of small town living, small town thinking, small town salaries. It comes with the territory."

"What territory is that? The Sinaloa Wild West Territory in Mexico? I've never paid a bribe to anyone here. What are you saying? That this is the new standard operating procedure now?"

"Think of it not as S.O.P. but as a T.I.P., Dad. You've paid plenty of tips in your life."

"Tip is an abbreviation for 'to insure promptness'. It never was meant as an under the table payoff to skirt the law."

"Times have changed, Dad. Just look at the dustup over the Trump indictments. While ordinary taxpayers like you and I are paying for the prosecuting attorneys, I've read that dedicated MAGA fanatics are instead paying into a Truth Social TIP fund to help Trump pay for his defense team."

"A slush fund, no?"

"Not really. It's more like GoFundMe but TIP stands for Trump In Prison. We're living in the final days of Trumpworld, remember. We're down to whatever spare change we have in our pockets."

There wasn't much more to say. Paul agreed that my next move was to find out exactly what the Town Board meeting notes said, and to make a copy at the Library in case Gene needed more info. But I was implored again to stay away from the woods. These people had no idea about how America works, trust in its laws and governance. And anarchy wasn't the way forward, given Trump's warning of 'Disciplined Order' for the newcomers and undocumented, as he put it.

But unlike turnover day in January 2025, the country wouldn't be holding its breath to see how much force would be needed to keep order in the streets. Now, four years later, I sensed a new optimism was setting in, a reach for calm and reasonableness. Peaceful Changeover was the watchword. The country desperately wanted to end the lingering stagflation with our new President, Gavin Newsom at the helm.

This was how I wanted my memoir to end. We had been through so much this past decade—from the pandemic to the demonic—and the country was ready to heal. Even the Z's had quieted down somewhat, although basic divisions remained involving AI job replacement and the exorbitant cost of living. The recession had knocked the wind out of those, not only in service industries and the uneducated masses of the migrant class, but the educated in-debt elite who could only find work in some relative's business, or in academia, or had collegiate contacts to fall back on. Inflation could only be tamed by less demand and more supply—but that would have to come after more job layoffs and a stunning uptick in two-working-parent families now living at, or below, the poverty level because the economy was slow to heal, slow to recover, slow to pay workers fair wages for a full day's work.

My way was clear: If my health held up, to live comfortably in Paul's—soon to be Gene's—co-op; maybe do some cruise traveling with an over-80 specialized tour group; play chess in Riverside Park;

and now that my memoir was about finished, get going on some other creative endeavor like a play or poetry—even take an art or music course at The 92nd St. 'Y', a short Uber drive across Central Park.

So getting a referral for a new Dr. Francona in NYC, preferably on the West Side in the Seventies was high on my list for Tuesday. Then the Library and its duplicating machine. Then to wrap things up, if I found any discrepancies in what Capt Collins had told me and the notes of the Town Board's meeting, leaving my circled and penciled notes with the nice lady police officer at the Station's front desk—but not to interface again with Collins. What Paul had told me about what went on at the wedding party after I had left for the hospital left me speechless. I opened a fresh bottle of white Chablis with my shrimp scampi dinner and went to bed early.

Caroline was up for the tasks of that morning, and after serving me breakfast we headed out in her car for Montclair. First off, a brief meeting with Dr. Francona to say my goodbyes and getting a referral for a GP on the West Side of Manhattan, in the Seventies if possible. Someone I could cane to if the need arose, since I wouldn't be driving. He was sorry to see me go and would email me with a list of doctors he knew in the area specializing in geriatric care. For that's what I needed now, not a GP but a specialist in aging bodies. And while I was there, for no cost he just wanted to check out a few things since his next patient would be late in arriving. So he looked at the knee, did the blood oxygen thing, stethoscope thing, blood pressure thing... and asked, "Are you getting enough exercise these days?"

"Well, with the cane I've cut back on a few things, like tennis."

"You should do more walking, more stairs, or try swimming. Your leg can take that now. Buy a treadmill or a stationary bike for the winter months or join a health club. Your blood flow isn't as robust as I'd like it to be. It's important to be in top shape now, now that you'll be in the City where everything is exhaust fumes, the food inedible and exercise is getting in and out of elevators."

"Okay," I said.

We said our goodbyes and I left his office and to Caroline sitting patiently in her car for the next round. I apologized for the delay, not knowing Francona would do a brief examination on me. But I supposed he needed to inform any future doctor of my general condition, and update my charts.

"I need to get more exercise," he told me.

She laughed. The Public Library is a block away. Do you want to meet me there?"

"No," I laughed along. "But I'll be in and out, ten minutes at the most. Promise."

The newspaper rack was right inside the main entrance, close to the librarian's desk. I saw the current Essex Examiner among the offerings, took it to an empty table and searched for the Montclair Town Board minutes. And yes! There they were on Page 3 and I quickly scanned them for what was voted on. And to my surprise Chief Collins was almost right. Here's the relevant portion...

".... [T]he Board recognizes a humanitarian crisis here. With the cold weather upon us, it is critical that these 500 newcomers to Upper Montclair be housed in warm and inviting surroundings. The Board

unanimously agrees that provable married families and non-married women and children up to and including the age of 14 be housed in the Upper Montclair Public School Gymnasium. Single men and children over the age of 14 can be housed elsewhere in private homes, or if no space is available, remain in their tents camping outside the School (but not in the park opposite the school) if the temperature is above 32-degrees during the nighttime. If the temperature falls below freezing, and if space allows, the newcomers have the option of moving indoors into the hallways of the Upper Montclair Public School, but must leave the premises before 8:15 AM on days the school is open to students. They may reenter the school and/or school grounds after 5PM. As a further option, the newcomers can camp along the Elizabeth Creek where there is now a hiking and bike trail. Porta-potties will be set up every 100 feet and the Salvation Army will supply a 24/7 food van. If the trail along the Elizabeth Creek becomes too congested, the newcomers can move their tents further away from the creek into the woods on both sides. We expect no serious problems but our Spanish-speaking teachers and counselors will be available by text and phone for the duration of the temporary placement of the newcomers until the Sears facility is open."

My attached note to Chief Collins read:

Chief Collins: The Board's minutes said nothing about camping on private property—only that the 'newcomers' can 'move their tents further away from the creek into the woods on both sides.'
Yes, there's a thin strip of wooded land between the creek and the edge of my property where the POSTED signs are placed but you

were being insincere when saying the Board had given permission for the newcomers to camp out on private property. The Board never addressed the issue.

Sincerely, Jerome Myer, Resident Owner, #1 Lois Lane.

I wrote the Collins note on a sheet of paper, then made two copies of the complete Board's minutes and my note. It had taken me a little longer than I expected, but again, Caroline was patiently waiting in the car, doing her nails.

"Last stop," I said, "back to Upper Montclair's Police Station. Mission Improbable is just about over."

"It's just starting," she corrected me.

So now everyone was on the same page, and I could tell Paul when he called at around 4:00 that Collins was exaggerating (to put it kindly) about the 'newcomers' being allowed to camp on private property without the owner's consent. I read the relevant Board's minutes and my note to Collins to Paul and he sounded somewhat concerned.

"That's what the Board is calling them? Newcomers?"

"Neutral enough, don't you think?"

"Well, it beats BIAS—what other towns are using to stir up the locals, as in BIAS parades on Main Street and BIAS sit-downs on highways, with BIAS caps, BIAS tee-shirts. It's amazing what internet chain reactions can do these days. How much money is being made off this highly charged issue."

"I've heard that BIAS has become an abbreviated slur," I added. Originally, it was Bussed *Illegal* Asylum Seekers, bad enough. But that morphed into Bussed *Insane* Asylum Seekers. The *Insane* part is too much, really. I can see how pissed people are—on both sides."

"Well, BIAS took care of MAGA, Dad. Look at it that way."

"And BIAS will soon go the way of MAGA, I'm sure, but the damage has been done."

"And don't think for one moment the 'newcomers' don't know about what's going on. It's getting very nasty in the suburbs, Dad. At least Montclair was flexible and compassionate enough to confront the crisis and had a plan in place to assist them. I give them credit for that. But I think you've made the right move at the right time to move out. And I want to emphasize again that you stay away from the shelter. Gene can deal with it. Or not. It's out of your hands."

"I've made a copy of the Board's minutes and my response to Collins and I'm leaving it with a bottle of champagne when he and Estelle get here on Saturday. I figure it will balance out."

"Yours and Mom's balance theory," Paul said, exasperated. "I hope you're on the ground level of the see-saw when it all comes crashing down."

I was hoping Paul would say he was coming out that night to keep me company, but I realized he had classes Wednesday and would have to be up around six for the commute into the city which was not a pleasant trip. And now with most of my things down there already, I could certainly manage if we moved the date up a few days.

Because, as usual, he was right. It was getting nasty in the suburbs of coastal cities around the country in old encrusted rich White enclaves still remembering, and still irrationally longing for, pre-desegregation days. What was missing, of course, was a fair national immigration policy promised by Trump but never delivered to his desk for signing. He wasn't entirely at fault. Congress was divided and Trump's 'executive orders' needed congressional approval for appropriations. And SCOTUS was tied up with lawsuits involving work, pay, housing and discrimination. They took so much time working their way through the courts and onto the Supreme Court's agenda, they were buried on page 6. Trump reluctantly came to the realization that his southern border security initiatives had been out-maneuvered by the Mexican cartels and their 'boat people' had stolen the headlines up and down the East and West coasts. It would begin on Trump's first day as Commander In Chief—and continues to this day.

So 'The Donald' had his work cut out for him. And although he had both Houses of Congress in his pocket during his first two years in office, he was stymied by a few Republican crossovers that made certain his immigration policies would fail. And he was even more outspoken as time beyond Day One extended itself, using his Truth Social blog as bully pulpit to castigate the 'handful of presidential wannabes' from his own party. It...

A gunshot! No, three gunshots! Not from a rifle this time but sounding more like from a handgun somewhere in the woods. Somewhere on the property. I can't go out there now, now that I'm alone here and it's getting dark already. So I'll end this for the day. Have some dinner that Caroline placed in the microwave. Have the rest of the bottle of the Chablis. Put the motion detector lights and

Puss'n'Bots on. Lower the venetian blinds in the bedroom and set the electric blanket on low. Have my nerves quieted down by a sleep-trank pill upon retiring. And hopefully get through the night.

Wishful thinking: It's now midnight, the sleep pill's effectiveness has expired and I'm restless as usual.

⁓◌◌◌⁓

I arose in chilly grayness, in a room further darkened by rain-laden clouds. Caroline was already making breakfast, I could hear her in the kitchen, so it had to be past nine. But it looked and felt like seven as I louvered the venetian blinds open.

My plan for the rest of the week was now plotted out in my head and on my calendar. I wanted to say goodbye to a couple of my chess-playing friends in the park today, but perhaps it was too cold out and they wouldn't be there. I would call them instead, especially Benjamin Finegold. We were known as Ben & Jerry to the Upper Montclair New Jersey chess world. And I know he'll be sad to know I'm moving. But what the hell: We could always play against each other on the Internet.

Tomorrow, Thursday, I would get a haircut and say goodbye to the Montclair barber who had trimmed what was left of my hair for more than a quarter-century now. And Friday, I would invite Caroline to lunch in Montclair at a formal place I knew that, in spite of the customer fallout, still did lunch and present her with a sealed envelope with my severance check and a note of my appreciation for her work over the years. That would be our last day together. Saturday, Paul would arrive in the late morning, pack up some odds and ends and that would be that.

Then I remembered the gunshots from the night before. I would leave this place today if I could, but as I said, the week was now plotted out. I got showered and dressed thinking how I would put this new development to Gene and Estelle, for they had to be forewarned about the people in the woods. But better; tell Paul who would tell Gene. He had a better way of handling things with Gene than did I.

Over breakfast I mentioned to Caroline I wanted to have lunch out with her on Friday in Montclair and she was delighted. There were still a few things she wanted to buy to leave in the cupboard for Estelle and Gene for the weekend. And so Thursday would be a perfect time to do a little shopping as well while I had my hair cut. Today's park visit was out, she agreed, because it was freezing cold and soon to rain and a perfect day for a last minute cleaning. Actually, she said, a fast moving snowstorm was on its way into Pennsylvania and would probably get here in the late afternoon or early evening. It might be a problem commuting tomorrow, but the roads should be cleared overnight and she might be a little late, but definitely here tomorrow to take me to the barber.

After breakfast, I returned to my room to write out my thank you note to Caroline, while she continued cleaning every nook and cranny of the house. She wanted to leave it in pristine condition and most everything she wanted to throw out or give to charity I accepted without question, even personal items of Ruthie's I still had emotional attachment to. She made sure I had some say on her 'leave it, put it in the cellar or garage, or throw it out' tri-choice of every item. Where I dithered, she put in a pile for a local charity she favored. For a week now, her car was overflowing with paints and brushes, frames, canvas and easels. I joked that she could open an art store. She joked that the music I was taking with me would shut down the co-op.

At 2:00 she left promptly because of the intensifying storm over Pennsylvania. The weather report for Northern New Jersey wasn't that good; two to four inches of snow was expected. We said our goodbyes with the understanding that she might be a little late with her commute Wednesday, depending on the overnight road crews. We'd keep in touch by phone.

And right after her departure, I went upstairs, lay down for a nap and fell deeply asleep—to make up for the dismal sleep of the night before.

I was dreaming about pickleball but awoke abruptly to gunshots. Three of them in a row from the same handgun I had heard at midnight the evening before. It sounded like some kind of signal, not an offensive or defensive move. I checked my watch; it was 3:00—I had slept for an hour, and felt somewhat refreshed. I lay back and thought about calling my chess friends then, Ben and Leon, but as I was searching for Leon's number in my telephone's directory, another three gunshots rang out. This time, a bit louder, a bit closer to the house. I went over to the side of the window, tilted the venetian blinds slightly, and peered out over the lawn and the woods beyond but saw no movement. Would Collins or one of his deputies come out if I called? Maybe there was a squad car in the O'Brien's driveway so I could report the shots. And surely my next door neighbors had also heard the gunfire, if they were home. That's what I needed to do:. Go over to Lew's house and see if anyone was there. Then with a neighbor's confirmation, make the call to the police.

So I got dressed in warm woolen pants and shirt. Put on my furry zippered winter boots, gloves, hooded parka and cap with earflaps and made sure I had my phone with me. I exited by the front door and caned over to Lew's, expecting to meet his wife, Debbie, or one of his daughters, but no one was home, for it was still working and school hours. I continued down Lois Lane almost to the O'Brien's—but I could see there was no squad car in the driveway. I walked back home, a bit disappointed.

And then another three-round display rang out. This was definitely a signal of some sort—now every fifteen minutes or so. What could it mean? Curiosity was there, but also fear. The possibility that I was being lured out into the woods crossed my mind. My heart was racing. I wouldn't take the bait. Paul's admonition to me not to get anywhere near the 'newcomers' was still foremost on my mind. He would soon be home from school. I'd tell him about the shots and that I didn't feel safe, and for him to come out and stay with me or drive me to his place before an expected snowstorm arrived that evening. He would do that for me, I felt certain. Tomorrow might even be a snow date and schools would be closed.

And there was Peter's gun in my safe... although there was no ammunition for it. He had somehow managed to secret the cartridge and either took it with him to Australia or dumped it. But it wasn't with the gun and holster, for I had checked that several times. The gun was useless, but might be used as a prop, just in case. All sorts of mind game scenarios were emerging, each one more upsetting than the last, as I thumbed my way into my house using the front door.

And now, back in my room and looking out the back window and across the lawn, there's a figure at the edge of the woods. It's the large mustachioed man who Paul and I had a discussion with when we first encountered the migrant group. Carlos. He's the one who was firing the pistol, for I could plainly see something in his right hand, and he made that a demonstrable fact as he raised his arm and fired three more rounds directly overhead while looking directly at me standing at the window. He's waiting for me to respond somehow.

Well, I don't have the time nor the energy to do a *Recission* analysis of the situation. And I don't want to be killed and have to relive my tragic ending for the rest of eternity—*Quantum Agnostic* style. Two completely absurd, useless, contradictory books when you think about it. And yet, curiosity is common to all animals, human or not, I'm afraid. So, here is where my written memoir ends for the moment, my dear Reader. I'll be using the voice recorder on my phone to keep you current in the interim before I return to my computer. For I've decided to take the bait, and go out and meet with Carlos, without Peter's pistol or any weapon of any kind, I may add. Why? Because if Carlos wants me dead for some reason, he's had plenty of opportunity before this. And all fingers would be pointing at him since Chief Collins probably has filled him in about our meeting.

I think Carlos needs to tell me something, to demonstrate he and his crew are only trying to survive until being moved into the Sears building. And if this is the case, I have nothing to fear from them. Yes, I'm still a NIMBY; I don't want them in my backyard. But I could easily see this was a humanitarian crisis of epic proportions. I didn't want to be the one, known throughout the neighborhood, who made a fuss. If I could somehow calm the situation by allowing them to stay over the Holidays I could then tell Paul and Gene this is only a temporary—and solvable—situation. After all, these newcomers deserve some respect for all the trials they have been through to finally wind up in, of all places... *Upper Montclair!*

So this is now being recorded on my new smartphone I've placed into the front breast pocket of my parka. And I'm caning my way through Ruthie's studio and out the back entrance down the stairs. Carlos is still at the edge of the woods and as I'm walking across the lawn it's beginning to snow. Just a few flakes but they're dry, not wet, which only means it will stick. I plan to just say 'hola' to him, listen to what he needs to tell me, try to understand, shake hands and that will be that.

"Hola, Carlos."

"Hola, Jerry. Me alegro de verlo. Vamos a ver el albergue por venado."

I didn't get all of it, but against my better judgment I'm following him through the woods and he stops occasionally for me to catch up. We're heading for the shelter, that much is clear.

And there it is! But there are no tents beneath or anywhere to be seen. Not a sign of anyone being there. It's all been cleaned up beautifully. The plastic tubs of pellets are gone as are the rainwater buckets—but everything else is back to where it was.

"Wow! Gracias!"

"Pero, un problema."

Carlos is over the fire pit covered by a burlap sack. He's now pulled it away to reveal—O God! The severed head of one of the does. A bloodied hole square in the middle of its forehead. The bastards!

"Shit!"

"No mi. Policía."

"Policia?"

"Si. El fusil." He's pointing to the wound. Now he's grabbed the head by an ear and has placed it in the burlap sack. And he's leaving.

"Adios."

"La chingada!" I call after him. It's the only swear word I know in Spanish.

He's stopped in his tracks and has put the sack down. He's coming at me. He's going to slug me...

"Dad? Can you hear me? Where are you? The screen is dark. Is the phone in your pocket?"

"I'm at the shelter. Let me take the phone out and show you. There. Can you see there are no tents any more. They've all cleared out and they left the place entirely clean, but over the fire pit... Oh, God, Paul!... they shot and decapitated a doe! See the blood on the rocks? I'm taking a picture of it. I can't believe it!"

"Dad, get out of there!"

"My God! Why would they do such a thing? For food or just to piss me off?"

"Listen to me, Dad. I'm on my way. Are you alright?"

"They dragged it over... purposely under the..."

"Dad, are you okay?"

"Yes, Paul! I'm fine."

"I thought we had a pact! Why are you at the shelter?"

"One of those we met—Carlos—led me here. He showed me the doe's head and I told him to go to hell. I thought he was going to slug me. He didn't touch me. He grabbed my cane, put it against a tree and stomped his foot down and broke it in two. He took off with the doe's head in a sack leaving me here. I'm okay. I just have to get back to the house somehow. I'm looking around for a long stick to lean on. They've used all the downed limbs around here as fuel for their fires."

"Push the buttons on your watch. That will bring..."

"I'm not wearing your watch, Paul. I haven't figured it all out yet."

"Then push the button on your pendant. You're wearing your pendant, right?"

"Yes."

"It will bring the police. I'm down in the garage now."

"Okay, I just did that. I'm trying to walk but there's a lot of pain in my knee. I still can't put full weight on that leg. I'm going to have.... to crawl back to the house. I can't stand..."

"Dad, stay under the shelter. They'll find you."

"They'll have to hurry. It's going to get dark soon and the snow is starting up again."

"Use the torch on your phone. They'll see the light."

"I'm going to try crawling back to the lawn. They'll see me there. They won't find me out here. I'm putting the phone back in my parka's chest pocket. I'll keep it unfolded, we can still talk. Don't worry."

"No, Dad, stay under the shelter. You can use the light on the phone to signal the police. If you put the phone in your parka, you won't be able to use the light. And I can't see you either."

"I can crawl down the path to the lawn, I know the way."

"Dad, stay where you are! I can't see you now. I'm calling the police just in case the pendant isn't working."

"I'm... crawling, slowly but surely. I... follow the path... before it starts to really come down."

"I'm going to put you on hold for a minute while I call the hospital and the police. I'm heading for the Lincoln Tunnel. Tenth Avenue isn't too bad, thank God. Don't hang up. Stay on the line."

"I'm okay, Paul. Good gloves, boots, cap, hood. Not too cold. Snow is starting to come down now a little more. Managing to... crawl... back along the... Not too bad. Making some progress but the trail is getting... harder to see.... Think I'm going to make it though. It's like... Paul? You still there?"

"I'm here, Dad. Trying to get through to the police. Ambulance is on its way. How are you doing?"

"...Like auditioning for 'The Shining', dear."

"What?"

"Getting a bit dizzy. It's winding me. Need to rest a bit. Why would they go after the doe? It really pisses me off. Whoever did this, it wasn't for the venison. It was out of spite, pure spite. Bastards!"

"Dad, stay where you are. Use the torch on the phone so they can spot you."

"Making.... some progress. The snow is starting to.... ohhh... ohhh shit!"

"Dad?"

"Ohhh... Paul.... I have.... this pain in my chest."

"Dad, stop moving! Don't go any further. Just lay there and catch your breath."

"They won't.... see me... here... need to go just a little further...to the... edge of the lawn."

"No, Dad. Stay still!"

"Almost there. Acchhh dammit... pain..."

"Take the phone out of your parka and put the torch on."

"Touch what?"

"No, Dad, Torch. The torch light."

"I.... how do... I..."

"Take your phone out of your pocket..."

"Phone out... my poc.... ohhhh."

"Dad!"

"Paul... I... need you... my heart is... hard to... pain. Ohhh ohhh... wait!"

"Dad?"

"I think... I see... the house!"

"DAD!"

"Ohhh... I... see the house...."

"Dad, turn on the light!"

"...See the light... in the... studio..."

"Dad... don't hang up!"

"....Ahh....ohh..ohh... ohhhhh the light! The light! Who? Is that you, Rachel?"

"DAD! LISTEN TO ME! I'm heading into the Lincoln Tunnel now. I'll be there..."

"Rachel... Rachel, help me, love!"

"Dad, stay...."

"Ohhhh.... Over by... the tree. Can't go... any... furth...."

"Dad? Dad?"

"Dad? I'm out of the tunnel now. Can you hear me now?"

"Hello? This is Steven Brower, Montclair Memorial's EMS team. Who am I speaking with?"

"I'm Paul Myer, Jerome Myer's son. I'm in Jersey now, on my way to Montclair."

"You're the son of the deceased?"

"Deceased! Oh, no, my God! What happened? Where is he?"

"He's lying right here beside us on a stretcher. He's passed away, I'm afraid. Most likely, cardiac arrest. We're in the middle of a snow shower so it took us about twenty minutes to get out here and locate him. We knew where the house was. We were here in August to transport him back and forth from Memorial."

"Oh, no. Oh, please try to resuscitate him."

"We've been trying that since we got here. His heart had already stopped when we arrived. He's not breathing and he hasn't a pulse. We've tried our defibrillator, a couple of dozen chest compressions followed by mouth-to-mouth resuscitation but he's unresponsive. He's turning cold. I'm afraid he's gone. There's nothing more we can do."

"O no no no Dad no... O my God! Where did you find him?"

"He had propped himself under a large tree just where the woods end."

"O Dad.... Dad... Dad..."

"Look, Mr. Myer. There's nothing else to be done now. We're bringing him to the hospital's morgue. You shouldn't come out tonight. The roads are too dangerous with all of this snow expected, and it's getting dark. But they'll have the roads cleared overnight, surely. Turn around and come out tomorrow."

"O my God… Dad… Dad…"

"We'll take good care of him."

"Ohhh, I know you will. O God! One… one thing, though. Please… please make sure all the doors to the house are secure. Can you do that?"

"Sure, don't worry. We'll check the house before we leave. We'll also make note he has his phone on him too. Be sure to ask for it."

"Thank you. Thank you so much. I'll be out there tomorrow morning early."

"Goodnight, Mr. Myer. We're signing off now. Sorry for your loss."

"My loss? My loss? My daughter's giving birth soon. It all balances out in the end."